THE MONSTER
IN THE BOX

D0964824

ruth rendell

THE MONSTER
IN THE BOX

HUTCHINSON
LONDON

Published by Hutchinson 2009

2 4 6 8 10 9 7 5 3 1

First published in Great Britain in 2009 by
Hutchinson
Random House, 20 Vauxhall Bridge Road,
London SW1V 2SA

www.rbooks.co.uk

Addresses for companies within The Random
House Group Limited can be found at:
www.randomhouse.co.uk/offices.htm

The Random House Group Limited Reg. No. 954009

A CIP catalogue record for this book
is available from the British Library

ISBN 9780091931490

Typeset by Palimpsest Book Production Ltd, Grangemouth, Stirlingshire
Printed and bound in Australia by Griffin Press

For Simon, my son, who told me about the box

CHAPTER ONE

He had never told anyone. The strange relationship, if it could be called that, had gone on for years, decades, and he had never breathed a word about it. He had kept silent because he knew no one would believe him. None of it could be proved, not the stalking, not the stares, the conspiratorial smiles, not the killings, not any of the signs Targo had made because he knew that Wexford knew and could do nothing about it.

It had gone on for years and then it had stopped. Or seemed to have stopped. Targo was gone. Back to Birmingham yet again or perhaps to Coventry. A long time had passed since he had been seen in Kingsmarkham and Wexford had thought it was all over. Thought with regret, not relief, because if Targo disappeared – more to the point, if Targo never did it again – what hope had he of bringing the man to justice? Still, he had almost made up his mind he would never see him any more. He would never again set eyes on that short, muscular figure with the broad shoulders and the thick sturdy legs, the coarse fairish hair, blunt features and bright blue eyes – and the mark that must always be kept covered up. Wexford had only once seen him without the scarf he wore wrapped round his neck, a wool scarf in winter, a cotton or silk one in summer, a scarf that belonged to one of his wives perhaps, no matter so long as it covered that purple-brown birthmark which disfigured his neck, crept up to his cheek and dribbled down to his chest. He had seen him only once without a scarf, never without a dog.

Eric Targo. Older than Wexford by seven or eight years, a much-married man, van driver, property developer, kennels proprietor, animal lover, murderer. It was coincidence or chance – Wexford favoured the latter – that he was thinking about Targo for the first time in weeks, wondering what had happened to him, pondering and dismissing the rumour that he was back living in the area, regretting that he had never proved anything against him, when the man appeared in front of him, a hundred yards ahead. There was no doubt in his mind, even at that distance, even though Targo's shock of hair was quite white now. He still strutted, straight-backed, the way a short man carries himself, and he still wore a scarf. In his left hand, on the side nearest to Wexford, he carried a laptop computer. Or, to be accurate, a case made to hold a laptop.

Wexford was in his car. He pulled in to the side of Glebe Road and switched off the engine. Targo had got out of a white van and gone into a house on the same side as Wexford was parked. No dog? Wexford had to decide whether he wanted Targo to see him. Perhaps it hardly mattered. How long was it? Ten years? More? He got out of the car and began to walk in the direction of the house Targo had gone into. It was one of a terrace between a jerry-built block of flats and a row of small shops, an estate agent, a nail bar, a newsagent and a shop called Webb and Cobb (a name Wexford found amusing) once selling pottery and kitchen utensils but now closed down and boarded up. Mike Burden had lived here once, when he was first married to his first wife; number 36, Wexford remembered. Number 34 was the house Targo had gone into. The front door of Burden's old house was painted purple now and the new residents had paved over their narrow strip of front garden to make a motorbike park, something Burden said he resented, as if he had any right to a say in what the present owners did to their property. It made Wexford smile to himself to think of it.

There was no sign of Targo. Wexford walked up to the offside of the van and looked through the driver's window. It was open about three inches, for the benefit of a smallish dog, white and a tawny colour, of a feathery-eared, long-coated breed he didn't recognise, sitting on the passenger seat. It turned its head to look at Wexford and let out a single sharp yap, not very loud, not at all angry. Wexford returned to his car and moved it up the road to a position on the opposite side to the white van, between a Honda and a Vauxhall. From there he could command a good view of number 34. How long would Targo stay in there? And what had he been doing with the laptop or the laptop case? It seemed an unlikely place for any friend of Targo's to live. When he had last seen the owner of the whitish-tawny dog and the white van, Targo had been doing well for himself, was a rich man, while Glebe Road was a humble street where several families of immigrants had settled and which Burden had moved out of as soon as he could afford to.

He noted the number of the white van. He waited. It was, he thought, a very English sort of day, the air still, the sky a uniform white. On such a day, at much the same time of year, late summer, he had visited Targo's boarding kennels and seen the snake. The scarf round Targo's neck had been of black, green and yellow silk, almost but not quite covering the birthmark, and the snake which he draped round it had been the same sort of colours, the pattern on its skin more intricate. Accident or design? Nothing Targo might do would

3

surprise him. The first time he had seen him, years and years ago when both were young but he, Wexford, was very young, Targo wore a brown wool scarf. It was winter and cold. The dog with him was a spaniel. What was it called? Wexford couldn't remember. He remembered the second time because that was the only time Targo had been for a few minutes without a scarf. He had opened the front door to Wexford, left him standing there while he picked a scarf, his wife's, off a hook and wound it round his neck. In those few seconds Wexford had seen the purple-brown naevus, shaped like a map of some unknown continent with peninsulas running out to his chest and headlands skimming his chin and cheek, uneven with valleys and mountain ranges, and then Targo had covered it . . .

Now the front door of number 34 opened and the man emerged. He stood on the doorstep talking to a young Asian, the occupant, or one of the occupants, of the house. The young man, who wore jeans and a dazzlingly white shirt, was at least six inches taller than Targo, handsome, his skin a pale amber colour, his hair jet black. Targo, Wexford noticed, might have grown old but he still had a young man's figure. The T-shirt he wore showed off his heavily muscled torso and the black jeans emphasised his flat stomach. He had left the laptop behind. While he was in the house he had taken off his blue-and-white scarf. Because it was warm, no doubt, and, incredibly, because it was no longer needed for concealment. The birthmark had gone.

For a moment Wexford asked himself if he could possibly have made the wrong identification. The yellow hair had gone white, he couldn't see the bright blue eyes. It was the purple naevus which had been the distinguishing mark and which primarily identified him. But no, this was Targo all right, squat, stocky, muscular Targo with his cocky walk and his confident stance. The Asian man walked a few steps down the short path with him. He held out his hand and, after a slight hesitation, Targo took it. Asians shook hands a lot, Wexford had noted, friends meeting by chance in the street, always men, though, never women. Someone had told him the Asians at number 34 owned the defunct Webb and Cobb next door – for what that was worth. No doubt they received rents from the tenants of the flats above.

Targo came across to the van, opened the driver's door and climbed in. Wexford could just about see him stroke the dog's head, then briefly put his arm round it and give it a squeeze. If there was any doubt left, the dog identified him. A memory came to him from the quite distant past; the first Mrs Targo, by then divorced, saying of her ex-husband, 'He likes animals better than people. Well, he doesn't like people at all.'

The white van moved off. It might be unwise to follow it, Wexford thought. He hadn't much faith in his powers of following a vehicle without its driver spotting him. It would be easy enough to find out where Targo now lived, harder to say what use discovering his address would be. He sat there for a few moments longer, reflecting on how the first effect of seeing Targo had been to make him aware of his own physical shortcomings. Yet when he had first seen him, all those years ago, he had been a tall young policeman, very young and very fit, while Targo was squat and over-muscled and with that horrible facial mark.

Sometime in the years since they had last encountered each other, Targo must have had the naevus removed. It could be done with a laser – Wexford had read in a magazine article about new remedies for disfigurement and deformity. The man had been making a lot of money and no doubt he had spent some of it on this improvement to his appearance as others had their noses reshaped and their breasts augmented.

5

The strange thing, he thought, was that Targo still sometimes wore a scarf even on a summer's day – until he remembered and stripped it off. Did he feel cold without that neck covering he had been wearing for most of his life?

A girl was walking past his car, starting to cross the street between it and the Honda. She looked about sixteen, wore the dark blue skirt and white blouse with a blazer which constituted the uniform of Kingsmarkham Comprehensive and, covering her head, the hijab. In her case it was a plain headscarf, the same colour as her skirt, but, unflattering as it was, it failed to spoil her looks. Her dark brown eyes, surmounted by fine shapely eyebrows, glanced briefly in his direction. She went towards the house Targo had come out of, took a key from the satchel she carried and let herself in. Too old to be the daughter of the handsome young man. His sister? Perhaps.

Five minutes later he was parking the car on his own garage drive. Instead of letting himself in by the front door, he walked round the back and surveyed his garden. It was a large garden which Dora had been doing her best to keep tidy and under control since their gardener had left three months before. It had been a losing battle. Those three months were the time of year when a garden needed constant attention, lawn-mowing, weeding, deadheading, cutting back. Very little of that had been done. I suppose I could spend the weekend making a real effort, he thought, and then added, no, I couldn't. We must get a gardener, and soon. He took a last look at the ragged lawn, the dead roses dropping petals, the nettles springing up vigorously among the dahlias, and went into the house by the back door. Dora was in the living room, reading the local evening paper.

'We have to get a gardener,' said Wexford.

She looked up, smiled, said in a fair imitation of his voice, 'Hallo, darling, how lovely to be home. How are you?'

He kissed her. 'OK, I know that's what I should have said. But we do need a gardener. I'll get you a drink.'

In the kitchen he poured her a glass of Sauvignon from the fridge and himself one of Merlot from the cupboard. No good putting nuts or crisps into a bowl because she'd snatch it away from him and hide it somewhere as soon as she saw it. He thought again of Targo's muscly body and then he carried the wine into the living room.

'What do you think about Muslim girls wearing the hijab?'

'Is that the headscarf? I think they should if they want to, really want to for themselves, I mean, but shouldn't be coerced into it, certainly not by fathers and brothers.'

'It must be the most unbecoming headgear for a woman to wear. But I suppose that's the point.'

'Or if you're Muslim you don't find it unattractive. Which brings me to Jenny. She's been here talking about some girl, a Muslim girl, she's sixteen, in her class at school. She seems to think you ought to know about it.'

'Know what?' Wexford liked Burden's wife, knew she was intelligent and a good teacher, but if only she wouldn't try to get him involved in investigations which wasted his time and usually came to nothing. 'What's wrong now?'

'This girl – she's called Tamima Something, Tamima Rahman, and she lives with her family in Glebe Road, next to where Mike and Jean used to live –'

'I've seen her. I saw her today.'

'How can you know, Reg?'

'Well, unless there are two sixteen-year-old Muslim girls living next to where Mike used to live in Glebe Road and attending Kingsmarkham Comp, I can be pretty sure I've seen her. What's Jenny's business with her?'

'She says Tamima got seven or eight GCSEs, A-stars and As and Bs, and if all goes well she'll be going on to sixth-form

7

college. But the girl seems unhappy, uneasy even, worried about something. She's got a boyfriend, a Muslim like herself, so that ought to be all right but Jenny doesn't think it is. She thinks you ought to see the family, find out what's going on. Mike, apparently, isn't interested.'

'Good for Mike,' said Wexford. 'He's better than I am at being firm with people who want to waste his time. Now, how about this gardener? Shall I put an ad in the *Courier*?'

H e couldn't get Targo out of his head. Incapable of doing much on a computer himself, he hesitated over asking DC Coleman or DS Goldsmith to find where the man was now living, his marital status, his means of livelihood. He had no real reason to know these things, only hunches, suspicions, speculations, built up over the years. Instead, he asked one of his grandsons and he, like all bright children, came up with the answers in a few minutes. Eric William Targo was now married to Mavis Jean Targo, née Sebright, and they lived at Wymondham Lodge, formerly the old vicarage of Stringfield.

Wexford knew the house, as he knew most of the big houses in the environs of Kingsmarkham. No vicar had lived in the place for many years. The Reverend James Neame, incumbent of the parish of Stringfield, now had four churches in his care, each one attended by no more than ten people at Sunday-morning service, that service itself taken by a lay reader when Mr Neame was preaching elsewhere. His home was a small red-brick house between the (now closed) village shop and the parish hall. Several families had occupied the vicarage since the last vicar left it for good but it was only dignified with its present name when a rich man from London bought it in the early nineties and gave it a rigorous makeover. It was now Wymondham Lodge with extensive grounds, sculpted gardens, two garages, three bathrooms and a guest suite when Targo bought it perhaps less than a year before.

The next day was Sunday and Wexford decided to drive over to Stringfield and – what? Spy out the land? The chances of seeing Targo just because he had his house in his sights were slim but he felt he couldn't rest until he at least went there and tried. Incongruously, he wondered how many animals and of what kind the man was keeping within the old stone walls of the vicarage garden. The day was fine, hazy and mild. Leaves were still a long way off falling but they had grown dark and tired-looking. Everywhere had that late-summer appearance of untidiness, grass long and brownish, flowers gone to seed, windfall plums lying rotting at the foot of trees. He took the bridge across the River Brede and was in Stringfield within ten minutes. There was very little traffic. The heart of the village had its usual neglected, even abandoned, look, the church tower in urgent need of repair, gravestones leaning over at angles, several of the once sought-after cottages with For Sale notices in their front gardens. He turned down the lane which led to Wymondham Lodge, a narrow byway in which it was impossible for two cars to pass each other. It widened a little when the edge of the stone-walled grounds was reached.

The land rose a little beyond the wall, giving Wexford a view of a pair of llamas grazing. He did a double take when he saw a Bambi-like creature, a miniature deer, nearby. He pulled the car onto the grass verge, thinking that he wouldn't be surprised to see a leopard or even an elephant. But there was nothing like that, though he caught a glimpse of tall wire fences, like the kind enclosing a tennis court, in the distance. The roar he heard he decided he must have imagined. Driving on towards the house itself, there was less to be seen. Not Targo or his wife, that was too much to expect.

But the white van he had seen in Glebe Road was parked on the gravel drive with a silver Mercedes beside it. The old vicarage looked as a dwelling only can when its owners are wealthy and able to spend money constantly on it. The brickwork had been repointed, the white trim recently repainted, the slate roof glossy and sleek, free of moss. There was no sound – but what sound could there be in this remote spot unless it might be a cry from some animal?

He moved the car along the road out of sight of Wymondham Lodge's windows. It was a former home of Targo's that he was thinking of, not the medium-sized detached place in Myringham where the kennels was, not old Mrs Targo's cottage in Glebe Road from which he had made himself a stalker, but the little place in Jewel Road, Stowerton, not much more than a cottage itself, where he had started out. Very young but a married man with a child and another one on the way and, of course, a dog, a spaniel.

Number 32 his had been and the Carrolls lived at 16. Wexford remembered perfectly now. They were all the same, those houses, a row of them, two tiny living rooms and a kitchen, two bedrooms upstairs. Some of them had a bathroom but most didn't. The gardens were small rectangles with a gate at the end, opening into a lane where dustbins were put out and deliveries made. Everyone had coal and coke delivered in those days.

Elsie Carroll had been found dead in her bedroom one evening while her husband was out at his whist club. Did anyone play whist any more? The police had come, Wexford with them, a very young policeman then, excited and a bit overawed. He hadn't seen the woman's body, only seen it carried out, covered in a sheet, after the pathologist had been. Leaving the house later, sent home by Ventura when George Carroll, the husband, had been found, he had encountered

Targo exercising his spaniel in the street. At midnight on a damp cold night. That had been his first sight, his very first, of the man who now lived in some grandeur behind those stone walls.

Of course he was wearing a scarf. A thick waterproof jacket, wellington boots and a scarf wound round his neck. The scarf had been brown wool with a lighter check pattern. The man looked at him, met his eyes, stared. He had the dog on a lead. While he stood still and stared, the dog was lifting its leg against a tree in the pavement. The stare was absurd, sinister, it went on so long. Wexford found himself making an impatient gesture, turned away towards the car which would take him home. Once he looked back and saw the man still there, still gazing at him. And he remembered saying to himself, that man, he did it. Whoever he is, he killed Elsie Carroll, and then he said, don't be ridiculous, don't talk – don't even think – such nonsense.

Driving home half a lifetime later, he thought, I've never told anyone but I'm going to. I'm going to tell Mike. I'll have my Sunday lunch with Dora and Sylvia and the kids, I'll contemplate my awful garden and I'll draft an ad to put in the *Courier* for a gardener. Then, after all that, I'll phone Mike and ask him to come out for a drink. Now Targo is back and I've seen him, the time has come to tell someone – and who but Mike?

'If it's about that Rahman girl, I'd rather not,' Burden said. Wexford had almost forgotten her, so full his mind had been of Targo. 'Who?'

'That schoolgirl Jenny seems to think is being victimised in some way. The one from the Asian family that live next door to my old house.'

'It's not about that, Mike. It's got nothing to do with that.

This is something quite different. I've never told anyone about it but it's not new, it's been going on for more years than I care to remember, and now I think it's going to start again. Doesn't that whet your appetite?'

'D'you mean you're going to tell me?'

'If you'll listen,' Wexford said.

They chose the Olive and Dove, the little room called the snug which over the years they had made almost their own private sanctum. Of course others used it, as the yellow-stained ceiling and lingering smell of a million cigarettes bore witness. In a few years' time a smoking ban would come in, the walls and ceiling be redecorated, new curtains hung at the clouded windows and ashtrays banished, but in the late nineties there was no hint of that. Outside the window it was mostly young people who could be seen sitting at tables under coloured umbrellas on the Olive's veranda, for the evening was as mild as the day had been, while their elders crowded into the saloon bar. All those people or those who succeeded them would ten years in the future be obliged to huddle on that veranda, rain or shine, snow or fog, if they wanted to smoke.

Wexford asked for his usual red wine, Burden for a half of lager. He was no big drinker, though he had a large appetite, and Wexford would have been surprised if he had eaten less before coming out than a two-course dinner with bread that he himself had given up and potatoes that he was forbidden. For all that, the inspector kept his slim elegant figure. To Wexford it was almost indecent that a man of Burden's age had no discernible belly and could still wear jeans without looking ridiculous.

Having said earlier that he wasn't coming if the conversation was about Tamima Rahman, Burden nevertheless plunged straight into the subject.

'I hope I'm not being disloyal but I sometimes think that people who are as intensely anti-racist as Jenny is, actually discover examples of Asian or black people being ill-treated where no ill-treatment exists. Moreover, I'm afraid I think, and I told her what I think, that if this Tamima was a white girl who seemed a bit depressed and, well, unable to concentrate, Jenny wouldn't take a blind bit of notice. There you are, I suppose that is a bit disloyal.'

'It's politically incorrect, Mike. I don't know about disloyal. As for this girl, I only know what Dora passed on to me from what Jenny said.'

'There isn't any more to know, as far as I can see.' Burden tasted his drink and gave a small approving nod. 'So what was it you wanted to tell me?'

'It will take quite a long time,' Wexford said reflectively. 'It can't all be told tonight.' He paused, then went on. 'You have to understand that I've never told anyone, I've kept it entirely to myself, and I thought I never would tell anyone. That was in part because the man in question had gone away. That wasn't the first time, he'd gone away before, but he'd never stayed away so long. I was beginning to think – no, I'd decided – that it was all over. Now he's come back. I've seen him.'

'What did you mean by "in part"?'

'Because I could think of no one to tell who would believe me,' Wexford said simply.

'And I will?'

'Probably not. No, I doubt if you'll believe me. But I know you'll listen and you'll keep it to yourself.'

'If that's what you want I will.'

The story he was going to tell started when he was very young, living at home with his mother and father as he couldn't really afford to live anywhere else. He got on with his parents, there were no difficulties there, but he moved away for two reasons: it wasn't 'grown-up' to live at home and, besides that, he was engaged. At twenty-one he was engaged. But he wouldn't tell any of that. He wouldn't talk about the sexual revolution which was coming but hadn't yet arrived, and how it was out of the question for his parents to let Alison stay the night. Even when he had found himself a room with a Baby Belling stove and use of the bathroom down the passage, he couldn't have had Alison to stay the night. Her parents would have expected her home by eleven at the latest. His landlady would have turned her out and him too probably. There would have been gossip. Girls still had a reputation to keep, girls still knew what the word meant and if they tried to forget it were still told by their fathers – never dads in those days – what would become of them if they lost it.

But he and Alison had their evenings. Mrs Brunton, his landlady, was one of those who believed that sexual intercourse only ever took place after ten at night. He was young and probably thought the way magazines were beginning to say men thought, that is about sex every six minutes. He had known Alison since they were sixteen and he liked the sex but not as much as he had thought he would. There must be more to it or what were all these people on about?

He tried not to think about it. He was *engaged,* and he had old-fashioned ideas about engagements. Not that he was quite back in the days when defaulting men got sued for breach of promise but still he would have thought it dishonourable for the man to break an engagement when the woman obviously wanted to keep it. Or did she? She said she loved him. He tried not to think about it but to think about his work instead.

And it was about that work that he would talk to Burden. The inspector waited, watching him and helping himself to the nuts Wexford was not allowed to eat.

'It was mostly taking statements,' he began, 'from people

who had been receiving stolen goods or knew someone who had or had broken into a house and stolen five pounds from a wallet. And making house-to-house calls and once, rather more excitingly, taking my turn in sitting beside a hospital bed in which lay a man who had been stabbed in the street. A very rare event in Kingsmarkham in those days. And then Elsie Carroll was murdered.'

It was the first murder in their area of mid Sussex for two years and the previous one hadn't really been murder at all but manslaughter. This one was murder all right. She was found by a next-door neighbour. The neighour, Mrs Dawn Morrow, had been expecting Elsie Carroll to come in and have a cup of coffee with her and a chat.

'Those were the days when a couple of women would never have met for a drink, that is wine or beer or spirits. No one drank wine, anyway, except French people or the sort that went to posh restaurants. Dawn had two children, three and one, her husband went to see his widowed mother on a Tuesday evening and she couldn't leave the house except perhaps to "pop next door". Elsie was invited for seven thirty one February evening and when she hadn't come by eight Dawn went to find her, leaving her children alone for a couple of minutes, as she put it. Both couples were on the phone but both believed it was wrong, absurdly extravagant, almost immoral to make a phone call to the house next door.'

At this point, Burden broke in. 'Where exactly was this?'

'Didn't I say? It was Jewel Road, Stowerton.'

'I know it. Smart cottages with different-coloured front doors, very popular with commuters to London.'

'It wasn't like that then. It was – it is – a terrace. Some people had outside lights either in the porch or on an exterior wall. The Carrolls at number 16 didn't. The back gardens were small and all of them had a gate in the rear wall leading into the lane where dustmen collected the rubbish and deliveries were made. No one locked these gates and everyone left their back doors unlocked. Nothing ever happened, it was neurotic to be afraid of some intruder coming in.

'Dawn rang the the Carrolls' front door bell and when she got no answer went back into her own house, out by the back way and into the Carrolls' garden by way of the lane and the gate in the rear wall. The back door had a glass panel in it and light was coming from the kitchen. That door was not, of course, locked. Dawn went in, calling out, "Hallo," and "Where are you, Elsie?" No one said "hi" then. When she got no answer she called out again and went through the kitchen into the hallway that everyone who lived in that terrace called "the passage". A light was on here too.

'I'd never previously been in any of those houses, all identical in layout, but by the evening of the next day I knew this one well. There were two small living rooms on the ground floor that subsequent owners have converted into one through room. Upstairs were two bedrooms, a bathroom and a tiny boxroom, big enough for a small child to sleep in. The Carrolls had no children so Dawn had no reason to keep her voice down as she went upstairs calling Elsie. It was just after eight.'

Wexford paused to drink some of his wine. 'Next day,' he went on, 'DC Miller, Cliff Miller, took a statement from Dawn Morrow and I sat in on it, learning the ropes. The next statement that was needed I'd have to do myself. Dawn said that a ceiling light was on in Mrs Carroll's bedroom and she went in there. At first she didn't see her. The bed was in a bit of a mess. It looked as if it hadn't been made. Pillows had been thrown about and the eiderdown had fallen half on to the floor. That was very unlike Elsie, leaving her bed unmade. Dawn walked round the bed and then she saw her lying on the floor between the bed and the window. "I thought she must have fainted," she said. "I went up to her and looked more closely but I didn't touch her. They told me afterwards that she was dead but I didn't know that. She was lying face downwards with her face turned into the rug so I couldn't see it."

'That's more or less what she said, Mike. Maybe I'm not remembering precisely. And I'm stating it coldly, leaving out what she must have felt, shock, amazement, fear. She went next door to number 18 where some people called Johnson lived and the Johnsons both came back with her. They went upstairs together. Mrs Johnson had been a nurse before she married, she looked at Elsie Carroll and said she thought she was dead but to go out of the room while she tried to see if she had a pulse. A bit later she came out and she told her husband Elsie was dead and to phone the police and he did.'

Elsie Carroll had been strangled with the belt of her dressing gown which had been lying across the bed. That was the opinion of Dr Crocker whom Wexford had never met before but who later became his friend. Crocker, who was there within not much more than half an hour, gave an approximate time of death as not more than an hour before and possibly as little as half an hour before. By this time Detective Sergeant Jim Ventura had arrived with DC Miller, DC Pendle and Wexford himself. Within a few minutes Detective Inspector Fulford had also joined them. This murder was something very out of the ordinary, a sensation, in that place and at that time.

'We had no scene-of-crimes officer at that time. DC Pendle – Dennis was his name – and I went around the house, paying particular attention to the bedroom, taking fingerprints. DNA had been discovered but Watson, Crick and Wilkins had yet to win the Nobel Prize for their discovery. It would be a long time before it could be put to forensic use and it's not foolproof yet, is it? But fingerprint detection had been around for a long time. While we examined that bedroom, a pretty little room which Elsie Carroll had papered in pink patterned with silver leaves, Ventura and DI Fulford waited downstairs for Elsie's husband George to come home.

'Almost the first thing Ventura had done was speak to Harold Johnson and Margaret, his wife, the former nurse. It was twenty minutes to nine. Johnson told him that George Carroll regularly attended the Stowerton whist club which met in St Mary's church hall and he would be there now. The church hall was no more than a mile away, if that, and George Carroll had gone there, as usual, on his bicycle. Margaret Johnson said he was usually home by nine thirty, though sometimes it was after ten. Ventura sent DC Miller – Cliff Miller – to St Mary's to find George Carroll, tell him what had happened and bring him home.'

'Things would be a bit different today, wouldn't they?' Burden said. 'The church hall would have a landline which it certainly hadn't then and all those whist players would have mobiles.'

'Elsie Carroll wouldn't have left her back door unlocked or the gate in the wall unbolted. There would be more street lights.'

'In other words,' said Burden, 'you could say, contrary to what one is always hearing, that life was actually *safer* then.'

'In some ways.'

'So are you going to tell me George Carroll couldn't be found?'

'Don't be so impatient. Let's say he couldn't be found immediately. D'you want another drink?'

'I'll get them.'

When he came back he found Wexford scrutinising the photocopy he had made in preparation for this meeting of the chapter on the Carroll murder in W. J. Chambers' *Unsolved Crimes and Some Solutions*. Looking up, he said, 'You didn't think I could remember all that after so long, did you?'

Burden laughed. 'Your memory is pretty good.'

'I'm giving you all this preamble because it's necessary but what I really want to talk about is the man I suspect committed the crime. No, not suspect. I know he did it as I know he did at least one other. His name is Eric Targo and we'll come to him in a minute.' Wexford said, almost humbly, 'You're happy for me to carry on?'

'Sure I am, Reg. Of course I am.'

'Miller came back to Jewel Road, having been unable to find Carroll, and we waited there for him, that is Fulford, Ventura and I. Elsie's body had been taken away. By our present-day standards, they were a bit cavalier about taking measurements and photographs, but I dare say what they did was adequate. The bedroom was sealed off as a crime scene. It was then that Harold Johnson dropped what Ventura called his bombshell. He asked if he could speak to Ventura, found him less intimidating than Fulford, I suppose. Fulford was more like an old-time army officer, a sort of Colonel Blimp, than a policeman.

'Johnson and his wife had been at home all the evening, watching television. Of all the residents of Jewel Road, they were one of the few families who had television and it sounded as if they were enthralled by it, glued to it every night. There were all sorts of rules and restrictions about television-watching at that time. For one thing, you were supposed to sit as many feet away from the set as there were inches in its diagonal, never sit without lights on and various other stuff that turned out to be nonsense. Still, the Johnsons wanted to do it properly and they believed they should draw the curtains and switch on what Margaret

Johnson called "soft lighting". But I suspect and thought so then, I remember, that although they would have denied this vehemently, they wanted to leave their curtains open as long as possible so that anyone passing could see the glow of the cathode tube and recognise it for what it was. Something I forgot to mention – the Johnsons were also among the few residents who had converted their two living rooms into one so that they had windows back and front with curtains to be drawn.

'It was about seven, he told Ventura, when he got up off the sofa to draw the curtains, he couldn't be sure of the time but he knew it was a bit after seven because the programme they wanted to watch had started. First he drew the curtains at the front bay window, then he moved to the back. These were French windows and the curtains floor-length and rather heavy. He pulled the curtains but the right-hand one got caught up on something, the back of a chair, and when he went back to free it he looked out into the darkness and saw the figure of a man coming away from the back door of number 16 and making for the gate in the rear wall. At the time he thought it was George Carroll who went out that way if he was going on his bicycle which he kept in the shed by the gate. But now he was less sure.

'He thought the man he had seen was short, no more than five feet four while George Carroll was five feet seven. But it was dark and Harold Johnson said he wouldn't be able to take his oath – that was his expression "take his oath" – on its being Carroll. The time he could be sure of: just after seven. Elsie, of course, couldn't say what time her husband had left the house but Dawn Morrow told Ventura next day that he usually left before seven, maybe as much as ten minutes before.'

'So when did Carroll come home?'

'A good deal later than was expected. About ten forty-five. It looked to me as if it was a terrible shock for him but as Pendle said to me afterwards, whether he'd killed her or not finding the place a blaze of light and his home full of cops would have been a shock anyway. Fulford told him he could see his wife's body if he wanted to but Carroll refused and began to cry. Fulford wasn't sympathetic. He said brusquely that he'd like to ask him some questions and he wanted to do it now, that was unavoidable. He and Ventura questioned the man and Pendle and I were sent home.

'If you're interested you can read what Carroll said in Chambers' book. You can have this photocopy I made for you. But the real thing of importance is that Carroll told Fulford he had spent the evening with a woman called Tina Malcolm. The term "girlfriend" wasn't used so much then and Carroll told Fulford he was the woman's "lover". That put Fulford against him from the start. He was exceptionally strait-laced and puritanical – worse than you.'

'Thanks a bunch.'

Wexford laughed. 'This woman, Carroll said, would confirm that he had been with her from seven thirty until ten and he was glad it had "all come out", it was better this way with his wife knowing. Then he remembered his wife was dead and began crying again.'

'My God,' said Burden. 'That's a bit grim.'

'Well, it was. I was glad to get out in the fresh air. The car we'd come in was parked outside. Pendle got into the driving seat – he lived fairly near me in Kingsmarkham High Street – and I went round to the passenger door. No remote opening of car doors then, of course . . .'

'I had been born, you know – I even remember the moon landings.'

'Sorry,' said Wexford. 'Though why I should apologise to a

man for treating him as if he were younger than he is I don't know. Pendle had to reach across and lift up the thing – don't know what it was called – that locked the door, and while he was doing that I noticed a man standing outside number 16. He had a dog with him on a lead and he was waiting while the dog took a pee up against a tree in the pavement. His name was Targo, Eric Targo, though I didn't know it then. Mostly someone you encounter like that will immediately look away when he knows you've seen him. Especially when you've been watching his dog foul the pavement. Targo didn't look away. He stared at me. You'll think I'm exaggerating but I'm not. You know how you sometimes read that someone's eyes pierced into your very soul?' Burden plainly hadn't read that and didn't know it. 'Well, never mind, but that's what Targo's did. He stared at me – it was under a street lamp – and then he nodded slightly. Oh, it was a very faint nod, not much more than a tremor, and as he turned away I saw the birth-mark. He had a scarf round his neck – he always wears a scarf or he did – but it slipped a little because he turned his head. At first I thought it was some sort of shadow, a trick of the light, but when he moved I saw it for what it was. Cancer the crab crawling across his neck, shaped like a crab with pincers or an island with promontories.' Wexford shrugged. 'Take your pick.'

They had been alone for the hour and a half it had taken to narrate all this but now three people came into the snug, a woman and two men. Although the room was small, it contained three tables, any one of which the newcomers might have chosen but they picked the one nearest to the policemen. Burden said quietly to Wexford, 'Shall we go back to my place and you can go on with the story there?'

Burden's house was nearer to the Olive than his. The difficulty was that Jenny would be there, unable to leave her young son on his own, but as it happened she said nothing to Wexford beyond, 'Can I come and see you about something, Reg? To the police station?'

He named a day and a time more to keep her quiet for the present than because he wanted to hear what she had to say. He knew it already. Burden and he went into a little room the Burdens called the study, though as is so often the case, nothing was studied there but it was a place where one of them could watch a different television programme from that showing in the living room. Burden left him there while he went to fetch drinks and the snack he could eat but Wexford must not.

Alone for a while, he reflected on that midnight so long ago. He had never forgotten that look, the light from the street lamp falling on the man's thick fair hair and his rather rugged coarse face with the scarf not quite hiding the dark stain mantling his neck. Then, the faint nod, as if to say, 'We know each other now. We are bound together now.' Of course that was nonsense, a nod couldn't mean all that.

Next day had been his day off. He would have preferred to go in, he didn't want to miss the next steps in the proceedings, but nor did he want to say that to Ventura. It sounded a bit – not overkeen but maybe *presumptuous*. He was too new in the job and too low down the scale to attract that sort of attention to himself. He spent the day with Alison instead, going for a drive (in her father's car) and the evening in his room. That was the time when he'd been doing the next best thing to going to university: reading, reading, reading. It was Chaucer that evening, 'The Squire's Tale'. But later on he lay awake a long while and his mind went back to the old worry, how he could marry a woman he didn't love and would soon, he was afraid, cease even to like any more.

Burden reappeared with a bottle of sparkling water and for Wexford a glass of red wine, the last of his self-imposed ration for that day. He poured himself a tumbler of water. From the array of bowls of nuts and cheese biscuits, he took a handful of salted almonds.

'You'd got to the bit where you and this Targo were staring at each other,' he said, his tone sceptical if not exactly scathing.

Wexford chose to ignore it. 'The following morning,' he began, 'at what Fulford called his tasks-for-the-day round-up, Ventura said he wanted me to come with him to interview Tina Malcolm, girlfriend or "lover" of George Carroll. Back at the mortuary the pathologist was carrying out a post-mortem on his murdered wife. Ventura and I went to Powys Road. This woman Tina Malcolm lived in a two-room flat with kitchen. No bathroom but that wasn't unusual in those days. There was a bath in the kitchen with a cover over it to make a table. It was neither shabby nor smart, just ordinary. It would have been interesting to a young person going in there today because, although the bedroom was quite a generous size, she slept in a single bed.'

'Have some more nuts.'

'You know I'd better not.' Wexford sighed but inaudibly.

'Tina Malcolm was about thirty-five, dyed blonde hair, heavily made up. Women wore much heavier make-up then than now. Lots of girls wouldn't let themselves be seen outdoors without it. More of it on the lips than on the eyes, though. Her heels were so high that they made you wonder, then as now, how women could take more than a couple of steps in them without falling over. She knew we were coming and I think she'd dressed up for us, not because we were policemen but because we were men.

26

'She took us into her sitting room and offered us tea which Ventura refused. You always think of Latins as being warm and effusive but he was a taciturn devil, dour and brusque. Accepting tea might have put her at ease. She was very nervous. As well she might have been in the circumstances.'

'In the circumstances? You mean she was involved with Elsie Carroll's death?'

'Well, no, rather the reverse. Or so it seemed. What happened next was extraordinary, Mike. It was the first time I'd ever come across anything like it, but more to the point, it was the first time Ventura had. He told me so in the car afterwards and mostly he hardly opened his mouth with lowlife like me.'

Burden laughed. 'So what was it? I can't bear the suspense.'

'She hadn't heard anything about the murder. Or said she hadn't. You have to remember that there was nothing like the proliferation of news then that there is now. Radio, yes, and TV, of course, but only two channels and no breakfast television. Newspapers, but no use to you if you didn't have one delivered by nine in the morning. It was half past when we got there and there was no paper to be seen. Ventura asked her if she had heard about the murder of Mrs Elsie Carroll and she just stared, her eyes went as big as saucers, and she whispered something about not knowing. Her hands had started to shake.

'Ventura gave me a look which indicated I was to say something, so I asked her if Mr George Carroll was a friend of hers. She nodded and whispered yes and Ventura told her to speak up. No one used that term "relationship", meaning "affair" in those days and Ventura asked her what was the nature of her friendship with Mr Carroll. This time she did speak up. "He's a good friend," she said. 'There's nothing wrong." That was the way people spoke then when they meant there was nothing sexual. Neither of us had told her when Elsie Carroll's death had taken place. Ventura asked her when she last saw George Carroll and she said she couldn't be sure, not very long ago. "Did you see him two evenings ago?" Ventura said. She drew herself up and looked shocked. I suddenly began to see that she was no shy violet, she was a clever woman. Ventura ignored that stuff about not seeing Carroll in the evenings. "Did you see him between seven thirty and nine thirty?"

'She shook her head quite calmly. "Please answer the question, Miss Malcolm," Ventura said. With a slight smile she said, "I have already told you I never saw Mr Carroll in the evenings. That wasn't the nature of our friendship. The answer's no." She was just a touch indignant by then. Another glance from Ventura and I said, "Are you absolutely sure of that, Miss Malcolm?" I got a nod and an impatient shrug.

'Ventura believed her. What astonished him was what he called the barefaced effrontery of Carroll trying to set up an alibi with an entirely innocent woman whose loyalty he thought he could count on. I thought it was a classic case of a woman who was happy to be having an affair with a married man when all went smoothly but the sky changed when a bad storm came up. I didn't say so, however. I knew it would be useless. Still, he was too good a policeman to leave this without further confirmation and I was left behind to call at all the flats in the block and ask if anyone had seen George Carroll on the previous night. In about three-quarters of the flats a woman was at home, a man in only one of them. I questioned them but no one had seen George Carroll or any man go into Tina Malcolm's flat. Or maybe I should say no one said they had.

'People like publicity these days, they're hungry for it. But not then. That fifteen minutes of fame – or is it fifteen seconds? – no one wanted it then. Then they wanted to keep themselves to themselves, keep out of the public eye. Don't get involved, was what mothers said to their children.

'It was next day that we did the house-to-house in Jewel Road and I encountered Kathleen Targo and her son. But not Eric Targo. Nearly all the men were at work as he was. Hardly any women were. Those of the men Ventura thought we ought to see we went back to talk to in the evening. No one was fingerprinted – there was no evidence pointing to anyone except perhaps George Carroll. These days we'd no doubt have taken DNA from everyone, men and women, on both sides of that street and streets beyond as well, but not then, not possible then.'

'So you saw Eric Targo in the evening?'

It had been an ordinary, seemingly insignificant, meeting. While Pendle was talking to a man called Green at number 25 on the other side of Jewel Road, he was knocking on the door of 32 and being admitted to the house by Targo. Somewhere at the back, probably in the kitchen, a child was screaming and there was a sound of water running.

'Don't like his bath,' said Targo.

Those were the first words Wexford ever heard him speak. As was often the case in marriages, his accent was uglier and coarser than hers, the local mixture of old Sussex and south London cockney. The man was short, just coming up to Wexford's shoulder, and had perhaps compensated for his lack of height by developing his body with weight-bearing exercises. Big muscles stood out on his arms and legs. He wore shorts – unheard of at that time of year in Kingsmarkham and its environs – which showed his thick thighs and bulging calves.

'He opened the door to me and the minute he did he remembered his neck was bare. As soon as he saw me he snatched up a scarf which was hanging from a hook with a lot of coats and tied it round his neck. The scarf made it even more odd that he should be wearing shorts. A woman's scarf it looked like, red and black and white. Then I had realised it was to hide the birthmark. Maybe I imagined it but I thought the look he gave me was full of hatred because I'd seen the birthmark.'

'You imagined it,' said Burden.

'Maybe, but you weren't there.'

Wexford had been led into a living room which, like every living room in that street, in the whole town probably, was heated either by a coal fire or an electric two-element heater. In this case it was the latter and the room was cold. The spaniel was stretched out in front of the 'fire'. Targo was the sort Wexford would have expected to be cruel to animals or at least callous with them, but to his surprise the man bent down and stroked the dog tenderly on its silky head before sitting down and asking him bluntly what he wanted.

'I asked him how well he knew Mrs Elsie Carroll. "That the woman what was murdered? Never spoken to her," he said. I didn't feel like calling him sir but I'd been told I had to. My personal assessment of someone didn't come into it. 'May I ask you where you were on the eighteenth of February, sir, between 7 and 8 p.m.?' I said.

'Targo stared at me. It wasn't the same sort of look he had given me under the street lamp, not a fleeting nod, but a brief stare of dislike and contempt. His eyes were a bright icy blue, still are, I dare say. "What d'you want to know for?" he said.

'I'd learnt the formula by that time. "Just routine, sir. To eliminate you from our inquiries."'

Burden laughed. 'What else?'

'Targo said he was at home with his son. I'll never forget his words. They were so expressive of the man's character.

"The wife had gone to her whatsit class – dressmaking. I don't mind that –" incredibly, he winked "– teach her to make her own clothes and the kid's, save my money." The screaming and splashing from the kitchen had stopped. There were footsteps out in the passage and Kathleen Targo came in with her son.

"Oh, pardon me." She recognised him. "Is anything wrong?'" It had amused him that people had begun to look on him, especially when on their home territory, as a harbinger of doom.

'I told her nothing was wrong and then I asked him if he'd mind telling me what he was doing while he was at home with his son. There was just an outside chance, Mike, that she'd deny that he had been – but, no. Not a flicker of wonder or doubt. "I was doing press-ups and leg curls – if you know what they are – in the kitchenette." They called kitchens kitchenettes then, even if they weren't particularly small.

'Mrs Targo told the boy to say goodnight to his dad and Alan went up to his father. He didn't say anything but – well, to my surprise, kissed him on the cheek. Then he fondled the dog's neck and that pleased Targo. He smiled and nodded. Alan went up to his mother and held up his arms but she shook her head. "Not the way I am now, Allie," she said. "You're too heavy."

'She was very unhappy with Targo. I guessed that then and what I thought was confirmed when I met her again by chance years later. She and Targo were divorced by that time and she'd remarried. That evening in Jewel Road I could see she was exhausted but he didn't get up. "You can make yourself useful for once, Kath," he said, "and show the officer out. I'm tired. Oh, wait, though," he said to me. "There's one thing you may want to know. I said I'd never spoken to that Elsie Carroll and I never did, but it's well known down this street that her two-timing husband was carrying on with a woman in Kingsmarkham. Dirty bitch. No better than a streetwalker."

"'Eric! Not in front of the boy," Kathleen said.

"'He don't understand. That Carroll'd have been happy as Larry to see the back of his wife, that I can tell you."

'I thanked Targo and said he'd been very helpful, the way we were supposed to, though he hadn't. All he'd done was teach me something about his own character. Kathleen took me out into the hall after that and sent the boy upstairs before she opened the front door and let the cold air in. I turned back on the doorstep and I asked her what she thought of the Tuesday-evening dressmaking class. I said my mother was thinking of signing up for it.

"'Oh, it's lovely," she said, showing more enthusiasm than I'd seen from her before. "Eric's so good staying here with Alan. I never miss." I had the impression she only said that to make me think all was fine with them on the domestic front. It was all part of that pretend-everything-in-the-garden's-lovely attitude people adhered to then. "Well, I'll have to miss it for my confinement."

'They still said that then. Well, some of them did, the really old-fashioned ones, the sort who still put on a hat to go to the shops. There were women in the villages round here, in the cottages without running water or electricity, where they referred to their husbands as "my master".'

'OK,' said Burden. 'I can see that Targo could have left his son for ten minutes, say, and gone along the back lane to number 16 – 16 right?'

Wexford nodded.

'And gone through the gate into the back garden – maybe even concealed himself and watched George Carroll leave on his bike before going into the house. He finds poor Mrs Carroll upstairs and kills her, strangles her. Then he leaves the way he came where he is seen by Harold Johnson, who doesn't recognise him in the dark. It could be done. Easily. But why, Reg? *Why?*'

CHAPTER FOUR

Burden was looking at the photocopy of the chapter from Chambers' book Wexford had given him. It was ten pages long. 'There's absolutely no motive,' he said at last. 'Of course, finding a motive's not strictly necessary but you have to admit it helps. Where's your circumstantial evidence? There's none against Targo unless you count Harold Johnson seeing a man cross the garden but, according to Chambers, he was never prepared to swear in court that it was George Carroll or anyone else. Or is Chambers wrong there and he took his oath it wasn't Carroll?'

'No, he never did,' Wexford said. 'All he would say was that he thought it was a short man but he was a very tall man himself and five feet seven or five feet four might have been equally short to him.'

'Targo's got the same sort of alibi as any other man in that street. He was at home with his family, in his case at home looking after his son. How old was the boy, by the way?'

'I wasn't very good on children's ages in those days. Four? Maybe a bit less.'

'So you're basing this theory on a look the man gave you, by night, in the light of a street lamp? Leave for a moment why he would – well, glare at you. Why would he kill Elsie Carroll? Revenge on George Carroll for something? But, apart from his apparently not knowing George Carroll except by sight, it wouldn't exactly be revenge, would it? If you think of Carroll as presumably being glad to have his wife out of the way, wouldn't it be doing him a favour?'

'I know all that,' Wexford said. 'I've thought of all that. It doesn't change my mind.' He got up. 'There's more to come, lots more, but I'm tired and I'm sure you are. That's enough for now. Say goodbye to Jenny for me.'

'I'll drive you home. I've only had that lager and it was all of three hours ago.'

'No, I'll walk, thanks. I'll see you tomorrow.'

The mild clear evening had become a cool night. When the sky was cloudless it was still possible to see the stars from the outskirts of Kingsmarkham. Brighton was just far enough away and London further. You could see the stars, see the constellations of Charles's Wain and Orion and Cassiopeia, but less clearly than he had from this same point when he was young. That might, of course, be as much due to the deterioration of his eyesight as to the pollution which misted the sky.

But the air revived him and his tiredness went. He recalled how those sightings of Eric Targo had affected him profoundly. He supposed it was because he wanted justice to be done and hated to see it fail to be done. If he could stop them the wicked must not be allowed to flourish like the green bay tree. Young as he had been, he had felt much like this when it became clear to him that the blimpish DI Fulford, and therefore Ventura, had made up their minds that George Carroll had killed his wife. It had been George Carroll that Harold Johnson had seen cross the dark garden towards the gate in the wall at seven that evening. George Carroll had a motive and a strong one. He wanted his wife out of the way so that he could marry Tina Malcolm. Dissolving a marriage

35

was difficult in those days, long before no-fault divorce came in, especially when it was a husband trying to part from an innocent wife. She would have had to divorce him and if she hadn't consented to that very little could be done about it. People remained bound to uncongenial spouses for the greater part of a lifetime. Wexford himself had known an old man who had been living with the woman he loved for thirty years but was unable to marry her because his wife refused him a divorce.

The fact that Tina denied being with George that evening, and therefore negated his alibi, was neither here nor there. Probably she had said she hadn't seen George because she was afraid of being involved – and this was very likely true. Where he might really have been, as far as Wexford could see, Fulford made no efforts to find out.

He could see too that it wouldn't be long before George Carroll was arrested and charged with Elsie Carroll's murder. Then another bombshell was dropped by Tina Malcolm. She came forward of her own accord, revoked her previous statement and said George had spent the evening with her. That did no good as no one believed her. It probably did harm, for it looked as if Carroll had coerced her, as perhaps he had. On the following day he was charged with the murder of his wife.

It was a day lodged firmly in Wexford's memory for other reasons as well. He saw Targo again, out with his spaniel, this time in the high street. He didn't speak and Wexford said nothing to him but their eyes met and Targo stared. It was after this that Wexford almost went to Ventura, told him about those glances and that unblinking stare, and suggested the man's movements might be investigated. He almost went. Perhaps it was never quite as close as 'almost'. His day's work done, as yet unaware that George Carroll was at that moment being charged with murder, he imagined what would happen at the interview. He envisaged Ventura's incredulity, turning to anger, that an underling as low-ranking and as new to the job as he, could have the presumption to suggest a solution to a murder case which, as far as he was concerned, had already been solved. If he condescended enough to ask for Wexford's evidence, that in itself unlikely, how would he react when told there was none, that it was all a matter of 'feeling', of glances and a *stare*?

No, it couldn't be done. It would be pointless. Apart from possibly damaging his career prospects, he would be set down as 'cocky', as 'cheeky' and getting above himself, even as showing off. He must forget it, put it out of his head. Strangely enough, that particular question came up again in the evening when he met Alison for a drink in Kingsmarkham's only wine bar. It precipitated their first real row. The following day would be a Friday and they always went out somewhere on a Friday night. A repertory company in Myringham were putting on, for one night, a production of Shaw's *St Joan*. Wexford very much wanted to see it, he saw very little live theatre then, and he had thought it might also appeal to Alison. Her hostility surprised him. She wanted a film, an Ealing comedy – strange that he remembered so much but he couldn't remember which one.

'But that will be on on Saturday too,' he had said, 'and in Stowerton next week.' There had been so many cinemas then, at least one in every small town.

'Reg,' she said, looking hard at him, 'isn't it time you faced up to it? You don't really want to see this highbrow stuff any more than you want to read those books you're always mooning over, Chaucer and Shakespeare and stuff. You're not an egghead, you're a cop. You do it to make an impression, don't you? It's just showing off.'

He had always had a short fuse but he was learning to control it, unplug it in time. 'You're wrong there,' he said. 'I read what I enjoy and when I get a chance to go to the theatre I try to choose what I shall enjoy.'

'Of course you would say that. It's not natural for a man always to have his head in a book.'

He asked her, his tone growing very cool, what would be natural for a man.

'Well, going to football or playing golf. Playing some sport. I've never known why you don't. One thing's for sure, when we're married you won't have time for books. We'll have a house and there'll be plenty to do. My dad's always painting and decorating, not to mention the gardening.'

'I've noticed. That's why we never see him when we go round there. He's always up a ladder or down a trench.'

'Better than having his nose in a book. That's useless if you ask me.'

'I don't ask you, Alison,' he said. 'And I shall go to *St Joan* tomorrow. You must do as you like.'

'I shall.' She got up to leave. 'And I shan't go alone.'

Finishing his drink, he thought that things had reached a grim stage when a man started hoping the girl he was engaged to would go to the cinema with another man. A football-watching, golf-playing, DIY expert – or hadn't that expression yet been coined? – a gardener who read the *Greyhound Express*. You are turning into an intellectual snob, he told himself, with no grounds for being so.

Next day he had learnt that George Carroll had been charged. It hadn't changed his opinion and he had believed that if the police charged a man with murder the chances were it was pretty certain that he would be found guilty and condemned to life imprisonment – if no longer to death. That made him shiver a bit. Was it cowardice then that stopped him speaking to Ventura or even Fulford? There was a difference between courage and foolhardiness. If he had had some evidence, a shred of evidence . . . But he had not. Forget it, he thought again. Put it behind you.

It hadn't occurred to him then that Carroll might appeal and on appeal be freed – not on the evidence or lack of it but due to the judge's misdirection of the jury. But that was a long way in the future, after many life-changing things had happened to him. In the present was *St Joan* to which he went alone. Even if he had wanted to take a girl he didn't really know any girls but Alison. He hadn't developed any critical faculty then and couldn't tell if the production was good or not, though he had thought that the Maid's (assumed) accent was a bit over the top and the Dauphin a bit too foolish and effeminate. At the interval he went out to buy himself a beer and when he came back, making for his seat at the rear of the stalls, he looked across the rows ahead and there, just taking their seats next to an older woman, were two girls, one fairish and plump, the other dark with fine brown eyes and a perfect figure in her red dress. And he thought, she is the woman for me, that's my type. I didn't know that till now but she is setting my type for me.

The room Wexford was renting was on the first floor of a house in Queen's Lane. Conditions were primitive by present-day standards. Using the bathroom was difficult because he shared it with two other tenants and he often used to go home to his parents' house for baths, taking his washing with him. His mother was the rare owner of a washing machine. He had a gas ring in his room and a kettle in which he heated up enough water to shave in. Shaving was carried out from a bowl on a little table by the window and one morning, as he was splashing water over his face, he saw Targo pass by.

Queen's Lane was the easiest route to the footpath across the meadows which led to the Kingsbrook Bridge. Dog walkers naturally chose it. Wexford thought very little more about it, though he did wonder why a man who lived in Stowerton would come all this way to find some open land when he could have reached woods and fields nearer home. But when it happened again the next day and again the day after that, always between seven thirty and eight in the morning, he began to suspect some other reason. The second time, Targo paused outside – apparently giving the dog the chance to sniff around the base of a lamp post and then relieve itself against it – but instead of watching the dog, he turned his eyes upwards and stared at Wexford's window. After that, this happened regularly. In today's parlance, Targo was stalking him.

The route he was now taking home from Burden's house under the stars, under a sky where now the moon, a three-quarters-full oval, had climbed above the trees, passed across Queen's Lane by way of York Passage. The whole place had changed beyond recognition. Not uglified (Wexford used Lewis Carroll's word to himself) because the few small shops had been given eighteenth century-style fronts, the late-Victorian houses pulled down and handsome new ones built and trees planted in the pavements. These trees were now big and shady and it struck Wexford, trying to locate exactly where, on the facade of the chalet-style house which now faced him, his window had been, that as things now were Targo's spaniel would have had to lift its leg against the trunk of an ash rather than against a lamp post. What had that spaniel been called?

He couldn't remember, though he had often heard Targo speak to it as he reached the footpath and let it off the lead. It hardly mattered. Targo didn't always use a name but sometimes a term of endearment. It had been chilling to hear this sinister creature, this murderer, call his dog 'honey' and 'sweetie'. He walked on through the lonely dark. There was no one about.

At home, his house was in darkness but for a glow from the front-bedroom window. He went upstairs. Dora was sitting up, reading in bed.

'Sylvia says she can get us a gardener,' she said, looking up from *The Way of All Flesh* which she was reading for the third time. 'He's the uncle of a friend of hers and he's an Old Etonian who's just retired from some government department.'

'Do Eton and the Civil Service qualify him to do our garden?'

'Probably not but she says his own garden's lovely, so that's a good recommendation.'

'We'll give him a go and I won't send off my ad,' Wexford said. He touched the cover of her book. 'I might read that again when you've done with it.'

His mind was too full of the past for immediate sleep. He lay in the dark and a picture of Targo appeared before his eyes: short, stocky, in those days wearing what looked like the trousers of a shabby old suit with an equally shabby raincoat. Every day when he passed Wexford's window he wore the same scarf, a brown wool thing with a fringe at each end. He walked stiffly, strutted really, and after the first few times he began whistling. The tunes he whistled were old, years and years old, 'It's a Long Way to Tipperary', 'Pack Up Your Troubles' and 'If You were the Only Girl in the World'. Wexford moved his bowl of water and his shaving things to another part of the room but still something compelled him to watch Targo and the spaniel walk by. The whistling would alert him and he would cross to the window, never moving the curtain.

No Internet in those days, none of the records which were kept today. The electoral register was on paper, kept in post offices and of course police stations. He decided to find out as much as he could about Eric Targo without letting it be known he was searching and, necessarily, without letting it interfere with his work and his duties. Soon he had discovered that Kathleen Targo, who had given birth to a girl, was in the process of divorcing her husband. He learnt this from a woman he interviewed in connection with the robbery of the shop on the corner of Jewel and Oval Roads – she was one of those to whom nothing is irrelevant. He didn't try to stem the tide and soon she had told him, without his asking a single a question about the Targos, that Kathleen had thrown her husband out after he blacked her eye and broke her arm.

'Mind you, he's strong,' he remembered her saying. 'She had to get help. It took three big strapping fellows from down here to get him out of the place and make sure he never went back.'

Those were the days when the police never interfered in a 'domestic', when violence towards women was generally regarded as all part of married life and private to the couple in question. Kathleen had apparently taken the law into her own hands while Targo, Wexford discovered, was back living with his widowed mother at 8 Glebe Road. According to what records he could find, Targo had been born in Kingsmarkham, the only child of Albert Targo and his wife Winifred, a woman who had come from Birmingham. Since leaving school at the age of fourteen he had worked for a market gardener in Stowerton, for two years in refuse collection for Kingsmarkham Borough Council and as soon as he had passed a driving test, become a van driver for a hardware firm.

Inescapable was the feeling that Targo was proud of what he had done, knew that Wexford knew it and was teasing him, defying him to come out with it to his superiors, knowing that without a shred of evidence against him he was safe. Wexford had an aunt who sometimes used the expression 'I wouldn't give her the satisfaction' and he steadily ignored the homicidal dog walker, refusing to give him the satisfaction. Ignored him, as far as Targo knew. But Wexford watched him proceeding towards the footpath, knowing that as soon as he reached the grass and trees he would let the spaniel off the lead, first stroking its sleek golden head. He learnt a lot about Targo in the few days he watched him, the stiff way he walked, strutted really, the cockiness that might have been put on for Wexford's benefit but which Wexford felt was natural to him. Then there was the attention he gave to the dog, stopping once or twice to pat it and say something, 'Good boy' or 'honey' perhaps, but Wexford was out of earshot.

After a few weeks Targo ceased to walk his dog that way. He had made his point, whatever that was. About that time a Kingsmarkham woman was murdered by strangling. Her name was Maureen Roberts and there was no doubt her husband was her killer. He was in their house when she died, he made no attempt to defend himself and on the following day he confessed to the crime. It was very different from the killing of Elsie Carroll. But she had been strangled. The murder weapon was one of her own stockings. The day after Christopher Roberts, her husband, was charged with her murder Targo reappeared, walking his dog to the Kingsbrook footpath past Wexford's window.

'This time,' Wexford said to Burden at lunch next day, 'I was looking out of the window. I mean, anyone passing could see me. I'd gone to the window to open it. I didn't expect to see Targo because it seemed he had given up exercising

43

his dog that way. But there he was, strutting along, bending down right outside my window to pat the dog on the head, and then looking right up at me. He had a blue-and-white-striped wool scarf wound round and round his neck.'

'Chelsea,' said Burden.

'Oh, possibly.' If he had taken the interest in football advocated by Alison he would have known about things like that. But he did know that it was the same scarf as Targo had been wearing when he went into the Rahmans' house in Glebe Road the other day. 'He didn't smile,' he went on. 'He seldom does but he stared at me and opened his eyes very wide. I knew he meant me to think he'd killed Maureen Roberts.'

'He must be mad.'

'At least you're not saying I must be mad.'

'No, but I'm tending that way.'

'It was a strangling, you see, and he meant to take the strangling of victims as his trademark, whether he did it or not. And in this case he certainly didn't do it. Well, he winked at me and then he walked on, the same walk he had always taken until a few weeks before. When he came to the field and the path he bent down, stroked the dog's head and let him off the lead and that was the last I saw of him for a long time. He moved away from Kingsmarkham to Birmingham where his mother came from. He had relatives there and soon one very good friend. He started a driving school and I thought I'd seen the last of him.

'I had until a few years later when the stalking began again.'

Burden was giving him the sort of look he would have given his wife when she raised once again the subject of Tamima Rahman. It was compounded of those two opposites, patience and exasperation.

'You aren't going to want to hear any more of this, are you?'

'There's more?'

'Oh, yes, lots more, but I'm not suggesting telling you now.'

They had left the restaurant and walked across to the Broadbridge Botanical Gardens. There on a seat along the main central path which led to the arboretum and the subtropical house, they sat down and contemplated the artificial lake with its island, its ducks and its two black swans. A squirrel ran down one tree, sat up on its haunches for a moment on the grass, before running up the trunk of another. A dog began to bark at the foot while the squirrel stared at it with loathing, making angry chattering sounds.

'I've got to go back,' Burden said. 'It's gone two and I'm due in court at half past when Scott Molloy comes up for perverting the course of justice. See you.'

Wexford watched him go, then got up himself. He seldom visited the botanical gardens these days but once he had been a frequent visitor. They had been designed and built to the specifications of a local philanthropist, who had died and left several of his millions to the town on condition they spent them on his dream gardens and called them after him, Samuel V. Broadbridge. A tropical house was to be included on the site, an absolute facsimile of the one on the campus of his alma mater, a fabulously wealthy Californian university, as well as an alpine garden, a miniature Red Rocks (in the Rockies) and a small Yosemite-like ravine.

That was in the late seventies and before that the acres had been open fields. Wexford had been all prepared to despise the place but once it began to mature and the fine trees to grow, the magnolias, locusts, cottonwoods and live oaks, all of which liked the mild south-of-England climate, he had begun to appreciate it. It was different, but difference need not mean worse. He should walk in here more often, he thought. He should walk *anywhere* more often. But where else could he find himself transported to a square mile of the western United States while no more than a mile from his own home?

After all, the open fields hadn't been very attractive, nor had the farm buildings on them. If Samuel V. Broadbridge hadn't stepped in with his dazzling millions, one of the several new housing estates would have been built on those fields. He watched a green woodpecker alight on the lawn which matched its feathers and begin pulling prey out of the grass. That was only one of the species of relatively rare birds which Sam V.B. (as he was known quite affectionately round here) had saved from expulsion if not destruction. Of course, there had been a worm in the bud and not the kind of worm the woodpecker would have appreciated. And Targo had been responsible for that too . . .

What was it Burden had said? 'There's absolutely no motive. Finding a motive's not necessary but you have to admit it helps. There's no evidence.'

All true and as true of what happened in Sam V.B.'s gardens twenty years later. His eyes went involuntarily towards the Red Rocks garden, though from here it was out of sight. It was time to go back. But he lingered, sat on a seat by the gate and gave himself to thinking about Kingsmarkham as it was now and had been then.

No council estates – or social housing as you were supposed to call them. No flats with fitted kitchens and bathrooms but cottages with outside privies huddled together along damp lanes, the like of which you only saw these days as a background to peasant appearances in costume dramas on television. The streets where his own house was were meadows then and at the end of his road the little wood, which some law decreed must remain in spite of the developers, had been the haunt of nightingales. The nightingales were all gone now. The high street was longer now than then with new buildings alternating with the Georgian frontages. And the police station was the first of these new buildings, assessed when it first went up as the *dernier cri* of modernity.

The Kingsbrook Precinct was yet to be built and Samuel V. Broadbridge was still at college in California. The open fields and woods were all the botanical gardens the citizens of Kingsmarkham needed. Apparently they didn't need cars either. Or they hadn't had them. Driving had been a pleasure, not a chore and a test of one's self-control and staying power. But that was common to the county and the country, not just Kingsmarkham. Such a small place then. No car parks encircling the town for they hadn't been needed. So was it better today? Were things better? The answer was always the same, some better, some worse. He got up and walked back to the police station, a building which had begun to look old and shabby, where the lifts went wrong and there wasn't an automatic door in the place.

He meant to leave early for home. A grandson was coming round to teach him how to use his CD Walkman. Do it for him more likely, Wexford thought, thinking too that he was certainly the only music lover his grandson had ever encountered whose CDs were all of Purcell and Handel.

A striking-looking woman with blue-green eyes, almost fanatically devoted to her job as a history teacher, Jenny Burden was a lot like Burden's first wife in appearance if not in character. Wexford found this rather satisfying. He was a great believer in men and women having a 'type' they adhered to in changing partners. Jean, who had been married to Burden when he came to Kingsmarkham and who had lived with him at 36 Glebe Road, he had first met when their children were small. She had died young of cancer and her widower had been devastated, to use a cliché word which no one used in that sense then. Within a few years he had married this pretty young woman with golden-brown hair who, seen from a distance, might have been Jean's twin; close to and when she spoke, the illusion was broken.

Wexford was thinking of his own type: hour-glass figure, dark hair, invitingly pretty rather than beautiful, the kind of woman of which his wife was the quintessence, when two things happened within moments of each other. Firstly, Hannah Goldsmith came into his office. Then, a call announced the arrival of Jenny Burden for her appointment which he had forgotten all about. In the interim Hannah gave him a rundown on her activities with the small Muslim community in Kingsmarkham. As a detective sergeant, she had more or less appointed herself the ethnic minorities officer, something to which Wexford had no objection. She made a principle of being intensely anti-racist, political correctness personified, a role which sometimes tied her in knots.

It was while she was telling him of her concerns at the possibility of forced marriages taking place locally when the call came. 'I think I've a job for you coming up in the lift at this moment, Hannah.'

Hannah turned round as Jenny came in. 'We've met before.'

'Yes, of course.' Jenny shook hands. 'At some school function, wasn't it?'

'Jenny, I'm going to ask you to talk to Hannah about this problem of yours. She'll be a lot better than I can be at dealing with it.' If there is a problem, he thought, but he didn't say it aloud. 'Hannah knows all the Muslim families in Kingsmarkham. She's also one of the few people I know who has actually read the Koran.'

Wexford remembered all too well a period of time, some year before, when Hannah had electrified (and embarrassed) his morning round-up of tasks meetings by breaking any short silences there might be with quotations she thought appropriate from this holy book. Smiling with relief, doing his best not to show too much haste, he sent Hannah away with Jenny in tow, and settled down to the mountain of paperwork which was just one day's accumulation.

Hannah shared office space with DC Damon Coleman and DC Lynn Fancourt. Both were there at their computers. 'Let's go up to the canteen,' she said, 'and we can talk over a coffee. Or a cup of tea which is marginally better. School not back yet?'

'We start on Thursday.' Jenny had never before been in the

police canteen, though she had heard her husband condemn the standard of its cooking, the service and its dismal appearance. 'I hope,' she said in the sort of meek tone she would never have used to a man, 'you won't think I'm wasting your time.'

'Oh God, no,' Hannah said, returning with two cups of coffee on a tray and two chocolate biscuits. 'I don't mind an excuse to come up here and have a break. I expect you eat biscuits, don't you? You're like me and don't have to worry about your weight.'

Jenny smiled. 'I'll go ahead then, shall I? A bit more has happened since I first talked to Reg – I mean Mr Wexford – about it. The girl's called Tamima Rahman –'

'I know the Rahmans,' Hannah interrupted. 'House in Glebe Road. They've done absolute wonders with that place. Extended it, had a new kitchen and added another bathroom. And Yasmin Rahman keeps it spotless. I just wish some of these people who condemn Muslims out of hand could see it.'

'Yes, well, Tamima was in my class at school. She was expected to do very well in her GCSEs. And she did. Very well. She told me immediately she got her results, even before I saw them for myself. Then, about a week after that, I met her in the street. I had the impression she tried to avoid me. She saw me coming and turned to look into a shop window. But I spoke to her and of course she had to turn round. We talked about her results and I told her how well she had done, I was very pleased with her. Then I asked her if her parents had applied to sixth-form colleges – you know what they are?'

'Sure. They're really what used to be called the sixth form in schools only they're a separate building. Kids go there from sixteen to eighteen, prior to doing their A levels. Right?'

Like experts in any field, Jenny was unwilling to take anyone else's estimate of that discipline without adding minor corrections. 'Well, more or less. They take their AS levels at the end of the first year. I was hoping Tamima would decide to do history – that's my subject – English and Spanish to AS and then go on to As. Of the sixth-form colleges available, I knew Carisbrooke was her favourite. But she said no, she wouldn't be going back to school next week. I thought she'd misunderstood me. I said of course she wouldn't be going back to *our* school, I meant had she applied to Carisbrooke because I thought she'd a very good chance of getting there with her exam results.

'You know how they say people can give you a stony look? Well, that was exactly the way she looked at me – stonily. I meant I'd be leaving school for good, she said. Any sort of school. That's a great pity, Tamima, I said. She looked down and muttered that she didn't want to talk about it.'

'You think this is her family's doing? Her dad's?'

Just as she disliked children being called 'kids', so Jenny disapproved of the current trend to call parents 'mums' and 'dads', but she let it pass. 'I'd heard her father was so progressive. He's got a degree himself, hasn't he? Why would he stop her going on to do A levels? It's not going to cost him anything. There's no reason to think he's against education for women, is there?'

Hannah almost gushed in her defence of Tamima's father. 'Oh, no, Mohammed Rahman is a lovely man. He's a social worker with Myringham Social Services and – a coincidence, I suppose – he has a special responsibility for teenagers in the borough. Of course, her going to a sixth-form college will cost him more than if she leaves and gets a job. That way she'd bring money into the household but I can't believe he'd let that weigh with him.'

'She's got a boyfriend,' said Jenny, making a face at her coffee, 'but he's half Pakistani. Would Mr Rahman object to that?'

'We don't know that he does.' As often happened, Hannah was now torn between militant feminism and anti-racism. But the Koran was not the only guide to Muslim ways she had read and she was never backward in showing off her knowledge. 'He isn't a relative, though, is he? The Rahmans may favour cousin marriage. He wouldn't be the right man for her because his parents came from Karachi, say, or Islamabad. They might want a family member for her.'

'Not at all a healthy thing,' said Jenny briskly.

Hannah was trapped again. 'The marriage of first cousins sometimes seems to result in children with disabilities, though it's a very controversial subject.'

'It's a well-known fact,' Jenny said sharply.

Hannah ignored this. 'I can't quite see how this can be a police matter. The school-leaving age is sixteen and she's sixteen. No one's breaking any laws. There's nothing to show the Rahmans are arranging a marriage for her and while forced marriage is against the law, arranged marriage isn't.'

'Do you think I should go and see them? The Rahmans, I mean. Talk to the parents?'

Hannah didn't care for this suggestion. It was all right for her to go as a police officer but she saw a teacher's visit as on a par with a social worker's snooping or an old-time lady bountiful's condescending to a peasant family. 'So long as you remember they're intelligent people, educated people – well, Mohammed Rahman and his sons are. I hope you don't mind me saying this but Mohammed wouldn't take kindly to being lectured.'

Mildly for her, Jenny said, 'I won't lecture him. I'll only say it's such a waste that a bright girl like Tamima isn't to go on to higher education. I mean, what's she going to do with her life? Work in some dead-end job until she can be a full-time housewife like her mother?'

The position of women in Islam was in conflict with Hannah's feminist views and this gave her a hard time. Still, she couldn't let that pass. She gave Jenny a pleasant smile. 'In the case of Tamima's mum I'm sure it's her choice to be a housewife. She's a very excellent one and absolutely the rock of that family. Can I get you another cup of coffee?'

After Kevin Styles, self-styled gang leader, aged twenty and of no fixed address, had been committed for trial on charges of breaking and entering and causing actual bodily harm, Burden went off to meet Wexford for lunch at the Kashmiri restaurant they currently favoured. On his way to the Dal Lake he had had an experience he could hardly wait to tell Wexford about. The Chief Inspector was already there, sitting at a table reading the menu.

'I can't see any difference between this food and Indian at the Indus down the road,' he said, looking up. 'Of course this may not be authentic Kashmiri. We wouldn't know one way or the other, would we?'

'I've seen him,' Burden said, sitting down.

'Seen who?'

'Your stalker.'

'How could you know?'

'Well, let's say your description was so detailed, not to mention the white van, that it was pretty obvious. The bushy white hair, piercing blue eyes, his height or lack of it, the way he walks or struts.'

'Scarf or no scarf?'

'No scarf. But close to you can sort of see where the naevus was. When you know there was a naevus, that is. The skin's paler than the rest and smoother.'

'You must have been very close to. Where was this?'

'Outside the police station. Well, outside the court which is more or less the same thing. The van was parked on a meter, all perfectly as it should be. I saw him put a coin into the meter and then he walked up to our forecourt and stood there, looking up at the windows. I went over to him. He didn't speak and nor did I. God knows what he was doing.'

'And not only God,' said Wexford. 'He was looking for me.'

'What, still?'

'Why not? He doesn't know whether I'm still here or retired or maybe I've died. He wants to find out.'

Soon after George Carroll had been released, Wexford was transferred from Kingsmarkham to a division on the south coast. He thought it was permanent but it turned out to be only temporary, lasting just two years, part of the preliminaries to his being made sergeant. It was a time of shifting change; everyone, it seemed to him, moving away.

That George Carroll should leave Stowerton was no surprise. He might have been acquitted but not because some startling piece of eleventh-hour evidence revealed him to be beyond doubt innocent. People were saying he got off on a technicality, just because some old judge who was probably senile had fallen down on the job. Carroll returned home for a while because he had nowhere else to go. In the present climate of social conduct, Wexford thought, his neighbours would at best have catcalled him and daubed abuse on his garden wall, at the more likely worst, smashed his windows and perhaps even stoned him. Then, all those years ago, he was treated with coolness and a few people turned away from him without a word or a nod. His house was put up for sale. Wexford had seen it advertised in an estate agent's window for two thousand, five hundred pounds. Its reputation had reduced its price but not, he thought, by more than, say, three hundred pounds. Now that same house would fetch two hundred thousand.

Targo moved too. He waited to see George Carroll come home, be ostracised and excluded, and then he and his family disappeared. Or that was the way Wexford had seen it. That was the way it looked. It might, of course, have been only co-incidence that when George Carroll returned to Jewel Road after the trial, an estate agent's board appeared outside number 32 advertising it for rent. Wexford had gone down there to look at the empty house and the board himself, though for what purpose he couldn't have said. He enquired of a neighbour and was told the Targo family had gone away, no one knew where, but Kathleen and her children had gone to one destination and Targo to another. Soon after that Wexford himself was leaving.

He said goodbye to Alison and gave a half-hearted promise to come back to Kingsmarkham at weekends when he was able to, fairly certain that he would hardly ever be able to. She was half-hearted too. She had gradually become so since their row over his intellectual pretensions and he could tell, to his relief, that the matter would be taken out of his hands, that she would soon break off their engagement. Strange that this made him fonder of her. Not fond enough to want them to be as they had been when they first met, but rather with a feeling of what might have been and what a pity it was that it could never come back.

As to the girl in the red dress, it had been only a glimpse he had had of her, not enough to make him go searching Sussex, just enough to make him think that one day he would like to marry a girl like her. Now he had his career to think of, his future. The breach with Alison came in a letter from her, the first letter he ever received in his new home, a room over a tobacconist's shop in Brighton. As he had thought, she had met another man, the one who had taken her to the pictures that night he went to *St Joan*. They were getting married almost at once. He wrote back, wished her happy and to keep the ring, hoping she wouldn't because he could do with the money he would sell it for, but she did keep it. Now, someone had told him, she had several grandchildren and no longer lived in this country.

One day, walking down the high street on his way to interview a man about the disappearance of a sackful of stolen goods, he passed Tina Malcolm. George Carroll's former girl-friend was with a man who wasn't Carroll and pushing a baby in a buggy. As people were always monotonously telling him, it was a small world, so it wasn't very surprising perhaps to see, on another occasion, Harold and Margaret Johnson, window-shopping in the Brighton Lanes. His friends he had left behind in Kingsmarkham and had so far made no new ones. Sometimes he went out to the pub in the evenings with DC Roger Phillips, but mostly he stayed in and read. Public libraries were in their heyday then, no nonsense about incorporating coffee shops and what technology there was, but lots and lots of good books. He read them, poetry and plays and novels. Worlds opened for him and far from distracting him from his duties (as Alison would have suggested) they seemed to make him a better policeman.

Considered kind and polite, the way to refer to black or Asian immigrants in those days was as 'coloured' people. Not that there were many of them. Wexford remembered a carpet seller who went from door to door with his wares. He wore a turban and must have been a Sikh but no one knew about that kind of thing then. A black man who swept the streets was probably from Africa but no one knew what brought him here or what misfortune made pushing a cart and plying a broom a preferable existence to any other he might find. After he hadn't been seen for several weeks Wexford heard that he had died, had been found dead of natural causes in the tiny squalid room he rented not far from where Targo had lived.

Years and years had passed before more immigrants came and now it was becoming unusual to walk along any Kingsmarkham road without seeing one Indian or Chinese face. The way some people, particularly politicians, talked about the situation, integration versus multiculturalism, it would appear to be simple, a straightforward matter of not being racist. But Wexford's experience had taught him what deep waters one struggles to swim in when plunging into the traditions of another culture. He had been told he was too sensitive to these issues and perhaps he was. Oversensitivity was likely to be Hannah's problem too, notably her propensity to bend over backwards to avoid uttering the slightest word that might be construed as criticism of some nasty (Wexford's word) custom. He had even heard her taking great care not to condemn, in a Chinese restaurateur's presence, the process of foot-binding which had ceased to be performed in China some forty years before the man was born. Useless to tell her that the restaurateur, who was no more than thirty, might not even know that women of his great-grandmother's generation had had their feet deliberately distorted and crippled from childhood.

She walked in now. Anyone ignorant of her profession might far more easily have taken her for a model or perhaps popular

TV presenter than a police officer. He wondered how acceptable it had been for a middle-aged Muslim like Mohammed Rahman to be questioned by a young woman in jeans and a rather too low-cut top. Hannah was sensitive only in patches.

'I felt I should call on the Rahmans,' she began. 'Their house is very nice inside, guv. It's small but they've built a beautiful extension and it's very tastefully decorated. Mr Rahman was eating his dinner. He'd just got in from work. I must say, it smelt fantastic. I suppose Yasmin Rahman had been preparing it all day and she didn't sit down with him, just stood behind his chair and waited on him.' Wexford waited to see how she would get out of that one. She smiled airily. 'Still, it's their tradition, of course, and you couldn't see her as in any way a victim. She seems a strong, even domineering sort of woman. I told Mohammed not to mind me but carry on with his meal, he must be hungry. I didn't think I'd find it awkward asking about Tamima and school and all that but strangely enough I did.'

'Not so strange considering the knots you tie yourself up in. What did you say?'

'Pretended not to know Tamima was leaving – well, had left, said we were a bit concerned that Asian girls with very good GCSEs weren't going on to higher education as they should be. He gave me a sceptical sort of look, guv – he's no fool – and I remembered a bit late in the day that he's a social worker. "Leaving school is Tamima's own choice," he said. "Maybe she will resume her education later, who knows? But children have their own way these days, don't they, Miss . . . ?" I said to call me Hannah. His wife hadn't said a word and I thought she might have no English when suddenly she spoke and very fluently. Not all girls were intellectuals, she said and she actually used that word. Some were homemakers as she had been and as Tamima was. She didn't want a career. It was only interfering people like her teacher, that Mrs Burden, who wanted it for her, and she *would*, having a career herself. Maybe *she* needed to earn money, but Tamima would not, her husband would do that.'

Wexford nearly laughed. 'You must have found yourself torn in two, Hannah, what with your adherence to militant feminism and your well-known defence of the multicultural society.'

To his delight, Hannah really did laugh, if in rather a shame-faced way. 'You've got to admit it's hard, guv. While Yasmin was going on about the virtues of being a housewife, Tamima came in. Yasmin said something to her in Urdu, I suppose it was, and whatever it was she looked mutinous – well, resentful. I couldn't help wondering if it had been something about the boyfriend they don't approve of . . .'

'Come on, Hannah, that's pure guesswork or else your Urdu's come on a lot.'

'OK, you're right, of course. I couldn't say anything to Tamima in her parents' presence, though I will. As soon as the chance comes along I will. Anyway, one of the brothers arrived and Yasmin started busying herself getting his food – I noticed she didn't get Tamima's, suppose she had to wait till the men were done. Oh, I know, but you can't excuse everything in every culture. So I left. It wasn't exactly satis-factory, was it, guv?'

He was preoccupied because he had been thinking, before she came in, of times long past. He asked himself how astonished he would have been if, when he was young, some soothsayer had told him forced marriage would one day be an issue in England. The answer was simple – he wouldn't have believed it.

But Hannah's visit hadn't been exactly satisfactory. It hadn't been satisfactory at all. It seemed to him that she and Jenny had manufactured a serious problem out of nothing. A girl had chosen to leave school at sixteen as the law said she could. No doubt she wanted to earn some money, the way they did. That same girl had been seen walking with a school-mate who happened to be male. Out of this, those two had composed a tragic romance. The girl was in love with a boy but snatched away from him into a forced marriage with a cousin. Perhaps she resisted, ran away with the boy, the result of which was that the two of them were murdered in horrible circumstances by one of the girl's brothers. It was a good thing neither of them knew of his sighting of Eric Targo, otherwise they would have hauled him into the plot, as the hired assassin employed by the brother.

He believed none of it. It was more than ever a pleasure to go home now work had begun on his garden. Andy Norton had done two afternoons' work on the flower-beds and twice mowed the lawn. No one had got around to pruning the roses the requisite six weeks prior to blooming so this year they were a failure. But red and yellow begonias were out in the tubs and purple and red salvias in the borders, now freed from weeds. Dora told him the names, otherwise he would have had no idea. It was enough for him to look, admire and be soothed. To forget for half an hour Targo the stalker, the murderer, the dog lover with the birthmark. The birthmark which was now gone. He'd like to know, he thought, when that naevus was removed and why, considering, to say the least, the man was no longer young.

He was to be best man at Roger Phillips's wedding. It was a sign, Wexford thought, of the almost friendless state the man found himself in, that Roger, who had known him for less than a year, should have no one closer available for this 'best friend' role. And he wasn't much better himself. He would have been lonely in Brighton if there had been less work to do and fewer books to read. And if he hadn't met Helen Rushford. He had been taking her out once or twice a week for the past three months.

Couples saved for years to give themselves a luxury wedding. He thought now of his younger daughter's fabulous feast, the marquee, the champagne and flowers, the dinner for two hundred. It had been different in the days when Phillips got married, a small affair paid for by the bride's father, the reception in a church hall, beer and lemonade to drink. No one drank wine then, sherry maybe and port but none of what they would have called 'table' wines. No gift lists deposited at a West End department store. No presents picked out and ordered on the Internet. Guests gave toast racks, tea trays or modest cheques. Wexford asked Helen what she thought he should give and she suggested bedlinen, a sensible practical gift. She was a sensible practical girl and he took her to the wedding with him.

He had handed the ring to the bridegroom and was turning round to take his seat in the front pew when a glance at the congregation on the other side nearly made him drop the little box the ring had been in. Sitting in a pew about halfway down was the girl in the red dress. Or a girl who looked a lot like her, a twin if not quite the same girl. And, no, it wasn't the same girl. But even prettier than the one in the red dress. The quintessence of his type, the type he now knew was his. Not a red dress but a pale pink suit with a tight top and full skirt and matching hat. Women habitually wore hats then and no woman would have gone to a wedding without a hat. Hers looked as if it were made of pale pink mist in which a rose half hid itself.

I shall speak to her as soon as we get out of here, Wexford said to himself. I'll start some sort of conversation with her at the reception. I shall think of something to say. Helen forgotten, he tried to think of what that something might be while the inimitable words of the Book of Common Prayer marriage service passed over him unheard and the congregation rose to sing 'Praise My Soul the King of Heaven'. It didn't occur to him then that, pretty as she might be, well dressed and elegant, she could be even less similar to himself in temperament, even less congenial, than Alison had proved to be. His mind was never crossed by the thought, as he sang a hymn in that church, that she might be anything other than as charming as she looked.

In the event he never got to speak to her. When the bride and groom emerged from the vestry they soon began the procession down the aisle followed by the four bridesmaids, her parents and his parents. Wexford found himself paired up with a girl who seemed to be Roger Phillips's sister and though he saw the girl in the pink hat as he passed her pew, she was whispering to an older woman who had sat beside her and he

62

could do no more than cast her an imploring glance. Outside the photographs began – in a bitter east wind and spitting rain – and no groups included the girl in pink. She had gone, and the people she was with had gone. He would see her at the reception but there were even more people than at the church and he did catch sight of her but only in the distance. Seeking her out was almost impossible with Helen on his arm. Besides, he had his speech to make and other speeches to listen to. But he managed to make his enquiries while Helen and a bevy of girls had accompanied Pauline to the room set aside for her to change into her 'going-away' clothes.

'Oh, that girl,' Roger's mother said. 'I've never seen her before. She was staying with some old friends of Pauline's parents but they've gone now. She was a friend of their daughter's but the daughter wasn't well and they asked if they could bring this girl with them. Someone said her name was Medora. Very unusual, I thought.'

Byron, he thought. Byron had a character in a poem called Medora. *The Giaour*? And wasn't the daughter of Augusta Leigh, his half-sister, that someone or other said was his child, wasn't she called it too? Strange choice for one's own daughter. But beautiful and romantic. Which parent was the Byron reader? He would ask her when they met – in the unlikely event of his ever getting to meet her.

Still, he mustn't be feeble for he knew that faint heart never won. Now for a way, once they came back from their honeymoon, to find out from Roger's new wife the name of her parents' friends and find it out without arousing suspicions. Even if he hadn't been going about with Helen, he would still have disliked the idea of himself and the girl in the rose-pink hat becoming the subject of teasing. He couldn't forget her and once or twice he dreamt about her. In the cold light of day he told himself what a fool he was, behaving like Dante over Beatrice. This was the twentieth century and he was a *policeman*, for God's sake. Forget her. Don't keep imagining you see her in her pink suit and her rose pink hat. He argued the case with himself the whole time Roger and Pauline were away and when they returned tried to discover the name of Pauline's parents' friends by a circuitous route, asking Roger to ask his wife if this couple were the Derwents his mother used to know in Coulsdon. He said he thought he recognised them from years back.

Of course this turned out to be the least pressing matter on Roger's mind. He had to be reminded twice. 'I hope you weren't expecting these people to be your long-lost aunt and uncle about to leave you a fortune,' he said, passing Wexford a slip of paper. 'As you see, they're not called Derwent, they're called Moffat and Pauline's got no idea where they live.'

'I think someone said the girl with them wasn't their daughter.'

'So that's it, is it?' Roger gave a crow of triumph. 'I might have known.'

Wexford had said there was nothing to know and resolved never to speak of it to Roger again. The name Moffat was written on the paper. There must be hundreds of Moffats in the country, perhaps not all that many on the south coast and Pauline's parents, Roger had told him, had moved to Brighton from Pomfret. So should he start on the East Sussex phone book? How much easier it would have been today, he reflected, when anyone could be run to earth via the Internet. Or could be if you knew how to do it or someone working for you did. For all his resolution not to think of the girl in the pink hat as any more than his type, he was hooked on that type now and on her as its representative . . .

'Reg.' Burden's voice broke rather harshly into his reverie. 'Are you going to sit there all night?'

He shook himself, blinked. 'Sorry. I was thinking about the past.'

'It's usually pleasanter than the present. I thought we might have a drink somewhere. It's gone seven and you said Dora was out. I finished that photocopy you gave me. It made me want to read more and I got Chambers' book out of the library. But your photocopy says it all and there's no more. He may call it *Unsolved Crimes and Some Solutions* but he doesn't offer many solutions and none in the Carroll case.'

They went into the Dragon rather than the Olive and Dove and found a quiet corner away from the crowd who had gone into the little room which used to be called the Saloon Bar to watch a football match.

'Claret or burgundy?'

'Doesn't matter,' Wexford said. 'Their red wine all tastes the same.'

His thoughts went back to those Burden's entry had interrupted. It was a big step he had taken from dreaming of the girl in the pink hat to actually hunting for her. He told himself that he had already done the preliminary work – he was already thinking in policeman mode – and now all he had to do was perform a few practical actions, starting with the electoral register for the Coulsdon district. You could go into a post office in those days, stand at the counter and look down the street numbers for the name you wanted. It was the Internet now, more difficult, he thought, more confusing. But to start on this while he was going about with Helen, taking her to the cinema, out for meals, for walks and a picnic in the countryside, kissing her goodnight – though no more than that – to do all this while she regarded him as her boyfriend, that seemed wrong to him. That seemed dishonourable. He told her he thought they should stop seeing each other. The look on her face appalled him, the tears that came into her eyes. She was five years younger than he and suddenly she looked very young, a child starting to cry. He told her he was too old for her, that she should find someone nearer her own age, and he sugared the unpalatable medicine by adding that she was so lovely she was wasting herself on him.

'But I love you,' she said. 'You're everything I want.'

Had any other woman ever said that to him? Had Dora, his wife? He thought not but he had broken with Helen just the same and he had never seen her again. Never seen her but occasionally heard of her. She lived in the village of Stoke Stringfield now with her husband and grown-up children, the village next to Stringfield where Targo had Wymondham Lodge. He knew of her and knew her married name was Conway. You should have been ashamed, he told himself, ashamed of treating the poor girl like that and even more of romantic fantasies which were bound to have a disastrous outcome.

He shook himself back into the present. 'You have to remember that there *was* a solution,' he said to Burden when their drinks came. 'Arresting and charging George Carroll with the murder of his wife was the solution. And it didn't cease to be the solution – that is in Fulford's and Ventura's and a lot of other people's eyes – when Carroll got off because the judge gave some direction to the jury he shouldn't have. The difference between them and me was that I had never believed Carroll guilty and believed him neither more nor less guilty after he was acquitted whereas Fulford and Ventura were pretty sure he was guilty and absolutely believed he was guilty after he was convicted. His acquittal made no difference to their belief but they were both very angry. That expression "hopping mad" describes them well. Ventura was positively jumping up and down with rage.

'He kept saying over and over, "This villain is to go free because some old fool in a wig doesn't know his job!"'

'So there were no other suspects?'

'Only in my mind. Targo was always there. While I was living in Hove I thought a lot about him and the wife he'd beaten up and the little boy Alan and the new baby. I knew they'd left Jewel Road and that they'd divorced but I wondered if he was paying her maintenance and the child support as he should have been. One day I bumped into Tina Malcolm, walking along with a baby and some man she may have married. Probably had as people rather shied away from having babies without benefit of wedlock in those days – as you'll remember. She didn't recognise me or didn't appear to. I used to wonder what she must have felt when her lover came up in court on a murder charge.'

'You mean he really was with her that night?'

'Oh, yes, I think so, don't you? He was with her and when he heard she had denied what he said – betrayed him, you might say, never mind the revocation he wouldn't have known about anyway – I imagine his world went to pieces. Perhaps he had loved her. Who knows?'

'You reckon he'd have got off the first time if she'd said he was with her?'

'I suppose so. It was an absolute alibi if she'd said he was with her for three hours. You see, although on Ventura's orders I questioned those neighbours who were at home, no one went back later and questioned the ones who hadn't been at home earlier. One of them might have seen Carroll go in there. But Ventura wasn't interested. Once Tina had said Carroll wasn't with her that only confirmed what he'd made up his mind to, that Carroll was guilty. But they were never asked, not after she denied it. Carroll couldn't have been in two places at once and he was never in 16 Jewel Road after 6.30 p.m.'

'Chambers says Carroll went up north somewhere. No one seemed to know what he did for a living, but he fell ill and died of pancreatic cancer about a year after his acquittal. What happened to Targo?'

Wexford shrugged. 'He started a driving school in Birmingham. He'd met a woman there who had quite a lot of money. Her name was Tracy Something. She was very young then, she'd been left the money by her father and she had a big house in Edgbaston. But he never married her and he came back here when his mother died and he inherited her little house in Glebe Road.'

'How do you know all this?'

'I made it my business to know. Just as I believe he made it his business to know about me. You see, if I was obsessed with him, as you'll say I was, he was obsessed with me. Oh, I don't mean in any sort of homosexual way, I mean he got it into his head that it would be – well, *fun*, to have a policeman in a way in his power, someone who knew what he'd done and, incidentally, would do in the future, but who could do nothing about it. But then I never suspected, for instance, that he might be a psychopath. I never considered he might be a serial killer and Elsie Carroll only the first of his victims *or an early one.*'

Burden began to expostulate, as he had done on the previous occasion this had been discussed. 'But you'd no evidence. Just a look and a man being fond of his dog. You'd *nothing.*'

Wexford shook his head. 'I had the stalking. It started again. I'd just got married and we were living in one of those houses near the Kingsbrook. You remember.'

'Sure I do. There was a meadow at the end of your garden that ran down to the river.' Burden added rather sadly, 'It's all built on now.'

'Well, people have to have places to live,' said Wexford. 'Targo began exercising his dog down there. It was the same dog, the golden spaniel, and it must have been very old by

68

then. There were a good many ways of getting into that meadow, one of them being the Kingsbrook towpath and another a gate to a path off the high street, but he chose to pass my house and take the footpath that ran down to the right of it. I got used to seeing him and I didn't like it.'

'What, just because he was walking his dog?'

'At that time, Mike, he was living – alone, I think – in his mother's old house at 8 Glebe Road. To have come into the meadow by any of a dozen entry points would have been easier than walking uphill to my house and using that footpath.'

'What did he do when he saw you?'

'Well, of course, he seldom did see me. It was summer when this started and very early in the morning. I'd see him from my bedroom window just after I'd got up. Sometimes he'd pause and look up at my windows the way he did when I had that single room. He always had a scarf tied round his neck. He always stared. Once and only once I was getting into my car – it was later because autumn had come – he said good morning and I said good morning and after that the stalking stopped. He didn't stay long. He sold the place he'd inherited and went back to Birmingham.'

'If it was stalking,' said Burden, 'you'd nothing to go on for calling him a psychopath.'

'I had the man who sneaked across the Carrolls' garden at seven o'clock, the short man, the man who lived so near the Carrolls that he could have left his sleeping child, done the deed and been back home in ten minutes.'

'It's a bit thin, isn't it, for calling someone a psychopath and a serial killer? Just that one murder and that of a woman he'd never even spoken to?'

'Ah, but there were his fantasy murders. I mean the killings he wanted me to think he'd done. Yes, I'm serious. Maureen

Roberts, for a start. The next real one – as far as I know – was years later after he'd done rather well for himself – inherited his mother's place, had money from that Tracy – bought a house and set himself up running a boarding kennels. You'll remember the case. Well, I know you do. You mentioned it the other day, that poor chap who was strangled in the botanical gardens. Billy Kenyon. Remember?'

'You mean you think Targo was responsible for *that*?'

'More than "think", Mike. I'm sure.'

'Are you going to tell me?'

'Maybe I'll wait till you ask.'

CHAPTER SEVEN

She was behind the counter at the checkout.

'And it wasn't even Tesco,' Burden said, as if the size or status of the supermarket where Tamima Rahman was working made any significant difference. 'It was one of those Indian places where you can buy everything you can think of in tins and they sell halal meat. They call them corner shops only it's not on a corner. Just one checkout and she was at it.'

'There's nothing we can do, Mike,' Wexford said. 'We couldn't stop her leaving school, we couldn't make the Rahmans apply to a sixth-form college and we can't ban the child from working. She's over sixteen.'

'But such work. It wouldn't be so bad if it was some sort of office job or something which involved training.'

'What a snob you are. I suppose the proprietor's a family friend. He offered the job and she was glad to take it. It may be only temporary.'

'Jenny says she's going to this place – it's called the Raj Emporium – and she's going to ask her. She could hardly believe it when I told her.'

Jenny must do as she likes, Wexford thought. If she wants to make private enquiries, let her, but I'm having no police interference. She is determined to stick to her romance, it's her own Romeo and Juliet, and she's hanging on to it. I never would have thought her so foolish. Three weeks passed before he heard any more and by that time it had largely passed from his mind. A boy had been stabbed in the street and the perpetrator, Neil Dusan, a Molloy gang member, was in custody while Kieran Upritchard lingered between life and death. A five-year-old had disappeared and turned up with an aunt in Macclesfield but not before everyone in Wexford's team had abandoned their other work to go out hunting for him. A petrol station owner had installed spikes to spring up from the tarmac if a customer left without paying for his fuel. One driver had called the police, the second had accepted the damage to his car and paid up, but the third had pulled a gun on the owner who was now in hospital with serious if not life-threatening injuries. Wexford had no time to concern himself with Tamima Rahman who had committed no offence, had nothing illegal done to her and made no complaints.

But meanwhile Jenny Burden had been several times to the Raj Emporium and extracted information from Tamima. Though the corner shop was busy in the evenings, for long hours only the occasional shopper visited the place and few who did weren't immigrants or the children of immigrants. Jenny wasn't quite the only white customer. On one occasion a youngish man with brown hair and blue eyes was in there, filling his wire basket with a selection of spices, his eyes lingering too long on the pretty Asian girl at the checkout. It was Tamima who lost patience with Jenny's visits but the proprietor, apparently her father's brother, was too good a businessman to tolerate her attempts to drive her former teacher away. His checkout girl got a severe dressing-down in Jenny's presence.

Wexford found her giving an indignant report of what had happened to Dora when he got home one evening.

'She gives the excuse that she needs the money. Apparently she's not satisfied with the pocket money she gets from her father. She insists it's temporary but she has no idea what other work is being arranged for her. If any is. It wasn't worth doing anything better than working for "uncle", she says, because her mother is taking her to Pakistan on holiday. They'll be away at least a month, staying with relatives, and she's looking forward to it. Why not look on this as a kind of gap year, I said, and get your parents to apply to Carisbrooke for next October. She didn't answer for a bit and then she said that wouldn't be possible. I asked her if she was still seeing her boyfriend.'

'That was a bit much, Jenny,' Wexford said. 'It wasn't exactly your business, was it?'

'You wouldn't say that if she were a white girl. You've got inverted race prejudice, you know. Caught it off Hannah Goldsmith, I suspect. I know the boy, he's a nice boy. His name's Rashid Hanif. He's going on to sixth-form college, but *he'd* be encouraged to. He's male.'

'Well, is she seeing him?'

'She says she hasn't got a boyfriend but I saw them together in the Kingsbrook Centre.'

The place was run-down now. Once a state-of-the-art pattern for all small shopping malls, it had gradually become rather shabby, its shops downmarket high-street chains mostly selling cheap clothes produced in South-East Asian sweatshops. It was rather sinister too, drug dealers operating in what had once been elegant passages leading into cafe gardens and which now stank of marijuana and urine. For Wexford it was a perpetual headache. His hope was that a promise (or threat) would at last be carried out, in spite of relentless opposition, and the place be demolished – even if demolition meant yet another supermarket and multi-storey car park taking its place.

73

'It's a dump,' Dora said. 'What on earth were they doing there?'

Jenny shrugged. 'How about hiding from her parents? Respectable Muslims won't go in there. They say it's dirty and it is. They prefer to buy from their own. Tamima and Rashid could wander about the place, maybe have cups of coffee in one of those cafes, sit on the seats by that so-called fountain that hasn't worked for months.'

Wexford fetched her and Dora glasses of white wine and a large red for himself. He helped himself to a handful of cashews before Dora snatched away the nut bowl. 'Jenny,' he said, 'whatever is going on, there is nothing to be done about it. There may come a day when higher education is as compulsory for school leavers as primary school is today for five-year-olds. It may come but it's a long way off yet. The time may come when it is an offence for a girl with seven GCSEs to work on a supermarket checkout but I doubt it. It's more likely that parents may be one day prohibited from arranging a marriage between their daughter and her first cousin but if there is no coercion applied, I doubt that too.

'Have the Rahmans locked Tamima up? Have they compelled her to work for her uncle? Are they forcing her to go on holiday to Pakistan? No to all those. I know why you think her mother is taking her to Pakistan. It's because when they get there you think she'll be made to meet a cousin who may be twenty or thirty or forty years older than she or hideous or unable to speak English, an illiterate peasant maybe, and forced into marriage with him. That what's in your mind, isn't it? Forced marriage?'

'If you put it like that, Reg, yes it is. I just don't think you know what lengths some of these people will go to in order to force marriage on a girl. I heard of one case where the parents tortured their daughter into consenting and another where a mother threatened a girl with being raped by her stepfather.'

Wexford was relieved when Jenny went. He wanted to talk to Dora about the gardener.

'It's true about him being an Old Etonian, but as far as I'm concerned that only means he speaks properly. You get so tired of people who can't speak their own language. Balliol as well as Eton, I think. He comes in that ancient Morris Minor he drives and gets straight on with things. I make us a cup of tea at four but he doesn't linger. He drinks it, refuses a second and gets back to work.'

'So he's a treasure?'

'He really is, darling.'

She went back to the book she had been reading before Jenny came. He thought about the past. Was he, already at his age, beginning to hark back there more than living in the present? It was Dora's saying she got tired of people being unable to speak their own language properly that set him off, that fired this train of thought.

Fancy-free, which was not quite the way he put it to himself, guilty over Helen, he had found Moffat, Edward P., Moffat, Josephine, and Moffat, Elizabeth M., all living at a house numbered 21 in a street which sounded rather posh. But now he had the address he didn't know what to do with it. Of course he looked in the phone book and found the Moffats' number but he had no idea what to do with that either. You can't write a letter to Edward Moffat Esq. – people addressed letters like that then – and ask him for the full name and home address of a Miss Medora Something who happened to take your fancy while you were being a best man. You can't phone Mrs Elizabeth Moffat, tell her you'd

done a sort of Dante and Beatrice thing and fallen in love
with a girl she'd brought to Roger Phillips's wedding.

But perhaps you could go to their house with some story,
some ploy. You could invent some tale – after all, hadn't you
a fertile imagination, fed with literature and romance?
Whatever the ploy was it must have nothing to do with his
life and his work as a police officer. That was out, utterly
banned. He would spend some thought-time, he decided, on
a careful plan, do nothing impetuous, though of all things he
wanted to do it as soon as he could think of it. He was greedy
for a sight of her. But before he had reached that point he
had been moved back to Kingsmarkham and promoted.

It was his home, his parents were there and a lot of old
friends. It also had the advantage of being nearer to Coulsdon.
Three months had passed since Roger Phillips's wedding –
the event that in his mind he called 'the fateful wedding'
because that was where he had seen her – but he thought
that not too long a period in which to carry out his plan.
When he presented himself at the Moffats' door it would
seem more casual, more a 'just passing' situation, than if he
had turned up with the little book on the following day.

It never occurred to him beforehand that a phone call would
appear to them a far more natural way of setting about things.
But because there was necessarily a delay in putting his plan
into action, he did ask himself if he wasn't assuming too
much, taking too much for granted, almost committing himself
to something from which there might be no going back.
Suppose she turned out to be cold and scornful or, worse,
laughed at him? Having good taste in clothes and walking
like a queen meant no more than that she took a pride in her
appearance. It might mean worse, that she was vain and narcis-
sistic. He would never know if he didn't try.

The little book he bought in what was then Kingsmarkham's

only bookshop was *Poems by Anne Finch, Countess of Winchilsea*. She was a poet before women were ever allowed to be poets. He read all the verse in the very slim volume because he read everything which came his way and also to give the book a slightly worn appearance. Its cover was a dark red suede and he rubbed at the suede a bit with his fingertips to mark it. This was for the Moffats' benefit, to make his story more convincing. After all, she, the unknown Medora, was hardly likely to be persuaded that she had left behind in a pew in a seaside town church a book of verse she had never seen before.

In the event his effort, if not a total failure, was a bit of a damp squib. It crackled for a split second and then fizzled out. Mrs Moffat opened the front door to him and listened to his excuses for being there in puzzlement. At first she hardly seemed to know who he meant by Medora, then she spoke. He expected patrician accents and got what they called now, but didn't call then, Estuary English.

'Oh, yes, my daughter's pal.' No explanation was forthcoming as to why she was staying in this house or why she came to the wedding. 'She lives in Cornwall,' she said. 'I haven't got the address but I reckon Josie could have. She's away right now, Josie, I mean.' She looked suspiciously at the book. 'Are you sure it was her left it behind?'

'Quite sure,' he lied. 'I saw it in her hand.'

'Well, leave it with me. I'll see what Josie says.'

He had no choice. But he knew enough of people and human nature by that time to be pretty sure of the little book's fate. It would lie about in that house for a few weeks. The daughter might come home, glance at it, say, 'What am I supposed to do with it?' and lay it down again until a cleaning lady, tidying up, stuffed it into a bookcase between a Dennis Wheatley and a Vicki Baum.

77

In the fiction he read so voraciously a character like himself might have got somewhere but not in life. He quelled his disappointment by thinking how grim it would have been had he met her and she turned out to be all those things he had considered but dismissed, vulgar and vain and empty-headed, so that a book of verses would only evoke an 'I've left school, thanks very much'. He had to forget her and get on with his work. It shouldn't be too difficult to forget someone you had never met, whatever the song said, and he repeated to himself, *'There is a lady sweet and kind, was ne'er a face so pleased my mind. I did but see her passing by, and yet I love her till I die.'* Well, of course he didn't. What nonsense. Never go back, he thought, otherwise he might have contacted Helen . . . But he had a flat in Kingsmarkham now, a quarter of a big house, and the girl who lived in the next flat on the same floor was attractive and unattached . . . Next time they met on the stairs he'd ask her in for coffee.

Meanwhile, there had been a murder in Pomfret and he was busy night and day questioning suspects. It was his first murder since Elsie Carroll and though Targo was long gone it was the thickset sturdy little man, the stalker with the spaniel, whose image came into his mind. Impossible, of course. Lilian Gray had been murdered by her husband. He had learnt that most people who meet a violent death have been dealt it by one of their nearest and dearest. The exception was a Mrs Parsons who had died in strange circumstances, killed by an old school friend who was in love with her.

'You were here by then, Mike,' he said to Burden. 'Do you remember the case?'

'I'll never forget it. People were still shocked by lesbianism then. I'm sorry to say I was a bit myself. You weren't, you took it all in your stride.'

'She wasn't really a lesbian, was she? Just a poor woman puzzled by her desire for another woman.'

'It's a long time ago,' said Burden.

He said nothing about wanting to hear more of Targo. Perhaps, Wexford thought, he never would. There had been few unsolved crimes in those years and no repetitions of the Carroll case with a man enduring a trial, a conviction and an appeal only to be ostracised for what Wexford was certain someone else had done.

By that time he had found the girl who was the quintessence of his type, married her and their children had been born. But he said nothing about that to Burden, that was his private thing, to be kept even from his best friends.

CHAPTER EIGHT

The Moffats' daughter phoned him. It was the last thing he expected. 'This is Josephine Moffat,' she said. 'You came to our house and brought a book for Medora.' She sounded nice and not much like her mother.

'We met when I was on holiday down in Cornwall with my parents,' she said. 'I don't see her very often because she lives so far away and mostly we just write. But she did come up to stay when we were going to that wedding, only I couldn't on account of I got flu.' Cornwall was thought of as far away then. The world had shrunk. 'I sent her the book.'

Now she would tell him Anne Finch's poems weren't Medora's. He had made a mistake. But, no.

'She was named after someone in a poem herself. She says she'd like to meet you but I told her you were a policeman in Sussex.'

He hardly recognised his own voice, it was so shy and hesitant. 'Would you give me her address? I don't even know her surname.'

'Don't you? How funny.' Suddenly the voice was coarser and less ladylike. 'It's Holland and she lives at 14 Denys Road, Port Ezra, Cornwall.' She gave him a phone number and he wondered if he would dare to use it.

No postcodes then. Just the town or village and the county.

Writing that letter was difficult but he did it, suggesting he might call and see her when he had a week's holiday in August. No answer came and he was deterred for a while. Then Ventura sent him to Cornwall to interview a man the Cornish police were holding on suspicion of his being involved in a bank robbery in Kingsmarkham. William Raw was taking refuge with his mother in St Austell when he was arrested and, with the interview fixed for the following morning, Wexford would have a free late afternoon and evening. Port Ezra was no more than seven miles away along the coast towards Plymouth.

It was now or never. This was a long-distance call, costly and not to be made lightly. He could have done it from the police station but too many of his colleagues did that sort of thing and he wasn't going to. Presumably, she lived with her parents. Most young girls did then and most young men too. But it was she who answered, her voice not quite what he had hoped for. What kind of a snob was he that he was daunted by a Cornish burr?

'I'd like to meet you,' she said. 'Could you come about six? Mum and Dad will be home by then.'

Meeting her parents wasn't part of his plan but he made enthusiastic noises and said he would like to take her out to dinner. Was there a restaurant nearby?

'Not in Port Ezra,' she said and she giggled. 'There's the Pomeroy Arms but that's just for drink.' It was long before the days when pubs did food. 'You could have supper here with us.'

He said he'd be with her by six. That giggle was another point against her but he castigated himself for his rigidity.

Port Ezra was a strange name, he said to his landlady before he left the boarding house where he and DC Bryson were staying. Not so strange for Cornwall, she said, where they had Cairo and Indian Queens, transliterations from the old

Cornish language. The nearest English equivalent to Medora's home town was Port Ezra, so that was how it was known.

He and Bryson had come to St Austell by train. They had no car at their disposal. He took the bus that followed the coast road to Port Ezra and beyond. It was less a town than a village with two shops and a pub, a dour grey church, white cottages with fuchsia hedges in full red and purple blossom, newish bungalows in its half-dozen streets leading off the cliff road and a magnificent view of dark blue sea pierced by jagged black rocks like a thousand islands. Number 14 Denys Road was one of the bungalows. The small car called the Mini had been on sale in Britain for a year or two, in just two colours at first, pale blue and red, and the Hollands had a red one standing on their driveway. Now he was outside the house Wexford hadn't the least idea as to what he would say. 'I did but see her passing by, and yet I love her till I die' would hardly serve as an opening move with her mother or father.

But it was she herself who opened the door.

'So here you are then,' she said in a broad Cornish accent, a burr as thick as a television actor might have with a part in *Jamaica Inn*. 'I never thought you'd actually come.'

He had to remind himself that he had a Sussex accent. For years he had thought he spoke the Queen's English, pure BBC, and then he had heard a recording made of his own voice and been disillusioned.

'Anyway, come on in,' she said.

She was wearing dark green trousers that they called slacks then and a low-cut green floral blouse. The clothes didn't suit the girl he had previously seen in tight-waisted full-skirted pink. His mother would have thought that blouse daring and even close on indecent. But her skin was perfect and her dark hair as glossy as satin. By this time he had been in dozens of strangers' living rooms and there was nothing out of the ordinary in this one, from the flying china mallards on the wall to the beige uncut moquette three-piece suite. Perhaps there were rather more framed photographs than usual. And which parent owned the *Complete Works of Byron* sitting among the cookery books and the Dennis Wheatleys? It comforted him to see it there, almost as if a sympathetic old friend were sitting in on their meeting.

'You're a cop, Josie says.' She smiled invitingly.

'Yes. A detective sergeant.'

Her perfume was musky and suitable for a woman twice her age. He sat down in one of the armchairs but when she patted the sofa cushion beside hers he moved to sit next to her.

'Fancy you seeing me and wanting to take me out. That's very romantic.' Now her face was quite close to his he could see how heavy was the make-up she wore. Had it been like that in the church but he not near enough to notice? Where were the parents? Not home yet? In another part of the house? 'I never lost that book. That was just a way of getting to meet me, wasn't it?'

He nodded. Her rather aggressive tone disconcerted him.

'Poems written by a woman hundreds of years ago. Not exactly my cup of tea.'

'Whose is the Byron then?' he had asked.

'Oh, that. My dad's. He's a bit of an egghead or used to be. Shall we have a drink? We've got sherry, Bristol Cream or Dry Fly?'

'Should we wait for your mother and father?' He was still anxious to do everything right. She must be nervous and that would account for the way she spoke and the words she used. 'They'll be home soon, won't they?'

'I don't know why you're bothered about them. I thought you'd like to be alone with me.'

Her face was very near to his now, the mouth half open. He edged backwards along the sofa, conscious of how this must look. It was no use any longer telling himself her behaviour was due to nerves. Then he heard a footstep overhead. So there was someone in the house, those parents or someone else? You're a cop, she had said, and it was being a cop that stood him in good stead now. But instead of standing up, leaving without ceremony, he turned back to face her and as he did so, she took him by the shoulders and pulled him down on top of her. At some point she must have ripped the green blouse because he saw her naked breasts and, in spite of himself, was excited by them.

It hardly mattered because she screamed, a shattering sound from strong young lungs. There was a pounding on the stairs, the door burst open and a man came in. Not her father, but a young man about his own age. He was big, burly and red-faced.

'What's going on here? Get off her.'

'With pleasure,' Wexford said, extricating himself.

'He assaulted me,' the girl said. 'Jumped on me and tore my blouse.'

She was holding the two sides of it together. 'Look at that, Jim. That's what he did.'

'You're going to pay for this,' Jim said.

Wexford stood up. 'And who are you?'

'He's my fiancé.'

'I see. I'd strongly advise you not to marry her,' he said to the man, 'not unless you fancy visiting your wife in prison.'

He expected this to have an inflammatory effect but instead a shifty look crossed Jim's face. 'Let's talk about this,' he said. 'There's no need to take it further. I mean, I was going to call the police . . .' He stopped when Wexford began to laugh. 'All right, all right. Only we'll need paying. Or Meddy will.

Her blouse is ruined for one thing and you've frightened her. We'll say fifty quid and we'll forget about it.'

It was an old trick. Wexford had been told about it but never personally come across it before. Usually, he understood, the players in the game were a prostitute, her pimp and a client. Perhaps the situation wasn't that different. 'Forget about it, is right. For one thing I don't carry fifty pounds about on me.' It was a very large sum then. Laughable as the price for a blouse which might have cost two pounds. 'And even if I did,' he said. 'I'd not hand it over to a thug like you when I've done nothing.'

The two of them, Medora still clutching her blouse, had moved over to bar the door. The man called Jim pressed himself against it with arms outspread. The girl stood next to him, glowering at Wexford.

'Open the door,' he said.

'Make me.'

'All right, I will.'

He grabbed Jim's left arm to pull him away when the other arm came up and struck him a glancing slap across the face. That was it. Wexford was young and strong and could throw a hefty punch. He took a step back and struck the other man a blow to his jaw. It wasn't all that hard, not half as hard as he could have made it, but Jim's knees buckled and he fell to the floor. Medora was screaming, real heartfelt terrified screams, quite different from the sounds she made when claiming to be raped.

'Stop that noise,' Wexford said. 'He's not hurt.' Jim was struggling to sit up. 'Well, not much hurt.'

'You've busted my jaw,' said Jim. Wexford knew he couldn't have if the man could speak. 'You've not heard the last of this.'

Wexford gave him a poke in the thigh with the toe of his

shoe. 'Goodnight,' he said and let himself out of the front door. Down the garden path, past the parked Mini. Jim's car? Out into the street, pulling the gate shut behind him. No one tried to stop him. He was quite sure he would hear no more about it and was in no doubt he had done the right thing in hitting Jim but he still felt all kinds of a fool. A fool for going there, a fool for not walking out when she said he'd like to be alone with her and most of all a fool for letting himself become obsessed with a girl he had never even spoken to just because she was pretty, wore a rose-pink hat and had a romantic name. Walking up Denys Road towards the beach and the bus stop, he resolved that he would never again let an obsession master him, not realising then that the peculiarities of our psyches are not so easily conquered and subdued. In those days, if he decided on something he was certain he would keep to it, for he was full of self-confidence. This particular resolution was doomed to failure from the start and even today Burden often cautioned him about another fixation. Hadn't he, after all, been obsessed for half his life with Eric Targo?

The buses from Port Ezra to St Austell were infrequent and he had walked for nearly two miles in sight of the sea before his reaching a bus stop coincided with the arrival of the bus. He had enjoyed walking in those days, walking fast and vigorously, in contrast to today when it was done purely for exercise and to offset the results of red wine and cashew nuts. In St Austell he found a pub and asked for a half of bitter. He took his drink to a table in the corner because he wanted to be alone to think. But when he was sitting down he realised that there was nothing to think about, he had done all the cogitation and recriminating that was necessary.

'Tomorrow to fresh woods and pastures new,' or in other words to interview William Raw and take him back to

Kingsmarkham. He looked forward to another ride on the Cornish Riviera back to Paddington.

His experience put him off Cornwall. Medora Holland and her boyfriend had tainted the county for him and when his mother wanted him to go on holiday to Newquay with her he contemplated a flat refusal. But his father had died six months before, her sister – the aunt who said she wouldn't give someone or other the satisfaction – six weeks before, and she seemed puzzled, forlorn and lost. Anywhere else, he said at first. Lyme Regis was supposed to be very nice (and he could see where Jane Austen's Louisa Musgrove jumped off the Cobb) or how about Teignmouth, where Keats had written about going over the hill and over the mead to Dawlish? Ultimately, he couldn't refuse her. Newquay on the north coast was quite a long way from Port Ezra on the south.

It was the first time in his life he had stayed in a hotel. Up till then it had been boarding houses which later on became B & Bs. The hotel wasn't very big and not at all grand but it had a dining room with separate tables and at one of them, not on their first evening but on their second, sat a middle-aged man and woman with their son and daughter. He could tell they were the couple's children because the boy looked exactly like the man and the girl very much like her mother. Doing Latin at school, he had come across the phrase, *mater pulchra, filia pulchrior*.

He said it aloud, not really intending to.

'What does that mean, dear?' his mother asked.

He laughed. 'Beautiful mother, more beautiful daughter.'

'Oh, yes. They are good-looking, aren't they? The girl is lovely. But I would never have thought dark hair and blue eyes your type.'

She was thinking of Alison, the last girlfriend of his he had thought it prudent for her to know about. 'Exactly my type,' he said, and then, as they were leaving the dining room he heard her mother call her Dora. That was enough to put him off for the night and half a day. The book he had brought with him to read was *David Copperfield*. He was about halfway through it when he came upon a highly relevant sentence. '"Dora," I thought. "What a beautiful name."' He had laughed, had his own version, 'What an ugly name.' He dreamt about Medora that night and her hateful embrace. Next day, while they were having lunch at a restaurant by the sea his mother told him she'd invited the couple, the boy and Dora to have a drink with them that evening.

How decorous it all was! How different from how it would be today, even if you could imagine people of their age – in their twenties – going on holiday with their parents. Even then he found it deeply dull and pedestrian. In the unlikely event of this Dora – horrible name – being the girl for him, would he want to meet her, his fate, his future, in company with his mother, her mother and father and her brother, over Dry Fly sherry in a hotel bar in Newquay? Who knew then that Newquay would one day become fashionable as a surfing resort and rival Ibiza as a venue for young people's raves and binge-drinking?

She had a pretty voice as well as a beautiful face and figure. She was witty and sharp. He fell in love three days later, forgot the awfulness of the name and came to love it, took her away from her family and abandoned his mother to the – acceptable and perhaps preferred – company of Dora's mother and father. It is said that we all have a peak experience, one day that is to be the best of our lives. Perhaps his was the fifth day since his meeting with Dora, when they were walking by the sea. When he told her he loved her she lifted her face to his and said she loved him too.

To meet your future wife in a hotel where you are on holiday with your mother and she on holiday with her parents seems the reverse of romantic. He was learning that romance has little to do with location or the exotic or glamorous circumstances and everything to do with feelings. And learning too that you like a name because you love the person who is called by it.

CHAPTER NINE

All the time he was engaged Wexford thought how wonderful it would be if Dora were living in his flat with him. She was often there, of course she was, but she always went home to Hastings where her parents lived. It became an obsession with him to long for her when he was alone, to imagine her letting herself in with her own key, making a phone call to a friend on his phone, running a bath and walking about the flat in his dressing gown. Because of this, because he wanted to see a dream made reality, they went back to Kingsbrook Court after their wedding – a small quiet affair – before going away on their honeymoon. And the real thing was better than the imagined cameos.

His expected promotion had come. This meant they could afford to take out a mortgage on a house and they had just moved in when their first daughter was born. It also meant more responsibility, longer hours and more travelling. Dora bore the evenings he was late, the evenings he had promised to take her out until work got in the way, the nights when it was his turn to get up for the baby but in the event was too tired even for her crying to wake him. She bore them with some resentment and he took her resentment patiently because it meant she loved him and wanted his company.

He was happy and doing well. Another baby was on the

way. He hadn't forgotten Targo and the man was always at the back of his mind, sometimes at the forefront. When Targo had sold his mother's house and was back in Birmingham, sometimes with Tracy Thompson and sometimes alone, later while he was in Coventry, Wexford had interested himself in the murders that took place in those particular areas of the Midlands. Several were of women who had plainly been killed by husbands or live-in partners. There were the inevitable child murders, most of them also associated with sexual abuse. Only one case was a strangling. The woman was a prostitute called Shirley Palmer, eighteen years old, and the suspect had previously been convicted of a serious assault on a woman in Stowerton, for which he had served a prison sentence. This gave Wexford a reason to go up to Coventry and sit in on the questioning.

To the investigating officers, and to a lesser extent himself, it was clear that Thomas Joseph Mullan was guilty, but Targo was always in his mind. Targo had killed once and would kill again. He was living nearby. He had strangled Elsie Carroll, or Wexford firmly believed he had, and that he had no apparent connection with the victim was in line with his part in the Carroll case. But this very fact made it impossible for Wexford to suggest to Detective Inspector Tillman that it might be worth questioning him or at least checking if Targo had an alibi. He could imagine the conversation.

'He stared at you? You think he stalked you?'

'I'm sure he did. On three separate occasions. There's no doubt about it.'

'And this goes to show he killed this woman he didn't know? You've no evidence, have you?'

It was impossible. He was starting to see that there was no one he could confide in, no one to whom he could tell that he believed Targo to be a murderer, and expect not to be met with incredulity. Of course he hadn't tried. He tried no one until he began telling the story to Burden all those years later.

At last, late in the evening, Mullan was charged with murder and Wexford went back to the hotel where he was staying the night. He phoned Dora to ask how she was and how his little girls were. Sheila had had a temperature when he left. Dora said she was fine now, both of them were fast asleep. In those days no one said 'I love you' as an invariable concomitant of a phone call to one's wife and no one said 'Lots of love' when terminating a conversation.

'I miss you,' Wexford said instead and she said, 'I miss you too and I haven't got all the excitement of a wet night in Coventry.'

After that he went downstairs to the bar and asked for a glass of red wine. People were just starting to drink wine instead of beer or spirits.

'Claret or burgundy, sir?'

'Oh, claret,' said Wexford, who didn't much care.

He was thin then and had no need to worry about his weight so he carried a dish of nuts and a bag of crisps to a table along with his wine. It wasn't the kind of place where the barman waited on you. The room was half empty. He sat down in a scuffed leather armchair. The only difference between this bar and one in a pub was that you sat in armchairs.

He helped himself to a handful of peanuts – no one seemed to have discovered cashews then – lifted the glass to his lips, drank, set it down and looked about him, as he always did in these circumstances, at the clientele. There was a group of four salesmen, then still called commercial travellers, three middle-aged couples he could tell were married because they didn't speak to each other – he made a mental resolution never to let himself and Dora get that way, never let them be identified as married by their silent indifference – and an over-made-up blonde woman sitting alone. Such was the state of things in those days that if this had been a pub it was doubtful if a woman on her own would have been served. He thought, by the look she gave him and a certain desperation in her eyes, that she would have liked to pick him up. He looked sharply away and saw that, seated at a table in the far corner, also alone, was Targo.

It gave him a bit of a shock. The last time he had seen him was some years before when he had passed Wexford's house on his way to the river and the water meadows, paused and stared up at his windows. And repeated that behaviour day after day. He had no dog with him in here. Targo was drinking something which might have been lager or pale ale. He was better dressed than in former days – or more showily dressed – in black jeans and a brown leather jacket. His shirt was black, he wore a black-and-white-chequered tie and his yellowish-brown hair, which had been clipped quite short in the stalking days, had been allowed to grow long, had developed a slight curl and reached to his shirt collar. But he still wore the scarf. It was black, brown and white stripes this time. The naevus was still there.

If gazing at someone will force him to look up and meet your eyes, Wexford's stare had this effect on Targo. Or maybe it didn't. Maybe the man had been sitting there waiting for him to come into the bar, was aware of every move he made and had calculated when he would arrive. It might even be that Targo was more aware of Wexford's movements than he was of Targo's.

They looked at each other. Targo stared. Staring at someone is usually a sign of recognition but of course there was no doubt that Targo recognised him. Once, years before, having his photograph taken for some identification requirement, the photographer had complained that Wexford blinked too much, but trying to hold his eyelids still only made things worse. Targo seemed to have no problem. Had he practised, even studied how to do it? As Wexford wondered, the man's gaze fell, he got up and walked out of the bar, leaving his glass half full.

Wexford started to go after him but stopped at the door and turned back. Go after him for what purpose? He already knew where the man lived and he knew from the notes Tillman had provided that Targo hadn't been among Shirley Palmer's regulars, that Targo's name wasn't mentioned at all. No one answering Targo's description had been seen in the neighbourhood of her beat either on the night she was killed or in previous days and weeks. How excited Wexford would have been if it had! Then he could have talked to Tillman about Elsie Carroll and the stalking, even about his conviction that Targo wanted him to believe himself responsible for murders where it was physically impossible he had been the perpetrator. As things were, there was nothing he could do. Or was it less a matter of doing anything but more of being able to confirm, now absolutely for sure, that Targo was pitting his wits against Wexford's? He was challenging him, saying in effect, you can do nothing but I can kill where I like or not kill, only make you believe I kill hecatombs of victims until you begin to doubt if I've killed anyone at all.

Something had been different about Targo and for a while Wexford had pondered what it was. Then he realised. No dog had been with him. He asked the barman if dogs were allowed.

'Oh, no, sir. We can't have dogs in here. There's a notice outside saying so.'

There was – outside the street door by which Targo had left and by which he no doubt had entered.

Burden came to Kingsmarkham soon afterwards and as they got to know each other well, becoming friends as well as colleagues, he thought that here was someone he could tell. But something stopped him. It was a while since Coventry and that sighting – you couldn't call it a meeting – of Targo in that hotel bar. He had never seen him again. He even thought sometimes, not that he had been wrong or mistaken, but that he must let it go, that justice could not always prevail and that there were some people, many perhaps, who had committed terrible crimes for which they would never be punished. If Targo was one of them, so be it. The man began to take on the aspect of a character in a recurring dream, someone who has no existence in life but only in the dream where he is vivid enough and haunting enough. Wexford actually did dream about him or had dreams in which he fleetingly appeared but never spoke and he understood that the reason for this might be because Targo himself, the real Targo, though they had encountered each other on several occasions, had only once had a real conversation with him. But Wexford knew where he lived, back in Birmingham now and with a woman who was not his second wife. He appeared not to have married again. The driving school was a success, had expanded and now he sold second-hand motor vehicles. He had also bought up several small slum properties for rent.

The illness Wexford had in the seventies, a thrombosis behind the eye, took him to London to convalesce. He stayed with his nephew, a detective superintendent in the Met called Howard Fortune, who lived with his wife Denise in Chelsea. Wexford hadn't expected to miss Dora specially, he certainly wouldn't get into the business he deplored in other men of phoning his wife every evening. That was what he thought.

The reality was that he slept badly. He hated sleeping alone. These days he sometimes thought how incredulous young people of the present day would be if they knew that, in spite of his relationships with several girlfriends, he had never slept a whole night in bed with a woman until he was married. Yet, after saying goodnight to those girls at some late hour, he had slept heavily until his alarm went off. In London, after his broken nights, he phoned Dora in the mornings and then went for long walks – doctor's orders – in the neighbourhood, often wondering if he might encounter Targo on one of them.

Targo was still living in Birmingham but it wasn't an outside possibility that he might come to London and look for him if he knew Wexford was there. And one day, in the King's Road, he saw a man ahead of him whose back, whose height or lack of height, whose walk were all Targo's but when he turned his head, showing where the birthmark should have been but wasn't, Wexford saw an aquiline face, a pointed chin and dark eyes.

It was as he had begun to think. Targo had grown older, had given up the wits-pitting and the challenge and lost all interest. It began to seem likely that Elsie Carroll, who had been his victim for some unknown reason, was also his only victim and there had been no hideous murder spree.

For all that, he thought of telling his story to Howard. He was very close to doing so some evenings when Denise had gone to bed early and he and his nephew were alone, having a late drink in Howard's study. But the moment passed and he no more told him than he told Burden. His health improved, he went back to Kingsmarkham, to Dora and the girls, and there he encountered Targo's wife – or the woman who had once been his wife.

It was in the then newly built Kingsbrook Precinct, later called the Kingsbrook Centre. Kathleen Targo was window-shopping, pushing a child of about three in a buggy. Two days before Christmas it had been and Wexford, as usual, was doing his last-minute Christmas shopping. He recognised Kathleen, noting how much healthier and happier she looked, though many years had passed, but was surprised when she recognised him and spoke to him in the sort of friendly way he never would have associated with her.

'It's DC Wexford, isn't it? Remember me?'

He didn't correct her, though he was a detective inspector by then. 'Mrs Targo,' he said.

'I was once.' She laughed. 'Good riddance to bad rubbish.'

'And this must be the baby you were expecting.'

As soon as he said it he realised that was impossible.

'No, that was Joanne. She's seventeen now. I got married again, I'm Mrs Varney now and this is Philippa. We've been living here since she was born. It's a wonder we haven't met before.'

She was a different woman, happy, placid. He remembered her as painfully thin apart from the swinging mound of pregnancy but now she had 'filled out', as they said, had 'middle-aged spread', as they also said. He had lost touch with Targo's whereabouts recently and he could ask where her ex-husband now was. Her answer surprised him and he felt a quickening of his pulse.

'Living in Myringham,' she said, turning up her nose, 'with some woman. I don't know what she's called and I don't want to. Alan and Joanne see him and that's how I get to know how he's doing. Not that I care. He was in Glebe Road for a bit after our marriage broke up, then it was Birmingham for years. But he's done well for himself, and he's got quite a big house. You never got anyone for poor Elsie Carroll, did you?'

97

Why did she ask? Like that, then, such a non sequitur. Because she *knew*? He would have loved to spend the rest of the day with her, take her and Philippa into one of the smart little cafes that were then a feature of the Kingsbrook Precinct, sit them down, order coffee and cakes and talk to her about Targo. Or, rather, get her to talk to him about Targo. But that was impossible. She would very likely say no, be astonished at such a request. It was Christmas and she had a family, she'd be busy. And once again he came up against the barrier – he had no reason to suspect her first husband of anything.

'I must get on,' she was saying. 'Nice to see you. Eric's got four dogs, Joanne says. That old spaniel lived to be seventeen but it's dead now and he's got more dogs and three cats and a couple of snakes. You wouldn't credit it, would you?' She hesitated, then said, 'He always did like animals more than people. Well, he didn't like people at all. That was the trouble.' And she laughed, the merry carefree laugh of a contented woman.

He had said goodbye to her and gone into the perfume shop to buy scent for his wife and his elder daughter. The one he tried – that he couldn't help trying because the assistant sprayed it on his wrist – reminded him of the perfume the girl in the pink hat had used. Medora. All that way across the years, it reminded him. He laughed, shaking his head, and bought a different kind. Was there any point in finding out Targo's precise address? No harm in knowing, he thought.

Dora was saying, 'Andy Norton knows a plant from a weed. That makes a change from some of them.'

Always interested in people, Wexford asked her what Norton had done in the Civil Service before his retirement. 'He was in some government department, apparently. Social Security, I think it was, only they called it something else then.'

'Well, on the subject of pensions, he must have a good one. Why's he doing our gardening?'

'He gets bored at home, I gather. And he likes to be out in the fresh air.'

It was a surprise when Burden arrived. He looked a little abashed, which was unusual for him. 'Not in the firm's time, you see,' he said.

'If you're saying what I think you are,' Wexford said, 'one day this is going to be the firm's business.'

'I've been in Sam V.B.'s Gardens. We got a call that someone had been stabbed but it was a false alarm or a hoax. But it reminded me of Billy Kenyon and what you said about Targo. Not,' he added, 'that I believe it. Not any of it.'

'But you want to hear?'

'I want to hear.'

Wexford smiled. He sat him down in an armchair, fetched wine and crisps. They had run out of nuts. When he had told him about the meeting with Kathleen Varney, he said, 'It was true that Targo was living in Myringham. In Hastings Avenue and in a much better house than the one in Jewel Road. It looked as if he and Kathleen were both doing well for themselves. But she wasn't quite right in one respect. He had all those pet animals but he was also running a boarding kennels for dogs.'

'At his home?'

'It had been a kennels before he took it on. Bought the place, rented it, I don't know. I went over there to have a look at it – and him.' The look on Burden's face prompted him to say, 'Not in the firm's time, I may add.'

'Well, I suppose you thought it was for the firm in a way.'

Wexford laughed. 'I didn't even have to invent a story.

Do you remember that dog Dora and I had? Sheila insisted on looking after it for some boyfriend called Sebastian, brought it home, adored it passionately for two days, fed it, walked it and then abandoned it to us the way kids do. We were going away – it was when we went to that Greek island – and I was genuinely enquiring what to do with the dog.'

'Targo recognised me at once. I had a feeling he knew all about me and was waiting for me to come. Nonsense, of course. He had – has, I suppose – an uncanny habit of absolutely meeting your eyes. When he talks to you he holds your gaze in an almost hypnotic way. That was the way he looked at me when I asked him about boarding Sebastian's dog. "I remember you," he said as if he'd never stalked me, as if he'd never stared at me in that hotel bar in Coventry. "You were on the case when that Mrs Carroll was murdered down Jewel Road," he said. "Must have been nearly twenty years ago." I tell you, Mike, he knew that I knew.'

'What, you mean he knew you knew he'd killed her?'

'Yes.'

Burden's tone could hardly have been more sceptical. 'A lot to read in a meeting of eyes.'

'He didn't care. He liked it. He knew I couldn't do anything. The house was full of his pets and it smelt of them. Have you ever smelt a marrow bone that's been lying around for a fortnight and every so often been chewed by a dog? Well, that's what the place smelt like. He had a snake and I can't say I was too keen on that. It wasn't in a cage or anything. Just lying curled up on a shelf next to a couple of books and a pot plant. One of the books was the *Bumper Book of Dogs*. Kathleen had said he was living with a woman and he was, the one called Adele he eventually married, but she wasn't around. There was a building outside in the grounds. They really were grounds, a couple of acres, I should think, and the building was a kind of glorified shed or stables. He took me out there. Everything was very neat and trim. "Shipshape" was the word he used for it. "Shipshape enough for you?" he said. There were about a dozen dogs in separate pens and of course they all came up to the wire, looking pathetic and whining and wagging their tails. The smell was there too but somewhat modified by the fresh air.

"'I do this because I love animals," he said. "It's not my main source of income. I'm in business." I didn't ask what business because I could see he expected me to ask. Something to do with cars or slum cottages, I expect. "Some of these boarding kennels are a disgrace. I like to think I run a luxury hotel for dogs." Well, I didn't comment on that. He showed me a pen where there was a mother dog with five puppies, all mongrels but very appealing. You needn't look like that as if I'm going soft on you. I assure you this is relevant.'

'OK. I believe you. Thousands wouldn't.'

'We went back into the house and he handed me a brochure setting out their terms. It was very expensive. I wasn't going to commit myself, though I stood there reading it, or pretending to read it, while I sort of sized up the place.' Then he did something rather nasty. It was obviously intended to tease or possibly frighten me.'

'What do you mean?'

'The snake was apparently asleep but he took it down from the shelf and draped it round his neck with its head right up against his face. Right up against the scarf he was wearing. He was fondling it like you might a kitten. He came up very close to me and I was determined not to flinch but it took a hell of a lot of self-control on my part to stay standing there and trying to look – well, unfazed. "What do you think, Mr Wexford?" he said. I don't know how calm I was. I hope I didn't tremble but I'm not sure. I just said, "Thanks very much. I'll let you know," or "I'll be in touch," something like that and I got out of there. When he'd closed the door after me I could hear him laughing.'

'Did you let him board the dog?'

'You must be joking. As it happened, the poor little beast died, got distemper. Had its injections too early or too late or something. I didn't speak to Targo again, didn't see him again, not until Billy Kenyon was killed. That must have been two or three years later.'

'Where was I? I mean, I remember the case but not being involved in it.'

'You were away doing that course. The forensics thing in Dover.'

'Of course I was. Are you going to tell me why that sentimental bit about the mother dog and the appealing puppies was relevant?'

'When he took in a pregnant bitch no one wanted – and he did a lot of that – Targo made a point of finding good homes for the puppies. Well, the good home he found for one of those puppies I saw was on the Muriel Campden Estate with Eileen Kenyon, Billy's mother.'

CHAPTER TEN

Kingsmarkham's botanical gardens, seven acres of them between Queen Street and Sussex Avenue, were still well maintained but had long been reduced in size to no more than half that by one of the lawns becoming a children's playground with swings and climbing frames and the tropical house turned into a coffee bar and brasserie. The picnic area had taken over most of the rose garden and Red Rocks fallen into disuse. It had not always been so. Once the place was looked after by a superintendent and deputy and five gardeners who took pride in their work. Visitors on their way to a day out at Leeds Castle or Sissinghurst would make a detour to take a look at Kingsmarkham's rock gardens in the spring or its prize blooms in the orchid house.

Those were the days when the botanical gardens were both a refuge and a pleasure ground for Billy Kenyon, a place to hide in and a place to enjoy, especially when the flowers were out. If he was capable of enjoyment. He was certainly capable of fear when his contemporaries shouted after him and he seemed never to get used to bullying and catcalls. What was wrong with Billy so that he never spoke, had never spoken, but still was able to look after himself? Harsh terms for someone like him were used in those days, 'mentally deficient', 'very low IQ', even 'moron'. But how could anyone be those things when he valued plants and flowers the way Billy did? When he learnt the names of plants and could write them all down if not utter them?

Today I think we'd call him autistic, Wexford thought. He would go to a special school for people with 'learning difficulties' – at least, I hope he would. His IQ might not have been low at all but quite high, as was often true of those with the Asperger's type of autism. The neighbours' children on the Muriel Campden Estate where he lived with his mother called him 'loony' and it was said that Eileen Kenyon did nothing to defend her son. He had left school at fifteen, the then school-leaving age, though he had seldom attended, and that was something else which Eileen failed to concern herself about. Even in his schooldays Billy had spent more time in the gardens than he had in class. The superintendent, George Clark, and deputy superintendent and the staff all knew him and knew him for a harmless innocent. On wet days they would let him sit on a chair in the temperate house and the deputy superintendent, a man called Denis Glaspell, often invited him into the big brick shed where the staff assembled in their tea breaks. Glaspell gave him a notebook and asked him to write down the Latin names of all the plants in, say, the rock garden, and Billy would do so, never making an error in identification or a spelling mistake. It was a pity, Wexford thought, when he was investigating the murder, that his teachers had never witnessed this. But would they have done anything if they had? Would they have had the time?

Billy was seventeen when he died. On the day of his death, in the hot summer of 1976, he left his mother's house in Leighton Close at nine in the morning, having made himself sandwiches of Mother's Pride and pre-sliced cheese. These with an overripe banana, which was the only item of fruit to be found, would be his lunch and mean he need not return till the gardens closed. His friend Denis Glaspell would give him a cup of tea. The dog came up to him, whining to be fed, but Billy left feeding him to his mother. The neighbours said she loved the dog much more than she loved him but if he knew this he gave no sign of it.

He had left her in bed with her lover, Bruce Mellor. How much of their relationship Billy understood no one seemed to know. But Billy's powers of comprehension were far greater than the people close to him believed and when Bruce said, and said frequently, that he'd like to live with or even marry Eileen Kenyon but he wasn't taking on a loony, not he, Billy no doubt had a very good idea of what he meant. Bruce didn't mind the dog, he liked the dog. Eileen too was in the habit of telling the neighbours that it was 'unfair on her' that she was 'lumbered' with Billy and it stopped her leading what she called a normal life. She'd like to get married before it was 'too late'.

It was the middle of June. The best of the flowers were past, they came in May, and the late-summer blooms had yet to blossom, but roses were still out and Billy made first for the rose garden. All the roses had their names in front of them on green metal tags pegged into the soil and Billy did his best to memorise the names: Rose Gaujard, Peace, Etoile d'Hollande, but when he forgot he checked with the green tag and wrote the name down in his notebook. One of the gardeners came along at about eleven – not that Billy wore a watch or had much idea of time – and told him Denis Glaspell had a cup of tea for him in the big shed they called the 'office'. Billy went along to the office, drank his tea and sat listening while the gardeners talked about football and snooker and what had been on TV the night before. He had another cup of tea in the office at three in the afternoon, by which time he had eaten his sandwiches and his banana. Another thing about Billy which endeared him to Denis Glaspell was his habit of taking his litter home with him or at least placing it in one of the waste bins. Too many visitors just dropped their food wrappings and fruit peel where they had been eating.

Denis noticed the plastic bag and the banana skin when Billy opened his backpack to put away his notebook.

'Let me dispose of that for you, Billy,' he said and Billy handed over the two items of rubbish without a smile and of course without a word. Denis had never seen him smile.

No one was quite sure where Billy had been after that. One of the gardeners had seen him in the hothouse but he hadn't stayed long. It was hot outside, though at about five the sky clouded over and it began to rain, a freak shower in a dry summer. Heavy rain always emptied the gardens and it did so that day, but lasted only half an hour before fading to a mist. There was no reason for any of the staff to keep a special eye on Billy Kenyon. He was their most frequent visitor, was entirely harmless and had an almost reverential attitude to the place. So it was never to be known who was the last person to have seen him, apart from his murderer.

George Clark, the superintendent, went round locking the gates at nine. It was still light, though going on dusk. George did as he always did and walked round the gardens, making sure that no one was left inside – occasionally a street sleeper would try to spend the night in there – and checking on the various designated areas that no damage had been done during the day. In Red Rocks he found Billy Kenyon's body, lying spreadeagled across the russet-coloured flat stones, one hand trailing in the water of a small pond, the other resting on his notebook. George felt for a pulse, laid his own face against the place where he thought the boy's heart must be. Then he looked more closely at his neck and the weals round it, at his face where the eyes protruded and knew for certain that he was dead, guessed he had been strangled. A leather belt, obviously the murder weapon, lay across his forehead where it had seemingly been draped.

No mobile phones then. George went back to his office and phoned the police, first taking a small swig from the miniature of brandy he kept there for emergencies. The little bottle was full because there had been no emergencies till now.

'If this death had happened today,' Wexford said, 'the press would have made much of Billy's notebook with the names of the flowers in it. They'd have called him "the dumb genius" and the "boy wonder failed by the education system". There was nothing like that then. I don't remember anything in the papers about Billy being other than a normal teenager. His mother and the man who wouldn't marry her while that meant taking on Billy – they didn't appear on television saying how Billy lit up their lives or what a saint he was. People didn't do that then. Nor did the press refer to Eileen Kenyon's on-and-off lover as Billy's stepfather the way they would now.'

'You're saying things were better then?' Burden raised his eyebrows.

'Yes and no. In some ways and in some ways not. I expect that's true whenever you contrast one period of time with another period of time. We have far more sophisticated forensic methods these days, as you know. If we haven't yet perfected tracing perpetrators by means of DNA, we're fast getting there. The mobile phone makes communication a whole lot easier. Parents ought to be able to keep a closer eye on where their children are – but do they? I don't know.

'To get back to Billy. He had been strangled with a leather belt. Those belts were on sale in the Saturday market but they were on sale in Pomfret market too and in Myringham market. Tracing it was impossible and there were no prints on it, though it could have taken prints. Our principal suspect was Bruce Mellor, the lover. But Eileen Kenyon ran him a close second.'

'Because Bruce Mellor wouldn't marry her while Billy was alive?'

'That's right. Neither of them had jobs and they were living on what in those days was called "assistance". They were both at home between 5 and 8 p.m. which according to the pathologist was when Billy died. Mellor took the dog out in the morning, returning after about an hour, and neither of them went out again. For the relevant time they alibied each other. But a next-door neighbour – I don't remember her name, Lucas or Lewis, I think – told me she had seen Bruce Mellor leave the house without the dog, this time at about six. This he denied, she had been mistaken, and Eileen denied it too.

'I asked her if she wasn't concerned when Billy hadn't come home by ten. As I said, the garden closed at nine in summer. It still closes at nine – what's left of it. Eileen said he was seventeen and able to look after himself. Besides, the body had been found by then and she had been informed by ten thirty.

'If Bruce Mellor had gone into the botanical gardens, no one remembered seeing him. If the neighbour's evidence was true and he had left the house next door at six he would have reached the gardens by about twenty past, by which time the rain had slackened and become a drizzle. Most visitors would have gone by then, so if Mellor had entered by either gate it was not surprising that no one had seen him. He would have been hard to ignore for he was exceptionally tall and thin and wore his yellow hair long – it was an unusual tawny colour – and either loose or tied back with an elastic band. Glaspell and his immediate superior George Clark, who found the body, and all the gardeners were closely questioned. None of them admitted to seeing Mellor. They were all, to a lesser degree, suspects but not for long. They had alibis a lot more sound than Mellor's or Eileen's.'

Burden had a question. 'Since you're going to say that you suspect Targo of this murder, how do you account for none of them seeing *him*? Or didn't you suspect him at that time?'

'I didn't because I couldn't find the connection,' Wexford said. 'The link between Targo and Elsie Carroll was tenuous enough but at least he lived in the same street. When Billy Kenyon was killed Targo was living miles away in Myringham in a big house in two acres of land and had at least one prosperous business going. Eileen Kenyon lived on what she called "the dole" on a council estate with a mentally incapacitated son. There was no reason even to consider Targo and, you know, Mike, how you sometimes label me an obsessive – well, I'm not blind to that in myself –' Medora Holland in her torn green blouse flitted across his mind's eye '– and I told myself to stop it, stop even imagining it while I had two quite feasible suspects.'

'There was the dog,' said Burden.

'Indeed there was the dog. But I didn't know that. When I went to the kennels to ask about boarding, Targo didn't tell me he'd given a woman called Eileen Kenyon in Kingsmarkham a puppy. Why would he? This was a while before the murder, no one had ever heard of Eileen Kenyon and Targo had no possible reason to tell me such a thing.'

'I came back,' said Burden, 'just about the time you gave up on the case. Sorry to put it like that.'

'Well, we did give up eventually, only we went on saying we would never give up. We always do say that, no matter how hopeless things look, don't we? We would never rest until we'd brought Billy's murderer to justice et cetera, et cetera.

But we knew we had given up. To recap a bit: the only evidence against Bruce Mellor was that he had possibly lied about going out that evening. But Mrs Lucas – she was called that, not Lewis – may have lied. She and he were at daggers drawn since there'd been some dispute about an all-night party the Lucases had for a son's twenty-first birthday. It may have been spite that made her say she had seen Mellor go out. Mellor alibied Eileen and she alibied him. Both had a motive of sorts but you know how unimportant motive is in preparing a sound case. It was one of our few unsolved murders.'

'When did you find out about the dog?'

'You mean that the dog came from Targo's place? Not until after we gave up. We questioned Mellor and Eileen exhaustively. I don't remember an interrogation like it – not one that came to nothing, at any rate. They were inarticulate and far from bright but they stuck to their story, that they had been in all that day.

'No one but Mrs Lucas claimed to have seen Mellor. Did we ever seriously suspect Eileen? Only perhaps as in cahoots with Mellor, supporting him, alibiing him, lying for him. She never denied wanting to be rid of Billy in order to marry Mellor but she said she only meant he should be in some sort of home. The trouble was that we had no evidence that Mellor had been in the gardens. No one had seen him and, as I've said, he was a memorable figure. Of course, we tried to trace the leather belt with which Billy was strangled. We failed. It might have belonged to Targo, may have been in his possession for years, but it might have come from any of those local markets. You try getting a market stallholder to identify something he's sold. All we did establish was that no shopkeeper in Kingsmarkham, Pomfret or Myringham had sold such a belt for years.'

'But the dog, Reg. What about the dog?'

'OK, I'm coming to that. Any case of strangling – and they were few – brought me back to Targo,' Wexford went on, 'as Billy's death did. I couldn't see any possible motive for his killing Billy. But then what motive was there in the case of Elsie Carroll? If it were just that Targo was a psychopath who killed at random, why those two? Why kill people when access is difficult if the place is full of loners, available as victims in the streets by night? Then I met him again.

'He'd told me he had what he called a business. It was a travel agent in Myringham High Street, a tiny little place grandly called Transglobe, and its walls were papered with advertisements for exotic places. People had started going to India and China for their holidays and he was cashing in on a new trend.'

'You mean you went there to book a holiday?'

'No, no, of course not. I went in there in connection with someone we suspected of smuggling raw opium out of Hong Kong. Opium! Those were the days.'

'I remember him. Berryman he was called. Raymond Berryman. He was sent down for a long time. So you went in there in all innocence and there was Targo.'

'That's right. There he was, sitting at the receipt of custom. No one else there but his dog. Mind you, there wasn't much room for anyone else. I saw him and it gave me quite a shock so that for a moment I thought I must be seeing things, confusing him with someone else. I'd never associated him with anything but dogs and driving. He seemed delighted to see me. Unnaturally delighted, I mean. That was one of the rare occasions when I saw him smile. He got up and put out his hand but of course I wasn't going to shake hands with him. The dog was a corgi and there in that tiny place it had its water bowl on the floor and a dish full of some sort of cooked entrails. Targo said, "Meet Princess," but I ignored this command just as I'd ignored his hand. He didn't appear offended. I asked him a few questions about our opium-running suspect and he answered them. Truthfully, I'm sure.

'He was looking more prosperous than I'd ever seen him. Very nice suit, expensive shoes I could just see under the desk, an Omega watch. A scarf, of course, but not a woollen one. This was more like a sort of cravat, grey, black and pink silk, not quite adequate to cover the birthmark. He was aware of that and he kept fidgeting with it, pushing the edge of it up to his cheek with his fingers, and each time it slipped down again.

'He hadn't put on weight, he was the same sturdy muscular type, unchanged except that his hair had receded a bit and there was more grey in it than fair. I was about to leave when he said, out of the blue as it seemed to me, "Funny how these cases fizzle out, isn't it? One week it's all over the papers and then when you people can't find the culprit it disappears and we never hear a word about it again." He fixed me with his staring eyes in that way he has. "I'm talking about the Billy Kenyon murder, of course."

'"I can't discuss that, Mr Targo," I said, and I thought "culprit" a funny word to use about a killer, too feeble a word. But of course I wasn't going to leave at that point. My eyes looked into his and he said, "I knew them, you know, that Mrs Kenyon and her fancy man." Another strange, and in this case old-fashioned, word to use. "No, I didn't know," I said. '"Oh, yes," he said. "That dog she's got, that was one of my puppies. My Dusty's young 'uns. I knew a dog would have a good home with her. Wouldn't like to say the same of anything human." And he laughed, Mike, he actually laughed. Laughing was something he did more than smiling. I can't quite say my blood ran cold because it never does but I had an idea what it would feel like.

'I asked him why he called the dog Princess. "She's a corgi, isn't she? They're royal dogs." He laughed again and was still laughing when I went, chuckling in an unpleasant way while he stroked the royal dog's head.'

'But you did nothing,' said Burden.

'I did what I could. I went back to questioning the staff at the gardens. I managed to get hold of a photograph of Targo, showed it to Glaspell and the rest. None of them remembered seeing him on the relevant day or any other. Once more I had nothing to go on, nothing but a laugh and his saying Eileen Kenyon wouldn't be fit to have charge of anything human.'

'He had an alibi?'

'I've no doubt he would have fixed one up or *already had one fixed up* if I'd asked him. He'd married again by then, that woman called Adele. It only lasted about six months but she would have alibied him. I gave up, in your useful phrase, because I couldn't see a motive. What was in it for Targo? Who benefits from Billy's death? Not Targo. Only Eileen Kenyon. So he did it for Eileen Kenyon's sake? He hardly knew the woman.'

'You're sure of that?'

'I'm sure. Come to that, he hardly knew Elsie Carroll. Well, he didn't know her at all except maybe by sight. I talked to Eileen Kenyon and Bruce Mellor about him. That conversation was the only one I had with them when they were transparently honest, not prevaricating or defensive. Eileen had met Targo three times, the first when she went to the boarding kennels because someone had told her he had puppies he'd give away to a suitable owner. The puppies were too young to leave their mother then but she could choose which one she wanted in advance. Targo had a talk with her about the proper care of a dog and said he'd come and inspect her place after she'd had the puppy two weeks. She came back to fetch the dog when it was eight weeks old and on that occasion he only spoke a few words to her. His wife attended to Eileen, putting the puppy in the dog carrier she'd brought with her and getting the carrier into Mellor's car.

'Two weeks later he called at the house in Leighton Close, was apparently satisfied with the dog's condition, its sleeping and feeding arrangements et cetera. He accepted a cup of tea and they chatted for a while, she said. I'd rather not imagine what having a chat with Targo would be like. Billy wasn't present. She didn't tell me what they talked about, she said she couldn't remember, but for Targo to have said she couldn't be trusted with the care of a human being has to mean that part of their talk was about the hardness of her lot in having a mentally incapacitated son and what a burden he was to her.

'Bruce Mellor never did marry Eileen. They fell out and he was seen no more in Leighton Close. Targo gave up the travel agency and the boarding kennels about a year after-wards and moved away with his menagerie but not with Adele. They'd split up and were divorced after a couple of years. He went back to Birmingham and that woman he'd been with off and on for years, Tracy Whatever-it-was.'

'And now he's back.'

'And now he's back. Living in some style. Is he still in the travel agency business? Does he still move around with a private zoo? I think he does. I saw signs of it when I went to Stringfield to have a look at his place. Perhaps it doesn't matter. I haven't a hope of proving any of this. He's got older and he may have given up this homicidal spree of his. But I've thought like that before. I thought like that when he followed me into that hotel in Coventry and when I ima-gined I'd seen him in London but I hadn't. Even if it's true now and he's changed, that wouldn't mean he hadn't done those things or justice shouldn't be done.'

'I don't believe it, you know, Reg. I'm sorry but I don't.'

'I know,' said Wexford, 'and I don't care. It makes no difference.'

CHAPTER ELEVEN

It was plain that the Rahman family disliked Hannah Goldsmith and she knew it. Not usually a sensitive woman, she did her utmost with Mohammed and Yasmin Rahman, their sons Ahmed and Osman and their daughter Tamima not to appear patronising; the more she tried the worse it got. Hannah's way of showing immigrants from Asia or the children of immigrants that she and they were all equally free citizens of the United Kingdom was to be excessively polite, flattering and considerate. Of course they saw through this at once, Mohammed with amusement, Yasmin with a kind of indignant suspiciousness and the sons with indifference.

She began, not for the first time, by telling them what a 'lovely home' they had. A pity the house was attached to that eyesore, Webb and Cobb next door. She was a little abashed when Yasmin said the defunct shop and flats above it was their property. But she made things worse by saying that building an extension at the rear, culminating in a conservatory, was such a marvellous improvement she couldn't understand why their neighbours hadn't done the same thing.

Mohammed smiled, said in his pleasant slightly sing-song voice, 'They are far from well off, Miss Goldsmith. I doubt if they could afford it. We have three incomes coming in here.'

Hannah had by then made up her mind that both sons probably lived on the benefit. 'Oh, what do you do then?' she asked Ahmed.

'Computers,' he said. 'I'm an IT consultant. Work from home.'

She looked enquiringly at his brother. Both were good-looking, dark; Ahmed clean-shaven, Osman with a beard like his father. All wore Western dress while Yasmin was in the long black gown of the traditional Muslim woman but hung with valuable-looking, heavy gold jewellery. Osman didn't answer her unspoken question, so she prompted him.

'I'm a psychiatric nurse at the Princess Diana.'

Hannah nearly gushed, 'How splendid!' but curbed herself just in time and said, 'Really?'

In the cold voice which was the only tone Hannah had ever heard from her, Yasmin said, 'If you wanted to see Tamima, Miss Goldsmith, she's not here. She's still at the shop.'

'Oh, do call me Hannah. Yes, I know she is, I've been there today. She told me you and she were going home to Pakistan for a holiday.'

'It is no longer home. This is home. But we are going there.'

Not easily daunted, Hannah was this time temporarily silenced by Yasmin Rahman's icy, clipped tone. Every word sounded like a snub. With a faint smile, probably intended as a tribute to his mother's handling of this interfering police officer, Ahmed picked up an armful of folders and other papers and moved to a desk at the far end of the extension. Osman followed him, settling in an armchair with the evening paper. Hannah rallied, asked Mohammed what future was planned for Tamima after her return.

'Perhaps she may go to London for a while to stay with her auntie. My sister, that is. There are girl cousins to go about with and have a good time. Fair enough, don't you think, when you have worked hard for your exams? Then, she says, she would like a gap year.'

'But people have gap years between school and university,' said Hannah, recalling her own.

'And why not between school and sixth-form college, then? Sixteen is a difficult age, you know. Teenage is a troubling time and we should all remember that. Oh, yes, she will probably go to sixth-form college. But we don't know yet for sure. Let her enjoy herself in Islamabad and London first and then we shall see.' With magnificent aplomb which Hannah was forced to admire, Mohammed said, 'We mustn't keep you any longer, Hannah. You are a busy woman.'

Hannah had hoped to have something significant to tell Wexford. She had nothing, yet she was convinced now, partly by the suave yet resolute behaviour of all the Rahmans, that the purpose of the Pakistan visit was to find a husband for Tamima. That, she thought as she walked along Glebe Lane towards her car, was exactly as such a family would behave if they intended to carry out some ancient traditional rite in defiance of laws they despised. She looked up at the windows of the flats above Webb and Cobb and a woman looked back at her, a white-skinned woman. Hannah wondered how well this woman knew the Rahmans. A future interview with her might yield useful information.

Street stabbings had until recently been confined to big cities. When the second happened and the victim, Nicky Dusan, died in hospital twelve hours later, Wexford feared a trend had started. People were imitative. They followed a fashion even if that fashion led to terrible consequences. DS Vine and DC Coleman were the investigating officers and three days after the knife attack Barry Vine arrested a sixteen-year-old called Tyler Pyke. Kathy Cooper and Brian Dusan, the dead boy's parents, had appeared on television with the customary emotional appeal for any witnesses, Kathy claiming that her son had been in a gang against his will. He had been forced into it, she said, by 'evil' contemporaries he had been at school with who told him he had to join to defend them all against the 'Pyke–Samuels gang'.

'Nicky Dusan,' Hannah told Wexford, 'is the first cousin of that boy Rashid Hanif who is Tamima Rahman's boyfriend and also cousin of Neil Dusan. He's Brian Dusan's sister's son.'

Wexford considered the name. 'You mean Brian Dusan and his sister are Muslims?'

Hannah was always happy to show off her extensive know-ledge of Islam and its history. 'They're Bosnians. Bosnians have been Muslim for centuries. It's a legacy the Turks left behind when they went. Brian Dusan is presumably lapsed, though it's hard for Muslims to lapse.' Wexford could see that Hannah was having problems here. A declared atheist herself and one who would have no hesitation in condemning any manifestation of Christianity out of hand, she steadily avoided criticism of Islam. 'The sister is a devout Muslim,' she said hastily. 'She married Akbar Hanif and Rashid is one of their seven children.'

How she would have condemned so large a family if the parents had been Roman Catholics! He smiled at her. 'You've really been into this, haven't you?'

'It wasn't difficult, guv. I knew it long before this stabbing happened. It's been part of my research into the antecedents of people connected with the Rahmans.'

'So you know as much about, say, Mr and Mrs Rahman's relatives as you do about their daughter's boyfriend's.'

'More. Much more. It's a very large extended family. Mohammed Rahman has at least two sisters living in London. Yasmin Rahman has a sister in Stowerton who didn't object at all to telling me her family's history. Among the things she told me was that they've got another sister living in Pakistan whose marriage was arranged, though it sounded more like forced to me. This woman has a son who may be lined up to marry Tamima.'

'May be? Not "is"?'

Hannah was a good police officer. She wasn't prepared to exaggerate to serve her own ends. 'Only "may be", guv. The sister thought this man a likely candidate but that's all. It was really guesswork.'

'Let's concentrate,' said Wexford, 'on Kingsmarkham's incipient gang warfare for now, shall we?'

He no more believed in the Rahman forced marriage theory than Burden believed in his insistence on Targo as a murderer. Hannah took a few steps towards the door and turned round. She was fond of having the last word.

'Tamima and her mother go to Pakistan on Thursday. I bought a loaf from her in the Raj Emporium yesterday and she told me.'

When he drove himself home the route Wexford took was along Glebe Road into Glebe Lane, into Orchard Road and then the Avenue. He stopped when he saw a white van he thought might be Targo's parked outside Webb and Cobb. He parked his own in front of the nail bar and looked up the white van's number in the notebook he still carried. It was Targo's but there was no sign of the van's owner. Hannah had told him one of the Rahman sons was a computer consultant and when he had seen Targo go in there back in August he had been carrying what was very likely a computer. Wexford's own skills in this particular technology were very limited but still he had an idea that a consultant or engineer or whatever the man was could make adjustments to what he called a machine by what he called remote control. Why then would Targo take the thing there? Or was he visiting for some other purpose?

Wexford disliked the thought of showing himself. From where he sat in his own car he could see that the driver's window in the van was open about four inches. No doubt the Tibetan spaniel was inside, no doubt waiting for an intruder to poke his face through that gap so that it could utter its single sharp yap. I shan't give it the satisfaction, thought Wexford, laughing at his aunt's phrase and driving off.

On the day Tamima Rahman and her mother left for Islamabad, Hannah went to call on Fata Hanif. With her husband and seven children she lived in a house in Rectangle Road, Stowerton, that had once been two houses but had been converted into one by the local authority. In spite of its size, and the car parked on concrete slabs in what had once been a front garden, the Hanifs were obviously doing far less well than the Rahmans. Akbar Hanif had no job, had been out of work for years, and he and his family lived on benefits.

He was not at home and nor were five of the children, for school had just returned after the summer holidays. Fata Hanif took her time answering the doorbell, possibly due to her pausing to tie a scarf round her head in case her caller were a man. There are many ways a woman can cover her hair but perhaps the most unflattering is when the scarf is brought low down over the forehead and high up to skim the chin. A pale face that had once been pretty peered out at Hannah from inside the black cotton oval. The voice was unexpected, south-east London which would be called cockney north of the river.

'What do you want?'

It was said diffidently rather than rudely. It sounded feebly frightened.

'May I come in?' Hannah produced her warrant card, wondering if it would mean anything to this woman. 'I'm a police officer but there's nothing for you to worry about. There's nothing wrong.'

The door opened a few inches wider. Fortunately, Hannah was very slim. She squeezed through the opening. 'This is just a friendly visit. I hope to have a talk with you about Tamima Rahman.'

Immediately Mrs Hanif said, 'I don't know her.'

They went into a living room. A baby lay asleep on the centre cushion of a three-seater sofa. An older child, perhaps two, was strapped into a high chair with, in front of it, a plateful of some sort of cereal he was slowly and almost ritualistically transferring to the floor, scooping it up in his fingers and smiling as it flopped on to a rug. Mrs Hanif took no notice of either child. It was the sort of room Hannah wouldn't want to stay in for more than ten minutes at the most. Though clean, it showed the signs on every article of furniture of the depredations of children. Everything was broken or battered or scuffed or chipped or cracked or torn or split or crushed or frayed. With all those children the Hanifs must be receiving considerable amounts of benefit, but whatever they did with it, they didn't spend it on improving their home.

Hannah sat down next to the baby. Every other seat in the place was damaged in some way. A leg missing and the chair propped up on bricks, the seat itself split or the cover ripped off to expose splintered wood and sharp nails beneath. Mrs Hanif sat in the chair on the bricks and, though it wobbled, it held her weight.

'I'd heard,' Hannah said carefully, 'that your son Rashid was friendly with her.'

'He's only a boy,' Fata Hanif said. 'He doesn't go out with girls. His dad and me, we wouldn't have it.'

Hannah could hardly say she had seen the boy and girl together. 'When he is older will you arrange a marriage for Rashid?'

For a moment she thought Fata Hanif would refuse to answer. She was silent for a long time. She got up and lifted the baby in her arms. Boy or girl, Hannah couldn't tell which it was. The child in the high chair had emptied his bowl and was looking with pride, Hannah thought, at the piles of rejected porridge on the floor.

At last Mrs Hanif spoke. 'I expect we will,' she said.

'Will it be with a local girl?'

Suddenly she became talkative. 'We've no relations round here except for that Nicky and his dad that's my brother. All my husband's relations are in Pakistan. He's got girl cousins there.'

Trying to treat it as if were a laughing matter no one would take seriously for a moment, Hannah said, 'So you wouldn't consider Tamima Rahman as a possible bride for your son?'

'We don't know the Rahmans. Her and Rashid go to the same school, that's all, and my sons Hussein and Khaled go there too and they're not any of them going to marry Tamima Rahman. You people think that because we're all Muslims we must know each other. Well, that's wrong, we don't. Is that all? Because I've got to feed the baby.'

Still asleep, the baby showed no sign of wanting to be fed

123

but Mrs Hanif was already unfastening the bodice of her long lilac-print dress. Hannah let herself out.

Concentrating on the murder of Nicky Dusan was hardly necessary now that Tyler Pyke had been charged and committed for trial. It would be months before that trial happened. Wexford sometimes thought how strange the system must be for the public, for the inveterate reader of newspapers or viewer of television news broadcasts. The killing happened and the media went mad. Photographs of the victim and the victim's family dominated front pages and screens. The 'quality' papers carried statistics, giving prominence to whatever number in the list of like murders this latest one was, the sixteenth or the eighteenth in as many weeks in the south of England. The victim's 'loved ones' were interviewed or appeared on television, giving appeals. Wexford dared to speculate – knowing how politically incorrect this would be – if there would ever be a death by violence after which the dead man or woman's relatives for once failed to describe them as perfect, the soul of kindness, loving, 'bubbly', helpful to all and the ideal son, daughter or sibling. No doubt, most of the dead had been in fact much like everyone else, a mixture of good and bad with virtues and faults. A few might be as saintly as their grieving relations said they were but others would balance that by being as satanic as – well, as Targo.

He hadn't set eyes on Targo since the day he had seen him carrying the laptop into 34 Glebe Road and seen too the spaniel in the passenger seat of the white van. Had he ever seen the man without a dog? Perhaps not. In the travel agency he had been accompanied by a corgi, in Myringham by his own pet dogs and those in the boarding kennels, in Jewel

Road, Stowerton, by what Wexford called 'the original spaniel' and with that same spaniel when he walked past Wexford's window on his way to the Kingsbrook meadows. But yes, there had been one occasion when he was without a dog. In the hotel bar in Coventry he had been on his own and this was no doubt only because the hotel banned dogs.

It must be over a month now since he had seen Targo sitting in his van on Glebe Road. Because Targo had seen and recognised him he had half expected the stalking to begin again. But it hadn't and now Wexford began to see that this supposition was unrealistic. The stalking had been confined to those early days in Kingsmarkham. Later there had been the incident of the snake. But he had never again been the subject of Targo's sustained surveillance and since the death of Billy Kenyon and subsequent investigation, he had encountered him only once. That had been when Targo told him how he had given the puppy to Billy's mother.

Mullan had got life imprisonment for the murder of Shirley Palmer in Coventry, but Wexford still wondered. Everyone he talked to about that murder, every police officer, said that if ever there was a justified penalty that was it. Mullan had killed Shirley just as Christopher Roberts had killed his wife Maureen. But he wondered. Although by this time Mullan had served decades in prison he had never admitted to the crime, though such an admission might have have resulted in his release. This was usually regarded as an argument against guilt.

Did this perhaps mean Targo had been responsible for Shirley Palmer's death? It was possible. The recent murders in the Kingsmarkham area had been knife crimes and Targo himself had only killed by strangling and claimed involvement in murders by strangling. Serial killers gave up when they got old, he thought. As he reflected on this, listing in his mind notorious killers who in age had left their life of crime behind them, he realised that there weren't so many. Most known killers had been caught before old age. Then the thought came that Targo couldn't be called a serial killer. Even Wexford, obsessed as he was, could hardly give that title to a man who was possibly responsible for only two deaths. Or perhaps three and others which Targo would have liked to be blamed for.

Now, with old age encroaching, would he be strong enough to strangle someone? It was a method which took physical strength. If his victim were a woman he would have. Wexford conjured up an image of him, short, sturdy, brawny with the muscles of a mini-sumo wrestler. Did he still lift weights, do press-ups? The question really was, would he want to? Perhaps he was satisfied now with the life he had made for himself, with his wife, his house, his cars and, of course, his dogs.

I will get him for what he's done, Wexford said to himself. Whatever it takes, I will get him. One day, no matter how far away and how long it takes. The murder of the innocent and harmless Billy Kenyon got to me like no other death by violence I have come across for a long time. If I let myself I could weep for Billy Kenyon, even now, after all these years, but I won't, of course I won't. I will watch him and wait and one day bring him to justice for Billy Kenyon and Elsie Carroll and perhaps too for Shirley Palmer.

CHAPTER TWELVE

hree weeks later they came to him with the same
subject on succeeding days. Hannah first, sand-
wiching her information between her report on Nicky
Dusan and the health or lack of it of Tyler Pyke. Jenny
avoided the police station and came to his home. But they
had the same thing to tell him. Yasmin Rahman had returned
from Pakistan and Tamima with her. Tamima was not
married, there was no husband and no marriage ceremony
had taken place. They had come home early because Tamima
was homesick.

'These children, they have their way these days, don't they?'
Yasmin had told Hannah, echoing her husband.

'I hoped to have a word with her,' Hannah had said.

But Tamima wasn't there. In spite of what her mother had
said, she was back working for her uncle at the Raj Emporium.
'She will soon be going to London to stay with her auntie in
Kingsbury.'

Hannah remembered that this was exactly what Mohammed
Rahman had told her would happen. She asked when that
would be but Mrs Rahman said she didn't know. She was
growing indignant by this time and Hannah finally had to
acknowledge that she hadn't a leg to stand on when Tamima's
mother said, 'I don't know why it interests you. She is free

to do what she wants. What wrong has she done? What wrong have me and her father done?'

'Nothing, Mrs Rahman, nothing at all.' Hannah was appalled that she of all police officers might appear to be victimising people for no more reason than that they were immigrants. 'I'm sorry. I'd no intention of upsetting you.'

'Tamima is over sixteen. She can leave home if she wants. You see, I know your law.'

Jenny had met with an even colder reception, in her case from Tamima's father. 'Tamima is working for her uncle. She's there because she likes to earn some money, as many young people do. Would you like to speak to her uncle? Or, better, would your *husband* like to speak to him? He, I think, is the policeman, not you.'

Shaken, Jenny said, 'No, no, of course not.' And, making matters worse, 'It's just that I've grown fond of Tamima and I want to see things turn out well for her.'

'And aren't I fond of my own daughter? My *only* daughter? Do you think I want her to be unhappy? Perhaps you should remember, Mrs Burden, that I am a childcare officer, specifically Myringham's teenage care manager. Don't you think maybe I know as much about adolescents' needs as you do?'

'Of course you do, of course.' Appalled, Jenny was admitting to herself that this man was too much for her. This man was a great deal cleverer, more sophisticated and astute than she had given him credit for. 'It's just that –'

He interrupted her. 'I'm sorry, Mrs Burden, but I am busy and cannot talk much longer. Tamima is planning to go to her auntie in London shortly. She will enjoy herself there, go out with her cousins. The length of time she stays is down to her and to my sister. Then she will come home and decide what her next move should be? OK? All right?'

'I had to be satisfied with that,' Jenny said.

'Aren't you?' Wexford raised his eyebrows. 'Dare I ask what all the fuss is about?'

'If that's your attitude, I give up,' said Jenny.

'I'm glad to hear it.' He changed the subject and spoke to Dora. 'Did Andy Norton come today?'

'He always comes on Thursdays. Well, twice he's changed to a Tuesday but he's always phoned well in advance to let me know. Three o'clock. You could set your watch by him.'

On the following Thursday he got home early. Andy Norton was still there, still engaged in cutting back the lushly over-grown shrubs and climbers which covered the rear garden wall. Wexford saw a tall thin man, white-haired and gaunt. He went outside, introduced himself and noted the mellifluous tones and fine enunciation conferred on its alumni by Eton College.

'You're doing overtime,' he said with a smile.

'I want to get things shipshape before the rain starts.'

'Shipshape', the word Targo had used long ago. He watched Norton get into his ancient but gleaming Morris Minor and drive away, waving as he went.

It was later in the evening that Dora told him. He had noticed when he got home from work how especially nice she looked in a new dark green dress and high-heeled dark green shoes. Her legs had always been one of her best features with their long calves and fine ankles. Round her neck she wore a necklace of gold and green garnets he had once given her. In his eyes she hadn't lost her looks at all; only in her own was she less attractive than she had been. He remembered how he used to compare her – was 'contrast' rather the word? – with other men's wives and how there was really no competition. He smiled and complimented her on her appearance.

She smiled back, thanked him, said, 'I've been meaning to

tell you. There's been a white van parked outside here for most of the afternoon. That's the second time this week. It was here on Tuesday too. I went out to check if it had a residents' parking pass in the windscreen but it hadn't. Still, the traffic warden didn't appear. They never do when you want them.'

Far from smiling now, he felt a sharp chill, like icy water trickling down his spine, the warmth her evident pleasure had brought him all gone.

'As a matter of fact, I took the number.'

He looked at the slip of paper she held out to him. It was Targo's. Of course it was.

'It comes of being married to a policeman,' she said.

He tried to speak casually, 'Dora, don't do that again. I mean, don't check up on a vehicle's right to park. Please.'

'But why, darling?'

'Suppose I said, because I say so? Would that be enough?'

'That's what you say to children. All right, then. But I would quite like to know.'

The white van didn't come back to Wexford's street the next day or the next. That meant little. Targo had at least one other car. Wexford decided not to frighten Dora by asking her if she had seen a silver Mercedes parked where the van had been. Nor was he going to ask her if there had been a dog in the van. Besides, Targo might well have a collection of motor vehicles. Or he might do his surveillance on foot, parking the van farther away and walking the Tibetan spaniel half a mile or so.

What puzzled Wexford was the question of whom Targo was keeping under observation and why. Not himself, surely. The man must know he was out of the house all day. So he was watching Dora. Wexford didn't like that at all. Only a few days ago, he had half made up his mind that Targo had abandoned his need to kill, had become a law-abiding citizen. Now he thought of the two occasions he had seen that van in Glebe Road. On both Targo had been calling on the Rahmans because one of the sons was an IT consultant, a legitimate reason for a visit. But Ahmed Rahman might have knowledge of Targo which would be invaluable to him. His thoughts went back to his wife.

Two years before, along with four other people, she had been abducted and held hostage by a group of countryside campaigners. He still thought of the three nights and four days as the worst period of his life. Suppose I lost her? was the question he kept asking himself. Suppose I never see her again? When she came back, he had sworn to himself that he would value her more, and for the most part he had stuck to that. He had appreciated her more and had shown it. But there was no reason to suppose that what had happened then would happen again. As far as he knew, Targo had never abducted anyone. He felt that cold trickle again when he spoke aloud what Targo did: 'He kills. It's a hobby with him'. He had killed at least one woman and one man, possibly two women. Maybe there had been others, 'unregistered in vulgar fame'. He remembered what Kathleen Targo had said to him when they met all those years ago in the Kingsbrook Precinct, 'He likes animals. He doesn't like people.'

What was to be done? He could hardly send a PC to keep an eye on the street outside his house. In the eyes of everyone but himself, Targo had done no wrong. Perhaps he should start again on proving that the man was not the innocent he looked to be. It was Friday afternoon, a mild day in October. The trees were turning brown and their leaves had begun to fall. The sunshine was rather thin and the pale blue sky streaked with strings of cloud.

The walk to Glebe Road constituted half his daily exercise but he was held up – almost swept up – by the crowd of Muslim men returning home or to their work from Stowerton mosque. They seemed remarkably happy, laughing and joking with each other, though not rowdily, and he thought how different a group of home-going church attenders would have been. Be careful not to be an inverted racist, he told himself, you're just as much a racist as Hannah if you favour immigrants over indigenous people. Letting the crowd go ahead of him, he fell in behind them. Most lived in this neighbourhood but by the time he was halfway up Glebe Road only two young men remained and an older man. Outside Webb and Cobb the older man paused to look between the boards which covered what had been a shop window and, apparently satisfied, passed on. They all turned into number 34. Mohammed Rahman and his sons, they must be, Tamima's father and brothers. He waited until they were inside before ringing the bell.

The door was opened by the son with the beard, the older one, Hannah had told him.

'Chief Inspector Wexford, Kingsmarkham Crime Management.' Wexford produced his warrant card. He had nearly said 'Kingsmarkham CID', for old habits died hard and to him the new title sounded like a mafioso managing a bunch of gangsters.

'You want my dad? He's inside with my brother. I'm off to work.'

Wexford walked in and was met in the narrow passage by a man of about fifty with black hair but a grey beard. He seemed to recognise Wexford, though Wexford had no recollection of ever having seen him before.

'Mohammed Rahman,' he said, held out his hand, and indicating the young man behind him, 'This is my son Ahmed.'

If the father seemed calm but wary, the son looked rather tense. He was a handsome man of perhaps twenty-five, pale-skinned with coal-black eyes and black hair. He had the face of a young Mogul emperor. They were absurdly crowded together in that narrow space, three tall men so close to each other that father and son had to shrink back to avoid touching Wexford while Wexford pressed himself against the wall.

'Come into the lounge,' said Mohammed Rahman.

A ridiculous word for a living room at any time, owing its provenance, Wexford thought, to early-twentieth-century Hollywood and luxury liners. Here it was less absurd than it might have been, for the room was unexpectedly spacious with ample light coming in through the conservatory. A large fireplace of stone blocks with a mantelpiece of polished granite held on its grate a bowl of dried flowers. Kelim rugs covered the floor and the conservatory was full of plants, a pale blue plumbago, a rose-pink oleander, which, had they been outside, would by now have been killed by frost. Apart from the rugs, not a single object was what Wexford would have called 'oriental'. He was rather ashamed to confess to himself that he had expected the decor of an Indian restaurant.

He was shown to a black leather armchair. The two Rahmans waited expectantly, the father managing a smile, the son still ill at ease. 'Do you know a man called Eric Targo?' he asked them.

The tension slackened. It was interesting to watch this lightening in each of them. Had they expected him to talk about Tamima? Ahmed spoke for the first time. 'He's a client,' he said.

'Your client? You're a computer consultant, aren't you?'

The young man nodded. 'I work from home. I have an office upstairs.'

'You look after Mr Targo's computer? Service it? Mend it if it goes wrong?' He was aware he was using the wrong terminology.

Evidently Ahmed was also aware of it for he smiled. 'Mr Targo has three PCs. If he has a problem I talk him through it or I call at his house.'

'He has sometimes brought a computer here, Ahmed,' his father reminded him.

'That's right. So he did. His Toshiba, his laptop, that was. Look, let me explain. Some of my clients – well, they're not exactly computer-illiterate, I wouldn't say that. But they get a bit nervous. They don't quite understand that when something's wrong I can put it right if we're – well, both of us get online. That's when I can talk him through what's bothering him.' He looked searchingly into Wexford's face, in case the Chief Inspector failed to follow him. 'Anyway, that's how it is but a lot of clients think I have to have the PC here to look at. And that's when he brings the Toshiba in for me to deal with it.'

'I see.'

What Wexford really meant was that he didn't see – it amounted to mending a machine without touching it or even seeing it – but he accepted it and was satisfied. He hardly knew what he had suspected, for, whatever Targo's murderous propensities, he must have constant contact in business and his personal life with people whom he knew in honesty and innocence.

The trees in Glebe Road had begun to shed their leaves. Wexford started the walk back to the police station, recalling how when he was a child he always made a point of treading on a fallen leaf, enjoying the crunching sensation underneath his feet. He tried it now, crushing a dried crinkled plane leaf, and was pleased to find it gave him much the same feeling. But back to the Rahmans. There was nothing sinister about the Targo–Rahman connection, he thought. Nevertheless, the fact remained that Targo had resumed his stalking of *him* or, rather, begun stalking his wife. It came to him then that, in accordance with the old marriage service, a married couple used to be called 'one flesh' and, thinking of that, he felt a pang, as if what seemed a threatened hurt were being done to himself. The first thing he did when he was in his office was to send for DC Damon Coleman and, wondering if he might be doing something indefensible, considering that in everyone's eyes but his own Targo was an innocent man, set him to keep his own house under surveillance. The stalker stalked, he thought.

Some years before, when his daughter Sylvia had been taking a course in psychotherapeutic counselling, she had taught him about the 'box' as a means of dealing with anxieties.

'If you've a problem weighing on your mind, Dad, you have to visualise a box – maybe quite small, the size of a matchbox. You open it and put your worry inside – now don't start laughing. It works. Close the box with the worry inside and put it away somewhere, inside a drawer, say.'

'Why not throw it in the sea?'

'That's a bit final. You may want to take it out again one day.'

'And this is going to take all problems away?'

'I don't say that, Dad, but it might help. If you find yourself thinking of the worry you also think it's locked away in the box so you can't touch it.'

He had scoffed. But still he tried it. Several times since then he had put Targo in a box and sometimes it had worked well. He tried it again now, carefully placing Targo and the white van and a bunch of dogs and his own fear into the box and hiding it in a drawer of the desk in his office. And the white van failed to reappear. No silver Mercedes was parked in Wexford's street and no man with cropped white hair walking a Tibetan spaniel had been seen. It had, of course, no longer been possible to tell Damon Coleman of the distinguishing mark, the naevus on the neck. That was gone.

Damon had seen Dora Wexford leave the house twice on foot and twice in her car but he was sure she hadn't seen him. Damon was an expert in the role of the invisible watcher. A woman he recognised as Wexford's daughter Sylvia came once and stayed about an hour. Jenny Burden called with her son. Apart from these, the only caller he had seen was a man in his sixties who arrived on Thursday at three in the afternoon in an ancient Morris Minor. Damon finished his surveillance at five by which time the visitor had not come out.

This wasn't quite what Wexford had wanted. His wife and her callers were not to be watched but, rather, whoever might be watching her. Damon's report reminded him of the kind of thing a private detective might produce for a husband who believed himself deceived. That made Wexford smile. The idea of Dora's infidelity was absurd, even the mildest disloyalty out of the question.

But his fear was in the box and the box was shut up inside the top left-hand drawer of his desk. As often, when he used the box – the invisible container created by his own mind – the apprehensiveness or anxiety locked inside it had faded away. Just as the box had no real existence so it seemed that the fear had none either.

Rashid Hanif had just come out of the gates of his sixth-form college on the Kingsmarkham bypass when Hannah spoke to him. If she had simply walked up to him he might not have been so obviously taken aback, but he had seen her car draw up and park ahead of him and this very good-looking young woman he recognised from the Raj Emporium step out of it, flourishing a warrant card. He was good-looking himself, a tall handsome boy with pale skin, brown hair and grey-blue eyes.

Hannah could tell he was frightened and she wondered why. After all, he might be only seventeen but he was a man and most men – at any rate the innocent ones – were happy to speak to her. 'I'd like to ask you about Tamima,' she said. 'We could talk in my car. I could give you a lift home.'

Making that offer was a mistake. 'Oh, no. No, thanks. I don't need a lift home. I can walk.'

'I know you can walk,' Hannah said. 'I don't have to take you to your house, just to the corner of the street. Come on. Those books you're carrying must be heavy.'

He allowed her to shepherd him into the passenger seat of the car. Hannah had no intention of driving off immediately. She sat in the driving seat and turned to face him. 'I've seen you talking to Tamima in the Raj Emporium, Rashid. I've seen you quite a few times. She's your girlfriend, isn't she?'

He shook his head, said in a low voice, 'I wish.'

'But she's not? Why is that? Because your parents are against it or hers are?'

There was a long pause during which his fingers tightened on the handle of the heavy bag. 'Both,' he said, and then, 'Look, I mustn't talk to you about that. I'll get into trouble. My dad's told me not to see her again. But I'm not to talk about it, OK?'

Hannah started the car, said nothing for a moment or two and then, when they were in Hartwell Lane heading for the Hart Estate, said, 'You can only see her in the shop, is that right?'

'I'm not to talk about it.' He immediately did so. 'They took her to Pakistan to keep her away from me but she missed me and she wanted to come back. Now they'll send her to her auntie in London.'

'Did she tell you this?'

'She didn't tell me but it's what I think. I told you, I'm not supposed to talk about it. Can I get out now? I can walk from here.'

'I'm sure you can,' said Hannah. 'If you'll tell me her auntie's name and where she lives I'll drive to the end of Hartwell Lane and drop you off.'

The boy shifted in his seat. Now he was clutching the bag of books. 'It's Kingsbury. But she's not gone yet. Maybe she won't go, I don't know.'

'And the name, Rashid?'

The house where his family lived was in sight. Hannah pulled over, leaving the engine running. 'The auntie's name, Rashid?'

The two words came out in a choked rush, 'Mrs Qasi,' and he flung open the car door and ran.

Hannah knew she must bide her time. It was true that Tamima might not go to London. If, for instance, she agreed to give Rashid up she might remain here. But that was unlikely. The Rahman parents wouldn't trust her to keep any promise she might make, especially if she were working in that shop where anyone might come in and have access to her. Besides, their aim was not only to divide her from Rashid but to marry her to someone else.

'It would be hard to force marriage on a girl here. In a place like this where everyone knows everyone else,' she said to Wexford.

'Used to,' said Wexford, thinking of the villagey town of his youth.

'Still does,' Hannah persisted. 'Especially if you're an immigrant. People are always on the watch for them to do something *un-English,* something bizarre or something *they* wouldn't do. Think of the drama there'd be if Tamima ran away on the steps of the mosque or the register office or wherever. In London she couldn't do that, she wouldn't know where she was or where to go. Think about it, guv.'

'Hannah,' he said, 'what I'm thinking about is the drama you're making out of a young girl's visit to London. To go shopping, no doubt. Maybe see a film or a show.' Smiling at Hannah's mutinous expression, 'She hasn't gone yet. But I've met those Rahmans and they impressed me as intelligent enlightened people, the last to force ancient traditions on a beloved daughter. I'll be very surprised if Tamima doesn't go away for a couple of weeks, have a good time and come back to take a better sort of job somewhere.'

On the way home he wondered if he had been rather rash in saying that. Was Hannah's theory so far-fetched? Perhaps what provoked his pacifying rejoinder was her vehement determination to prove that a forced marriage was intended without any evidence for it. But that was not so different from his certainty that Targo was at least twice a murderer. He had no evidence either. Yet he constantly said to himself that he knew it for a fact. Hannah, too, probably was even now telling herself the same: that, though she had no evidence, she was still convinced that the Rahmans were planning Tamima's marriage to some old man she had never seen before. If Hannah's theory was a fantasy, wasn't his just as likely to be one too?

For once, very few cars were parked along his street. No white van or silver Mercedes was numbered among them. Of the few that were there, not one had a dog sitting on the passenger seat, the driver's window a few inches open to give it air. He let himself into his house, called out, 'It's me,' as if others existed who had keys.

Dora came out into the hall. He put his arms round her and kissed her with a little more than his usual fervour.

'I suppose that's because you've been imagining me lying dead somewhere,' she said.

'Don't.'

'And don't you set Damon Coleman to watch this house without telling me. Poor chap, he looked so bored. I nearly went out and told him my lover wouldn't be round before two.'

Wexford laughed. The laughter was a bit forced.

'It was that white van,' Dora said, 'wasn't it?'

'It seems to have stopped. That's something to celebrate, so let's have a drink.'

CHAPTER THIRTEEN

A second glass of red wine had been tempting but he had refused it. Not because he had some sort of premonition he would be called out – that hardly crossed his mind – but because it was early, he had only just sat down to his dinner, and if he had more claret now he would want another before bed. So he left the silver stopper his daughter Sheila had given him in the neck of the bottle and applied himself to the fusilli alla carbonara and roquette salad he didn't much like but which Dora deemed good for him. As you got older, he thought, your taste reverted to the food of your youth. In your middle years you had quite liked deep-fried melon flowers and filo pastry and chorizo but now you wanted what you never got, sausages and steak-and-kidney pudding and stewed plums and custard. On the other hand, his preferred drink used to be beer but now he hardly touched it. He was musing on this, wondering if Dora felt the same but somehow feeling sure she didn't, was on the point of asking her, when the phone rang.

She knew it would be for him. She passed it to him without answering it herself.

'I have to go.' He got up, leaving half his fusilli. 'Something serious,' he said. It was the phrase he always used to her when he was called out to an unexplained death or a lethal attack. So it had been when Billy Kenyon's body was found in the botanical gardens, so it was when Nicky Dusan was stabbed. It was this economy of explanation he was later glad he adhered to. Telling her the address he was called out to this evening, though at the time it meant nothing to him, would have shocked and horrified her so that he would have baulked at leaving her alone.

She nodded, accepting. The days when she would have lamented his failing to finish his dinner were long gone. Now, his girth staying the same if not exactly increasing, she was pleased when he missed a meal or only ate half of it.

Again glad his evening's drinking had been limited to one small glass of red wine, he drove himself to Pomfret. Two police cars, a police van and an ambulance – not to be needed – were already parked outside the row of white stucco cottages. He left his car fifty yards up Cambridge Road. A blue-and-white-striped canvas barrier with a doorway in it had already been erected to cover most of the front of number 6. Barry Vine lifted the flap over the doorway and came out as he approached.

'Pathologist's just come, sir,' he said. 'He's with the deceased now.'

'Who is it?'

'Dr Mavrikian,' Barry said.

'I don't mean the pathologist,' said Wexford. 'Who cares, anyway? I mean who's what you call "the deceased"?'

Barry knew very well Wexford's hatred of jargon and verbiage, so said, 'Sorry, sir. The dead man is called Andrew Norton. This is his home and a neighbour . . .' The look on Wexford's face stopped him. 'You know him?'

'What did you say the name is?'

'Andrew Norton.'

142

Wexford felt his heart pound. He could almost hear it. 'He does – did – gardening for me.'

'Someone put a rope round his neck and strangled him.'

'I think we'll wait to hear what Dr Mavrikian says before we make statements like that,' said Wexford.

He was very taken aback. Thank God he hadn't mentioned that address to Dora. She had liked the man, they had had tea together when he took his break on Thursday afternoons. Damon Coleman had seen him come and go in his ancient Morris Minor. Wexford walked along to the living room where the body was lying on the floor between a sofa and the television set. Mavrikian got up from his knees and gave Wexford one of his impassive stares. He was a tall, thin, humourless man of Armenian origin with lined white skin and blond, very nearly white, hair. The only time he had been seen to be even slightly moved was when the news had been brought to him that his wife had given birth to a daughter.

In Wexford's estimation any faults he might have were compensated for by the swift (and accurate) assessment he made of the time of a victim's death and the cause of that death.

'He's been dead since between seven and nine this morning, let's say twelve hours ago. Someone put a rope round his neck and pulled it tight. All the details to come in my report. Good evening.'

As he was leaving Hannah Goldsmith arrived. 'He was my gardener, poor chap,' Wexford said to her.

'My God, guv.'

'He was at my house yesterday afternoon.'

'Your partner may know something relevant then.'

'She's my wife,' said Wexford, annoyed.

Andy Norton had been a good-looking man, his regular features and still smooth skin bloated by what had been done

143

to him. His head of white hair was as thick and glossy as a wig but it wasn't a wig. The scene-of-crimes officer was anxious to get on with his job so Wexford turned to Hannah and told her they would go next door to speak to the neighbour.

'She's a Mrs Catherine Lister, sir,' said Barry Vine. 'She's a widow and she lives alone. Her and the dead chap, they seem to have been good friends.'

'What does that mean?'

'Oh, nothing. Only what I said, sir. She's very upset.'

Mrs Lister's daughter opened the door. She was a woman of about forty, very thin, her dark hair drawn back into a ponytail.

'I came over to Mum this afternoon,' she said, 'and I've been here ever since. I'd like to take her home with me tonight. Is that OK?'

'Once we've had a word with her it will be quite OK,' said Wexford.

He had a strong sensation of déjà vu. He had been here before yet he knew he never had. For almost his whole life, while he had lived in the Kingsmarkham neighbourhood, he could never remember having even seen this terrace of cottages, tucked away in the hinterland of Pomfret. Yet the little hallway, the stairs going straight up opposite the front door, the single living room that had once been two, the garden with its door in the wall beyond . . . He forced himself back to speak to the older woman.

She was rather like his own wife, the same type, the type that was *his*. Her figure was still shapely, her waist small and ankles fine. She had hair which had once been very dark and was now iron grey, large dark eyes and the clear skin and good colour of a woman who has known very little illness. If she had cried her eyes were dry now and there was no puffiness in her face. She suddenly spoke without waiting for questions.

'We were very close, Andy and I,' she began. 'We were more or less living together but these cottages are a bit small for that. I have a key to his house and he had one to mine.' She looked down at the hands in her lap. 'I spent last night with Andy, as I did two or three times a week, but I came back here at about seven this morning.'

Her voice was steady and cool. The daughter took one of her hands but Catherine Lister didn't press hers in return.

'What time did you go back next door?' Hannah asked.

'Not till afternoon. I did some housework, cleaned the place, put my washing and Andy's in the machine. He didn't have a washing machine. I was going shopping for both of us later on . . .' Her voice broke and she shook herself, steadied herself. 'It was about four. I went in to him to see if there was anything special he wanted.' Again her voice wavered but she kept on, 'I let myself in and I – I found him on the floor. Dead. I could see he was dead.'

'Did you touch him, Mrs Lister?' Wexford asked.

She turned her face away. 'I lifted up his head. I – I kissed him.'

The crying began then. Her daughter put her arms round her and Catherine Lister sobbed into her shoulder. Wexford and Hannah exchanged glances. They were silent for perhaps a minute. The only sound was the sobs and gulps from the weeping woman.

'I'm sorry, Mrs Lister,' Wexford said. 'I'm very sorry but I do have to ask you a few more questions.'

'Surely you can leave Mum in peace for now!'

'No, I'm afraid not. Did you hear anything from this house during the morning?'

'Nothing,' she said, her voice hoarse from crying. 'I heard nothing and I didn't see anyone.'

'Did Mr Norton have any enemies?' This was Hannah. 'I mean people he disliked or who disliked him?'

'Everyone loved him,' said Catherine Lister.

But she rubbed the tears from her eyes and gave them all the information about Andy Norton that they wanted. Wexford left her then. The clocks had gone back and it was dark but light from the French windows of number 6 showed him Andy Norton's garden, beautifully tended, with still a few chrysanthemums and Michaelmas daisies remaining in bloom. The grass exemplified the phrase 'a manicured lawn'. He walked down the path past the shed in the right-hand corner to the green-painted door in the rear wall. It had no lock or bolts. He opened it and stepped out into the cobbled lane at the back. Now he knew what this house reminded him of, what this terrace of houses reminded him of.

These cottages were the same as the row of houses in Jewel Road, Stowerton. This house had the same structure as the Carrolls' at number 16, from the narrow hallway to the shed in the garden and the door in the rear wall leading to a lane outside. Or they had once been the same when they were first built. When would that have been? 1870? 1880? Something like that. Probably there were other terraces in Kingsmarkham and Stowerton and Pomfret of the same vintage. Much had been done to these and no doubt by now to those in Jewel Road since he had first been in the Carrolls' house. A pair of single rooms had been turned into one double room, French windows had been put in, as had central heating and new kitchens and bathrooms. But if you had known one of these houses forty years before, if you had *lived* in one of these houses, you would know the configuration of all of them wherever they might be.

He went back into Andy Norton's garden and shut the door in the wall. The moon was rising, a red ball, streaked with bands of dark cloud. With the coming of the moon the air seemed to grow colder. He closed his eyes momentarily and was back in Jewel Road where a man opened the door to him and showed, for a few brief seconds, a birthmark like a crimson crab climbing down his cheek and his neck, before he snatched up a woman's scarf and covered himself.

There was no more for Wexford to do tonight. DS Vine and DC Coleman were busy interviewing the neighbours. The scene-of-crimes officer had finished. He walked out through the blue-and-white tent that covered most of the front of the house and opened the gate. A man was walking his dog in the direction of the cross street. He was an elderly man, well above medium height, not wearing a scarf and the dog he had on a lead was a boxer. But it made his spine tingle.

He half expected cold blue eyes to stare into his. The man looked curiously at the tent and the police tape and passed on.

Wexford went home to tell Dora before anyone else did or she saw it on the news, and when he turned into his garage drive and switched off the engine, saw an image of Targo opening that door in the wall in the dark and seeking a hiding place in the shed until the time was ripe. He was a man of such self-confidence that he would see no need to bring the instrument of death with him. The world was full of strips of cloth, rope cut-offs, pieces of cord, scarves, ties, straps and belts. Such a thing would be waiting in Andy Norton's house or garden for him to lay his hands on.

Andy Norton was a widower. He had three children from his marriage, only one of which, a daughter, was living in England. Of his sons, one was in the United States, the other in Italy. Prior to his retirement he had been an official – with one of those permanent or private secretary titles – in the Department of Social Security. His wife had died fifteen years before. He and she had lived in a south London suburb but he had sold the house when he retired and bought this Pomfret cottage. Mrs Lister, a widow, was already living next door.

Mary Norton, a teacher whose home was in Leicester, arrived next morning. Talking to her in his office, Wexford found himself with a not uncommon dilemma, how to avoid asking her when had she last seen her father. He slightly changed it.

'When did you last see your dad, Miss Norton?'

She had a hard crisp voice, was a thin fair-haired woman. No one could be less like Mrs Lister. 'He came up to stay with me the weekend before last. That often happened. Or I came down to stay with him.' Her tone remained the same, steady, clear and calm, when she said, 'We were very close, father and daughter the way a father and daughter should be.

'I don't know how much you know about him. He had been a civil servant – that is, an official in a government depart-ment. Dad retired eight years ago and came to live here. He had an excellent pension but he liked to keep himself busy and he went out gardening. He was a good gardener and he loved it. He enjoyed the chats he had with elderly housewives over a cup of tea.'

Though he knew it was unreasonable, Wexford resented her patronising words. When she had finished he kept silent for a while, moved a pen on his desk, straightened the blotter. 'And Mrs Lister,' he said quietly, 'how did you feel about her?'

Mary Norton plainly resented the question. She had calcu-lated, Wexford thought, that she would have everything her own way in this interview. She would fix the time of it, organise the structure of it, pass on the information she thought the police should have, deliver her planned speech and then terminate it. Though she wasn't in the least like him, the way she stared, her blue gaze steady and unblinking, reminded him of Eric Targo.

'What's that got to do with Dad's death?'

'I ask the questions, Miss Norton.' The words were harsh but the tone was gentle. 'Would you answer the one I asked you?'

'If you must know, she's a pleasant enough woman. It was good for him to have companionship.'

It was more than that, Wexford thought, much more. He asked her if her father had made a will and, if so, what was in it.

Incredibly, she answered him in lawyer's jargon. 'His testamentary dispositions divided everything he left between my brothers and myself. There was this cottage and his savings, not a great deal.' She hesitated, then softened a little. 'My father gave away most of what he had to his children. He sold his house and got a good price which enabled him to leave quite large sums to each of us under the seven-year rule. You know what that is? The beneficiaries get a tax concession if the donor lives for seven years. He did, in fact. Just.'

'Very well, Miss Norton. That will be all for now.'

Even though he hadn't yet received Mavrikian's report, he knew Andy Norton had been strangled. What he had at first thought to be a length of rope, but which turned out to be a window-sash cord, had been used.

'All the sash cords were in place, sir,' DS Vine said to him.

'This one wasn't new. It had been in a window somewhere, it was a bit worn and frayed at one end, and my guess is it was lying in a kitchen drawer or cupboard.'

'Your guess?'

'I realise we're going to have to find precisely where it came from, sir. They're doing a house-to-house in Cambridge Road now.'

'Yes, well, don't let me hear of any more guesswork, right?'

He went back to Pomfret. The house-to-house, which he could see going on, reminded him of Jewel Road all those years ago. How many house-to-house inquiries had he instigated since then? Yet the procedure taking place again brought Targo to mind. Andy Norton had been strangled and Targo was the arch-strangler. It was absurd. Why should Targo kill the harmless and innocent Andy Norton? Come to that, why had he killed Elsie Carroll and Billy Kenyon? They also had been harmless and innocent.

Damon Coleman and Lynn Fancourt were doing the house-to-house at this end of Cambridge Road. He went up to meet them when Damon came away from the doorstep of number 18 and Lynn from number 20.

'Any luck?'

'A woman opposite, sir, at number 5, seems to have kept the house under surveillance, especially in the early mornings and late evenings.' Lynn Fancourt smiled. 'She disapproves of Andy Norton's relationship with Mrs Lister. She watched their comings and goings.'

'She'll have to look elsewhere for her kicks now,' said Wexford.

'Yes, sir. She swears no one went into the house this morning. She was watching from the moment it got light and that's at about seven. She saw Mrs Lister come out and go into her own house next door at seven fifteen.'

Wexford went back to number 6 and made his way in through the blue-and-white-striped awning. Barry Vine was inside with a PC from the uniformed branch.

'Suppose,' he said to Vine, 'the perpetrator came into the back garden here while it was still dark. Say at five. Come with me.'

They went out by way of the back door into Andy Norton's garden. There was something particularly dreadful about looking at this trim and lovely place, the small lawn weedless and neatly mown, the borders rich with autumn flowers, the four sculpted stone tubs still holding their cargos of red and apricot and pink begonias. From the moment the cultivator of this garden had died – it too had begun to die, gradually withering, abandoned to its untended state. Tomorrow it would be a little drier, the grass a little longer, or a little wetter, nearer to drowning, the dying petals starting to fall.

'He could have come through the gate from the lane. And suppose he came in before it got light. That means before seven. Let's say he waited out here, with his sash cord. He could have hidden in the shed. He would have seen a light go on in the house and taken that as a signal. Did he know about Mrs Lister? It doesn't really matter. If she had been there would he have killed her too? But she wasn't. She had gone.'

'You sound as if you know the perpetrator, sir?'

'Do I, Barry?' Wexford shook his head. 'What happened next? He went up to the back door and knocked. There's a knocker but no bell. When he heard someone knock at his back door Andy Norton went to answer it and admitted him. Why? We don't know. Perhaps because it's natural for older people, brought up in a safer age, to open their doors to whoever knocks. Maybe it wasn't like that and the back door had been left unlocked overnight. Maybe it always was. We shall know more than that when I get the pathologist's report.'

It was Targo's murder of Elsie Carroll all over again. So many small properties in these towns had lanes running at the backs of houses. So many gardens were impossible of entry except over or through those walls if the doors were locked or bolted. All the houses had back doors. Many householders still left theirs unlocked. Wexford thought of 32 Jewel Road where Targo had once lived, of 8 Glebe Road where he had lived later on in his stalking days. He would know the layout, he would know which moves were feasible.

He rang Mrs Lister's doorbell. Her daughter let him in,

explaining that instead of taking her mother away, she had stayed the night.

'Mum's lying down.'

'I'd like you to go up to your mother and ask her two questions: whether Mr Norton's back door was left unlocked overnight and whether there was a piece of sash cord in Mr Norton's house. You know what sash cord is?'

'A kind of rope that opens and shuts windows.'

'That's right. Now your mother will probably guess what this cord was used for if she didn't actually see it when she found the body. I hope she didn't see it and won't guess but if she does that can't be helped. Is all this clear?'

'Yes, of course. I suppose it was used to strangle the poor man.'

'What I want to know is, did this sash cord belong in the house or was it – well, brought there?'

She went upstairs. Wexford sat there, thinking about Targo. This was more than obsession, this was paranoia. It was impossible Targo was responsible for this; wild imaginings, fixation, a kind of madness. The daughter came back into the room.

'Mum did see it when she – found him. She recognised it. It was a piece of sash cord that had been rolled up and put in the garden shed along with balls of string and a length of rope. She says she's glad to help. She wants whoever did this caught.'

'And the back door? Was in left unlocked?'

'She doesn't know. She says it often was and she told Andy she thought that wasn't a good idea but he said this was the country and there wasn't much crime in the country.'

Wexford sighed.

The box had burst open and Targo come out of it, strutting, staring, defying him. His dilemma was the same one, the old one. How to interview – interrogate – a man lacking even a tenuous connection with the murder victim whose death he was investigating.

'This woman,' said Burden, 'the one who lives at number 5, she saw no one but Catherine Lister when she left just after seven?'

'She wouldn't have seen Targo if he came into the garden from the lane. If he came the same way as he came when he killed Elsie Carroll all those years ago.'

'A *man* who came into the garden, Reg. A man or a woman but not Eric Targo. He's old now. If he did in fact kill Elsie Carroll – and I have my doubts about that and about Billy Kenyon – would he have the strength to strangle a man a head taller than him? Would he have the strength to strangle anyone?'

'*He* would,' said Wexford. 'What excuse can I have for going to talk to him?'

'A white van parked outside Andy Norton's house on two occasions – how about that? Or a silver Mercedes?'

'They weren't, though. Not so far as we know. And no, Mike, we're not going in for fictitious scenarios because the fact is we don't need them. We don't need an excuse. What's to stop us questioning anyone we choose about any crime committed on our patch?'

The day after Andy Norton's death, Donaldson, who was Wexford's driver, took him and DC Lynn Fancourt to Stringfield. Passing through Stoke Stringfield village, Wexford thought briefly of Helen Rushford, his girlfriend of a few months when he lived in Brighton, she who had told him she loved him and that he was everything she wanted. She lived here somewhere, a grandmother no doubt, and he would long have ceased to be what she wanted. In that house by the green or down that lane? In one of those pretty cottages? If she came out of one of those houses, would he recognise her? Probably not.

They drew up outside Wymondham Lodge. No cars were on the driveway but the big garage had space for two vehicles so they might have been hidden from view.

'Look, sir,' Lynn said, 'those animals. Aren't they lovely? Are they llamas or alpacas?'

'No idea,' Wexford said, smiling at the benign-looking creatures who came up to the fence in quest perhaps of treats. 'Targo's got some big felines too, I think. Only they're behind bars.'

When he rang the doorbell a dog started to bark. It sounded, as Lynn remarked, like two dogs, and so it was, the Tibetan spaniel and a Staffordshire bull terrier puppy, the latter on a lead held by a woman in late-middle age with the brightest red hair Wexford had ever seen. He had seen geraniums that colour but, not previously, hair. It was woven into a helmet shape that fitted over a large head and a face not resembling the terrier's or the spaniel's but with its squashed features and a turned-up nose, perhaps a Pekinese's. Thickset and stocky, she was expensively dressed in a beaded brocade jacket and black trousers. She looked impassively at their warrant cards. Her eyes, prominent and very blue like Targo's, met Wexford's.

'Oh, yes,' she said, 'I've heard him mention you.'

This was unexpected. 'Mrs Targo?'

'I'm Mavis Targo, yes.'

Her manner was charmless, her voice gruff.

'We'd like to speak to your husband.'

She unfastened the lead on the bull terrier and it immediately jumped up at Wexford. She gave it an indulgent smile
which she switched off when she spoke. 'He's not in.'

He gave the dog a push. It was unexpectedly strong. 'When
do you expect him home?'

'I don't. He comes when he's ready. He pleases himself.'

'May we come in, please?'

Wexford put his foot over the threshold and she had no
choice but to let him in. Lynn followed quickly to avoid the
door being slammed in her face. The old house had a gracious-
ness its furnishings did their best to diminish. They found
themselves in a big hall out of which an elegant curved stair-
case climbed, but it was furnished with gilded tables and
chairs of the imitation eighteenth-century French variety, set
about on a pink-and-white Chinese carpet. A large chande-
lier, a glittering waterfall of prisms, was suspended from the
ceiling. The puppy jumped on one of the tables and stood
there, wagging its tail.

'Get down, sweetheart,' said Mrs Targo in a half-hearted way.

'I don't know what you want to come in for,' she said to
Wexford. 'I said he's not here and I don't know when he will
be. I haven't seen him since yesterday morning.'

'Sixty per cent of the population of this country has a mobile
phone,' said Wexford. 'I think that's the correct figure. I'm
sure your husband is one of them. Would you like to call him
and let me speak to him?'

'What, now?'

'Now.'

'You'd better come through.'

'Coming through' meant entering a large living room,
furnished in much the same style as the hall but with a blue
carpet. A blue, white and pink silk rug, spread across quite
a big area of this carpet, had been extensively chewed and

most of its fringe was missing. The puppy homed in at once on the rug and, applying its teeth to the edge where the fringe had been, began gnawing at it with gusto.

'Leave it, sweetheart,' said Mrs Targo, unperturbed when the dog took no notice. She picked up a pink-and-silver mobile phone from one of the tables and dialled a number in a lethargic, vaguely depressed way. Her fingernails were the same colour as her hair.

When there appeared to be no reply she dialled a second number, beginning to shake her head. Targo stared at Wexford from a silver-framed photograph standing on a piano. It had been taken not long ago and after the treatment to remove the birthmark. Targo was smiling – *smiling* – proud, no doubt, of his new unblemished appearance. In anyone but this monster it would have been pathetic, even touching. For the one of him, there were four of his wife, taken when she was younger and slimmer, in one of the photographs wearing a wedding dress embroidered in sequins.

'He's not answering,' she said. 'D'you want me to leave a message?'

'I'll do that,' said Wexford. 'Give me the phone.'

He asked Targo to contact him and gave him a number to call. If it was Targo, if the numbers she had called had been his.

'Where was he going when he left here yesterday morning?'

'He had a call to make in Kingsmarkham. I do know that. He did say that much but not when he'd be back or nothing.'

'What does your husband do for a living?'

'He's mostly retired but he still does a bit of property.'

'You mean he's a property developer?'

'All those right-to-buy flats, that sort of thing.'

'So where is he, Mrs Targo?'

'I don't know, do I? I've tried to get him for you and he's not answering. What more can I do?'

'Your dog is eating the flowers in that vase,' said Lynn.

Wexford suppressed a smile. 'It's now ten past three. I shall phone you at six, but whether he is back or not, we shall come back at seven. If your husband phones you please tell him I shall see him here at seven.'

At this point, as they were returning to the hall, a disconcerting thing happened. There came from somewhere in the grounds behind the house a deep-throated roar.

Lynn said, 'That sounded like a lion.'

'It *is* a lion.' Mavis Targo sighed. 'That's King. My husband's crazy about him but I don't know . . . Well, I'll have to feed him before Eric gets back or he'll go on like that for hours.'

'Is he allowed to keep a lion like that?' Lynn asked when they were outside.

'God knows. I'm not going to worry about that now.' Another roar and another sounded more loudly. 'Good thing he hasn't any near neighbours.' Put the lion in a box and shut it up in a drawer . . .

At seven, when he and Lynn went back, the lion was silent and in the darkness no other animals could be seen. The sky appeared starless, the land an undulating grey expanse dotted with black trees which the imaginative might have compared to the plains of Africa. Targo was still out. He had phoned, his wife said, or someone had phoned, and left her a message on the landline.

'You mean you were out when this person phoned?'

'I had to feed King, didn't I? And that scares me to death. And then I had to take the dogs out.'

'Who was it left you a message?'

'I don't know. I thought it was someone in his office but he's told me he's got no one working for him just now.'

'Are you saying it was Mr Targo himself disguising his voice?'

'It could have been. I couldn't tell, I was in a state worrying about King.'

Perhaps you need a box of your own, Wexford thought. 'What did the message say?'

'Just that he was OK and he'd call me.'

'What, this mysterious voice simply said it was speaking on behalf of your husband and he'd call you tomorrow?'

'That's right.'

'I'd like to listen to it, please.'

'Oh, it's not there now. I erased it. I always do that with messages to avoid getting in a muddle.'

'All right. I want the address of his office, the numbers of all the phones he has. The number of his car. DC Fancourt will take those numbers from you. Come along now, Mrs Targo.'

When Lynn had taken the numbers down, having some difficulty in extracting that of the Mercedes from her, she asked about the white van and was told it was in the garage. Mavis Targo was at last beginning to show signs of agitation. It had taken a long time to shake her out of her apathy but she was shaken now.

'I keep telling you I don't know where he is. I don't keep tabs on him. I wouldn't be here long,' she added with a flash of bitterness, 'if I did.'

'His son and daughter live here or near here. I'd like their addresses and phone numbers.'

'I haven't got them! I've hardly ever seen them. He doesn't have them here, he goes to them. I don't know where they live.'

'Then I suggest you get busy with the phone book. I suppose you know his daughter's married name?'

She did. Eventually, it was Lynn who found the phone book and looked up the names while Mrs Targo smoked a cigarette and, fetching herself a gin and tonic, asked Wexford if he and 'the young lady' would like a drink. This was refused. The Tibetan spaniel began to whine, its note growing shriller until the puppy followed suit, first yapping, then emitting a full-throated bark.

'They're asking for their dinner,' said Mavis Targo.

Lynn patted the puppy on its head. 'Missing his master too, I expect.'

The office address was in Sewingbury, three or four miles away, in a small two-storey building on the edge of the industrial estate. Street lamps were on but most buildings were in darkness, including Targo's office. Like the place he had had in Myringham when he was a travel agent, it appeared to consist of one room. The door was of glass and the window a sheet of plate glass, through which, as at Myringham, a desk and two chairs could be seen by the light of Lynn's torch. On the floor were two empty bowls, one for water, the other for dogfood. All that was missing were the posters of exotic locations and the proprietor. Neither Targo nor anyone else was about and the door was locked. No cars were on the parking spaces adjacent to the building. The whole place seemed infinitely desolate.

Back in his own office, Wexford phoned all the numbers he had been given. On Targo's he was put on to message. Alan Targo answered his own phone, was polite and pleasant but had no idea where his father was. He hadn't seen him for three weeks.

'I'm a solicitor,' he said. 'My firm's in Queen Street.'

Wexford thought of telling him they had last met when Alan was a child of four but he thought better of it.

'My sister's here, as a matter of fact, if you want to talk to her. But I know she hasn't seen Dad for weeks.'

She hadn't. He recalled that other evening, long ago, when Alan had been sitting at his father's feet stroking the dog and

159

this woman he was talking to had been still in her mother's womb. Nothing odd about that, though. Half the people he talked to had been yet unborn when he was young . . .

He was wasting his time, Burden said when they met for a drink. When they met for a drink and dinner, Wexford corrected him, for they couldn't go home yet. He had phoned Mrs Targo five minutes before to be told her husband was still out.

'I shall go back to the zoo. You can come with me if you feel like it. He has to get home sometime.'

They had deserted the Indus for the restaurant whose gimmick was that it served only old-fashioned British food. Not 'English' because haggis was sometimes on the menu and so were Cornish pasties.

'Cornwall's in England,' said Burden.

'Not according to the Cornish. They say England starts when you cross the Tamar.' Wexford had less than happy memories of the county (or country) and the awful Medora in Port Ezra, but happy memories too in that his first meeting with his wife was in Newquay. Strange, though, to remember that he had already come across Targo in those days, that Targo had been with him for the greater part of his life.

'*Why* does he do it, Mike? Elsie Carroll, Billy Kenyon, and now Andy Norton. He didn't know any of these people. All he had in common with them was that they happened to live in the same neighbourhood. But why those? Would anyone have done for him? Oh, I know I've yet to convince you that he killed them.'

If a reply was needed, Burden failed to give it. 'I'm going to have the fish pie. I fancy all that sauce and mashed potatoes. My mum would have called it nourishing, though I don't know if nutritionists would agree with her these days. Too much fat, probably. Not that I have to worry about that.'

'Please don't preen yourself. I've enough to bear without that.'

Burden laughed.'A glass of Sauvignon, I think. Shall I have potatoes as well or just the sprouts and the carrots?'

'Potatoes would be adding insult to injury.' He looked up from the menu, said to the waitress, 'Fish pie over there, please, and roast beef without the Yorkshire pudding, sadly, for me. Oh, and a glass of *tap* water. I shall be driving us back there. But I'm not wasting money on bottled fizz, the biggest ramp of all in these extravagant days.'

Burden studied the decor. A mural of Morris dancers covered half a wall, jousting knights the other half. 'On the wall behind you that you can't see they're changing the guard at Buckingham Palace.'

'*Christopher Robin went down with Alice,*' said Wexford. '*Alice is marrying one of the guard. "A soldier's life is terrible hard," said Alice.* That's the first poem I ever remember reading.'

Burden sighed a little. 'Are we really going back there tonight? What *for?*'

'Well, in part to ask Targo where he was between seven fifteen and nine thirty yesterday morning.' Their drinks came, Burden's Sauvignon filling a large glass. 'Have you ever thought how much less depressing water would be if it had a colour? I mean, if it was light blue or pink like rosé. A natural colour, of course, not some sort of dye they put in.'

'No, I haven't. If we weren't going back there on a wild goose chase you could have a big glass like mine full of burgundy.'

'I have often wondered,' said Wexford, 'why it should be so difficult, if not impossible, to catch a wild goose. A tame goose is quite easy to catch and it's hard to understand why catching a wild one should be so different.' The waitress brought their food and another came with vegetables. 'I wish I'd had the Yorkshire pudding but it's too late now.' He applied his knife to a slice of beef. 'I asked you why he does it. Why does he kill people he doesn't know? It was a rhetorical question really because I know how he chooses the people if not what impels him to kill them.'

'Go on then, tell me. This fish pie is very good.'

'He picks a person,' said Wexford, 'that someone wants to be rid of.'

'He *what*?'

'You heard me, Mike. He doesn't have to know the person but he has to know something about them. First there was Elsie Carroll. It was quite well known in the neighbourhood, if not to poor Mrs Carroll, that her husband wanted shot of her in order to have a free run with Tina Malcolm. Billy Kenyon was expendable because it was only if he was out of the way that Bruce Mellor would marry Eileen Kenyon. Possibly there were others in Birmingham and Coventry similarly in need of someone to rid them of an encumbrance but if there were we don't know about them. And so to Andy Norton . . .'

'His girlfriend said everyone who knew him loved him. No one wanted to get rid of him, that's for sure.'

'*I* did, Mike,' said Wexford, 'or Targo thinks I did.'

'You? Why you?' said Burden. 'What on earth do you mean?'

'I'll tell you. Targo, though quite sane, is a psychopath. He is a monster, entirely callous, indifferent to others' pain. But for some reason and I don't know what that reason is – he needs to give people in need of it some help in dealing with their trouble. Perhaps he has a conscience of a kind. Perhaps he does it so that he can say to himself, "I'm not so bad. I did him a service." Or maybe it gives him a reason for what he does. He needs a death and he needs a hook to hang a death on to.'

'It sounds mad to me. What sort of service are you saying he did you?'

'Think about it,' said Wexford, drinking an inch down the glass of his tap water. 'He was parked outside my house day after day, watching. He must have seen Andy Norton go in – not by the front door, mind, but what he would think of as sneaking round the back. He would have seen him park his car, go in the back way and stay for three hours. He'd never see Dora but he would have known she was in. Do you see now?'

'I don't believe it!'

'That means you do. It always means that. Look, I hate thinking like this because I know what would be impossible to my wife, but to Targo it would be all in the day's work. It's possible too that he saw Damon Coleman watching my house and if he didn't know he was a police officer he may well have set him down as a private detective, employed by me. I was the deceived husband and Andy Norton my wife's lover.'

Burden shook his head, but in wonder rather than disbelief. 'Do you mean he likes you? He cares about you?'

'Liking and caring don't come into it with him. It's dogs he likes and cares for. And llamas and lions. He was performing a service or restoring order where before there was chaos. Or maybe doing this makes him see himself as a just judge, a justified executioner. I rather prefer that line.' Wexford laid down his knife and fork. 'I don't want a pudding. All this speculating about Targo takes away my appetite. He's my new slimming regime. My thin guru. If we don't get him for killing Andy Norton what do we do? Keep searching the town, maybe the country, for people other people want out of the way? Such is the sorry state of the world that there'll be thousands.'

'But he doesn't ask people if they want rid of someone, so how can he be sure?'

'He didn't ask me but maybe he sometimes asks. Perhaps he's asked others. When, for instance, he's sure the husband or parent or whoever it is will be thankful and keep quiet about his part in it.'

Burden sat in silence. After a couple of minutes – a very long time for two people sitting at a table not to speak – he made a signal to the waiter and when the man came over, asked for a crème brûlée. Wexford was looking at his watch.

'It's ten past nine.'

'All right. I won't be long. It's not as if we've an appointment set in stone with the man.'

'I've a feeling he'll be there. I wonder if he still exercises. Works out, as they say these days.'

'What if he does?'

Wexford was good on feelings. His intuition usually served him well. But not this time. Last night's moon, a little thinner but just as red, loomed half risen when Burden rang the Wymondham Lodge doorbell. There was no sound from the menagerie. More lights came on inside the house and the dogs set up an optimistic barking. The puppy rushed out when Mavis Targo open the door.

'Disappointed, are you, poor chap?' Burden said to it and it plainly was, sadly slinking away when scent and sight told it someone not Targo was on the threshold.

'He's not here.'

Once again Wexford had to force his way into the house. 'Where is he, Mrs Targo?'

'I haven't heard from him. I don't know where he is.'

'Has he got a passport?'

'Of course he has.'

'Then would you like to see if you can find it?'

She had not far to look, lifted the lid of a bureau and produced Targo's passport, the small red booklet sheathed in a leather and gilt case. 'He wouldn't go abroad if that's what you're thinking. He hates abroad. He took me to Spain on our honeymoon and he hated it so much we came back early and he said he'd never go again.'

Wexford was unconvinced by this but the passport bore out what she said. It was almost unused, in pristine condition. 'Has he ever been absent from home this long before without letting you know?'

'Oh, God, yes,' she said. 'He's a law unto himself, he is. He'll have business dealings somewhere. Birmingham, Manchester, Cardiff, you name it. He could be away for days, maybe a week. And when he comes back it won't be to see me. It'll be to see if King and his dogs are OK.'

Wexford pondered for a moment. 'These right-to-buy flats you mentioned. Where are they?'

'Some are round here and there's some in Birmingham, I reckon. I don't really know. I never had anything to do with them. Why would he go there, anyway? He's not a rent collector.'

Nothing more was to be done at Wymondham Lodge.

'What's this about right-to-buy-flats?' Burden asked when they were in the car. 'Some property dealing of Targo's?'

'I don't know but I can guess. It works like this. There was a housing bill which made it possible for council tenants to buy their homes. As sitting tenants you got your flat at the market value minus 3 per cent and a couple of million people bought their homes. There was some sort of time limit on when you could sell your house or flat on but when you did you could make an enormous profit.'

'OK, where does Targo come in?'

'Well, suppose you knew of some particular block or, better still, terrace of houses and you know there are ten original tenants in them. Each can exercise his or her right to buy. So you give each one a big cash enticement to buy on your behalf. That way, even allowing for the bribe, you get a property for half what you'd pay on the open market. Then you lease them back to the council who put people from their housing list in. You can make a packet. From what Mavis Targo says I think that's what he's been doing.'

'So that's the business he's got in Cardiff or Birmingham or whatever and, allowing for what you've said, there's no reason to suppose it isn't legitimate. As far as staying away, his wife isn't worried about him. She's used to this behaviour.'

'I've phoned both those mobile numbers repeatedly and they're always on message. Since we went there I've phoned his office landline and it doesn't even have an answerphone, it just rings and rings. Why would a man live like that if his business was legitimate?'

'I don't know, Reg, but nor do you. People are peculiar. How many times have I heard you say that there's nowt so queer as folk?'

'I'm going to trace that Mercedes of his and put out a call for him. Oh, all right, I know I've no grounds, no evidence, as you keep telling me but I'll see Freeborn first. I'll get to see him first thing tomorrow.' Freeborn was the Assistant Chief Constable. 'I think I've got a case.'

'I don't,' said Burden. 'Listen to me. You'll tell him that God knows over how many decades Targo murdered three people in Kingsmarkham and environs. How do you know? You intuited it. Where's the evidence, he'll say, and you'll give him all that stuff about Targo killing people other people want out of the way and how once upon a time he stalked you. So now you'd like to track his car and put a watch on all UK exits in case he tries to go abroad on a fake passport. You what, he'll say, and then he'll say, go away and stop wasting my time.'

And this was what happened – with small variations. Freeborn didn't tell Wexford to stop wasting his time or to go away but he did tell him there could be no question of putting a watch on ports and airports. Targo was not even a missing person. Old he might be but, if what Wexford said about his physical health and strength was accurate, to believe that his disappearance was in any way age-related was nonsense.

'Has his wife reported him as missing, Reg?'

Wexford shook his head. 'She says that going off like this and switching off mobiles isn't unusual with him.'

'Well, then.'

There was no more to be said.

Damon Coleman and Lynn Fancourt had questioned everyone in the Pomfret neighbourhood of Cambridge Road without any positive result. Wexford went back to Cambridge Cottages and carried out, purely for his own satisfaction, a reconstruction of what he thought had happened on the morning Andy Norton was murdered. He played Targo's part himself. Being Targo, he let himself into the shed and found the box of rope coils and balls of string from which the killer had taken the window-sash cord. Straightening up, he banged his head on the roof. Targo was about seven inches shorter than he, so he wouldn't have done that. Holding a short length of rope – a length just short enough and long enough to strangle someone – he sat down on a stool and asked himself what sort of time he was trying to recreate. Five thirty? No, too early. Six, then. And how had Targo got here? In one of his vehicles, parked it anywhere in Pomfret and walked to Cambridge Road. It wasn't a very big place.

The back door was unlocked but when had it been unlocked? Wexford got off his seat and, carrying the length of rope, walked down the path past the chrysanthemums and the Michaelmas daisies to the small area of yard between the back door, the wall and the kitchen window. Targo would only have wanted to be invisible while he was doing that under the cover of darkness but once there was no hiding place for him. It seemed likely that the back door was unlocked. Did he go in without knocking? Or knock and fetch Norton down? How did he know Catherine Lister had left? Because he saw a light come on in the house next door. Wexford looked over the dividing wall and saw that this would have been quite possible. Wexford did what Targo may have done and rapped on the glass with his fist. Lynn came to open it and Wexford stepped inside.

Surely the first thing Andy Norton would have said was to ask him what he was doing there and how had he got in. Well, no doubt he had asked. That wouldn't have deterred Targo once he was inside. It hardly mattered what he said, for the grim truth was that Norton would never see him again.

Wexford walked into the living room as Targo must have done, following Norton, and there got the sash cord round his neck from behind, the way the thuggee of India had once done with their garrottes. He felt his anger rise as he thought of this gentle and innocent man becoming another of Targo's victims.

All I want, he thought, sitting in the car, is a small break-through. Just something to make one other person believe me or approach believing me. One person to give me the benefit of the doubt. I don't know what to do now, short of trying to call all those numbers all over again, short of going back to Wymondham Lodge and talking to that woman and being assaulted by a pack of crazy dogs. I don't know what to do unless I get a breakthrough.

Lynn Fancourt had seen him sitting there and was coming up to the car. He opened the driver's window.

'I've been talking to a woman in Oxford Road, sir,' she said. 'That's the street that runs parallel to this one. The lane's between the gardens. But maybe you know that.'

'I know that, Lynn. What have you got to tell me that I don't know?' Make it good, he didn't say aloud.

'She's called Wentworth, Pauline Wentworth. On the

morning Andy Norton was killed she came downstairs to answer her phone just before six. She hasn't got an extension upstairs. She answered the phone because her daughter's due to have a baby and she thought that was what it was about. It wasn't, it was a wrong number. But she didn't go back to bed because she knew she wouldn't go to sleep again. It was dark, of course, but there was a big moon if you remember. She went into the kitchen and put the kettle on for tea. It was then she looked down the garden and noticed that the door in her rear wall was flapping open. No mystery about that, she'd left it open the night before. She went down the garden to close it and as she did so she saw someone go through the door in the wall into Andy Norton's garden.'

'Why didn't she call us?'

Lynn cast up her eyes. 'She says because she thought she recognised him. This person, she meant. She *thought* she recognised him as a man she'd seen a couple of years ago out walking his dogs. One of his dogs had gone after her cat and she'd told him to put it on a lead. She said he was a small man, no taller than her, and not young, but – listen to this, sir – and when she'd seen him before he had a big birthmark on his neck but this man didn't.'

Wexford kept his excitement under control and spoke calmly. 'She could see that in the dark – well, moonlight?'

'She keeps a light on all night at the end of her garden. Apparently we told her – I mean, uniform did – to do that after she'd had a break-in.'

'What did she think this man was doing?'

'She didn't know, of course. But she thought it was all right because he was what she called "a respectable person" and an animal lover. Maybe, she said, one of his dogs had got into the garden and he wanted to get it back without disturbing the householder. In my opinion, sir, these animal people are a bit nuts.'

He laughed. 'Thank you, Lynn,' he said. 'Well done.'

I know him, Wexford said to himself. I know the way he works and the way his mind works but this new scenario I am imagining, it can't be that way. And, letting himself into his house, he went to find his wife.

CHAPTER FOURTEEN

'I felt I knew him really well,' she said slowly. 'He was a friend. As you know, I don't usually feel like that about someone I've only known a few weeks.' She suddenly thought of something. He guessed what it was from her face and knew it was the very thing he wanted her not to feel. 'He wasn't killed because of anything to do with this house and – well, me, was he?'

'I don't know why he was killed,' he said truthfully and then he lied. 'But it couldn't have had anything to do with you. That's out of the question.'

'Only I'd hate to think that. I'd never get over that. Oh, Reg . . .'

He held her close. She put up her face for a kiss. It was just the way she had done this the second time they had gone for one of those evening walks at Newquay. The most trusting act he had ever known . . .

Later he was back in Pomfret. 'Can you describe him?'

'Not very tall,' said Mrs Wentworth. 'I mean, nowhere near your height.' The look she gave Wexford, wondering, unflattering, slightly disapproving, made him feel like a giant in a freak show. 'I used to live in Stringfield and I'd seen him about once or twice, always with a dog, but not for years. I mean I hadn't seen him since I came here. I told the young lady I thought it was him but then I wasn't sure because he used to have a birthmark and this man didn't. You can't get rid of something like that, can you?'

'Wonderful things are done with plastic surgery these days, Mrs Wentworth,' said Wexford.

'When I saw him in Stringfield he used to wear a scarf. Even in the summer in quite hot weather he wore a scarf. And then someone told me he wore it to cover up that mark and one day he took the scarf off when I was looking at him and I saw it. So you say he had it removed?'

'It's possible.'

'Well, then, it was him. I could see quite clearly what with my light and the moonlight. I did think it was him but when I saw he didn't have that awful birthmark I said to myself, well, it can't be him, can it? But it must have been. He wasn't with a dog that morning, though. I thought that's why he was going into Mr Norton's garden. I thought, maybe his dog's got in there and he's looking for it.'

Would that be enough to persuade Freeborn of the need for a call to locate Targo's car? Enough to put out a watch for him at Heathrow, at Gatwick and other possible airports? That he had left his passport behind meant nothing. He was the sort to have several passports. And a lot of time had been lost. It was now two days since Andy Norton's body had been found. But Wexford had got his breakthrough. For the first time in all his years of watching Targo and being stalked by Targo, of suspecting him and of being certain of his repeated guilt, he had concrete evidence that Targo was a murderer.

'Are you convinced now?' he said to Burden.

'Well, yes, I'm coming close to it. And I'm sorry, Reg, for doubting you all this time. I'm convinced because you've given me so much background, but I don't know that anyone else will be. The Wentworth woman's evidence is a bit shaky, isn't it? Imagine it in court, an even moderately clever counsel telling her it would still have been dark at six in the morning at the end of October – never mind the moon and her light – and asking her how she could have seen a birthmark or the lack of one. She couldn't see, could she? Surely she should be wearing glasses? She's seventy-two years old and all lawyers are ageist.'

'We've got enough,' said Wexford, 'for me to start a country-wide search. Don't look so worried. I'll go back to Freeborn and ask him first. But he'll say yes when he knows the facts.'

He said yes. A reluctant yes but a considered one, put into a word after several minutes' thought. The first thing was to find that missing Mercedes. But who had made that phone call to Mavis and left a message? Was it possible that a man could disguise his voice so that even his wife wouldn't recognise it?

Targo had left home, Wexford thought, on the same day he had killed Andy Norton, within hours probably. He marvelled at a man so removed from all human feeling, from shock, from simple self-questioning, that he could ~~could~~ go about his normal business after committing a crime of such magnitude. It wasn't quite normal business, though. He had gone without a dog and he had gone in the Mercedes. What was the significance of that? Perhaps only that he had intended to stay away for a while. Where had he gone first? To his children? No, Targo hadn't been to see his children.

Had he been to see his first wife? When Wexford had last seen her, that day in the Kingsbrook Precinct, she had said of their divorce that it was 'good riddance to bad rubbish', but people change, people become reconciled to those they would once have passed in the street without speaking.

It was a long time since he too had seen her. In her late sixties now, she appeared to be a strong healthy woman, very pleased to see him.

'You haven't changed a bit,' Kathleen Targo said.

Gallantly, he told her she looked younger than when he had seen her all those years ago in the Kingsbrook Precinct. 'I know you're called Mrs Varney now but I had a bit of a job finding you with only Sewingbury to go on.'

'That's because I married again. Jack died a few years back and I married his best friend. He'd been a widower for about the same time.'

She took him into a living room and offered him coffee. 'I won't, thanks. Things are a bit rushed at present.' He remembered the child in the pushchair. 'How's Philippa?'

'Just qualified as a doctor. Working all hours but you have to, don't you, your first year or two?'

'You must be proud of her.'

'No doubt of that. I'm a very lucky woman, Mr Wexford. All my children have done well for themselves. I've got my health and strength and I've had two good husbands after starting off with a rotter. I can't complain and I don't.'

She invited him to sit down. Photographs of her children were on the mantelpiece, tables, the top of an upright piano, and alone, on what looked like an old-fashioned music console, one of her as a bride for the second time. He wondered how he would have felt if Dora had been married before and kept a photograph of her earlier wedding in the living room. He would have hated it but then he and Dora had been young and in love, not like this couple marrying for companionship in impending old age.

'You're no longer Mrs Varney,' he said, 'so what do I call you?'

'I'm Mrs Jones now but you call me Kathleen.'

'Your first husband is missing.'

That made her laugh. 'A good miss, I should think. If he's disappeared you can bet your life it's on purpose.'

'I don't suppose you know where he is.'

'You don't suppose right. I don't know where he is. He'd go to any one of his women before he'd come to me. Left Mavis, has he? They weren't getting on, I know that. Joanne tells me. Alan won't have a word said against his dad, God knows why not, but you've got to hand it to him.'

Strange and interesting, Wexford thought, how grown-up children can be devoted to a bad parent – more devoted often than to a good one. Because they still hoped to please them, even so late in the day, and thus at last win their love? 'He's left his wife only in the sense that he's gone away somewhere. Do you have a name and address for the woman he was living with in Birmingham?'

'Tracy something. Wait a minute. Tracy Cole. After I threw him out, he was with his mum in Glebe Road for a bit and then he went to her. I've got the address she was living at then. Well, I've got it somewhere. I'm one of those people who never throw anything away so I reckon I can find it.'

'I think I will have that coffee,' said Wexford, 'if it's not too much trouble.'

'No trouble at all.'

Did this propensity of hers extend to never forgetting anything? Perhaps. People who hoard, people who save every useless scrap and fragment, the anal ones, as psychologists call them, usually have good memories, he had noticed. He would ask her. Those hard times – hard in more ways than one – in Jewel Road, Stowerton, might not be lost in the mists of time. In his mind's eye, as in a dream, he saw Targo sitting by the appliance everyone in those days called 'an electric fire', the little boy Alan, who was loyal to him still, going up to him, kissing him goodnight and then stroking the spaniel's silky head . . .

She came back with coffee and two cups on a tray. Also on the tray was a yellowing sheet of paper on which, long ago, someone had printed an address. 'He wouldn't write me a proper letter. Wouldn't even buy a stamp and stamps weren't the price then they are now. He put this bit of paper through my front door without even an envelope to show me where he was living. He knew I'd see the address was in the best part of Birmingham. That Tracy Cole was loaded. Her dad had died and left her the house and wads of money. Her and him, Eric, I mean, it was one of those cases of a couple who never really get away from each other, one or other of them will always go back.'

If she still lived there, Wexford thought, if she did after so long, could Targo have taken refuge with her?

'Kathleen,' he said, feeling a little awkward as everyone does when using a given name for the first time, 'do you remember the evening I came to talk to Mr Targo when you were living in Jewel Road? It was in connection with the murder of Mrs Elsie Carroll. Do you remember that?'

'Of course I do. I remembered you, didn't I? And that was the only time we met till we ran into each other in the precinct, apart from me being rude to you on the doorstep.'

He laughed. 'You weren't rude, just a bit sharp,' he said. 'This is very good coffee. Do you also remember that I asked your husband where he was on the night Mrs Carroll was killed and he said he was babysitting Alan?'

'I'd been giving Alan his bath,' she said, and incredibly to Wexford, so excellent was her memory, 'and I wasn't there

176

when you asked that. I came in and heard him say that bit about me being at my dressmaking class. I didn't say anything when he said he'd been here all the time doing press-ups and all that rubbish. I didn't because I was scared of him. You could tell that, couldn't you?'

'I was very young, Kathleen. I didn't know about domestic violence. Well, no one did much then. It was talked about as a private thing in a marriage, not to be interfered with by outsiders.'

'That suited men all right, didn't it? Eric didn't knock me about much in those days but I didn't want him hitting me at all when I was so near my time. I mean, I didn't want to fall over. What I'm trying to say is that night you were asking about, I came back early from my class because the teacher was taken ill. Oh, I remember all this even though it was so long ago. When I came back Eric wasn't there, he'd left Alan alone. Only for ten minutes maybe but he had left him and it was that made me think I'm not putting up with this, him leaving his kid alone at night, him hitting me if I step out of line and making more fuss about that dog than he ever would about the baby I was expecting.'

His belief needed no confirmation but she had made assurance doubly sure.

'I did put up with it a bit longer,' she said. 'Joanne was born two weeks later. You stayed in hospital a lot longer then that they do now but he came to see me just the once. Once in ten days when I'd just had his child. He wasn't at home looking after Alan. He was at home looking after the dog while Alan stopped with my mum. I did put up with it for nearly two years more. Alan was six and Joanne was getting on for two. He hit me then, a punch in the breast. They thought punching a woman's breast brought on cancer – it doesn't, they know that now, but I believed it then and I said to him, that's it, what you've done is going to kill me anyway but this is the end. Next day me and the neighbours threw him out and he went to his mum and to Tracy who was another mum to him.'

Wexford's next call was to an old people's home. It might still have been called that but political correctness had renamed it the Seniors' Sanctuary. He had been directed there by the woman who had lived next door to Eileen Kenyon on the Muriel Campden Estate.

'Alzheimer's is what it is,' she said to Wexford on her doorstep. 'She's only in her sixties but that's what it is. You won't get any sense out of her. I know, I've tried, and you'll just be wasting your time.'

He didn't get anything out of her and he was wasting his time. It wasn't the first time he had visited such a place and this one depressed him anew. The decor, the smell, the half-circle of chairs in front of the television set in which sat the elderly inmates, all dressed in a jumble of ill-fitting bizarrely coloured clothes, not one of which looked as if it had originally been bought for its wearer. But perhaps the worst thing was the programme which was showing on the screen, a display of acrobatic dancing by beautiful teenagers in tight-fitting sequinned costumes, their lustrous hair flowing, their skin like a new-picked peach.

Like half the spectators, Eileen Kenyon was in a wheelchair, sitting in that characteristic pose of the sick elderly, her shoulders slumped, her back rounded almost to a hump and her head lolling to one side. Like most of them, she seemed to be staring at something, but not the screen. The sequinned young people cavorted and performed impossible leaps and gyrations while the old sat, twisted and sunken, not watching them.

Golden lads and girls all must, thought Wexford, *as chimney sweepers come to dust*. A carer whispered to him that he would get nothing out of Eileen Kenyon. She no longer knew who she was or where she was. And when the carer moved her wheelchair away from the semicircle of viewers over to the window where he was, he realised she was right. Eileen Kenyon was now only dimly recognisable as the woman she had been. It was as if a hand, dipped in some viscous greyish matter, had passed over her head, whitening and thinning her hair, dimming her eyes and slurring her features.

'Do you remember me, Mrs Kenyon?'

No response at all. The eyes which had gazed at the wall some ten feet away from the television, now stared at the floor.

Inspiration led him to ask, 'Do you remember your dog, the dog you got from Mr Targo?'

One of her eyelids flickered. He tried to remember the dog's name. It was maddening that he remembered the names of Targo's own dogs, Buster, Princess, Braveheart, but not the one Eileen Kenyon had had when Billy was killed. But then it was true that he had almost total recall of the things Targo had said to him.

'Dusty's puppy,' he said. 'Do you remember Dusty's puppy? Dusty was Mr Targo's.'

She lifted her head a little. The eyes opened. 'Snake,' she said quite clearly, and mumbling, 'Snake he had. Scary snake, don't like snake.' Then, 'He asked . . .'

'What did he ask?'

But there was to be no more. He had been given nothing to make him think Eileen Kenyon would have finished her sentence with the words 'if she wanted Billy killed.' Asking her if she knew where Targo might be now seemed ludicrous. He thanked the carer and made his way out along a gloomy corridor to the stained-glass double doors which were the entrance to this place. There must be more places in Kingsmarkham he might have gone to. Something Kathleen Jones had said had briefly alerted him. But what was it?

Of course she had told him, not what he came for, but what was almost more important, that Targo hadn't stayed in babysitting that evening so long ago. What else was it? Philippa becoming a doctor? No. Tracy Cole? Yes, definitely, but that could wait. Glebe Road, he thought, she had mentioned Glebe Road. That was where the Rahmans lived. Nothing had happened to make him think it possible except the knowledge that Targo had visited Ahmed several times in the past. So suppose he had called at the Rahmans after he had killed Andy Norton?

CHAPTER FIFTEEN

He took Hannah with him. They knew her and, if she was to be believed, they hadn't resented her suspiciousness. Hannah was honest and quite openly confessed that Mohammed Rahman had firmly but amiably put her down. He was, she told Wexford, a master of the smiling snub. Wexford expected Mohammed to be at work but Yasmin told him that her husband was ill in bed with flu. He had come down with a virus a couple of days before.

Ahmed was upstairs, taking his father a hot drink, but he came down after a few minutes. On the previous occasion that he had seen him, when he and his brother had just come back from the mosque, he had been struck by Ahmed's good looks and air of health, perhaps too of contentment. All that had changed. Both sons had pale skin while Tamima's was a dark gold, but today Ahmed was white with a sickly pallor. Under his eyes were dark shadows and there was a day's growth of beard on his chin. This of course was becoming a fashionable way for a young man to look but Ahmed's seemed the result of indifference to his appearance, as if something more important than trends and style brought about that careworn look. Probably he had picked up the virus that had laid his father low.

'Yes, Mr Targo came here in the afternoon,' he said in answer to Wexford's inquiry.

'You were expecting him?'

'No, we weren't. When the doorbell rang I thought it was the doctor for Dad.' Ahmed hesitated, then said, 'I was surprised to see Mr Targo. He wanted to order some software.'

Aware that this left Wexford in the dark, Hannah said, 'He didn't do that himself? He asked you to do it for him?'

'Oh, yes.'

Ahmed looked at his mother. She was sitting very stiffly in a straight-backed chair, no jewellery but for her rings to be seen this morning, her head covered in Wexford's presence. Her expression was rather stern, her hands clasped together, but she got up at Ahmed's glance and said she would make coffee.

'What kind of software?' Hannah asked.

'Some floppy disks and a home manager CD.'

'What exactly is that?'

'A home manager CD?' Ahmed suddenly seemed on surer ground. 'Put simply, you plug it into your PC and you can control your lights and electrical appliances by sending a signal from your PC to the switch modules. It goes via the electrical circuit of your home. It turns on the radio if that's what you want. It even sticks the kettle on.'

'And that's what Mr Targo wanted?'

'So he said. He'd read about it somewhere.'

'You could get it for him?' Wexford asked.

'Oh, yes,' Ahmed said confidently. 'The point is I know where to get it and how to order it, that sort of thing. You can buy the floppies anywhere but he always likes me to do that stuff.'

Yasmin came back with the coffee. When she had handed

the cups to them, Wexford noticed her eyes go to the polished granite mantelpiece. She looked at it as if she detected something not quite right about it and then she looked sharply away. As she sat down again, picked up the sugar basin to pass to them, her hands were shaking. Not strongly but the merest tremor which she conquered by stiffening the fingers and holding them out straight.

'Do you know where Mr Targo went when he left here?'

'Home, I suppose. I didn't ask him.'

'Were you surprised,' Wexford asked, 'that he didn't have a dog with him?'

'I wouldn't allow a dog in my house,' Yasmin said.

How would Targo have reacted to that? Her remark caused a silence. Hannah broke it. 'Is Tamima still working at the Raj Emporium?'

The sternness of Yasmin's expression concentrated itself on two deeply cut parallel lines between her dark eyes. 'My daughter has gone away to stay with her auntie. We have told you she was going many times before. Now she has gone. My son Osman had the day off work and drove her there.'

They drank their coffee, Ahmed filling up the silence by giving a gratuitous lecture on innovative autonomous robotic kits with forward, backup and turn actions. To Wexford it might as well have been delivered in Swahili and he got up to leave before his cup was empty. But before going to the door he crossed purposefully to the fireplace, put one hand on the shiny granite and looked closely at the right-angled corner of the mantelpiece. He touched it with one finger and, at a soft indrawing of breath from Ahmed, turned away with a polite smile. Mrs Rahman's expression was unchanged. Ahmed got up to show them out.

'What was all that with the fireplace, guv?' Hannah asked outside.

Wexford was contemplating the Harley-Davidson which had joined the other vehicles on Burden's former front garden. 'Something happened there not long ago,' he said. 'I don't know what it was but Yasmin and her son know. They're scared it may have left some sort of mark.'

'Has it?'

'Not so far as I could see.'

'Tamima's aunt is called Mrs Qasi and she lives in Farmstead Way, Kingsbury, London NW9. Do you think Tamima really has gone there?'

'I don't know, Hannah, and I don't care. At present the missing Targo occupies all my thoughts.'

Wexford had decided that unsatisfactory though she was, Mavis Targo must be the best source of information available on her husband. She opened the door of Wymondham Lodge, said, 'He's pining away. He won't eat.'

These were the first words she addressed to him. There had been no greeting, not even an enquiry to know what he wanted. For a moment he had thought she was speaking of her husband, that he had come home, that he was ill and somewhere in the house. He should have known better, he told himself. Of course it was a dog she was talking about, probably the cream-and-white fluffy one which sat disconsolately in its basket in a corner of the ornate living room. And he wondered if it was a shared passion for canines which had brought this ill-assorted pair together. But perhaps it was not so incongruous a match; for now, looking at her, he saw that she and Targo were rather alike, they might have been brother and sister, the same sort of height, the same stocky build, coarse features, staring blue eyes. If this were horror fiction, he thought, she would turn out to be Targo himself in disguise and she a corpse in the cellar. But how then had he achieved that formidable cleavage which showed at her neckline? He almost laughed.

She was still talking about the Tibetan spaniel missing Targo when the puppy appeared at the French windows, yapping and flinging itself against the glass. She rushed to let it in, opened the doors and as she did so there came from somewhere in the grounds a shrill chattering sound and a low resounding roar. The puppy scampered about, jumping up at Wexford and covering the pale carpet with muddy footprints.

'He doesn't miss his master,' she said. 'He's too young, aren't you, sweetheart? I can't say I'm sorry. I couldn't be doing with two of them breaking their hearts.'

'I don't suppose you've heard from your husband?'

'Nothing. Not a word. It's a long time now, even for him.'

'I am sorry to have to ask you this, Mrs Targo, but I'm afraid it's necessary. Does the name Tracy Cole mean anything to you?'

'Oh, God, yes. You needn't be sorry. She wasn't the last one before me, she was the last but one. She's not called Tracy Cole now, she's been married twice since him and her split up.'

'Would you have a phone number for her? An address?'

'You're barking up the wrong tree if you think he'd go to her.'

The hackneyed metaphor, used in this house, made him smile.

'Just the same, do you have a number?'

Her answer came reluctantly. 'He's got her number on his mobile. I know he has, though he denies it. It's not written down anywhere, I wouldn't have that. I've got her married name somewhere. She wasn't married when he was with her, in case you didn't know.' Wexford said nothing. He waited. 'I don't know if you do know, but she was very young. Her dad had just died and left her that big house and what they call a portfolio of shares. She was only eighteen and she had to wait till she was twenty-one to inherit the rest.'

Mavis Targo was no Kathleen. She boasted that she never kept anything, often threw things away and regretted it afterwards. Tracy Cole's second married name couldn't be found but Mrs Targo said she had remembered it. She remembered it because it was the same surname as Targo's own second wife: Thompson. She was Tracy Thompson and the second wife had been Adele Thompson.

'He was married to her when he was living in Myringham?' Wexford thought how odd this conversation would have sounded to him in the days when he first met Targo. Not merely odd but bizarre, incredible, having no possible connection with an English middle class as it then was, in which the great majority married and remained married until one of them died. Today's serial polygamy would then have been associated only with Hollywood. 'When he had the boarding kennels?'

'What, Adele? I suppose he was. I hadn't met him then. It didn't last long that marriage. She didn't like dogs. She kept it from him when they met but after a time it showed. Well, it would, wouldn't it?'

Wexford said nothing, only looked encouraging. He welcomed Mrs Targo's new loquaciousness. 'The other Thompson,' she said, 'Tracy, I mean, she lived in Edgbaston, still does for all I know. That's the poshest part of Birmingham. He brags about that. Lovely house she had, he says, more a palace than a house. It's nothing for him to be proud of, is it?'

'You said he wouldn't go to her but are you sure of that? He wouldn't hide out with her?'

At last some kind of realisation dawned. 'What d'you want him for? You've never said. What d'you think he's done?'

'We need him to help us with our inquiries into the death of Mr Andrew Norton.'

'Who's he? I've never heard of him and I'll bet Eric hasn't.'

Wexford got up. His rising to his feet was a signal for the bull terrier puppy to rush over and jump up at him. Addressing the dog as 'sweetheart' – perhaps it had no other name – Mavis Targo told it in the gentlest possible tone, quite unlike her rough manner with Wexford, to get down.

'Tell me something,' he said as he was leaving, 'when did your husband have the naevus removed?'

She laughed. 'When we were first married. I asked him to. He did what I asked him in those days.'

Wexford made no comment. 'You'll let us know if you hear from your husband, won't you, Mrs Targo?'

If she was to be found, if she was still alive. He suddenly had one of his hunches that Tracy Cole, the rich woman, the woman who lived in the best part of Birmingham, she to whom Targo fled when his wife turned him out, was the refuge to whom he had gone now. Alan Targo had been six, his mother had said, and now he was what? Forty? Would Targo still want the woman he had wanted thirty-four years ago? He might. People do, and Wexford thought of his own wife to whom he had been married for so long. Kathleen had said that, no matter who else intervened, Eric Targo and Tracy Cole always went back to each other . . .

With the information he had Tracy wasn't hard to find. Over the phone she said she hadn't seen Eric Targo for more than a year but had several times spoken to him. Wexford wondered if Mavis Targo knew that and doubted it. Tracy, who called herself Miss Thompson, said that she had quite a lot she could tell Wexford about her former lover but she would prefer to do it face to face. Would he come and see her?

First he cleared it with West Midlands Police. The officer he spoke to on the phone was a Detective Superintendent Roger Phillips. It had to be the same one. After all this time, the occasional phone call, one or two letters, then years of silence.

'I was best man at your wedding,' he said.

'So you were. And a very good one, as I remember. I'm still married to Pauline and will be till death do us part. How about you?'

'The same. Still married to the same woman, thank God.' Wexford told him about Tracy Thompson and the hunt for Targo. 'I'd like to talk to her if it's OK with you.'

'Sure. You want me to send a DC with you?'

'Thanks but I'll have my sergeant.'

'Bring him in afterwards for a cup of tea.'

Wexford said he would, tried to remember, when the call was ended, what Roger had looked like, failed but recalled perfectly the pretty face of his wife. It was her parents who had been friends of the people who brought Medora Holland to the Phillips wedding . . .

He took Barry Vine with him and they went up by train, a long journey if you start from Sussex. Wexford seldom went anywhere by rail but he read his newspapers and watched television and he knew how liable trains were to delays and cancellations and he feared the worst. But the train from Euston to Birmingham, if not on time, was only five minutes late and they made it to the place that was 'more a palace than a house' at the appointed time.

This added up to four women with strong connections to Targo he had talked to and of them Tracy Thompson was the youngest and the smallest. A tiny woman, no bigger than a child of ten, she could have been taken for a teenager until seen close to. Then the lines which criss-crossed her face showed, the white threads in her limp brown hair. She was dressed like a teenager in jeans and a Disney T-shirt printed with Dalmatians and in the setting of this house she looked an even more incongruous figure than if she had been living in a social housing flat.

Palatial it was, grand and somewhat awe-inspiring, but as Barry Vine remarked to Wexford afterwards, also 'weird'. The furniture in the large high-ceilinged rooms looked as if it had been there, standing precisely where it was now, through several generations, untouched, never renovated, the wood surfaces never polished, curtains, though intact, faded to a grey pallor by decades of sunlight, carpets bleached or irredeemably stained. If the place was not quite Miss Havisham's abode it was Satis House after a half-hearted cleaning.

There was no suggestion, Wexford thought, of Tracy Thompson having been left at the altar and abandoned to the life of a recluse. Rather, she had inherited this place with everything in it but was simply indifferent to her surroundings so long as she might be warm and comfortable when she chose.

She saw him looking, said, 'It's a bit shabby, isn't it? Shame really. I keep meaning to do something about it but I don't suppose I ever shall. You see, I don't like having people in unless they're my friends; I can't stand cleaners, builders, whatever.' She flicked back her long little-girl's hair. 'What did you want to ask me?'

'It's more a matter of what you want to tell us, Miss Thompson.'

189

'Well, the first thing is, what d'you want Eric *for*?'

And then she said something which nearly made Wexford shoot out of the shabby floral armchair he was sitting in. 'He hasn't gone and killed someone, has he?'

Barry Vine was nearly as astonished as Wexford. He had gone a little pale. 'What exactly do you mean by that?' he asked her. 'Were you serious?'

'I think I was,' she said. She seemed not in the least alarmed. 'I don't know if he was when he asked me.'

'What did he ask you?'

'Perhaps I'd better start by telling you about us, Eric and me, that is,' she said. 'I suppose I ought to offer you something but I don't drink tea or coffee. I expect there's some Coke.'

'Please don't bother,' Wexford said. 'You were going to talk about your relationship with Mr Targo.'

'Yes, well, we've known each other since for ever. He'd just come to Birmingham and my dad had just died. I was feeling pretty low. I was only just eighteen, you see, and I'd no one. My mother was dead, I'd no relatives. Everyone kept telling me how lucky I was to have so much money and this house. I was sitting on a bench in the park, thinking about things, what loneliness was and not being able to see any future, when this dog came up to me. It was a spaniel, quite old but so *sweet* and gentle. It licked my hand and when I stroked it it climbed up on to the bench and snuggled up beside me. It put its head in my lap. And then the owner – it was Eric – came up and he said his dog was like that with people he liked. We talked and I told him about myself and he said I ought to get a dog, he'd get me a dog. And, well, he did.'

It didn't sound much like Targo and yet it did. It wasn't quite true that he liked dogs and disliked people but rather that he only liked people who liked dogs. 'Go on,' Wexford said.

'We started seeing each other. I suppose you could say we fell in love. He wasn't my type and I wasn't his but we sort of clicked. His wife had left him, he wanted sometimes to see his kids but he didn't want a share of their house. I had enough for both of us, you see, but if you think he took up with me because I was rich you'd be wrong. He was crazy about me. And I was the one who got tired of it first. I gave Eric the price of a house and enough to start a business – a driving school it was – paid him off, you could say, and I married someone else. But I could never get Eric out of my head. His divorce had come through and then I got divorced. Eric didn't move back with me, he had his own house, and when I found out he'd a woman living with him there, I was so mad I got married to someone else on the rebound.

'Well, after that it was sort of on and off with us, though you could say he was really the only one for me as I was for him. I've been single for years now and there's never been anyone else. Eric married this Adele he'd been living with and moved to Myringham in Sussex. She came from there. And he came from a place called Stowerton. He'd already got property he let out and he started a dogs' boarding kennels. Just up his street that was with him being so mad about dogs. I helped him with the money to set it up. I thought we might get back together because Adele only lasted a few months more but he'd met that Mavis and married her and that was like the end for me. I'd invested in this property development of his, getting hold of right-to-buy properties it was, and it was doing well, but he still married Mavis and bought a big house somewhere with her money. And that's it really. Up to a year ago we were still meeting sometimes and still talking on the phone but when he asked me if there was anyone I wanted rid of – well, that was the end, the really final end.'

Wexford had listened to all this in silence. Now he said, speaking quite slowly, 'What exactly did he ask you, Miss Thompson?'

'You want the details?'

'Please.'

'He phoned and said he had to come up here on business and he'd like to see me. Time was when he'd have come up to see me and found a bit of business to do while he was here. But never mind, that's all water under the bridge. He came and I asked him if he'd be staying. No, he said, and he wanted to tell me that we wouldn't see each other again. He was with Mavis now and they'd settled down. He was getting on and having a bit on the side was no longer on. I said to him, is that what I was, a bit on the side, and all he said was, you know what I mean. He was always saying that, that I knew what he meant – especially when it was hurtful, what he said. Then he said he'd like to do something for me as a kind of thanks for all the years. Was there anyone I wanted rid of? I didn't understand him – well, no one would. He said he'd put it more plainly. Was there anyone I wanted out of the way, disposed of, and no questions asked. I thought he'd gone mad, I really did.'

'He meant, did you want someone killed, is that what he was saying?'

'That's what he was saying. As a kind of *compensation* for leaving me and maybe for us not getting married in the past.'

'What did you say to him?' Vine asked.

'What do you think? I said I was glad he'd said he wouldn't see me again because I felt exactly the same about him and if there was anyone I wanted rid of it was him.'

'You didn't think of contacting us?'

'Well, I did. But what had I got to go on? It would be my word against his. I thought they'd say it was a case of a woman scorned. I mean, look at it this way. He was married, doing well, living with his wife. I was a single woman with two failed marriages behind me, a woman who'd given him God knows how much money over the years and now he'd rejected me. How would that look to the police? Like revenge, don't you think?'

'You've told us now,' said Wexford.

'Because you asked about him. And I thought you wouldn't if you hadn't good reason. Right? And you do believe me, don't you? You don't see me as a woman scorned?'

'I believe you.'

Tea with Roger Phillips terminated in a bottle of port being brought out. Wexford had resolved some years before never to drink port again but he had one glass with Roger while he told him about the interview with Tracy Thompson and the 'compensation' Targo had offered her, told him too about Elsie Carroll and Billy Kenyon and Andy Norton. Roger echoed the words Wexford himself had used to Tracy.

'I believe you.'

'She says she hasn't seen him since. He's tried to phone her, left messages, but she hasn't answered them. That offer he made shocked her to the core.'

'Well, it would, Reg. We're used to violent death and death threats so we often fail to appreciate how shocking ordinary members of the public find that sort of thing. Society hasn't really become depraved, whatever the media says. Most people lead pretty sheltered and certainly law-abiding lives. Are you thinking that he may have made that sort of offer in the past to the people who would benefit from what he was about to do?'

'He didn't make it to me,' said Wexford, 'and he expected me to benefit from the death of Norton. I'm sure he didn't make it to George Carroll. If he had, what would have stopped Carroll telling us about it when he was charged with murder? But it may well be that Eileen Kenyon knew. He could have suggested it to Eileen Kenyon after he'd given her a puppy and seen how she was with Billy. If she knew he'd killed Billy it was in her interest to keep quiet about it.'

'And now he's disappeared?'

'I don't think he's with a woman. There's only this Adele left and we'll contact her but it appears she was with him for a shorter time than any other woman in his life. He could be anywhere.'

'He must be getting money. Have you looked at his bank account?'

'I've had no grounds to do that till now. It's my next step.'

With undertakings (neither would adhere to) to keep in touch, meet for a meal when the Phillipses were in Sussex visiting Pauline's aged mother, they parted. Wexford took the *Birmingham Post* he had bought that morning out of his raincoat pocket and read it in the train while Vine, afficionado of Donizetti, listened to *L'Elisir d'Amore* on his CD Walkman.

When he was reading a newspaper belonging to a distant city or even specifically to London, he always looked at the births, marriages and deaths. Time was when people he knew were getting married, then having babies, now some of them were dying. The last name in the deaths column was Trelawney. He knew no one called that, yet . . . '*Trelawney, Medora Anne, beloved wife of James, on 31 October at Sutton Coldfield, sadly missed. Funeral at All Saints' Church, 3 November at 10 a.m., no flowers, please. Donations to the British Heart Foundation.*'

It was almost certainly the same one. The boyfriend who had tried to blackmail him she had called Jim and Trelawney was a Cornish name. No age was given for her, he noticed. It looked as if she had died of heart disease. What had she been doing in Sutton Coldfield? Living there with Jim, no doubt, and maybe children who sadly missed her. He folded up the newspaper and went back to thinking about Targo. There was very little doubt now that Targo had disappeared.

CHAPTER SIXTEEN

Hannah Goldsmith picked Jenny Burden up at the school gates at four thirty in the afternoon. It was pouring with rain which meant that everyone had covered their heads or put up umbrellas and was scurrying through the downpour. This suited Hannah well. She didn't much want to be seen having secret or at any rate private meetings with Mike Burden's wife. The cafe they went to in a side turning off Queen Street would have been called when Wexford was young a 'pull-up for carmen'. If they had heard the phrase they would have supposed it something to do with the opera.

It was a shabby little place, ill-ventilated and with condensation running down the windows. The tea was the mahogany-coloured kind they used to say you could stand a spoon up in but now was called 'builder's'.

'I wanted to share with you what I'm doing,' Hannah began, 'because I know you're concerned about Tamima Rahman the way I am. I went along to see the family with the guv yesterday – it was about something quite different – but Yasmin Rahman happened to say that Tamima had gone to London to stay with her auntie. Her brother Osman – he's the nurse – drove her up there the day before.'

Jenny nodded. 'So she's there, is she? Where exactly is she?'

'Auntie's called Mrs Qasi and she lives in Kingsbury. That's a London suburb in the north-west, sort of west of Hendon if you know where that is. But as to whether she's there I don't know. They say she is and maybe it's all right. But I found Mrs Qasi's phone number and called her and asked to speak to Tamima. That was this morning. She said Tamima was out with her cousin. Apparently she's got a lot of cousins, all of them in that sort of area. They'd gone to Oxford Street shopping, she said. I asked when she'd be back but Mrs Qasi didn't know. I phoned again at three and this time there was no answer. I left a message.'

'What is it you suspect?' Jenny asked.

'I don't know. All these weeks since Tamima left school in July I've thought there was a possibility the Rahmans would arrange a marriage for her.'

'Not force a marriage?'

'I think they are anxious to keep her and Rashid Hanif apart but sending her to London shows they haven't succeeded. Now this is perhaps the point where the idea of an arranged marriage becomes a forced marriage.'

'You mean send her to London and introduce her to some relative, of whom there are dozens up there, and if she's OK about the idea so well and good but if not . . .'

'If not it would be much easier to compel her to marry in London than down here where everyone would know what's going on.'

'And if she won't, she refuses, what then?'

'I don't want to go there. Not yet. First of all I want to find if Tamima's with Mrs Qasi and more to the point if she's happy to be there.'

But Tamima didn't call her back as Hannah had asked her. Nor did she call Jenny, though she had her number. Teenagers don't write letters but they send emails. Jenny got an email from her, though there was nothing to prove Tamima was the source of it.

Hi Mrs Burden. I am having a great time in London with my auntie Mrs Qasi at 46 Farmstead Way, Kingsbury, and my cousins. I didn't really know them till now and it's so cool. I may decide to stay for a while and get a job.
   Tamima

'Anyone might have sent that,' Hannah said

'Yes, I don't know *why* she would send it. After all, I haven't made any enquiries about her since before she went to Pakistan. Why not contact you?'

Hannah said thoughtfully, 'Let's give it a few days. If we haven't heard any more would you feel like going to London on Friday or Saturday and paying this Mrs Qasi a visit?'

'Saturday would be best for me. No school.'

But on Friday, when Hannah went with Wexford, to check with the Rahmans that Ahmed had heard nothing from the missing Eric Targo, Osman had the day off and was at home.

Looking very much like his father and half smiling in the same supercilious way, he told Hannah that he knew she 'took a great interest in Tamima's activities'. 'You may care to know that she's going to share a flat with her cousin and a friend for a while and get a job. Quite enterprising, don't you think?'

It was one of those areas of not-quite-outer London that still retain vestiges of countryside, spoilt countryside where chain-link fencing, concrete and abandoned factory buildings scar the fields but where the fields still exist. You could see how Farmstead Way got its name. The road Hannah drove along to reach it skirted the Brent reservoir and there was even a small herd of black-and-white cows chewing the cud under a stand of chestnut trees. The rain had cleared away but only temporarily and the blue sky would be short-lived. It was Saturday when Hannah should have had a day off and Jenny had no school

Faduma Qasi's home was a bungalow, semi-detached, as were all the houses in the street, though their designs had been varied and there were green-tiled roofs among the red. Hannah had phoned to warn Mrs Qasi of their coming and she let them in very promptly. Both she and Jenny had expected a black-robed woman who would have covered her head before answering the door, but Tamima's aunt was dressed very much as her non-Muslim neighbours might be in a black-and-white dogstooth check skirt, black sandals and a red polo-neck sweater.

When the introductions had been made, she said she would make tea. Jenny and Hannah sat down in a living room in which not a piece of furniture or ornament had its provenance in an Asian subcontinental culture. Hannah was reminded that Mrs Qasi was Mohammed Rahman's sister. His home had taken on a similarly indigenous British end-of-the-twentieth-century atmosphere. A bookcase was full of English books and, even more to Hannah's astonishment, a bottle of sherry stood on a tray next to two glasses.

The tea came, much like the tea in the Queen Street cafe, strong, aromatic, dark chestnut colour when a drop of milk is added to it.

'Now,' said Faduma Qasi, sitting down to pour, 'I'd like to begin by setting you right on a few matters. I know what you're thinking. I can see it in your faces. It's written all over them, if you don't mind me putting it that way.' She passed Jenny's cup, indicated the bowl of loaf sugar. 'You expected to see a downtrodden old woman in a burka, didn't you?

You think all Muslim women are like that and your mission in life is to set them free and emancipate them. But I don't quite fit the picture, do I? I'm a teacher –' she looked at Jenny '– like you. But I'm not married. I was and my marriage was arranged but we were each shown pictures of possible people to marry and we chose each other. We met and liked each other and went out together. Arranged marriages are a tradition in our family. My brother's marriage with Yasmin was arranged and you couldn't find a happier one. I'm divorced now. My husband didn't say "I divorce you" three times and throw me out, like the newspapers say. We were divorced properly in the court. I've a man friend – I refuse to call a man of fifty a boyfriend – and eventually we shall get married.'

Hannah received her teacup and the sugar pushed towards her. 'My brother was born in Pakistan but I was born here and English is my native tongue. I was born a British citizen of enlightened intelligent parents. I don't cover up my head because there's nothing in the holy Koran about a woman having to cover her head. I try to be a good Muslim and I don't drink alcohol. Yes, I've seen you looking at the sherry bottle – that's for guests. Would you like a glass? No? A bit early in the morning, I expect.'

'Mrs Qasi,' Hannah began, 'we don't mean to –'

'No, I know you don't mean to. I know you think you're quite without prejudice but you're racists like English people are. Benevolent racists, is what I call you. OK? Now we'll talk about what you came for.'

Jenny said, 'I think you've taken the wind out of our sails a bit. Out of mine, at any rate. What we came for was really to ask if your niece Tamima is all right, if she's staying here, and if – well, if you're happy about her sharing a flat with your daughter and a friend. I mean, they're very young, aren't they? Tamima's only sixteen and I don't suppose your daughter's much older.'

'My daughter is also sixteen,' Mrs Qasi said, 'but when Tamima speaks of her cousin she doesn't mean Mia. She means her cousin who is my sister's daughter – we are a large and united family, Mrs Burden – and who is twenty-seven. The friend is my niece's friend Clare and they have been sharing a flat for five years.'

Hannah asked, 'Would you give us the address of that flat and your other niece's name, Mrs Qasi?'

'My niece who owns the flat is called Jacqueline. Her father is an Englishman, you see. But I don't think I shall give you the address. I would if you had an order or a warrant or what-ever you call it but you haven't. Tamima has done nothing wrong and nor have Jacqueline or Clare. As you must know, Tamima is in London with the full approval of her father and mother. She intends to return home at the end of the year. At Christmas, I believe. You see, I celebrate that like any other British citizen while not believing in the faith behind it – again like most British citizens. Incidentally, Tamima was here until yesterday. She left with Jacqueline and Clare just about the time you phoned to make this appointment. If you want her address I suggest you ask my brother for it.

'By the way,' she added, speaking to Jenny, 'the email Tamima sent you was written at my suggestion. It seemed a sensible and polite thing to do.'

The interview had turned out very differently from the way Hannah had expected. Much as she hated being called a 'benevolent racist', she was obliged to admit, if only to herself, that Faduma Qasi had been precisely correct when she described – in cringe-making detail – the kind of woman she and Jenny had expected to find. Some of the expressions she had used, especially with regard to dress and marriage, were the very things they had discussed while driving along the road from west Hendon. She, who had prided herself on her utter lack of race prejudice, her persuading of herself that all people, regardless of race and skin colour and origin, were equal, must now thoroughly examine her attitudes and revise them. She felt humiliated, an unusual sensation for her. But she was anxious not to show it.

'Tamima lived here with you for how long?' she said.

'About a week. It was like a holiday for her. Jacqueline works from home so she could take days off and she took Tamima about in London. To a theatre matinee, you know, and the cinema and to museums. We are not entirely un-cultured, our family. Then she and Clare suggested Tamima get a job at the Asian supermarket Spicefield and moved in with them. She asked her parents if that would be all right and they agreed.'

'I believe,' said Jenny, 'that it's a fact that Mr and Mrs Rahman were anxious to separate Tamima from a boy she was friendly with, Rashid Hanif.'

'I know nothing about that. Tamima never mentioned him.'

Hannah spent the rest of the weekend preparing a report for Wexford. It outlined her suspicions but also contained incontrovertible facts. There was no proof that Tamima Rahman had ever been in London, only the word of her parents and her aunt Faduma Qasi. Mrs Qasi had refused to give the details of her niece Jacqueline's flat so Hannah had no idea where it was, who the friend was apart from her being called Clare, or which branch of Spicefield was supposed to be employing Tamima.

Preoccupied with Targo, Wexford nevertheless took the time to read it.

'I've asked you this before, Hannah, but I'll ask you again. What is it you suspect?'

'That they're forcing her to marry someone.'

'But what makes you think so?'

'It's in the report, guv.'

'I've read the report. Now I'd like you to answer a few questions I'm going to put to you. Has Tamima or anyone in the family ever spoken to you of forced marriage, as something they favour or, conversely, are opposed to? Have any of them ever told you they disapprove of Rashid Hanif? Or named someone they prefer over him to be a boyfriend or fiancé or husband for Tamima? You say – though not in the report – that the Rahmans are an enlightened Westernised family, yet you suspect them of inflicting on their daughter a cruel and ancient custom. Why? Above all, why have you, whom I always take to be particularly pro-Muslim and anti-racist, suddenly begun showing what seems to me like unreasoning prejudice?'

This last was too much for Hannah. She burst out with a passionate rejoinder. 'Oh, guv, I haven't. It's not like that. I'm trying to be open-minded. I'm afraid that if I – well, veer too much to being pro-Muslim I'll lose my judgement.'

'No fear of that,' Wexford said briskly. 'Now there's a lot to do here. We've got someone missing who's almost certainly committed at least one murder. And I've just heard that the Mercedes has been found, parked at the roadside in a village in Essex. Apart from Targo, wherever he is, crime goes on. Petty crime if you like but you wouldn't call it petty if it was your house that had been broken into and pillaged and wrecked. So you can have one more go at finding where Tamima Rahman lives and works and if that fails you have to give up. Are you happy with that?'

'I have to be if you say so, guv,' said Hannah. But she made a mental note that on her own, without backup, without even Jenny's support, she would pursue her enquiries into Tamima's whereabouts. She would start with the supermarket and find which, if any, of their branches employed her.

CHAPTER SEVENTEEN

This time it was in the Olive and Dove's 'snug' that they met. Ashtrays on the tables were piled with ash and cigarette ends, the ceiling yellow and polished with tar deposits.

'If the day ever comes when they bring in a smoking ban,' Wexford said, 'this place will get a clean-up. They might even get new curtains.'

'More likely to close down. People won't come. Smokers like to smoke while they drink.'

'Or we shall have the place to ourselves.'

Wexford went to get their drinks. The saloon bar was quieter than usual as if in anticipation of restrictions to come. Two girls sat chatting and smoking at a corner table. In his youth, Wexford thought, they would have been in a teashop but they would have offered each other cigarettes then as now. The elderly man who sat alone with his yellow Labrador – did people now refer to *him* as an elderly man? – had a pipe in his mouth. Pipes would disappear. Even now his grandsons talked of seeing someone smoke a pipe as he when a boy might have spoken of seeing an eccentric in galoshes or using a monocle. The man with the dog brought Targo to mind – not that he was ever far away.

'What we need to know,' he said to Burden, 'is what he

was up to in Kingsmarkham between the time he left the Rahmans at around three – say three thirty – and came back to fetch the Mercedes *sometime after eight fifteen*. We know it was still there after eight fifteen because the girl from the nail bar saw it. So even if he drove it away at half past eight it had been there for getting on for six hours.

'He didn't go home. Mavis Targo says he didn't and why should she lie? He didn't call on his children. He didn't go to his Sewingbury office. Because if he had he would have gone in his car. It's too far even for him to walk.'

Burden took a sip of his wine. He wrinkled his nose but made no comment on the quality or taste of what he was drinking. 'Why didn't he have a dog with him? Oh, I know Mrs Rahman wouldn't have a dog in the house but when he'd been there on at least one previous occasion he brought the dog but left it in the car. Why didn't he have a dog this time? Because of what he intended to do *after* he'd been to the Rahmans? He left the car where it was because there are no parking restrictions in Glebe Road and he went off to do whatever he did.'

'Yes, but what was that? His not bringing a dog suggests to me that he knew he wouldn't be going back home. He was running away. He'd committed another murder and this time he knew he'd been seen going into his victim's garden.'

'But did he know that, Reg? Surely he didn't. If he had he wouldn't have wasted time ordering fancy computer equipment. Wouldn't he have been off as soon as he could pack a bag and be off?'

'You're right,' said Wexford. 'He couldn't have known. He wasn't in a hurry. It looks as if he expected to return home. His wife says he took no clothes with him. So did something happen while he was at the Rahmans or soon after he left the Rahmans to make him realise he might have been seen?

Perhaps. Maybe we should go and ask what used to be called "gentlemen's outfitters", but no doubt aren't any longer, if they sold a whole new wardrobe to a single customer that afternoon.'

'What, and carry the stuff all the way back up Glebe Road to the car?'

'I know it's not a brilliant theory, Mike. How about he went to get a false passport from some mate?'

'I know this place has degenerated along with the rest of the countryside but surely you'd have to do that kind of thing in London or maybe his other favourite haunt, Birmingham?'

'Mike, I just don't know. The whole thing doesn't add up. But I've been busy with a map of Essex before we came down here. Melstead where the Mercedes was found, is about seven miles from Stansted airport. That's why I thought about the clothes and the passport. He could have got out of the country before anyone started looking for him. Of course that doesn't answer why he left the car where he did. It was bound to be found so why not leave it in the long-stay car park at Stansted?'

'Come to that,' said Burden, 'why go to Stansted at all when Gatwick is on our doorstep?'

'I know. I thought of that. I phoned Mavis Targo and told her about finding the Mercedes. She just said, "Abroad?" in the sort of tone a woman might use if I'd suggested her husband had gone to Mars. Then she repeated that stuff about him hating abroad. He's only once been out of this country and that was to Spain on their honeymoon.

'I said he'd renewed his passport just the same. That was because they were going to New York, she said. Her daughter was getting married in New York and she wanted to go to the wedding. I didn't know she had a daughter. She's not Targo's of course. Targo was apparently going too but when it came

207

to the crunch he couldn't face flying and he's seasick on boats. When I said it was still possible he'd left the country all she said was *she* was left to feed the bloody animals. Every time she goes in the cage to feed the lion she's so frightened her hands shake and she can hardly hold his steak dinner.'

Burden laughed. 'I don't hold with keeping wild animals – dangerous animals – as pets. Why does he do it?'

'I suppose he has an affinity with them. He's a dangerous animal himself. He's a monster.'

'What d'you think made him leave the country – if he has?'

'While the car was parked outside the Rahmans' and while he was walking about Kingsmarkham, shopping or seeing someone or, for all I know, revisiting the scenes of his past crimes, he spoke to someone or saw or read something and realised he was in danger. I don't know what that something was but it's the only thing that accounts for his not going home as he planned. Instead he had to get away fast.'

'Yes but, Reg, he didn't get out fast even then. This discovery of his – I mean that he would be a suspect – was probably made during the afternoon, at latest by about six when it's dark and the only people about are in the pubs. But we know he didn't leave Glebe Road until after eight fifteen. When he did leave he drove, not to the nearest airport, but up to north Essex, a long way, taking in the Dartford Crossing and endless miles of motorway. That's not getting out fast.'

'No, you're right. And what we haven't considered is how did he get from where he parked the car to Stansted, if he did. Walked? In the middle of the night? If it's anything like most of these country places – think of the villages round here – he'd be walking along narrow totally unlit lanes, some-times no houses for miles and if there were any they'd be in darkness at that hour. Did he know the way? Had he ever been there before? I asked Mavis that and she said not that she knew of. She did know he'd never been anywhere from Stansted airport.'

'The prints on the Mercedes – I take it they're his?'

'His and Mavis's. Whatever she says, Mike, he's left the country now and he's not planning on coming back. There's only one thing that really worries me about that theory. Would he leave all those animals? Would he leave his *dogs*? Oh, he could rely on her to look after them but surely only for a while. The dogs permanently maybe but the llamas? The lion? That's the part I don't understand. I have to see this place where the car was parked. I'm going up to Melstead tomorrow.'

The route from the Dartford Crossing along the M25 and the M11 was almost uniformly ugly and spoilt. But beyond the hoardings and the proliferation of road signs, behind the flower stalls, the prefab cafes and the golf courses, meadows and untouched woodland could be distantly seen, with here and there a church spire or an ancient half-timbered house. The scenery improved once Donaldson took the turning for Braintree, and Wexford, who had heard, along with most Sussex people, that Essex was generally a flat eyesore, was surprised. He had only previously been to Colchester and hadn't expected gently hilly country, willow-bordered streams and pretty villages boasting more thatched cottages than in his own county.

Melstead was such a place. It was approached – and apparently exclusively approached – along a network of narrow lanes without pavements. At one point Donaldson was forced on to the verge and halfway into the hedge when a woman sped past them without any relaxation of speed. Wexford considered doing something about it, then told himself he wasn't a traffic cop and had better things to occupy his time with.

The street where Targo's Mercedes had been found ran from the heart of the village, where there was a green with a war memorial, the church and the vicarage, up to a pub called the Prince of Wales Feathers and a small council estate. Donaldson parked the car and Wexford and Lynn Fancourt walked up to the middle point of the street. Here were the only two shops remaining in the village, a butcher's which had about it that indefinable atmosphere of pride and conceit that proclaims its reputation as 'the best butcher in Essex' and a general store and post office.

Recently converted to vegetarianism, Lynn shuddered theatrically at Mr Parkinson's display of locally shot pheasants and turned her face away to follow Wexford into the general store. Another surprise was in store for him. Out here, in this rustic and intensely English spot, the proprietor and postmaster was Asian. And a particularly dark-skinned hook-nosed Asian at that. Wexford wondered if it was politically incorrect even to think these things. He showed Anil Mansoor his warrant card and introduced Lynn.

'Sussex, eh? I have cousins in Sussex. Maybe you know them?'

This reminded Wexford of the sort of people who when you tell them you're going to Sydney, say that maybe you'll see their brother who emigrated to Perth ten years before. He ignored the remark and asked about the car.

Mr Mansoor said he hadn't noticed it until a customer told him it had been there four days and asked him what he thought should be done about it. Minding one's own business seemed to be a watchword of the postmaster's.

'I said it was nothing to do with us. There are no parking restrictions in this street. Anyone could leave a car here if he wished, plenty of room for us remains.'

'Do you live over the shop, Mr Mansoor?' Wexford asked.

A note of pride came into Mansoor's voice. 'No. I have a home in Thaxted. I drive here each day, it isn't far.'

'You didn't see the man who parked the Mercedes here?'

'As I say, I go home to Thaxted each evening sharp at five. Indeed, you might call that afternoon rather than evening, but that is when I drive to my home.'

'If someone wanted to get to Stansted airport from here and had no car, what would he or she do?'

'He could walk.' This was such an alien notion to Mr Mansoor that he burst out laughing as if he had been exceptionally witty. 'If he was mad or stricken by poverty, yes, he could walk. It is seven miles. Better to get a taxi. You will find the taxi man's home opposite the pub. It says Tip-Top Taxis on the gate which is rather a silly name, in my opinion.'

Today Mr Mansoor's side of the street was parked with cars almost nose to tail, there being just two gaps large enough for someone to squeeze a vehicle in. If there had been even a single car or van on the other side the space left between would have been wide enough for no more than a bicycle.

'What happens when something comes the other way, Lynn?'

'That happens, sir,' she said, pointing.

The van which had just about passed the halfway mark in the street moved relentlessly on while the Fiat coming towards it was forced to reverse, a manoeuvre which was a challenge to the old man at the wheel who was several times in danger of scraping the bodywork of a Rolls-Royce, a VW and a Transit van. They watched with interest but desisted from applause when the older driver succeeded in escaping with no damage to his own car or the others. They walked up the path to Tip-Top Taxis.

Wexford was almost certain the taxi driver was going to tell him he had received a phone call from someone requesting to be driven to Stansted airport or even to a station on the

London to Cambridge mainline at midnight on the relevant date. But the owner of Tip-Top Taxis disappointed him. Mr Davis kept his books efficiently. No such call and no such appointment were recorded.

'I'd have remembered anyway.'

'Why is that, Mr Davis?'

'Because I'm sixty-five years old and I reckon I'm past driving some lazy sod to Stansted at that hour when there's no flights before six in the morning.'

'It could have been in the morning,' said Lynn, thinking of Targo sleeping in his car. 'Have you any bookings to the airport or a train the next morning?'

'Not a sausage, Miss. I do a regular run Wednesday mornings without fail. Take a lady to see her mum in an old folks' place in Newmarket, wait for her and bring her back. That satisfy you?'

So Targo had parked his car and vanished. He was strong and fit and resourceful. He could have walked. 'Along those lanes, sir?' Lynn asked as they walked back to the car. 'In the dark? You noticed how fast the locals drive. He'd have been lucky not to be killed. Do you remember that woman that passed us on the way here?'

'I do. A pedestrian would get short shrift from someone like her.'

Hannah was put on to someone called a personnel co-ordinator at the Spicewell supermarket headquarters. This was far from London and even farther from Kingsmarkham on an industrial estate outside Peterborough.

'Kingsmarkham Crime Management. This is Detective Sergeant Goldsmith. Can you tell me if you're employing a Tamima Rahman at any of your branches? R-A-H-MA-N.'

'I'll check.'

In the days when such information was kept in files she would have had to call Hannah back. As it was she didn't even have to ask her to hold the line. She knew within thirty seconds. 'No, we don't employ anyone of that name.'

Hannah was always thorough. 'Would you check again, please?'

The second check afforded no different data. Hannah's next call was to Mrs Qasi. Her tone was waspish. 'Don't ask me. I haven't seen Tamima since she left here. I've told you. She's living with Jacqueline and Clare in Wandsworth.'

As soon as the words were out Faduma Qasi realised she had inadvertently let out Tamima's place of residence. Using a wheedling tone usually foreign to her, Hannah asked if Mrs Qasi could, *please*, be more specific.

Tamima's aunt hesitated – or had she put the receiver down?

'Are you there, Mrs Qasi?'

'Oh, well, I suppose it won't do any harm. Mancunia Road, Wandsworth, SW18. It's number 46.'

'Thank you very much.'

While she had been checking on supermarkets, Damon Coleman had also been round the shops. When Wexford was young, engaged to Alison, Kingsmarkham's men had only one shop in which to buy their clothes, an old-fashioned (even then) outfitters in the centre of the high street. This was Prior's, where women also bought skirts and suits and their children's school uniform. Now there were six, one of them in the run-down Kingsbrook Centre, one (very trendy) in York Street, the rest in the high street where Prior's still held a pre-eminent place but under its new name, minus the apostrophe, of Priors Prime of Life. Damon went there first and met with no success. The smart place in York Street was no help and nor was Young Adult three shops along from Priors.

The last shop he visited was called Heyday, its window full of jeans, sweaters, baseball caps, heavy metal-studded belts and Wild West ten-gallon hats.

No, Mr Targo hadn't bought anything there on the afternoon in question but they knew him. He wasn't what you'd call a regular customer but he had bought a couple of pairs of jeans there, one pair two or three weeks before.

'You're a snappy dresser, Damon,' Wexford said. 'Is that expression still used?'

'Not so far as I know, sir.'

'You'd know. Let's say you care how you look. Would you leave the country with only the clothes you stood up in?'

'No, I wouldn't. But then I wouldn't be fleeing from justice, would I?'

'Fleeing' was hardly the word. Shilly-shallying, loitering, hanging about, would be more appropriate. Targo hadn't even been shopping. Surely if you embarked on a flight without a suitcase full of clothes, Wexford thought, you would only do so because you'd find clothes at your destination. Not necessarily in the shops of some foreign city but because you kept them there in a friend's home. He phoned Mavis Targo.

'My daughter? Lois? He wouldn't go to her. The only time they met they didn't get on. It was here and she's allergic to dogs. She only stayed one night but I had to lock the dogs up and you can imagine the sort of fuss Eric made.'

'Just the same, I'd like her phone number, please.'

'What time is it? 2 p.m.? Well, it's only seven where she lives. I'll give you the number but you'll have to wait till a more civilised hour.'

Wexford didn't bother with civilised hours but called Mrs Lois Lidgett in Colorado Springs five minutes later. Her 'I wouldn't have him in the house' had a familiar ring. He remembered that Adele Thompson had said she wouldn't be in the same room with Targo and Mrs Rahman wouldn't allow his dog to cross the threshold.

People had been telling him over the years that a good way to think clearly was to go for a walk. If you sat down in a chair and tried to think the chances were you'd go to sleep. First put the monster in the box, he thought. Throw the box away – but he couldn't do that, it was the monster he had to think about. He had always considered walking as therapeutic in that if you did enough of it it would use up some of the calories you put in by means of red wine, cashew nuts, Chinese food, fruit pies and snacks. Might it also be beneficial in a psychological way? That is, affect the mind so that it concentrated on the problem in hand?

Beautiful the botanical gardens were no longer. Or perhaps it was only the time of year, the untidiest time when lawns are brown with scattered leaves and a few dying roses linger on straggly bushes. The tropical house had become a coffee bar, the pinetum had been vandalised by those such as the Molloy gang and the rare trees enclosure turned into a (seldom used) children's playground with swings and see-saws. The grass was too wet to walk on so he kept first to the main drive, then turned off along a path between lawns shaded by great cedars and beeches shedding copper-coloured leaves.

A woman was coming towards him and because he was always aware of women's fear when encountering a lone man in a lonely place, he took a few steps off the path on to the wet turf. He smelt her scent, then heard her say, 'Keep off the grass, Reg. Do you remember saying that to me before these gardens were here?'

He had no idea who she was, a tall thin woman, very upright, white hair piled on her head in a chignon. Unrecognisable – yet she had recognised him.

'Why did I say that?'

'Most of those words weren't needed, you said. Cut out "keep" first and you get "off the grass", then "the" which isn't necessary, finally "grass" because what else? You've just got "off" left and that says it all. I've never forgotten it. You don't know who I am, do you?'

He did now. 'Yes, Alison, of course I do. How are you? Tell me you don't live here and I couldn't have seen you all these years.'

She laughed. 'I live in France. I lost my first husband and married a Frenchman. I'm here because my mother died. She was immensely old but it's still awful, it's still a shock.'

'Let's walk,' he said.

They went back the way he had come. So much for thinking and concentrating on his problem. He was telling her about his life, his children, his grandchildren, when she took his arm and, looking down at her right hand resting on his sleeve, he saw the ring she wore on her third finger. It was the engagement ring he had given her when he was twenty-one and she had kept when he offered it. He looked at it and she saw him look but neither of them said anything.

At the gates she said, 'I'm staying at the Olive. Where else? Back to France tomorrow on the Eurostar.'

'Goodbye, my dear,' he said and he took her in his arms and kissed her. She walked away, waving once.

Back to the police station and back to earth. DS Goldsmith, he was told, had gone to London in pursuit of Tamima Rahman but was expected back shortly. He felt vaguely annoyed. He had told her to have one more go at finding Tamima's whereabouts. Perhaps it was that word 'shortly' which irritated him. What was wrong with 'soon'? He was trying to do the thinking which the fortuitous meeting with

Alison had put an end to, when Burden walked in frowning, the corners of his mouth turned down. He seldom swore but he did now.

'That bloody lion's escaped.'

'What?'

'King or whatever it's called, it's escaped. Mavis Targo's been on. She went to feed it and it got out.'

'For God's sake, Mike. When did this happen?'

'Early this morning. She was scared to tell us, thought it might come back of its own accord. She phoned the RSPCA first and then something called the Feline Foundation, then us. We were a poor third. The media haven't got it yet but they will without help from us. I've been on to Myringham Zoo and they've got someone coming over, their Big Cats expert apparently.'

'How did it get out?'

'Well, normally, she says, she wouldn't go into its enclosure. Targo does and apparently he strokes the thing. She throws half a side of lamb or whatever over the wire – he hangs it on that hook thing – only she missed and it caught on the top. She unlocked the gate, went in and tried to reach it but failed. The lion was in its cave. She fetched a pair of steps to climb up, forgetting that the gate was unlocked. When she came back the gate was open and she saw the lion out in the meadow where the muntjac deer are. She was so frightened she ran back to the house, locked herself in and drank some brandy. I don't know what she hoped for, some miracle, some waking up from a nightmare maybe, but it wasn't till half an hour ago that she phoned us.'

Wexford's phone was ringing. He picked it up.

'*Kingsmarkham Courier* here. Lionel Smith speaking. What can you tell us about this escaped lion?'

The widespread publicity was welcomed by Wexford. If anything could bring Targo back, this might. The news that his wife was missing or one of his children would very likely leave him indifferent, but the loss of one of his precious pets would be a major disaster in his life.

Of course the story figured mostly in the British media but Damon Coleman found, via the World Wide Web, references to it in French, German and Spanish newspapers. Bulls might stampede through the streets, wandering bears terrorise the unwary or animals resembling a lynx be spotted on the moors, but this was a lion, a man-eater, truly the king of the beasts. British newspapers loved it. The *Sun's* front page was all lion, a magnificent full-page photograph under the single word headline ESCAPED! Whether this was a picture of King hardly mattered. One lion is very much like another and this one had the recognised leonine attributes, a noble head, a flowing mane and a powerful muscular torso. The *Guardian* scooped with a photograph of Targo inside his lion's cage, the animal standing six feet away from him. Mavis must have dug that out of her archives, Wexford thought. He liked the *Daily Mail's* version best, its headline A DOUBLE FLIT with a picture of Targo jogging in shorts, T-shirt and scarf and another of some unnamed lion crouching and poised to spring.

Kingsmarkham filled with reporters and photographers, all hoping, Wexford said, for King to emerge from his hiding place to attack and devour some unsuspecting citizen, preferably in public, preferably a woman and preferably a blonde.

Burden laughed. 'I don't know about "unsuspecting". The whole place is galvanised with terror. Down the high street half the shops aren't opening. Their staff haven't come in to work. There's no one about on foot but the traffic's heavier than usual. Everyone who's got a car is out in it.'

'He'll come back, won't he, Mike? He won't be afraid of the wretched beast not being found. He'll be afraid of it being seen and shot.'

'What good would his coming back do? He'll no more know where his lion is than we do.'

'Maybe not. But you say that because you can't imagine being as attached to any animal the way Targo is to that lion. And to his dogs, come to that. If you were abroad and one of your children was missing you'd come home, wouldn't you?'

'Well, of course,' said Burden. 'But that's different. They're my children and they're human beings.'

'It's not different for Targo. He's got children too but his animals are more important to him. Always have been. Once, long ago, I saw him smile fondly at his son Alan. Not because he felt tenderly towards the boy but because the boy was being specially nice to his spaniel. I think he'll come back.'

'The Big Cats bloke's told me he'll shoot it with an anaesthetic dart if he gets the chance. The trouble is he knows how it's done but he's had no experience of actually doing it. The chap from the Feline Foundation's got a twelve-bore and a licence for it. That was the first thing I asked. He doesn't want to have to use it but he will if it's a matter of saving human lives. I hope they don't have to kill the poor thing.'

'So do I,' said Wexford.

At the last minute Hannah had decided to take Jenny Burden with her to Wandsworth if Jenny would come. She would and the two women set off for London in Hannah's car, threading their way through late-afternoon traffic but finding Mancunia Road, which abutted on to Wandsworth Common, without difficulty.

The flat was the top one in a Victorian terraced house. The nameplate under the bell said Clare Cooper and Jacquie Clarke.

'I expected to take longer getting here,' Hannah said. 'We may be in for a long wait.'

She had parked rather nervously on a space where a ticket from a machine on the pavement was required. Or that was how it seemed. Things were very different from what prevailed in Kingsmarkham. The horrors of possibly having her car clamped had occurred to Hannah even before she got here. But she put her coins into the machine and a ticket emerged, entitling her to park for two hours. She and Jenny went up the steps to the front door of number 46 and rang Clare Cooper and Jacquie Clarke's bell. Rather to their surprise a voice answered, said it was Clare Cooper and would open the door. Hannah felt sure their luck wouldn't hold and she was right.

A tall fair-haired young woman admitted them to the light and airy flat. She looked for rather a long time and with great interest at Hannah's warrant card. 'Tamima's not here,' she said. 'She left – oh, a week ago at least.'

'What, just left?' Hannah said. 'On her own? Where did she go?'

'Home to her parents, I suppose. I didn't ask. She's Jacquie's cousin. I never met her before she came here. She tried to get a job in a supermarket, I do know that, but she didn't get it. That was when she started going out every evening with some boy. I think Jacquie saw him but I don't really know. Anyway, she said she was leaving and she packed her cases and went.'

'When will Jacquie be home?' Jenny asked.

'Not till Monday. She's gone away for the weekend.'

They hadn't come near to using up the allotted two hours' car parking. They sat inside the car, at a loss for what to do next.

'She's definitely not at home with her parents,' Hannah said. 'I spoke to Mohammed Rahman this morning. He was a bit cold with me but there's no doubt she wasn't there. He said she'd be home for Eid ul-Adha, whenever that is.' She caught herself up and blushed. She had done the unforgivable thing, the counter-PC thing and spoken in a disparaging tone, if not in disparaging words, of a time-honoured Islamic tradition. 'I mean, she'll be home for a holy festival.'

'Then where is she now?'

'I don't know. Do you think we should go over to Kingsbury and see if Mrs Qasi can tell us anything?'

'It's miles,' said Jenny rather dismally. 'It's not so much the distance as going right through central London in the rush hour. But it's not for me to say. You're the one that's driving.'

Hannah never let a little difficulty like driving through London at five in the afternoon on a Friday put her off. 'That's OK. Let's go.'

It took a very long time. Hannah would no more have talked on her mobile while at the wheel than she would have parked on a double yellow line. She gave the phone to Jenny and told her Mrs Qasi's number. By this time they were crossing

Wandsworth Bridge so almost committed to going northwards. And Faduma Qasi was at home. Her tone sounded amused when she told Jenny that of course they could come. She would be delighted to see them and would get tea ready.

'I thought she was going to start laughing,' Jenny said. 'It was really very odd. 'I could almost think there was a conspiracy going on between all these people to keep Tamima hidden somewhere.'

'Not "almost". I expect there is. What did that Clare woman mean by "out with some boy"? Tell me if what I'm saying is too far-fetched but it's not a forced marriage I'm thinking of now. It's an honour killing.'

Jenny was silent for a moment. Then she said, 'There was a story in the paper yesterday about some Indian widow who'd committed sati and thrown herself on her husband's funeral pyre with all the relatives standing round.'

'It's "become" sati, not "commit",' Hannah corrected her, 'and it's Hindus who do that, not Muslims. It's been against the law for about two hundred years.'

'Come to that, honour killings are against the law but they happen.'

'I know.'

Next day Hannah managed to see Faduma Qasi again and this time she went alone. As had happened the day before, Mrs Qasi refused to discuss Tamima and her questions met with silence. Not, of course, absolute silence, for Mrs Qasi, once more offering tea or coffee or, with a half-amused glance, Oloroso sherry, was happy to talk about the weather, a small earthquake in Pakistan and the long hours of fasting she and her family observed at Ramadan. But when Hannah took the conversation on to the subject of Tamima, she said she really couldn't discuss family matters.

'You seemed quite willing to talk about her the first time I came.'

'Yes. Perhaps that was a mistake on my part. I've reason to believe my brother objects very strongly to his private affairs being discussed.'

'If it's a matter of breaking the law, Mrs Qasi,' said Hannah, 'these aren't his private affairs. I've reason to believe Tamima has antagonised her family by meeting a young man her father and mother can't accept and that they may take steps to stop it.'

'I really can't say.'

'Perhaps you can say where she is now. Clare Cooper, your other niece's flatmate, told me she was no longer living with them. She hasn't succeeded in getting a job. She isn't at home in Kingsmarkham. Clare mentioned some involvement with a boy. Tamima is only sixteen years old.'

'I know nothing about this.' Faduma Qasi got up. 'I think you should go.'

Hannah had no choice about it and she went. But every word on the subject that Mrs Qasi had uttered increased her anxieties. The picture that formed before her eyes was as yet only of Tamima imprisoned, Tamima in the home of some relative unknown to Hannah, not restrained to the point of being tied up like an animal, but possibly locked in a bedroom belonging to this jailer until she 'came to her senses'. The boy she was involved with must surely be Rashid Hanif and it was to the Hanifs' house that Hannah went as soon as she was back in the Kingsmarkham neighbourhood.

At first, parking her car in the only vacant space she could find in Rectangle Road, Stowerton, Hannah wondered why there were so few people about. Cars, yes, pedestrians, no.

She was halfway to the Hanifs' house when a car pulled up alongside her and a woman put her head out of the driver's window.

'You don't want to be outside,' she said. 'The lion's been seen in Oval Road. I'd get inside somewhere if I were you.'

Hannah thanked her, resisted saying she wasn't her and walked up to the Hanifs' front door. It was opened by Fata Hanif, her head bare. 'I saw you coming,' she said. 'I thought, maybe she's seen the lion. Come in quick. My husband just came home. He says it's been seen in the high street.'

'I've come to talk to you, Mrs Hanif. It's nothing to do with the lion.'

Akbar Hanif was sitting in the living room, the baby on his lap, an older child on either side of him. He was a heavily bearded, rather fat man, wearing a loose white shirt over black trousers. He nodded to Hannah, looked at her warrant card with an amiable smile and asked her what the police were doing about the lion, an enquiry Hannah ignored.

'I hoped your son Rashid might be at home,' she said. 'Or isn't he back from college yet?'

'They are on half-term.'

This was a fact already known to Hannah. 'But he's not at home?'

Fata, a small girl now in her arms, said, 'No, he is not at home because he has gone away camping with his cousin. He works hard. He's entitled to a break sometimes. Now his great-auntie has died and left him some money, a little bit of money, so he is spending it on a tent and other equipment for camping. Is there something you don't like about that?'

'Fata,' said her husband, the intervention evidently intended as a reproof but uttered in a tone of gentle mildness.

'Where is he camping?'

'In somewhere called the Peak District if it's any business of yours.'

This time the reproach came in a sad shaking of Akbar's head.

'When do you expect him back?' She addressed her question to Rashid's father.

'Wednesday or Thursday.' Fata spoke for her husband. 'I don't want him back here while that lion's about. I don't want any of my children out on the streets.'

Hannah was heartily sick of the lion. 'And this camping is just with his cousin?' What numbers of relatives these people had, Hannah found herself thinking, a reflection she caught up short, horrified at yet another example of racism in her uncontrolled thoughts. 'Just he and the cousin on their own?'

'Oh, no,' said Mrs Hanif. 'There are four or five of them, another cousin and two friends from college.' She gave Hannah a penetrating glance. 'But if you're trying to make out a *girl* is with them you are wrong. And now I think you should go,' thus making her the second woman to have addressed those words to Hannah in the space of four hours.

The street was empty. It was late afternoon and already growing dark. She drove back to Kingsmarkham where she encountered Lynn Fancourt in the police station car park.

'I'm really scared of this lion,' Lynn said, 'especially after dark. Cats are nocturnal, aren't they? I expect it only really starts prowling around, looking for something to eat, in the night-time.'

'It won't come into urban areas. It's probably more frightened of people than they are of it.'

'I hope you're right.'

Hannah went up to Wexford's office.

He was looking at his computer screen with Damon there

to guide him through the Web. The glance he gave Hannah was less than pleasant.

'Well?'

Damon was going and Wexford said nothing to encourage him to stay.

'I've been in London, guv,' Hannah said, 'and since I got back I've had a talk with Rashid Hanif's parents. I think Tamima Rahman's gone off with Rashid, they're hiding out somewhere. I don't believe for a moment his parents' story that Rashid's gone camping with a bunch of friends and relations.'

'So she's somewhere, as you put it, with her boyfriend. She's over sixteen. I've yet to learn that fornication's against the law in this country.'

'It's against sharia law. Asian people have killed a daughter for less. They may have killed her or be planning to do that. May I tell you what I've found out?'

'You'd better sit down,' said Wexford rather sourly.

Hannah told him about Clare Cooper, her two visits to Mrs Qasi and the reaction of the Hanifs to her questioning. 'You can see why I'm anxious, guv. No one's seen the girl for days, weeks maybe. Everyone's got excuses for her not being where she's supposed to be. But Clare Cooper did mention her being involved with a boy and as Rashid Hanif's gone off some-where too, surely it's obvious they're together. Or they've been together until –'

'All right, I see all that. But none of it leads me to your conclusion, that she's a victim of an honour killing. You've absolutely no evidence for thinking that way. It's pure assumption.'

'Would you OK it if I went to see the Rahmans tomorrow and put it to them. Asked them, I mean, if Tamima's away because she's with Rashid.'

Wexford was silent for a moment. Then he said, 'Let me tell you what I should really like, Hannah. Firstly, never again to hear the name Tamima Rahman coupled with the term 'forced marriage' or 'honour killing'. Then, if you go to talk to the Rahmans, I'd like you to find Tamima there, alive and well and in the bosom of her family. But preferably not to tell me about it.'

'All right, guv. I get the message.' In the doorway, Hannah turned. 'D'you know, guv, you're the only person I've talked to since I've been back here who hasn't mentioned that lion?'

Perhaps he hadn't mentioned it because he had heard little else all day. When Hannah came in he had been looking at lion pictures on the Internet, a video that claimed – surely erroneously – to be of King ranging the open space outside its cave in the days of its captivity. He phoned Mavis Targo. No, she had heard nothing from her husband. She would have told him if she had. At present she was afraid to go outside and did so only to reach the white van in which she went shopping. This meant a walk of maybe three yards. She described to Wexford the agonies she went through each time she made that short journey, waiting for King to spring at her from out of the bushes.

'And one of the muntjacs has gone.'

Wexford had to think what a muntjac was. A sort of small deer? 'You mean one of yours?'

'Excuse *me*. One of Eric's. He had three and now there's only two. I watched them through binoculars. I was scared to go out there.'

He would be with her next morning, he told her. It was now nearly two weeks since her husband had departed.

CHAPTER NINETEEN

The lion was still at liberty. In this countryside, Wexford thought, there was very little reason why it shouldn't retain its freedom for weeks, months even, provided it found enough small animals to feed on. The area abounded in wildlife, badgers, foxes, hares and rabbits, pheasants and partridges. On his way to Stringfield, he found himself noticing all the roadkill, squashed bloody pelts and bundles of black and brown feathers. Would a lion eat carrion? Probably, if it was hungry.

While Donaldson stopped at a red light at the Local Traffic exit, Wexford made a phone call to the Rahmans. It was Yasmin who answered and once again her magisterial tone and economy of speech impressed him.

'Hallo? Who is speaking?'

Wexford said he wanted to talk to her and her husband, her son Ahmed too if that was possible.

'My husband will be here,' she said. 'My son Ahmed also.' The faintest hint of humour came into her voice. 'And my son Osman too if you want the whole family.'

'That must include Tamima, of course.'

She was annoyed. 'How many times do we have to tell you? Tamima is in London with her cousin.'

'No, she isn't, Mrs Rahman. But we can talk about that later.'

It was a fine sunny day, the grounds of Wymondham Lodge and the downs beyond looking at their autumn best. English woods have few trees in them which turn red in November. That display is confined to North America where forests have a preponderance of maples. Here, in Sussex, the fields were green and the woods dark green and yellow and brown, the gold coming from the birches and the tawny colour from beech and oak. A little breeze ruffled the treetops, making the different shades mingle and shiver. On some distant slopes sheep grazed and there were black-and-white cattle in the meadows by the Brim. But nearer home was more exotic fauna, the llamas enjoying the sunshine, the two remaining muntjacs running for the cover of the hedge at the sound of Wexford's car. No lion, of course, to greet him with a roar.

The front door wasn't opened immediately. Mavis Targo called out, 'Who is it?' Wexford couldn't help smiling as he answered. Did she imagine the lion would reply with 'It's me, King!'

She was very much dressed up for his visit. Or dressed up for her own satisfaction. A tight black suit and green blouse set off her heavy gold jewellery, several necklaces, earrings as large as coat buttons. Her thick fingers were stiff with gold and diamond rings. Wexford imagined her, forced by her fear to stay at home, diverting herself by trying on various outfits and hanging jewellery on to some designer creation, experimenting with colours and shapes in front of the mirror, like a little girl playing with mother's clothes.

'I haven't heard from him,' she began, and she didn't mean the lion. 'Not a word since he went off that morning. I don't believe he's abroad. He wouldn't go abroad. And now Ming's ill. He's pining for Eric, that's what it is. I had to take him to the vet yesterday and she says it's a virus. It's no virus, it's missing Eric.'

The Tibetan spaniel lay curled up on a pile of silk cushions in the corner. 'Poor lamb, he won't go in his basket. All he wants are those cushions and Sweetheart keeps annoying him. Well, he's only a puppy, he wants to play.'

'May I sit down, Mrs Targo? I want you to tell me all over again but in greater detail this time what happened on the day your husband went missing. Starting with first thing in the morning, please.'

They went into the ornate drawing room.

'Eric was up very early,' she began. 'But he often was. He went out somewhere – in the van, I think it was.'

To take himself to Pomfret and what he meant to do in Cambridge Cottages, Wexford thought. 'Did he take a dog with him?'

'I don't know. It was five in the morning. I woke up when he left and then I went to sleep again. When I got up he was back and both the dogs were there. Oh, yes, I remember he said he'd taken them out for a walk. I went shopping later on and when I got back he was out in the grounds with the animals.' She gave Wexford an exasperated look. 'You don't know how many times I've been over this in my mind. I've nearly done my head in, trying to think what he said and if he said where he was going. But he never did say, I'm certain of that.'

'When did he go out again?'

'It would have been two or three in the afternoon. He phoned someone on his mobile first but I don't know who that was. Then he went off in the Merc.'

'Not taking a dog with him?'

'I didn't know that till he'd been gone half an hour. I hadn't seen Ming for a bit, I'd seen Sweetheart, so I thought, he'll have taken Ming. But he hadn't because Ming came in from the garden soon after that.'

'He said nothing to you about where he was going?'

'No, but he often didn't. If I thought about it I'd have said he went over to the Sewingbury office or maybe to see a tenant. And when he didn't come back I thought, no, he's gone to Birmingham and he's stopping overnight.'

'I know this is very personal, Mrs Targo,' he said, 'but I have to ask it. Yours wasn't a very happy marriage, was it?'

Very cagily, she said, 'What makes you say that?'

'What, when a man goes off without a word to his wife as to where he's going, no phone call to her from wherever that is or from his car on the way there? He stays away for days on end and doesn't contact her?'

'It's just his way,' she said. 'He's always been like that. Maybe you'll say most women wouldn't put up with it but I don't care that much, I'm OK. I've got this place and the dogs and most of what I want. I don't complain.'

It was useless pursuing this line. 'The phone call you received, the message from someone whose voice you didn't recognise, are you sure of that? Are you sure you didn't know the voice?'

'It wasn't Eric's and it wasn't Alan's, I do know that. But I do think I'd heard it before. It sounds a funny thing to say but I think it was the voice of someone who's been here to do some work, a builder or a gardener or maybe someone to do with the animals.'

'Can you be more specific?'

'I don't think so. I just know it was a voice I'd heard before.'

'Someone employed by your husband at the Sewingbury office?'

'I never met them – well, there was only one and he left before Eric went missing. I never heard his voice.'

Wexford sighed internally. 'The forensic tests on your car – that is the Mercedes – have been completed. It will be brought back tomorrow.'

She nodded indifferently. 'I never drive it.' Sweetheart came padding in, its tail wagging when it saw Wexford. Mavis picked it up and held it in her arms. 'Poor lamb hasn't been out walkies for three days. But what can I do? I can't risk my life to take a dog out.'

Targo would, Wexford thought irrelevantly. With nothing more in view than to provide her with some reassurance, nothing but to look at the quiet, empty, sunlit land, Wexford got up and approached the French windows. He put his hand to the doorknob. 'May I?'

'You can if you want but be careful.'

'Mrs Targo, your lion isn't going to be waiting outside, enjoying the sunshine.'

But it was.

Wexford stepped back, closed the door again. King was fast asleep. It lay curled up on the terrace like the big cat it was, at the foot of its marble facsimile and its woman attendant, a yard or so from him the pathetic remains of what had once been a small deer. Only the deer's almost fleshless long legs had been rejected. The rest had been King's breakfast or perhaps the previous night's supper.

'I phoned the Big Cats man from the zoo,' Wexford told Burden several hours later. 'I'm probably being unfair but I thought the Feline Foundation chap might be a bit trigger-happy. Then I sat down with Mavis in that awful pseudo-Versailles room and she kept saying over and over, "What am I going to do?" I kept telling her to do nothing, just wait for the man with the anaesthetic to come. "You could make us a cup of tea," I said, but she's no Yasmin Rahman. It took her a good fifteen minutes and when the tea came it was pale grey and tepid. Made me wonder if she'd ever made tea before. While I was drinking it or pretending to, Ming the spaniel was sick.'

'But the zoo man did come?'

'Oh, yes, he came. By that time I was wondering how long that lion would stay asleep and what if he woke up before Big Cats arrived. However, King stayed asleep, the man came – accompanied by two other chaps, maybe what we used to call zookeepers – a shot was fired into King's flank, he rolled over quietly and sort of collapsed into unconsciousness. Mavis started screaming that he was dead and what would Eric say when he came back. I felt like saying, "He won't come back here, he'll be in custody," but of course I didn't.'

'What's happened to the lion?'

'Big Cats and his mates lifted him up on to a sort of stretcher and put him into the back of their van. A black van, incidentally, with Myringham Zoo's logo on the side, a giraffe gobbling up the top of a tree. One of the mates came back and cleared up the remains of the unfortunate muntjac. He told me that if no one claimed him they'd keep King. Apparently, they're looking for a stud male for their three lionesses.'

'So a happy ending for King and his harem.'

'Yes. At least there's been something good coming out of Targo's disappearance. Have we time for lunch before I go to the Rahmans?'

'I've ordered Indian takeaway,' said Burden.

Wexford sat behind his rosewood desk which was his own private possession and Burden – his attempts to perch himself on one corner of it meeting with a frown – took the only other comfortable chair in the office.

'I'm going to see the Rahmans, all of them except Tamima of course, to try and lay to rest this obsession of Hannah's with Tamima's forced marriage or honour killing. But if I get nothing out of them except denials we're still left with the dilemma of where the girl is. Now what I think is that she's simply gone off with Rashid Hanif. His mother told Hannah he'd inherited "a little bit" of money. That might be ten thousand pounds or fifty, depending on whether you yourself are rich or poor. Whatever it is I don't think he's camping as his mother says he is. I think he's having a teenage honeymoon with Tamima somewhere.'

'You mean her parents know this?'

'I doubt it. But they must know ~~not~~ she's not in any of the places she's supposed to be, that is with her aunt Mrs Qasi, or with the two girls who share a flat in Wandsworth. In any event, I expect them to be worried and therefore glad to see me. I'm also going to ask Ahmed and his mother – she was in the house at the time while Osman was out and their father was ill – exactly what happened when Targo called at their house in Glebe Road some eight or nine hours after he'd killed Andy Norton.'

The takeaway that arrived came from the Dal Lake, chicken korma, aloo gobi, rice and mango chutney plus a plateful of chapattis, all brought up by Lynn Fancourt, who also provided on the tray a jug of iced water and a packet of paper napkins, rather incongruously printed with a design of holly and mistletoe berries.

'Left over from someone's Christmas party, I suppose.'

'You're out of date,' said Burden. 'Shops in the high street have been selling Christmas stuff since September.' He spooned out some rice and korma for himself. 'Surely,' he said, returning to the subject of Targo, 'we know why he went there. He wanted that computerised thing that switches lights and heating on.'

'Yes, maybe. But doesn't it strike you as very odd that a man who apparently hasn't basic computer skills – like me – a man who needs help with using the equipment in his office, wants to buy a device that presumably demands those skills for its functioning? His wife is at home all day to see to switching things on and making the heating work. Also, there's the matter of why he stayed so long. He came in the afternoon – half past two or three, nobody seems sure – but it's sure when he left. Not till at least eight fifteen because the nail bar lady and Mrs Scott saw his car still there "after eight fifteen".'

'It looks as if he didn't want to leave until after dark.'

'Yes, but it would have been dark at five, so that doesn't really answer the question.'

'We've thought he might have been buying clothes and maybe a suitcase and just left the car there.'

'But we know he wasn't buying clothes, Mike. No one sold him clothes in Kingsmarkham that afternoon and if he went to Stowerton or Myringham to buy them why would he, for instance, take a taxi or a bus when he could have used his own car? I'm starting to wonder something quite different. Suppose he was with Ahmed and his mother for only an hour or two and when he left he left on foot? Took himself off somewhere by train or took a taxi to Gatwick?'

'He can't have done that.' Burden took some more spinach on the grounds that his wife, though she wasn't there to see, would approve of healthy eating. 'He can't have gone on foot because his car was found up in north Essex.'

'He isn't the only person in the Kingsmarkham area who can drive a car, Mike. Suppose he went off walking and someone else – later on in the dark to avoid being seen – drove the Mercedes up to within easy distance of Stansted to make it look as if he had gone there.'

'Some pal, d'you mean? Some accomplice? How about his wife?'

'Mavis says she never drives the Mercedes. But that means nothing. She could have driven it. Her prints were all over the interior, as they would be whether she drove it that day or not, and no one else's were. She could have taken the van down to Glebe Road at nine, say, or ten, left it somewhere not in Glebe Road and driven the Mercedes up the M11 to north Essex.'

'Wait a minute, Reg. We always come back to the problem of whoever drove the car up to that village having to get to Stansted or, harder, get back to London. Say she drove the car away from Glebe Road at nine she'd have had a three-hour journey ahead of her, through the Dartford Crossing, up the M25, onto the M11, *past* Stansted airport, out along the A120 to Thaxted or Braintree and then to that village. So she gets there at midnight more or less. How does she get back?'

Wexford looked out at the gathering clouds, uniformly grey overhead but on the distant horizon black and thick. A storm was coming. He turned back to Burden. 'There are trains early in the morning from Stansted into London. But she wouldn't be in Stansted. And the Tip-Top man I saw drove no one out of Melstead that night and no one the following morning. Besides, we saw her in Stringfield at ten the following morning. No, you're right, it can't be done. Besides, I don't believe her capable of doing it. The answer has to be that whoever drove that car up there had an accomplice driving another car in which to fetch him or her back. Who these people are we don't know and are no nearer knowing than we were a week ago.'

A sudden gust of wind blew the half-open window wide. Wexford went to close it as thunder rattled.

'Is it true that when I was young storms only happened in the summer or am I imagining it?'

'Well,' said Burden, 'as I often tell you, you've got too much imagination.'

CHAPTER TWENTY

No roofs were torn off, no building collapsed. Perhaps a dozen trees were blown over, one of which blocked the Kingsmarkham to Brimhurst road, another wrecking Burden's rock garden. Heavy rain swelled the Kingsbrook and it burst its banks at the point where Wexford's old garden used to reach, flooding a small area where nothing much grew and nothing grazed.

'It's like that joke about the dullest headline you can think of,' he said to Burden. '"Small Earthquake in Chile, None Injured."'

Burden smiled politely, the way he did when Wexford's humour failed to amuse him. 'I know it's going to cost me a fortune to have that tree moved.'

Wexford reflected on his own garden, which was fast returning to its normal condition of untidiness and neglect, and then he thought of Andy Norton who, however you looked at it, had died because of him.

Like some character in nineteenth-century fiction, searching the metropolis for a fallen woman, for some girl who had gone astray, Hannah Goldsmith was scouring London for Tamima Rahman. She actually told herself this as she drove from Mrs Qasi in Kingsbury to Mrs Clarke in Acton, reflecting that these days it was only among Muslims (or perhaps Orthodox Jewry) that a young girl's chastity would be so valued or its loss so productive of danger and even death. She had started with an optimistic view. Wexford didn't believe Tamima was in danger either of a forced marriage or, much worse, of being injured or even killed for the honour of the family. He was usually right while she was often wrong. What she wanted now was simply to find Tamima – in almost any circumstances – find her alive and well and with Rashid Hanif. Sympathetic to a Muslim culture she might be, but still she found it impossible to believe that there was anything wrong in a girl who was over the age of consent spending a week or two alone with her boyfriend. In her view, the only fault would lie in their missing out on their education.

Rashid Hanif had money. Not much probably but enough to take Tamima to some cheap hotel for a couple of weeks. That the pair could be staying with relations was not to be considered. No good Muslim would give sanctuary to Rashid and Tamima in defiance of their parents. But a relative might have some clue as to where they would be likely to go. That was why Hannah was seeking out a small colony of Rahman relatives living in Acton as well as Akbar Hanif's sister in Ealing. For all that, a small voice echoing somewhere inside her head kept telling her, 'You won't find Tamima. You know you won't. She's dead. Rashid may be dead too. They're a modern-day Romeo and Juliet.'

Mrs Clarke, née Rahman, lived in a small semi-detached house and appeared to be the only one at home. In her fifties, she was a handsome woman if rather too thin, her eyes midnight brown, her hair unnaturally black, the rainbow-shaded trousers and silk top she wore she could just carry off with that colouring. No, she hadn't seen her niece Tamima for four or five years. Of course she knew the girl was staying with her daughter, she and her daughter were very close, but she couldn't recall that the subject of Tamima had ever been discussed between them. From what her daughter Jacquie had told her, she understood Tamima had stayed for a while in the flat Jacquie shared with a friend she had known since university. 'Uni' was what she called it, a term that grated on Hannah's ears. I'm getting as precious and fussy as the guv, she told herself. It must be catching.

Next door lived Amran Ibrahim, Yasmin Rahman's brother, with his wife Asha. Both insisted to Hannah that they hardly knew Tamima and hadn't seen her since she was a little girl. She drove to Ealing. Akbar Hanif's sister Amina lived in a handsome detached house of 1920s vintage, a far cry from his home in Rectangle Road, Stowerton. She was a big, expensively dressed woman in her late forties and she had no objection to talking about family matters. Childless herself, she was very attached to her brother's children.

'I'd be very surprised if Rashid did what you're suggesting,' she said over the coffee she made for herself and Hannah. 'He's not only a good boy who works hard at school – gets very good exam results – but, well, he's been brought up to respect his parents. It wouldn't be too much to say *fear* his parents, especially his mum. They'll arrange a marriage for him one day and he's told me he's happy with that. It won't be till he's finished university anyway. What makes you think he's not camping in Derbyshire the way Fata says he is?'

Hannah had been in contact with Derbyshire police, suggested they should find Rashid Hanif (while certain they wouldn't be able to) and been told, though very politely, that they had no time to waste on such things.

'I think he's somewhere else with Tamima Rahman. Or he has been.'

'It seems very unlikely to me. He's simply not that sort of boy.'

It was Rashid's uncle, Fata's brother in Hounslow who gave her the first clue. He and his wife had twice been to Brighton where they had stayed in a B & B. 'Very lovely,' he said. 'Very good. Nice people run it. You know they are not allowed by the law to turn people away because they are Asian – my wife is from south India. They are not allowed but some people when they see a brown face – well, they make it clear one isn't wanted. But Mr and Mrs Peddar at the Channel View showed us nothing like that. They welcomed us.'

'And you told your sister and her husband?'

'Yes, we did. But they never went there. How can you have holidays when you have seven children?' He laughed. 'You can do nothing when you have seven children.'

Would Rashid take Tamima there? Hannah thought it possible. She took the precise address from Rashid's uncle and, in high hopes that they had at least been there, phoned the Channel View. Mrs Peddar at once came over the line as an indiscreet woman.

'We have many Asian visitors. I really like them, they're so well behaved. In fact, we've thought of specially advertising for Asians but we can't, it's against the law.'

'The people I have in mind,' said Hannah, 'are very young, a man and a young woman.' It went against the grain with her to refer to any female person as a girl.

'That sounds like Mr and Mrs Khan. To tell you the truth, I don't think they're Mr and Mrs at all, I'm sure they're not married, but nobody cares any more about that sort of thing, do they? I think it's rather nice, calling themselves Mr and Mrs, it sort of shows – well, *respect*.'

Hannah thought she came across some daft opinions in the course of her work but few dafter than that. 'I'd like to come down and see them, Mrs Peddar.'

'They haven't done anything wrong, have they? I'd find that hard to believe.'

'No, nothing wrong,' said Hannah.

'I've been going over what we talked about yesterday,' Wexford said when Damon brought in tea for himself and Burden. 'and I've been thinking some very politically incorrect thoughts.'

'I think them all the time,' said Burden rather gloomily. 'What are yours?'

'I told you that when I went up to Melstead I talked to the Asian man called Anil Mansoor who runs the general shop and post office. It's in the street where Targo's Mercedes was found. Nothing he said was much help and certainly nothing was suspicious. But one thing he did say I ignored at the time but it's come back to me now. He said, "Sussex? I have cousins in Sussex. Maybe you know them."'

Burden had begun taking sugar in his tea. It was a new departure that had been going on for perhaps a couple of months. He fancied a change, he said when asked, which Wexford thought an inadequate explanation. He watched Burden wistfully, hoping to see him put on weight but if anything he seemed thinner than before. Now, as if in defiance, he loaded three spoonfuls into his teacup.

'So?' he said.

'This is where the political incorrectness comes in. If he'd been – well, white, I'd not have stored that remark of his in my mind. So he had cousins in Sussex? So what? But because he's Asian I'm thinking of other Asians, I'm thinking of the Rahmans.'

'But there are hundreds if not thousands of Asians in Sussex.'

'I told you it was politically incorrect.'

Burden drank some of his syrupy tea with evident enjoyment. 'OK, but what are you getting at?'

'We'd considered that Targo might not have driven the Mercedes himself. Suppose one of the Rahmans drove it? Drove it to Melstead because he knew the place, knew how to get there down all those narrow lanes, because he had been there before to visit his cousin, the postmaster?'

'That's pure speculation.'

'A lot of what we do is.'

'Are you saying that the Rahmans and this postmaster – what's his name? Mansoor? – were in cahoots with Targo and this was done to help him with his getaway? Make us think he'd left from Stansted when in fact he left from some other airport or exit or never left at all but is still in this country?'

Burden poured himself another cup of tea. And with a glance at Wexford which the latter interpreted as challenging, ladled in the sugar. 'There's no sign they're in need of money, is there?'

'Well, you could say that everyone is in need of money. Often for reasons one knows nothing about.'

'If you're right,' Burden said thoughtfully, 'and more than one member of the Rahman family is involved, it solves the problem of how Targo got from Melstead to Stansted airport in the middle of the night. Targo, accompanied, say, by Osman, drove the Mercedes to Stansted from Sussex. Osman, on his own, drove it to Melstead, left it there and was taken back to Sussex by Ahmed or their father in their own car.'

'I'm going to talk to them. Come with me, why don't you?'

The fallen trees had been cleared away but the back-streets of Kingsmarkham, thickly treed, were littered with broken branches and twigs, the last of the fallen leaves, and here and there a dislodged roof tile. Wexford and Burden encountered Hannah standing outside Webb and Cobb, facing the window, part of which was exposed by a board which had come adrift in the previous night's storm. She seemed fascinated by the interior that was already familiar to Wexford, the crates, the boxes, the stepladder and the tray on the table filled with shards of crockery.

'I was just about to go into the Rahmans, guv,' she said.

As she spoke the front door of number 34 opened and Ahmed came out, holding a hammer and a bag of nails. In a rather hoarse – perhaps nervous? – voice, he said he wouldn't be more than five minutes. He had come out to nail the board back in place.

'We're in no hurry,' said Burden in a cold tone.

Mohammed was sitting in the armchair the family seemed to regard as exclusively for his use while Osman was in the conservatory watering plant pots. He set down the can, came in as his father said, 'I'm glad you've come. We're worried about my daughter. She's disappeared.'

'At least you acknowledge it,' Wexford said. 'I confess I was afraid you would stick to this story of yours that she is happily spending time in London with this relative and that.'

He looked from one to the other of them, Yasmin sitting statue-still, her hands, heavily beringed, lying in her lap, her head wrapped more strictly than usual in scarves, one black, one Prussian blue; Osman, as handsome as his brother but bearded, still in his nurse's attire of dark blue trousers and Mandarin jacket; Ahmed and his father both dressed like businessmen in white shirts and dark suits. He glanced at Hannah, said, 'Detective Sergeant Goldsmith believes Tamima is in Brighton with Rashid Hanif but I don't. What do you think?'

The elder Rahmans were silent. Like one putting off the evil day as long as he could, Osman said, 'I've seen Rashid today. He's been camping but he came back last night and his mum brought him into A & E with a suspected broken ankle. He hasn't seen Tamima for weeks.'

'I believe that,' Yasmin said reluctantly, as if the words were being forced out of her. Wexford turned to Ahmed.

'Tamima will have to be reported as a missing person. But I warn you that if she is not missing and you in fact know where she is, you will be arrested and charged with wasting police time. Is that clear?'

Ahmed nodded. Silent, he seemed in a trance-like state or hypnotised. By fear? By knowledge? Yasmin wore one of her habitual expressions, scorn this time. She looked down at the hands in her lap as if admiring the load of rings which adorned them.

'I'd like you to tell me the truth about what happened when Mr Targo came here that afternoon, ostensibly to talk about you ordering some remote-control device for him. What was the real reason, Mr Rahman?'

Ahmed tried to clear his throat. He appeared to be one of those people whose voice apprehension paralyses. The throat-clearing served its purpose but only up to a point and when he did speak his voice was hoarse. 'He did want that – that software.'

'And what was the other purpose of his visit?'

Yasmin's voice was quite clear, unimpeded by nervousness. 'You had better tell him, Ahmed.' She paused, stared Wexford in the eyes, said, 'It wasn't my son's fault.'

'What your mother says is sound,' Burden said. 'You had better tell us. Just you without your family if that's what you want, here or at the police station. Which is it to be?'

'I'll tell you.' Ahmed took a deep breath, exhaled and spoke in a steadier voice. 'I haven't told my father this. My brother doesn't know either. My mother was here. She knows. Targo – I don't want to call him Mister any more – he came here and asked about the software. Then he said he knew my sister was going about with a boy our family didn't like. He'd seen her, he said. That was Rashid Hanif, of course. He said a white boy but Rashid's not really white, he's just pale-skinned because his mother's Bosnian.'

'What else did he say, Ahmed?'

Ahmed looked from one to the other of them as if he expected the help that was not forthcoming. He lowered his head and shook it. 'All right, I'll tell you. He said he knew we wanted my sister killed to save the family honour and if that was what we wanted he'd do it. He'd kill her, he said. We didn't have to pay him. He'd do an honour killing and no one would suspect him or us if we kept quiet. There, I've told you.'

'Not everything, Ahmed,' said Wexford. 'Not by a long chalk. You can't leave it there. You have to go on.'

Ahmed put his head in his hands. Through his fingers he whispered, 'I can't, I can't.'

'I can,' said Yasmin.

Seeing the shock and distress in his father's face, Osman had gone to sit beside him. Wexford asked himself if he had ever before seen a grown-up son take his father's hand as Osman took Mohammed's now, holding it tightly in his own.

There was a solidarity in this family he had seldom seen before the immigrants came. He turned his eyes to Yasmin.

'Well, Mrs Rahman?'

'I was there,' she said. 'What Ahmed says is true.' Her tone changed and the note of her speech altered subtly. Wexford wondered if it were a fact that lying raised the blood pressure. She looked suddenly as if her systolic had gone up to two hundred. 'He was disgusted by what the man had said to him. So was I.' She repeated it. 'So was I. We are not the kind of ignorant cruel people who would want a daughter killed for the sake of some outdated honour.' The last word she came dangerously near to spitting out. 'Honour!'

Incongruously, a line from Anne Finch, Countess of Winchilsea, came into Wexford's head from that little book he had given to the now dead Medora: *The pale, the fall'n, th'untimely sacrifice / To your mistaken shrine, to your false idol Honour!* All he said was, 'Well?'

'Ahmed told him to go. He said we would have nothing to do with what he said. Go, he told him, and he left.'

'How did he go, Mrs Rahman?'

'In his car, of course. He came in his car and he went in it.'

Ahmed spoke again. 'He went in his car, he drove off in it. I saw him. But he must have come back later.'

Mohammed spoke. His voice sounded small and subdued. 'I wasn't well, I was in my bedroom. I looked out of the window at six thirty, I know it was six thirty, I looked at the clock. That car was there. It was still there.'

'Very well,' said Wexford. 'I want this house searched and, if necessary, the building next door searched. You can either give me permission to do that now or I can get a warrant. A warrant will delay things but it's your choice.'

'We are law-abiding people,' Mohammed said. 'All we want is to do what is right. You may search.'

247

'You're looking for my sister's body?' Osman had perhaps misunderstood or had failed to follow what had gone before. He suddenly looked years older than he was. 'You think he killed her just the same?'

Damon Coleman and Lynn Fancourt carried out the search with a uniformed officer. Lynn said afterwards she had never searched such a clean house, all the furniture polished to a high gloss, baths and sinks gleaming, linen sweet-smelling and carefully ironed. Tamima's room distressed her when she contemplated what she was sure had become of the girl. Posters of pop singers were on the walls. Tamima had a tiny pink radio, a pink straw basket lined with pink and white fabric and laden with teenagers' cosmetics. The room Ahmed shared with his brother – the largest in the house – was a temple of technology, full of cables and computer attachments as well as a desktop and a laptop, while Osman had apparently left no mark of his personality on the place. Perhaps he did no more than sleep there, bed down for seven or eight hours each night in the small single bed which seemed removed by design as far as possible from Ahmed's way of life and means of livelihood. Wexford, looking in there, while the search progressed, thought that if what he believed was true and Ahmed and his mother had been lying, if Ahmed himself had assisted at Tamima's murder, the Rahman sons would soon each have a room to himself. Or there would be only one son remaining to take his pick of the rooms.

It had been dusk growing dark when they arrived and now in the deep dark of a winter's evening the rain had begun. The search of 34 Glebe Road had been completed and nothing had been found. All the time it was going on, the Rahman family had sat in their living room, Wexford, Burden and

Hannah Goldsmith with them, and for once Yasmin had made no offers of tea or coffee. The lights were on, mainly from table lamps, and after a while Ahmed had picked up the evening paper. He sat looking at it. Reading it? Wexford wasn't sure. Perhaps he merely stared at the print with unseeing eyes. Yasmin got up and drew the curtains on the dark, wet night.

For his part, he was turning over in his mind the extraordinary phenomenon of Eric Targo. The man had killed three people or possibly more but the ones Wexford was convinced about were Elsie Carroll, Billy Kenyon and Andy Norton. In all those cases he had killed someone he presumed another person very much wanted out of the way. Tamima Rahman was someone another person or people might well want out of the way, if the propensities of some immigrant families for killing a daughter who had dishonoured them were taken into consideration. But if he had killed her – if, come to that, she were dead – why had he broken away from his usual procedure of carrying out the act without asking for leave, without seeking permission? It seemed a total break from custom, a departure from the way he usually acted that kept him safe. Except that it wasn't total. Wexford remembered what Tracy Thompson had told him, that it was Targo's asking her if he could kill someone for her which put an end to their relationship.

Wexford got up and, saying nothing to the silent people in the room, went outside into the front garden and the street. A thin drizzle was falling. Strangely, someone had parked a Mercedes at the kerb directly outside the Rahmans' house, but this one was black. He thought, Ahmed's story isn't right but it's right in parts. That's why Targo didn't bring a dog; he was going to drive off, find Tamima and kill her. Because Ahmed and his mother were lying in one respect? They had wanted Tamima killed to save the family honour and if it had been done they would never have spoken out, never have betrayed Targo. But Targo might have had another reason for asking permission, in other words for telling them what he meant to do. They would be blamed for her death and not he. No one would believe that he, a mere client of Ahmed's, had been involved . . .

He went back indoors as Lynn, Damon and the uniformed officer came downstairs.

'Nothing, sir,' Lynn said.

'All right. We'll start next door in the shop called Webb and Cobb.' He went into the living room and asked Mohammed for the key.

Tamima's father handed it to him in silence. Wexford gave the key to Damon and they all went to the brown-painted door which Damon unlocked.

'Cobb means a spider, doesn't it?' Damon asked.

'When it's only got one B,' said Wexford.

They went in, Burden with them. There was a strong smell of musty airlessness, paint and a hint of mildew, nothing else. The mushroomy scent would have been from rising damp which had made a kind of tide of black fungus climbing up the wall. Burden switched on lights which were the kind that hang from a lead in the middle of the ceiling. There were no spiders to be seen and no cobwebs. This ground floor, the area which had been the shop, comprised three rooms, the large front one, a smaller one behind and beyond the stairs a kind of dilapidated kitchen. It was all clean in here too and Wexford concluded that Yasmin made a practice of keeping this place almost as spotless as her house. Almost, for she hadn't attempted to clean off the fungus, or had attempted and failed, nor had she had much success with removing dark grey stains from the kitchen tiles.

The larger of the rooms was of course the one which could be seen from the street between the window boards. Two built-in cupboards were empty but for a cracked jug and a spoutless teapot standing on shelves. Stacked up on the floor were perhaps twenty large wooden crates and as many cardboard boxes. There was nothing on the table except a trayful of broken pottery and nothing at all in the table drawer. They opened crate after crate and box after box, found nothing.

The kitchen was bare but in the back room were several crates of the same type as those in the shop room. Only one cupboard here, only the crates. Again the crates were opened, this time by Lynch. She lifted out pieces of china, a flowered tea set, about twenty tiny coffee cups, each one wrapped in tissue paper. Underneath or in the next crate she expected to find Tamima's body. She had been sure she must find it here ever since she had driven away from Brighton, leaving behind an indignant couple in their thirties who had insisted in angry tones that their name really was Khan and offered to show her their marriage certificate.

The crates were empty now and there was nothing for it but to put everything back. Wexford had opened the only cupboard in this room which, because it was without shelves and was no more than a foot wide and less than that deep, seemed to serve no useful purpose. He had such a shallow narrow cupboard in his own house but it housed the electricity meter and fuse box. No such equipment occupied this space. On the left-hand side the wall was not of brick but of hardboard, as was the wall between it and the window. He now noticed that the whole room had recently been painted. That accounted for one of the ingredients of the smell. The painting had been done in that creamy-ivory shade famous among builders' merchants as 'magnolia'.

'How has that board been – well, fixed there?' he asked Damon.

'With screws, I should think, sir. Under the paint you'd probably find screws hidden under some sort of filler.'

'Then find them, will you? I want that wall taken down. Just the bit between the cupboard and the window.'

The uniformed officer, whose name was Moyle, took over. As Damon had said, he soon exposed the screws, eight of them. He went back to the van he had come in and returned with a screwdriver. Hannah, watching, found that she was shivering. PC Moyle began methodically removing the screws and the hardboard panel loosened until he was able to take hold of it with both hands, free it and set it against the opposite wall. An empty space was revealed with another such panel screwed in at the back. It was now possible to see that this had once been a large walk-in cupboard, including the one next to it.

Moyle said, 'D'you want me to take the screws out here, sir?'

'Yes, please.'

Hannah smelt it first. Not a strong smell, not yet, but enough to conflict with paint and mildew scents. Charnel house, Wexford thought because long ago he had read the expression somewhere. It strengthened when Moyle lifted away the rear panel, became a reek, a stench. Hannah covered her nose and mouth with her hands and Burden screwed up his face in distaste. Inside the compartment at the back, a parcel tightly wrapped in green plastic sheeting and brown sacking, perhaps five feet six or seven long and tied with rope and electricity cable, was leaning against the wall.

While Moyle cut the ropes and he and Damon started to remove the mummy-like wrappings, Wexford examined the inside of the cupboard. But it was totally empty. The thing inside its shroud of man-made materials had left nothing of itself behind. The foul smell of corruption assailed him as he stepped back into the room and the corpse was exposed.

He found himself looking into the contorted face and the staring eyes no one had bothered to close of Eric Targo.

CHAPTER TWENTY-ONE

I t was almost the middle of the night. The police station car park was empty but for Wexford's own car and Hannah Goldsmith's. Ahmed Rahman would not be going home that night.

Walking down the stairs to Interview Room 2, Wexford thought how he had been thwarted of the great coup he had hoped for most of his life to bring about. No longer a creator of victims, Targo had become a victim himself. He would soon be remembered as a respected citizen and no doubt whatever obituary he earned would dwell on his successes as a self-made man, his 'beautiful home', his menagerie, his dogs, and his love of animals.

Ahmed sat on one side of the table with a cup of tea in front of him. Standing behind him beside the recording equipment was PC Moyle, keeping an eye. Wexford thought of the days when everyone questioned in this room or the one next to it – where Yasmin Rahman would soon be questioned by Burden and Damon – smoked like furnaces, chain-smoked, and had to be supplied with Rothman's King Size or Player's as well as tea and, sooner or later, sandwiches. As a non-smoker himself, he had suffered, had coughed and grown hoarse. But there was nothing to be done about it until now when they had a comprehensive smoking ban throughout the police station.

Hannah came in, sat down opposite Ahmed and, rather slowly and deliberately, Wexford joined them. It had been a shock for Hannah, finding dead Targo encased and swathed like a mummy. She had been sure the unwrapping would reveal the slender pathetic body of Tamima and now her hunt had to begin again. Wexford hoped what she said was true, that she was enormously relieved, but knowing her need always to be right, her often unjustified certainties, he wondered.

Having told Ahmed that the interview would be recorded, that they were Detective Chief Inspector Wexford and Detective Sergeant Goldsmith and that the time was 11.37 p.m., he began by asking Ahmed to tell him what had really happened at 34 Glebe Road that afternoon when Targo called.

'You can forget that stuff about the home management device and forget too about Targo driving off but coming back before six thirty. Inspector Burden is questioning your mother next door and I don't think your mother will lie, will she?'

'No, she won't lie,' said Ahmed.

'So tell me.'

'I shall have to, I suppose. Will I go to prison?'

'Probably. That depends on what you did.'

'I killed him,' said Ahmed, 'but I didn't mean to. It was an accident.'

Hannah said, 'Begin with what he said when he made the offer to kill Tamima.'

Ahmed nodded. He pushed away his half-empty teacup. 'My mother was there. She was sewing something. I think Targo wanted me to send her away but I couldn't do that in her own home. Then he sort of shrugged as if he was saying, "OK then, if that's what you want. Let her stay." After that he asked about this office-manager thing and I showed him some pictures in a brochure I had. "Get one for me, will you?"

255

he said and I said I'd send off for it and it'd be about ten days. Well, what I said was, five to ten working days. Then he said, quite pleasantly, in the same sort of voice, "Your sister's going about with a white man, isn't she?"

'I was so surprised I just stared. My mother laid down her sewing but she didn't say anything, not then. Targo said, "You people don't like that kind of thing, do you? It's bad for your family honour or whatever." Those were his words, "honour or whatever". My mother spoke then. She said, "We can't discuss that with you." He took no notice. He said, "You'll want her out of the way, won't you? Dead and gone and no questions asked. I'll see to that and it won't cost you a penny."'

'What did you say to that?' Wexford asked.

'I said I thought he should go. My mother got up. She was wearing the hijab, of course, and a shawl round her shoulders. But when she looked at him she pulled the shawl over her head as well and held it in front of her face. I think she wanted to hide herself from him, he was such a monster.'

Yes, thought Wexford, that is what he was, a monster. A chimera, an abomination. 'Go on,' he said.

'He didn't go. He laughed. He said, "I know that's what you want. I've seen them kissing – that's not the way a good little Muslim girl behaves, is it? You won't want her in your home again and you need not. Just leave things to me. I'll find her wherever she is."

'I hit him then. He was an old man and shorter than me and I know I shouldn't have done that but I was so angry. I saw red, I really did, red in front of my eyes. I hit him on the jaw and he fell backwards.' Ahmed was speaking now at great speed. 'He fell backwards and crashed against the fire-place and hit the back of his head on that marble shelf, the what-d'you-call-it.'

'The mantelpiece,' said Wexford.

In Interview Room 1 Yasmin Rahman had reached much the same point in her account. She was heavily veiled, much as she had been when Ahmed described her, the shawl on top of the hijab pulled down to form a peak over her forehead. Her strong handsome face, with the long straight nose and dark liquid eyes, was almost hidden but for the mouth.

'My son Ahmed hit him. He asked for it – isn't that what you say in this country? He asked for it. That man – Targo – he fell down and there was blood coming from his head. I thought he was dead – how would I know? I went to the kitchen to get water and something to wipe away the blood and when I came back Ahmed was feeling his heart and listening to his heart and he said he was dead.'

'While this was going on,' Burden said, 'where were your husband and your other son?'

'Osman was at work. My husband was upstairs in bed. He was ill with flu. He heard that man fall and he called out to me to ask what the sound was. I went up and told him it was something out in the street. It was ten minutes to four and Ahmed said we must hide the man's body while we thought what to do next. We had to put it somewhere Osman wouldn't see it. We carried it through into the place next door.'

She was very cool and calm. Burden thought this was probably the way she had been when Ahmed hit Targo and later found he had killed him. He had noticed her extraordinary dignity before, the way she could sit still for long periods without fidgeting, without even moving her eyes. 'So what did you do next?' he asked.

'Took the car away,' she said calmly. 'We waited till the night-time. Took it a long way to where my cousin Mr Mansoor who is the postmaster lives. It is a place called Melstead. Mr Mansoor knows nothing. He wasn't even there, he was at his home in Thaxted.'

In the next room Wexford was saying, 'If he wasn't dead when he fell on the floor why didn't you call an ambulance? You say it was an accident, it wasn't your fault.'

'I don't know if he was dead then but he soon was. I knew that because the blood stopped flowing. That means a person is dead, doesn't it?' Ahmed didn't wait for an answer. 'I thought no one would believe me if I said it was an accident.'

Wexford said drily, 'We sometimes believe what people tell us. It's more difficult to believe when those same people try to cover up an offence by concealing a body and going to considerable lengths to deceive as you did. I refer to the little games you played with Mr Targo's car. What did you do? Drive it up to the place in Essex where some cousin of yours lives to make it look as if Mr Targo had left the country through Stansted airport?'

'I'll tell you what we did. As soon as we knew he was dead we took the body next door into the shop. There's a door in our living room that leads into the room where we hid him. We had it put in when we had the conversion done. Then we waited till it got late and there was no one about. I drove Targo's Mercedes and my mother followed, driving our car. It was a piece of luck that my father was ill with an infectious illness, so my mother was sleeping in Tamima's room and my father didn't notice she wasn't there.'

'Why not go to Gatwick?'

'It was too near,' Ahmed said. 'The car would have been found next day.'

'Who worked on the cupboard in the shop next door? You, I suppose.'

'I wrapped the body up, made a sort of parcel of it and put it in the back of the cupboard. Then I sort of boarded it up. I used some sheets of hardboard, screwed them in place and painted over the lot.'

Wexford sat back in his chair, silent. It was Hannah who said, 'Where is your sister, Ahmed?'

'I don't know. I only wish I knew. He didn't kill her, I know that. At least I prevented that.'

Unless he did it before he spoke to you, Wexford thought. 'It was you who phoned Mrs Targo with a message allegedly coming from her husband?' The strangely familiar voice, he thought. The voice of someone who had worked in the house as Ahmed had when he set up the computer.

'Oh, yes,' Ahmed said wearily. 'That was me.'

Later that night Yasmin Rahman was released on police bail but her son remained in one of the station's two cells for further questioning in the morning.

CHAPTER TWENTY-TWO

Manslaughter would be the charge, or perhaps unlawful killing, consistent with Dr Mavrikian's findings when he examined Targo's body. Death had resulted from that single deep wound to the skull which corresponded to the sharp corner of the granite mantelpiece at 34 Glebe Road. There was also bruising to the left-hand side of Targo's jaw – incidentally in the centre of where the naevus had been – where right-handed Ahmed Rahman had struck him. Yasmin Rahman would be charged only with assisting an offender in a death and would probably, Wexford thought, receive a suspended sentence. He hoped Ahmed would serve no more than two or three years in prison and if it were less he wouldn't be sorry. The man had rid the world of a monster who, though old, had been strong, and might have lived another twenty years of natural life. This, of course, was no way for a detective chief inspector to think.

He himself took to Mavis Targo the details of her husband's death and as much of an explanation as he thought good for her to hear. Sentimentality would have it that Ming the Tibetan spaniel should die of grief but it seemed to have got over missing its master and when Wexford called was helping Sweetheart eat the Chinese carpet. Mavis may have been equally indifferent to Targo's passing. At any rate, she showed no emotion but spoke only of her worries as to how to dispose of the menagerie. Although Targo had left most of his properties and his stock to his children, the house was hers and as soon as she could she intended to sell it and buy a flat in central London.

'You asked me if my marriage was happy,' she said to Wexford, 'and of course I wasn't going to say it wasn't, was I? The fact is we were going to split up. What I say is, thank God we never got around to it. Once we'd done that he'd have changed his will.'

'What I can't understand,' Burden said later, 'is how he got all those women to marry him. Ugly little chap with that birthmark before he had it taken off, it's beyond comprehension.'

'Anthony Powell,' said Wexford, the reader, 'says somewhere that while women are rather choosy about whom they sleep with, they will marry anyone. Women are said to like power in a man and Targo exuded that.'

They were on their way to pay a first visit to Rectangle Road, Stowerton, and the Hanif family. It was four thirty in the afternoon and Rashid was due home from Carisbrooke Sixth Form College and his formidable A-level programme of maths, biology and physics. After they had listened for about fifteen minutes to Fata Hanif's highly laudatory curriculum vitae of her eldest son while she spooned puréed apple into the mouth of her youngest, Rashid hobbled in on a single crutch, his leg in plaster up to the knee.

Before either of them could say a word, he had plunged into a defence of himself, his mother backing him up as soon as he drew breath.

'I haven't seen her for weeks, not for months. I don't know where she is so it's no good asking me.'

'Of course he hasn't. My son's a good boy. He's obedient, he respects his parents.'

'All right,' Wexford said. 'Wait a minute. Tamima is missing. Her parents have no idea where she is. None of her relatives have any idea where she may be. Now, I must tell you that we have witnesses who have seen you about with her, at one time if not recently. They may not be reliable, I don't know. Certainly, Tamima has been seen about with a white man or boy and you are white, Rashid.'

Mrs Hanif set down the apple-purée spoon, wiped the child's face and said, almost spitting the words, 'The police are institutionally racist, that's a well-known fact.'

'And you,' said Burden, 'are a British citizen, a white woman from a family in the former Yugoslavia. Where's the racism?'

'My husband's Asian.'

'Maybe. But Rashid is pale-skinned and blue-eyed,' said Wexford. 'If witnesses say they've seen Tamima with a white boy the chances are it's Rashid but he says no and for the present we must take his word for it. You would like Tamima to be found, wouldn't you, Rashid?'

'He doesn't care!' Mrs Hanif shouted.

Equally loudly, Rashid forgot respect and said, 'Oh, do shut up, Mum!'

The baby began to cry, drumming his heels on the footrest of the high chair. 'See what you've done.' But Mrs Hanif spoke in a low petulant tone, subdued by Rashid's unaccustomed defiance.

'Tamima has to be found,' Wexford said. 'I think you'd like to help us, Rashid, I want you to come down to the station and make a statement.'

Rashid's mouth fell open. 'What about?'

'The last time you saw Tamima, what she said to you, any

phone calls you've had from her, that sort of thing. You can come with us now. No need for you to walk anywhere.'

Wexford considered asking Mohammed and Yasmin Rahman to go on television and appeal to the public to find their lost daughter – considered and rejected it. Clever gentle Mohammed might make a good impression but his wife would not. Viewers would tend to be set against her by her stern features, steady eyes and rigidity of expression. She reminded him of a bust he had once seen in Greece of Athene and he thought that the helmet the goddess had been wearing would have become her. Besides, she was associated with her son in the unlawful killing of Targo. Better to send out photographs of Tamima, which the Rahmans were happy to provide. She was a good-looking girl if rather too like her mother ever to be called pretty, yet with her dark skin and black eyes and the hijab she often if not invariably wore, a big percentage of the public would fail to distinguish her from any other Asian girl.

Rashid said in his statement that he and Tamima had once been good friends but 'nothing more'. The last time he saw her had been a month ago when he talked to her in her uncle's shop, the Raj Emporium. That had been just before she went to London to stay with her aunt, Mrs Qasi.

The newspaper photographs had no effect or none of the kind Wexford wanted. A great many people claimed to have seen Tamima but in every case it was a different Asian girl they had seen. He began to wonder again if it was possible Targo had murdered Tamima *before* he made his offer to Ahmed and he recalled what Osman had said. 'You think he killed her just the same?' It was possible and in a strange way it would have been just like Targo. Suppose he had found Tamima, had strangled her – what had he done with her body? – and then gone to Ahmed to ask if he wanted his sister killed. If the answer had been yes, he would have said the deed was already done. Wexford could almost hear him saying, 'It's all done. I don't want payment. Glad to be of service.'

It made him shiver because it seemed possible. Then he thought of the menagerie, the carnivorous animals, and began to feel sick. No, he was imagining too much . . . When he was younger he had never felt like this. He had been tougher. Banish ugly and dreadful images, he thought, put them in a box and send the box to the deep recesses of his psyche – but this faculty seemed to be deserting him now.

He went to London to see Jacqueline Clarke and Clare Cooper and learnt more from them than Hannah had. It seemed that though Tamima had come to their flat intending to get a job and stay there for some weeks, even until Christmas, she had in fact left after a week, saying she was going home to Kingsmarkham.

'Did she ever mention a man called Eric Targo, an old man?'

'I don't think so,' Clare said. 'She didn't mention anyone much when she first came and then after a day or two she was always on her mobile, answering calls more than making them, I think.'

'Were any of those calls from Rashid Hanif?'

'I don't know who they were from. We didn't like to ask.'

Jacqueline Clarke said, as if she had just remembered, 'There was a man came here once to call for her. He wouldn't come in, I don't know why not. Tamima went down to answer the door and came back upstairs for something. She left him standing on the doorstep. I looked out of the window and saw him. It was dark, though.'

'What was he like?' Wexford asked quickly.

'Young. Quite tall. I think his hair was brown, not very dark. I couldn't tell you the colour of his eyes.'

Definitely not Targo, he thought. Rashid Hanif? Quite possibly. But wherever she was, if she was alive, she wasn't with Rashid now. But it was impossible. The timing was wrong. But why would he go at that stage? He could only have killed her if he could have been absolutely confident that Ahmed would leap at his offer and not go to the police.

Every day he had got into the habit of calling on the Rahmans. It was unorthodox behaviour, though not against the rules. Released on police bail, Yasmin was at home but he never saw her. She seemed to know it was wise to keep out of the way when he called and not to speak to him. She made tea or coffee and sent it in by one of her menfolk. Mohammed and Osman had both gone back to work, so he called on his way home in the early evening. Nothing much was said – nothing at all, that is, about the killing of Targo and the concealment of the body. When they talked it was about Tamima. Sometimes Hannah came too and then they would ask questions as to all the people the missing girl had ever known right back into her early childhood, trying to find out who she might now be with and where she might have gone, always supposing she was still alive.

Webb and Cobb was no longer a crime scene and Mohammed's plan was to decorate the shop area and try to let it, to paint the exterior at the same time after replacing the windows in the top flat. This was necessarily delayed and Sharon Scott moved out, leaving the tenancy to the husband she was divorcing, Ian Scott.

Yasmin Rahman's strict morality made her disapprove of Scott's bringing to live there with him a woman he wasn't married to. In Yasmin's absence one evening, this was a topic of conversation between Wexford, Hannah, Mohammed and Osman. The Rahman men were more easy-going. Osman took the robust view that Scott's morals were no concern of theirs so long as he paid the rent. Mohammed was against sitting in judgement. Besides, times had changed and we must change with them, but he didn't know how to talk his wife round. Not for the first time, Wexford marvelled at people's selective morality. Presumably, it was all right for Yasmin to help her son conceal the body of a man he had killed and attempt to deceive the police by taking part in a plan to hide that dead man's car, while all wrong to rent out her property to a cohabiting couple.

He had no intention of visiting Mavis Targo again but one day, a week or so before Christmas, he met her in Kingsmarkham High Street. With two full shopping bags on the pavement beside her, she was contemplating the Mercedes, recently returned to her, and the yellow-painted metal clamp fastened to its rear nearside wheel. Ming and Sweetheart, bouncing about on the back seat, were both barking hysterically.

'Do something, can't you?' she said to Wexford.

'Nothing to do with me, Mrs Targo.' Resisting the temptation to tell her he was not a traffic cop, he took a little pity on her. 'Just phone the number they give and pay the fine and they'll release you in no time.'

'I knew it was a mistake to drive that bloody car. It's always brought me bad luck.'

He said nothing about the menagerie or the house. The sight of her reminded him of his failure. Targo might be dead but he had died in what was an accident, no more retributive or judicial than if he had met his death in a road crash. And now, even if they ultimately found Tamima's body concealed somewhere, buried or at the bottom of a lake or river or butchered and therefore more easily hidden, Targo could not be responsible. Yet he felt he must find the girl, dead or alive, he must find her. It was terrible to him that the police forces of the whole country had searched for her, her picture had been all over the media, but she remained missing. He tried to comfort himself with the knowledge that it is much easier to hide a living person or for that living person to hide herself, than to conceal a corpse. The dead body cannot move, cannot pick itself up and find a new hiding place. Inert, it lies where it has been left or placed, but that place may be deep under the earth.

The windows at Webb and Cobb had been replaced and the exterior painted before Ian Scott moved in. Apparently, his private life no longer concerned Yasmin Rahman. She had other things to worry about. Her son Ahmed would come up for trial in February and she had no reason to think that her daughter Tamima would be found before that – if found she ever was.

Christmas came and went. Mavis Targo sold Wymondham Lodge and moved. Dora Wexford got flu and had to stay in bed while her daughter Sylvia came in to look after her. While he manfully limped to his sixth-form college, Rashid Hanif's broken ankle refused to mend and required an operation. A vast overhaul of the police station started with builders and decorators moving in and the working lives of a dozen officers disrupted. Then at the end of January when the weather had turned very cold, the trees were silvered with hoar frost and the pavements disappeared under a light covering of snow, Wexford met Yasmin Rahman crossing the high street from Glebe Road.

He was on his way to meet Burden for lunch at the Dal Lake when he saw her. He had spotted her on the other side of the road, noticed the thick black scarf she wore wound round her head and the unflattering floor-length belted black coat, buttoned from neck to foot and just exposing clumping black brogues. In spite of all this, how beautiful she must have been when young, he thought, reflecting at the same time that this was a truly dreadful thing to say of a woman, as if beauty were necessarily and invariably confined to youth.

She crossed the street when the light turned red and advanced on him. He could see something in her face he couldn't at first define. Her first words gave an explanation.

'I've had a shock. I don't know what to do.' She frowned, shifting blame on to him as was her way. 'If you are going out, I suppose I shall have to go back home.'

He had no idea what could have happened. They were outside a small cafe that specialised in 'natural' foods but also served coffee and tea. 'Let me buy you a cup of coffee, Mrs Rahman. You've made enough for me in recent months.'

If she had refused it would have come as no surprise. Negativity seemed to be something she enjoyed. But she accepted with a reluctant nod. 'I think perhaps I shouldn't be talking to you,' she said. 'I am a convict now, aren't I?'

If she meant she would soon have a criminal record, he was bound to agree with her, but all he said was, 'That's all right. Don't worry about it,' and pulled out a chair for her close to the window.

There were only two other people in the cafe but still she looked to either side of her and over her shoulder to make sure she wasn't overheard. Wexford ordered two coffees which the waitress insisted on calling 'Americanos'. Yasmin Rahman preserved silence until she had gone, then said in a steady determined voice, 'I've seen my daughter. I've seen Tamima.'

He said nothing, looked at her.

'I saw her yesterday but I couldn't quite believe my eyes.' She spoke slowly and deliberately. 'I thought I was having a delusion, I've been so worried, you see.'

'Of course you have,' he said.

'But I saw her again this morning. At the window. She was half behind the curtain but I saw her, I knew her. Of course I know my own child.'

As others had disbelieved him, so he gave this no credence. 'Are you quite sure, Mrs Rahman?'

'I'm sure. I know my child. It was Tamima.'

'Which window was this? Where did you see her?'

The waitress chose this moment to arrive with their coffee. As soon as she appeared Yasmin Rahman clamped her lips together, sat statue-still, staring at the roadworks outside the window. The waitress seemed to be purposely taking her time, setting out milk and sugar, then recalling that the bowl of packet sweeteners was still on her tray. Yasmin continued to watch the man with the mechanical digger and the man with the pneumatic drill.

'Which window was this?' Wexford repeated once the waitress had finally gone.

Yasmin expelled a heavy sigh as she turned her head back. 'One of the new ones. In the top flat, Mr Scott's flat.'

'Above Webb and Cobb, do you mean?'

'If you choose to put it like that.' Yasmin's black sleeve fell back a little, exposing several heavy gold bracelets on her narrow fragile-looking wrist. He noticed how impossibly long and thin her hands were. 'I thought that man had killed her. From the moment he made that offer to me and Ahmed I feared he had already killed her. And then I saw my daughter at that window. She was looking out between the curtains.'

'Did she see you?'

'I don't know. I haven't said anything to my husband. It was only an hour ago and he was at work.'

Wexford finished his coffee, said, 'We'll go there now. I'll take Detective Sergeant Goldsmith with us.'

He went to pay the bill, returned to hear her say, 'Can it be someone else?' She spoke in her usual austere dignified way but her words were harsh. 'I dislike that woman. I dislike being patronised.'

How upset Hannah would be, he thought, that she of all police officers might be found wanting in the very area of race relations where she so much desired to meet her own standard of treating black, Asian and white people all with perfect equity. At the same time he admired this woman's nerve in attempting to make the rules for the law. But he gave in. A call to Burden fetched him to the cafe and they all went up Glebe Road together on foot. Glancing at the black-robed figure beside him, Wexford wondered if this were the first time Yasmin Rahman had ever walked in the public streets accompanied by two men other than close male relatives.

A sign attached to the ground-floor window of Webb and Cobb proclaimed it as shop premises to let with, underneath, the name of a firm of agents to apply to. The flat immediately above looked empty. At the top, because the winter's day had turned dull, a light was on behind the drawn curtains in Ian Scott's.

'Someone's in,' Burden said. 'We ring the bell, do we?'

'It's the top one.'

Yasmin proceeded to ring it but nothing happened and no one came. She pressed the bell again. The light upstairs went out and the curtain was twitched. There was no entryphone but there was a letter box. Wexford pushed the flap inwards and called in his strong resonant voice, 'Police. Open the door, please.'

Again there was no response.

'Please, may I try?' Yasmin's humble words were at variance with her imperious tone. She called through the letter box, 'Tamima, this is your mother. You must open the door.' She turned to Wexford. 'Or you'll break it down, is that right?'

'I hope we shan't have to do that.'

But as she called out, 'They will break it down!' a youngish man with blue eyes and brown hair opened the door. He wore a white vest and jeans, a bath towel draped over his shoulders. 'I was having a shave. It's bloody freezing out here,' he said. 'What do you want?'

'You know what we want, Mr Scott.' Wexford didn't wait for further discussion but headed for the stairs, followed by Yasmin and Burden. The stairs twisted round outside the lower flat before going on up. When he had set foot on the second stair of the second flight he looked up and saw, standing at the top, the girl he had last seen coming home from school with a satchel on her back.

CHAPTER TWENTY-THREE

At the top, in Scott's sparsely furnished flat, Tamima sat on one end of the bed, her mother on the other. They avoided looking at each other. Wexford sat on the only chair in the room, Burden and Scott on stools Scott brought in from the kitchen. It was Wexford who broke the silence.

'How long have you been living here, Mr Scott?'

'Since the middle of November.' He spoke sullenly, then with energy. 'I've a right to be here. I'm the tenant.'

'And you have been here with him all this time?' Wexford addressed Tamima.

She shrugged. 'Since maybe the end of November, whatever.' As in the case of her lover, speaking spurred her on to animation. 'I've been so bored of everything. I'm bored out of my head. He said he was taking me to a luxury apartment. But he never did, he brought me to this shithole, and in the night too, so nobody would see.'

She met her mother's eyes. Veiled and gowned in austere black, Yasmin Rahman was taking in every detail of Tamima's clothes. Probably she had never seen her daughter dressed like this before, had never seen any good Muslim girl dressed like this, from the low-cut top and the ultra-short miniskirt to the fishnet tights and the cheap high-heeled scarlet shoes. She lifted her head gracefully and turned away.

'Didn't you see any newspapers? Didn't you watch tele-vision?' This was Burden. 'There's been a nationwide search for you. Didn't you know?' He looked at Scott. 'Didn't *you*?'

'She was scared of her family.'

'I was going to tell them,' Tamima said. 'I *was*. Every day I meant to go next door and tell them. But I don't know, I don't know why I didn't. Well, yes, I do. I didn't want my mum and dad to hate me. It wasn't that I was scared of them taking me away from *him*. I'm sick of him.'

'Charming,' said Scott. 'Thanks very much.'

'I suppose you first saw Miss Rahman while you were living here with your wife,' Wexford said.

'That's one way of putting it,' Scott said.

'Is there another?'

'I don't know what I've done to be questioned like this. I've done nothing wrong.' A frightening thought occurred to him. 'She is over sixteen, isn't she?'

'Of course I bloody am. I don't know how many times I've told you.' Tamima's bravado suddenly left her. Her face turned red and she stuck out her lower lip like a child half her age. 'I want to go home,' she wailed, and turning to her mother, threw herself upon her, clutching her shoulders.

Yasmin remained stiff and unresponsive for a moment. Then, her expression softening, she slowly put her arms round Tamima, holding the girl's cheek against her own. She stroked the long black hair and began whispering to her in what must have been Urdu. Wexford watched them for a moment. Then he turned his eyes on Ian Scott. The man had been correct to say he had done nothing wrong. His small follies were minor compared to what Tamima's brother had done, what her mother had done. He got up.

'There's nothing for us to do here,' he said to Burden and together they went down the stairs and out into Glebe Road.

'Jenny will be pleased nothing's happened to her,' Burden said when they were partaking of the lunch that had been long postponed. 'She was worried about a forced marriage if not an honour killing.'

Hoping for the drama of it, Wexford thought uncharitably.

'Not that I ever believed in either,' said Burden.

'I am going to have kedgeree,' said Wexford, 'which I don't believe is Indian at all, let alone Kashmiri. I think we invented it in the days of our supremacy.' They ordered. 'We shall be able to tell Hannah we told her so.'

'I suppose it was Scott she saw hanging around in the Raj Emporium.'

'And Scott Targo saw with her which made him think the Rahmans would want her killed.'

'I'm afraid the kedgeree is off,' said the waitress. 'There has been quite a run on it.'

'All right. I'll have the chicken tikka masala which I believe is another colonial invention.'

'So will I,' said Burden. 'All this has made me wonder just how common these forced marriages are. Or these honour killings, come to that.'

'Common enough in Asia, I fear, less so here. I dare say we shall hear no more of them.'

Some undefined unease took away his appetite. He left half his main course and wanted nothing more. Burden ate heartily as usual, finishing with what he called that well-known Kashmiri speciality, a large slice of apple pie with cream. It was half past two. While they had been in the restaurant the winter's afternoon had turned colder and an

274

icy north wind blew out of every narrow side street and alley. Wexford had no belief in telepathy, premonitions, clairvoyance or portents, yet as he walked along in the bitter cold he was increasingly aware of some foreboding, some horror which lay ahead, and he quickened his pace, prompting Burden to ask what was the hurry.

The warmth which met them as they passed through the swing doors into the police station foyer was so relieving as for a moment to banish all other sensation. Then Wexford saw Hannah bearing down upon them, phone in hand. Something in her face told him he wouldn't be passing on triumphant news about Tamima that day.

'I was just calling you, guv,' and as she spoke his phone began to ring.

'There's been an honour killing. It's really happened. A woman in Stowerton found dead in the room she was renting, her throat cut. She'd left her husband of a year and the husband and her father swore they'd kill her. I'm going there now.'

'We'll all go there now,' said Wexford and, silently, to himself, at least I know it can't be Targo this time.

AFTERWARDS

The years passed, two or three of them. As Wexford had predicted, Yasmin Rahman received a suspended sentence for assisting an offender, the offender being her son Ahmed, convicted for the unlawful killing of Eric Targo. Ahmed spent the last year of his sentence in an open prison and was released on licence. By that time his family had moved away from Glebe Road, where some of their neighbours, notably Ian Scott – now with a new partner – and the occupants of Burden's old home, had made life un-comfortable for them. Having secured three fairly good A levels at Carisbrooke Sixth Form College, Tamima had just begun a four-year course in Islamic studies at a university in the Midlands.

The Rahmans now lived in Myringham where Mohammed still worked but inside the office, the head of social services having decided it would be unwise for him to risk catcalls and other abuse from clients. Yasmin's criminal record made very little difference to her life. As for Osman, he had given up nursing and was at University College London, studying for a medical degree.

It was a Sunday in summer when Ahmed came to Wexford's house. Once more without a gardener, Wexford was at home mowing the lawn, or, rather, after half mowing the lawn, had given up in disgust and was sitting in a deeply cushioned cane chair outside the French windows, reading a novel by Ivy Compton-Burnett. Ahmed hadn't come through the house. He must have entered the front garden on his way to the front door and seen Wexford from there. He walked softly over to within a few feet of him and cleared his throat. Wexford looked up.

'I'm afraid I'm disturbing you,' Ahmed said.

'That's all right. How are you?'

'Not bad. Better than I have been.'

Wexford laid his book face down on the table beside him. 'What brings you here?'

'I want to tell you something. A confession really. May I sit down?'

For a moment the sun seemed to have darkened and someone else, something invisible yet grimly present, appeared to have entered the garden and strutted up on to the paving. No one was there, yet Wexford could see a shadow fall, the stocky muscular figure, the white hair and the thick blue-and-white scarf wound round its neck. Ahmed repeated his last words.

'May I sit down?'

'No, Ahmed,' Wexford said, 'I don't think you may because I don't want to hear what you have to say.'

'I have to tell you. I think you'll be pleased. You hated him too. When my mother was out of the room, I did –'

Wexford interrupted quietly but with firmness. 'I'm not hearing this,' he said, getting up. 'I'm hearing none of it. I haven't even seen you.' He went into the house by way of the French windows, closing them behind him.

Ahmed stood outside for a moment, mouthing something, holding up his hands, but the image of Targo, which had never really been visible, had gone. Was he going to say what

I think he was? Wexford asked himself. What else could he have been about to confess? But I won't think of it. I will never think of it again but put the monster back in its box and throw the box onto the rubbish heap. The best place, the only place, for him.

SPIRITUAL LIFE
IN THE EARLY
CHURCH

SPIRITUAL LIFE IN THE EARLY CHURCH

The Witness of Acts and Ephesians

BONNIE THURSTON

FORTRESS PRESS   MINNEAPOLIS

SPIRITUAL LIFE IN THE EARLY CHURCH
The Witness of Acts and Ephesians

Interior design: Publishers' WorkGroup
Cover design: Patricia Boman

Library of Congress Cataloging-in-Publication Data

Thurston, Bonnie Bowman.
   Spiritual life in the early church : the witness of Acts and
Ephesians / Bonnie Thurston.
     p.   cm.
   Includes bibliographical references and index.
   ISBN 0-8006-2616-8 (alk. paper) :
   1. Spiritual life—Biblical teaching.   2. Spiritual life—History
of doctrines—Early church, ca. 30-600.   3. Bible. N.T. Acts—
Criticism, interpretation, etc.   4. Bible. N.T. Ephesians—
Criticism, interpretation, etc.   I. Title.
BS2545.S65T485   1993
248'.09'015—dc20   93-11516
                                                                  CIP

The paper used in this publication meets the minimum requirements of American National Standard for Information Sciences—Permanence of Paper for Printed Library Materials, ANSI Z329.48-1984.   ∞™

Manufactured in the U.S.A.   1–2616
97   96   95   94   93   1   2   3   4   5   6   7   8   9   10

This book is dedicated with gratitude
to my parents
Eleanor King Bowman
E. V. "Bonny" Bowman
on the occasion of their
50th Wedding Anniversary
March 14, 1992

Contents

Preface

In recent years there has been a great hunger in the churches for a more profound spiritual life. Either because we have lost touch with our brothers and sisters in the pews or because we somehow view the field of spirituality as at best suspect and at worst beneath our notice, we in the academy have done little to feed that hunger.

In this book I attempt to speak to the pastoral need for a deeper relationship to the God of Christian faith. Its aim is modest: to introduce the general reader to the spiritual life of the early church by presenting some of its attitudes and practices, and to do so without the encumbrances of an unduly daunting apparatus.

Chapter 1 develops a working definition of *spirituality* as the term is used in this book. Then in chapter 2 the religious backgrounds of the New Testament are examined to help orient nonspecialists to the religious environment of the early Christians; this material is not intended to be definitive.

The remainder of the book (chapters 3–9) focuses mainly on the church as it is depicted in the Acts of the Apostles which, while not used uncritically as a historical source for early Christianity, at least presents one early Christian's view of his church. A general essay on the spiritual life of the Jerusalem church is followed by specific studies of the use of the name of Jesus, of the Lord's Supper, and of Acts 4:23-31 as an example of the prayer of the early church. Moving from the Jewish environment of Christianity in Jerusalem to its Hellenistic background in Asia Minor, I note the relationship between Acts and Ephesians and then turn to a discussion of Ephesians 3:14-21 as an example of how an early Christian writer used prayer in the production of Christian literature. The conclusion suggests how the spiritual life of the early church can inform our practice today.

In the initial chapters, scholarly apparatus has been deliberately kept to a minimum. Generally speaking, only direct quotations are noted; instead, chapter 2 closes with a bibliography of works consulted, which may be of use for further exploration the reader may wish to pursue. The later chapters have more extensive notation, as I assume the reader will want a more complete presentation of the specific subjects treated.

Unless otherwise noted, Scripture quotations are from the New Revised Standard Version of the Bible.

My gratitude goes to my late husband, Burton B. Thurston, Sr., who was a constant source of encouragement; to Marshall D. Johnson, my editor at Fortress Press; to George Miller for his help in proofreading; to the librarians at Wheeling Jesuit College, especially interlibrary loan librarian Mary Gasiorowski; to the New Testament Prayer in Historical Context group of the Society of Biblical Literature who heard early drafts of some of this work; and to the New Testament Section of the South East Regional Society of Biblical Literature who provided helpful commentary on chapter 4.

1

What Is
Spirituality?

Let us begin at the beginning. "In the beginning God created the heavens and the earth. Now the earth was formless and empty, darkness was over the surface of the deep, and the Spirit of God was hovering over the waters" (Gen. 1:1-2, NIV). "The Lord God formed the man from the dust of the ground and breathed into his nostrils the breath of life, and the man became a living being" (Gen. 2:7, NIV).

These familiar words from Genesis stress two ideas that are formative in understanding the term *spirituality* as it applies to the early Christians. First, in the light of the experience and understanding of the first followers of Jesus, Christianity today must be understood to be countercultural because it does not share the root assumption of the scientific age. Second, spirituality has its origins in and is as basic as breath and breathing.

Because of our connection to our roots in the early church, we Christians today cannot share fully the dominant assumptions of our world about the origin and destiny of human life. In *Jesus: A New Vision*, Marcus Borg puts it this way:

> Those of us socialized in the modern world have grown up in a culture with a largely secularized and one-dimensional understanding of reality. . . . The dominant worldview in the modern period flows from the scientific and technological revolution of the last few centuries. . . . Perceiving reality within the framework of this worldview, what is real is essentially the material, the visible world of time and space. What is real is ultimately made up of tiny bits and pieces of "stuff," all operating in accord with laws of cause and effect which can be known. Reality is constituted by matter and energy interacting to form the visible world.[1]

This is precisely not the worldview of early Christianity (as I hope this study will demonstrate). In the mind of the writer of Genesis, the origin of the things in the world is God, not a random play of physics and chemistry. Likewise, the origin of human life is God—indeed, God's

1

very breath. What this means is that for the early Christians, what is seen is not "all there is." Life is not reducible to a series of scientific principles or rules. Life is shot through with the mystery of God who is at its foundation.

Because its origin is God, the creation was understood to be, as the nineteenth-century poet Gerard Manley Hopkins put it, "charged with the grandeur of God." When Jesus looked at the lilies of the field and the birds of the air, he did not see photosynthesis and aerodynamics. He saw examples of God's generosity and care for God's creatures. Paul put it this way: "Ever since the creation of the world [God's] eternal power and divine nature, invisible though they are, have been understood and seen through the things he has made" (Rom. 1:20).

First, then, we need to understand that the early Christians did not live in a one-dimensional and mechanistic universe but in a dual world, a world of matter and of spirit, a world of created things and their Creator. In our scientific age, we need to recall that the unseen, spiritual world was understood to be "real" and to exert power and shaping influence on the seen, material world. (For proof of this assertion one need only recall the number of exorcisms and "spirit world" encounters in the Synoptic Gospels.)

Human beings seem to be religious animals insofar as one of our basic needs is to be in communion with the reality of the unseen world. We humans are aware of our own death. We are capable of self-transcendence. We can become the objects of our own consciousness and go beyond it. This process leads to the fundamental theological questions, Who am I? Why am I here? Where am I going? Answers to these questions are usually given in some symbolic form. "Rational" and "scientific" reasons have never been enough. People have always looked to a wider world of ideal possibilities. That wider world of possibility, according to the biblical record, is as basic as breath.

The etymological root of *spirituality* is the Latin word *spirare*, to breathe, and *spiritus*, breath. It is the same root word that the Bible uses for "spirit." In the biblical record, the image of the stirring of breath is associated with the Holy, with God. Before creation, the Spirit of God hovered over the primal chaos. God's breath brought human beings into existence. John 4 personifies God as spirit, and in John 15 truth comes as a spirit. In the Ephesian letter Paul says that we have access to God through the Spirit.

Spirituality as associated with breath suggests two things. First, spirituality in this sense is an animating life principle. Second, the spirit is the human person in his or her devotional aspect. Thus in the biblical sense, a "spiritual person" is one attracted to and in communion with the reality within and beyond the visible one. She or he is sensitive to and attached to "things of the spirit." Spirituality in this sense is the practice of religion. What a person does with what that person believes is "spirituality."

We are now ready for a functional definition of spirituality as it applies to the early church. Spirituality was what the early Christians did to put into practice what they believed. It was what they did to respond to a world filled with the presence of God and the risen Christ. Therefore, it included private prayer and public worship, devotion and fasting, almsgiving, art, and social action. In short, spirituality encompassed practically the whole realm of human activity, because all of life was understood to be under the lordship of Christ. Here we shall examine in detail only the most distinctively Christian of those activities. (Baptism has been excluded from this work. While it is certainly a spiritual "practice," it represents initiation into the Christian life.)

This study of spirituality in the early church assumes that humans live an amphibious life of sense and spirit, that in their daily lives Christians of the first century lived in communion with God and worked to conform themselves to God's unseen reality. In *The Spiritual Life* Evelyn Underhill described the process: "A spiritual life is simply a life in which all that we do comes from the center, where we are anchored in God: a life soaked through . . . by a sense of His reality and claim, and self-given to the great movement of His will."[2]

What follows is not a crash course in first-century personal religion. It is more nearly a crash course in New Testament history. But it does assume sympathy with the movement toward God, seeking to answer the question, How did the early Christians set out and journey in God's direction?

2

The Spiritual
Backgrounds of
the New Testament Church

Christianity as a religion was not foreign to its environment. Many beliefs and practices from that environment were adopted and adapted by the early Christians. This is why it is important to know something of the forces that shaped Christianity as the New Testament presents it. The religious environment in which the New Testament church found itself was by no means monolithic. Judaism, Hellenism, and the Roman religions were all clearly in evidence. If we are to understand the spiritual life of the early Christian community, we must know something of the diversity of belief and practice against which it defined itself. The following is intended as the briefest of overviews of the Jewish and Greco-Roman religious backgrounds of the New Testament. For more detailed information, the reader is referred to the bibliography at the end of the chapter.

Jewish Backgrounds
of Christian Spirituality

The study of the Jewish backgrounds of Christianity is complicated by many factors. First, the period of direct contact and influence was relatively short, roughly that of the first century of this era. Second, there were at least three major "schools" of Judaism in this time period, Pharisees, Sadducees, and Essenes, and these were to some degree divided by geography. Most of our evidence about Jewish practice in the first century is from Palestinian, Semitic worship, not that of the dispersion (although the distinction between diaspora and Palestinian Judaism has been broken down in recent scholarship), and is dominated by Pharisaism, which was the prevailing school of thought.[1]

Jewish worship itself was radically disturbed by the destruction of the Temple in 70 C.E., and this resulted in a spiritualized idea of sacrifice.

4

Finally, the earliest liturgical texts now extant are more fluid than later ones, so that echoes of wording must be treated with caution, even if structure and themes show remarkable stability.[2]

Outside Palestine, there were two major centers of Jewish settlement: Babylon and Alexandria, the latter perhaps the largest city in the ancient world, with fully one-fourth of the population Jewish. Scholars estimate that 8 percent of the Roman Empire was Jewish, with only one-fourth of that number in Palestine. So the distribution of the Jews in the empire was widespread. In the first century there were between six and seven million persons of the Jewish faith, about a million in Egypt. In 14 C.E., Rome had between fifty and sixty thousand Jews. The Roman approach was to try to maintain good relations with such a large "minority group."

The legal status of the Jews was problematic, but they did have certain rights as *religio licita*. As members of a legal religion, Jews could organize associations for synagogue worship and levy a tax for Jerusalem (which was a mixed blessing, because it is estimated that, with the Roman tax, 30 to 40 percent of a Jew's income in the first century went to taxes). They were exempt from military service, and their holy books were protected. Certain aspects of the imperial cult were modified to suit Jewish monotheism, and they were allowed to marry according to Jewish custom rather than Roman law. Such special favors were a mixed blessing, because they had a tendency to make Jews unpopular with the general citizenry.

This was compounded by the fact that Judaism in this period was a missionary religion. The Jews had maintained their unity in Babylonian exile and now, with their Scripture translated into Greek, they adopted a policy of being "light to the Gentiles." Pagans heard of their praise of God and took instruction in righteousness. There were numbers of proselytes and what the Acts of the Apostles calls "Godfearers," those who practiced Judaism but did not formally convert. Both the beliefs and the literature of Judaism contributed to its mission.

Beliefs and Literature

The fundamental Jewish belief was and is radically monotheistic. The Jews believed in one God who had created and given meaning to life and demanded from his people love and obedience. The Jews believed that "the same God who is the God of heaven, the supremely transcendent God, is yet the God of his people. . . . He is the God who concerns himself with the people whom he chose in the covenant, but also the God who lives with them, who makes himself their travelling-companion here below."[3]

Chosenness is the prevailing characteristic of the one people. There is a special relationship between God and Israel, because Israel belongs to God by God's initiative and is bound by covenant to God. That covenant was expressed in the law, Torah, which means "direction" or "moral instruction" and is the totality of God's will for God's people as it is revealed in the Ten Commandments, the Pentateuch, the whole written Scripture, and, according to some circles, the oral interpretation of those Scriptures.

The one people chosen by the one God shared one hope, the hope of a Messiah. It was generally held that the depressed state of Israel was due to disobedience. Jews looked forward to a day of deliverance when God would intervene with a Messiah and Jerusalem would become the center of the world to which all the nations would come to receive the law.

To understand the expectations of the early Jewish-Christian community, we need to review the development of the idea of "Messiah," for it had passed through several stages before the New Testament period. The earliest messianic thinking originated in God's promise to the house of David in 2 Samuel 7. God made a special covenant with David to establish his "house" forever and unconditionally ("Your house and your kingdom shall be made sure forever before me; your throne shall be established forever," 2 Sam. 7:16). Second, up to the time of the Babylonian exile, the prophets spoke of the Messiah in terms of a better, indeed ideal, king who was to come because of God's power. He is described as "Emmanuel." After the exile, when Davidic kingship no longer existed, the prophets began to think in terms of some far-distant time when God would directly intervene to rule the world. This shift from an understanding of a human king under God to a divine ruler on a cosmic scale is paralleled by the shift in literature from what is called classical prophetism to apocalyptic writing.

Apocalyptic was part and parcel of the milieu of Jewish religious literature in the first century B.C.E. and the first century C.E. It is the literature of visions, symbolism, and supernatural happenings. Its central, eschatological theme is God's revelation concerning the end of time and the coming of his kingdom. In apocalyptic literature, a golden age will dawn when the world is overcome and the Messiah rules. This golden age will be preceded by tribulation, cataclysm, and the return of Elijah. Then the Messiah will come from the clouds and issue cosmic judgment. Daniel 7, 2 Esdras 13, and the *Apocalypse of Baruch* provide examples of the sort of apocalyptic literature that provided the models for Mark 13 and the Revelation to John.[4]

Psalms of Solomon 17:23-36 gives a vivid picture of messianic expectation at the time of Jesus.

> Behold, O Lord, and raise up unto them their king, the son of David,
> At the time in which Thou seest, O God, that he may reign over Israel Thy servant,
> And gird him with strength, that he may shatter unrighteous rulers,
> And that he may purge Jerusalem from nations that trample her down to destruction.
> Wisely, righteously, he shall thrust out sinners from the inheritance,
> He shall destroy the pride of the sinner as a potter's vessel . . .
> He shall destroy the godless nations with the word of his mouth;
> At his rebuke nations shall flee before him,
> And he shall reprove sinners for the thoughts of their heart.

The point is that memory of God's deliverance in the past gave hope for the future. That hope was for a cosmic leader, understood in military terms after the Davidic model, as well as for the Day of the Lord, understood in apocalyptic terms. Historical catastrophe, then, could be seen as a new and divine intervention in history.[5]

The beliefs of Judaism were spread by its literature. It was mentioned above that Hebrew Scriptures was translated into Greek between 250 B.C.E. and the first century C.E. This means that Hebraic words and ideas were already in the Greek intellectual stream before Christianity appeared. Philo of Alexandria (ca. 25 B.C.E.–50 C.E.) produced philosophical and theological works on Jewish life and law from a Hellenized point of view. He attempted to show how Jewish law was completely reasonable and compatible with Greco-Roman philosophy. Josephus (37–ca. 100 C.E.) first commanded Jewish rebels against the Roman army in Galilee in 66 C.E. and then turned himself over to the Romans. His *Antiquities of the Jews* (written in 81–96 C.E.) refute charges against Judaism and give a nearly contemporary history of the "Jewish War." Finally, the Talmud, a collection of postbiblical laws, teachings, and interpretations that originated with the rabbis in Babylon and Palestine in the first four centuries of this era, provides information about the beliefs and practices in the period under consideration.

Practices and Images

Practices of Judaism included public worship in the Temple and the synagogue, private worship in the home, and observance of circumcision, Sabbath, and the festivals (Passover, Tabernacles, Succoth, Hannukah, and Purim). Temple worship was based on regulations of Mosaic law, was carried out daily, and was primarily sacrificial. The Temple was the only place where sacrifices were made. It was understood that in the Holy of Holies in the Temple God dwelled in a special way. Thus Jerusalem, and in particular the Temple, was the spiritual center for all Jews. Sacrifices offered in thanksgiving and guilt offerings for sins unintentionally committed could only be offered there. Apparently, the Temple cult was especially brilliant at the major festivals, Pentecost and Tabernacles.

Scholars once suggested that the synagogue developed as a substitute for the Temple during the Babylonian exile, but this is not certain. All the elements of synagogue worship (prayer, Scripture reading, and teaching) had Temple backgrounds, but the ministry of word and prayer was more highly developed in the synagogue. Whether this was because the priests in the Temple had other duties or because the Temple declined and then was destroyed in this period cannot be determined.

Sabbath services of the synagogue were four: the most important, morning prayer; additional prayer; afternoon prayer; and evening prayer, at each of which the Tephillah (Eighteen Benedictions) was used. Three hours correspond to the hours of daily prayer for individuals (see Ps. 55:17 and Dan. 6:10, 13), and two seem linked to the daily hours of sacrifice in the Temple.

Since it was the standard pattern of first-century Jewish worship to use the Shema (Deut. 6:4-9) twice daily (morning and evening) and the Tephillah three times (morning, afternoon, and evening), it will be helpful to review both. Shema means "hear," and the text of the prayer is preserved for us in Deuteronomy 6:4-9, which begins, "Hear, O Israel: The Lord is our God, the Lord alone. You shall love the Lord your God with all your heart, and with all your soul, and with all your might" (Deut. 6:4-5). The verses have been seen as a confession of faith, as a thanksgiving for deliverance from the land of Egypt, and as an act of self-dedication. The most ancient interpretation of the prayer is that it is an act of thanksgiving for redemption. It is recited when one lies down and rises, so recitation at the beginning and at the end of the day represented the minimum obligation. Men recited the Shema from their twelfth year on; women and slaves were exempt from the obligation.

Tephillah, or eighteen benedictions, comes from a word that means "prayer," sometimes called *amidah* in reference to the standing position in which the prayers are recited. The Tephillah is a great petitionary prayer asking the blessings of God on various activities. It is characterized by *berakah*, blessing-thanksgiving, the purpose of which was to make every activity of the devout Jew a sacred, liturgical action. The formula of the Tephillah runs, "Blessed be thou, O Lord our God, King of eternity, thou who hast . . . " It is to be said by all men, women, children, and slaves.

Characteristic of Jewish spirituality of the time was the "ministry of the word," Scripture reading and teaching in both synagogue and home. In many ways, the primary spirituality of the first-century Jew was domestic, centered in the duties of home life, circumcision, Sabbath meals, and festivals.

Urban T. Holmes's description of the dominant images of Judaism at the time will serve as a summary closing of this overview of Jewish belief and practice. Holmes lists three primary images in Judaism, *da'ath, shekinah,* and *berakah.*[6] *Da'ath* is knowledge that takes possession of the person known. It is received primarily to discern God's plan and will and comes from the study of Scripture. In Jewish and Hellenistic intellectual history, it appears as the concept of wisdom, which had its own fascinating development. *Shekinah* is the dwelling of God with God's people. It is the manifestation of God in provisional presence, the holy in the midst of the profane. Understood to reside in the Holy of Holies in the Temple, it is also present when several people are gathered to study Torah and where the righteous judge and make decisions. The *shekinah* was the source of mystical thinking about God present with people. Finally, *berakah* was mentioned in connection with the Tephillah. *Berakah* is blessing or thanksgiving. It is the characteristic response to God and involves blessing God's name and being thankful for all God has done. It is a blessing of God and an act of praise and thanksgiving as persons and things and all creation are understood as belonging to God.

Hellenistic Backgrounds of
Christian Spirituality[7]

The original meaning of *hellēnismos* was simply "use of the Greek language," from the verb *hellēnizō,* to speak Greek. Later it came to mean the Greek way of life and culture, that dominant force in both ancient Greece and, later, in the Roman Empire.

The Hellenistic period extends from the conquests of Alexander the Great (356–323 B.C.E.) in the fourth century B.C.E. to about 30 B.C.E., the date of the final incorporation into the Roman Empire of the lands once ruled by Alexander. Alexander's goals were as much cultural as military. His dream was that of one, vast empire unified by Greek language and culture which he believed was superior to any then in existence. The date 30 B.C.E. may be the beginning of Roman political history, but Hellenism as a cultural force persisted with surprising strength, and the "Hellenistic age" extends to at least 300 C.E.

The Pax Romana was the dominant political factor of the New Testament period. As a result of the Punic Wars, Rome controlled the western Mediterranean. Julius Caesar (100–44 B.C.E.) extended the territory, and on his death Rome entered the period of peace. In 27 B.C.E., Octavian (Augustus Caesar, 63 B.C.E.–14 C.E.) began to rule as the first Roman emperor.

Several factors increased the power and stability of Rome. First, imperial policy set up rulers of provinces who were directly responsible for their conduct. Senatorial provinces were senate-appointed offices answerable to the Senate. Imperial provinces were administered by a governor appointed by the emperor. They were frequently on frontiers (as was Judea) and had standing armies.

The presence of established land and sea routes made travel and communication easier than before. A courier could go fifty miles a day on Roman roads, with the promise of shelter (however dangerous) and entertainment in the evenings. There was a consolidated system of law and, in theory, common justice for all who were Roman citizens. Finally, language was uniform, with Latin used in the West and Greek in the East (here, again, is the legacy of Alexander).

The Religious and Philosophical Environment

During the political and cultural expansions of the time, another revolution, a cosmological one, was occurring. To understand it, we need to be familiar with Western culture's three understandings of "the structure of the universe." First there existed the classical model with its three "layers": heaven, earth, and an underworld. Second was the Ptolemaic, earth-centered cosmic image, and, finally, our modern Copernican view of the sun as the center of our solar system. The Hellenistic-Roman world witnessed the shift from the classical to the Ptolemaic views.

Euripides (ca. 485–406 B.C.E.) expressed the classical image when he wrote, "Heaven and earth were once one form, and when they had been separated from one another, they gave birth and brought up into the light all things" (frag. 484, Melanippe). This view of the cosmos was maintained by homage to the gods at the center of the world, which was marked by a sacred mountain or omphalos like that at Delphi. Living in proximity to such a center, humans were at home with the gods who protected them and nourished their world.

This view was challenged in the sixth century B.C.E. by the pre-Socratic philosophers. Anaximander (611–547 B.C.E.), for example, argued that earth was an unsupported cylinder in the middle of the universe. Ptolemaic cosmology as developed by Claudius Ptolemy (ca. 100–178 B.C.E.) kept the earth center of the traditional understanding but extended the view to the realm of the planets. His new cosmic architecture defined the universe hierarchically. The point is that we are looking at a period of time in which the basic understanding of the universe was in flux. This had far-reaching implications for religion and spirituality.

Traditional Olympian religion, which had been associated with the polis (the city-state), belonged to the sociopolitical order. If one was born in a geographical area, the person was born into its religion. For example, Athenians worshiped Athena. (Modern sociology of religion calls this a natural religious group.) The new religion, however, was in response to what was newly understood as the spontaneity of the sacred. God no longer was bound to a single geographic location. Thus, religion became a voluntary association of individuals that challenged the sociopolitical order.

Furthermore, Hellenistic internationalism led to the expansion of the Eastern deities like Egyptian Isis and Syrian Atargatis into Hellenistic cities and society which had previously known only Greek expressions of religion. Inevitably, transformations in both the traditional Greek and the new Eastern religions occurred. History of religions calls this phenomenon syncretism. The word was first used to designate a federation of Cretan cities that had previously lived in enmity with each other, but it came to mean "to mix or join together," from the Greek verb *kerannymi* ("to mix"). "Mixture," however, is a misleading term in the religious sphere. It would be better to think of Hellenistic religions as a response that preserved the richness of the new political internationalism in the religious sphere than to think simplistically of "mixing religions."

The process of syncretism worked something like this: Oriental religions were Hellenized. Rites and practices of the original may have been preserved, but myths and cult legends were translated into Greek. Second, concepts from Hellenistic religious experience invaded all religions of any origins. Third, ancient concepts separated from local traditions and were reinterpreted to fit the new world culture. The final syncretistic phenomenon was the creation of new religions out of Greek and non-Greek elements of older religions. This happened, for example, with the formation of the cult of Serapis, and some might say in early Christianity.

Obviously, Hellenistic religion cannot be understood apart from Greek philosophy which, in some measure, is responsible for the demise of traditional Greek religion. Greek religion had been polytheistic and anthropomorphic. The gods were essentially overgrown humans who sometimes acted in the worst way humans can act but on a cosmic scale. The sophisticated philosophies of Socrates, Plato, and, later, Aristotle made such religion seem infantile. To understand the spiritual climate of the time, an acquaintance with three crucial philosophic "schools"— Platonism, Epicureanism, and Stoicism is helpful.

Greek philosophy exhibits two main approaches. One is the speculative and scientific, which attempts to explain the universe in which humans live. The other is the practical, which speaks to ethical and political issues. In Greece, the first preceded the second. Pre-Socratic thought speculated about the cosmos, and in the lifetime of Socrates, the philosophic interest shifted to human affairs.

Platonism is, in actuality, the union of the teachings of Socrates which were recorded by his pupil, Plato (428–347 B.C.E.), with ideas from the Heraclitean system, particularly those centering around the belief that all things are endlessly flowing and thus cannot be known. Platonism is heavily epistemological, that is, interested in the ways of and limits to human knowing. It argues that sense perception does not reveal the true nature of things. Sensible things are separate from, yet participate in, the Ideas. The realm of the Ideas is One and changeless; thus God must be part of the world of Ideas. The notion of the soul is closely tied to the intellect, since the soul is understood to be the affective center of human personality. After the death of Plato, his students Xenocrates and Speusippus created the Platonic system, which is reflected in popular Platonism of succeeding centuries. The dualism of Neoplatonism is widely seen in early Christian thought.

Epicureanism is often misunderstood and misrepresented in popular literature. It is certainly not synonymous with hedonism. Epicurus (341–270 B.C.E.) was unwilling to give up belief in the gods who were needed in his system to embody the perfection of human happiness. (One might say the Epicurean gods were created in human image.) Epicureanism argues that only our experiences have meaning, and only the pleasurable ones are meaningful. The aim of life is to follow the natural, pleasurable instincts as they arise. Only the practice of virtue and the avoidance of vice, however, give true pleasure. Happiness is the goal of human life, but true happiness is found only in a life guided by intelligence that can rise above the life of the senses. Epicureanism enjoyed its greatest popularity between 100 B.C.E. and 50 C.E., although by the end of this period its popularity was greatly diminished (there was, however, a public chair of Epicureanism in the schools at Athens in the second century C.E.).

Stoicism may well have exerted the greatest influence on early Christianity. It certainly inspired great personalities of the early Roman Empire (Seneca, Epictetus, and Marcus Aurelius were its proponents). Stoicism was a new stream in Greek thought, but practically none of its great teachers before the Christian era were Greeks. Zeno was a Cypriot; Cleanthes was from Asos in the Troad; Chrysippus, from Soli or Tarsus; Ariso, from Chios; Herillus, from Carthage; Dionysus, from Heraclea in Pontus; and Saphaerus, from the Bosporus. Perhaps this influx from the East gave the philosophy its prophetic note. It certainly exhibited a development parallel to the voluntary character of the new religions mentioned above.

Zeno (332–264 B.C.E.) talked to those who came to a public colonnade, a porch or stoa. He argued that virtue is the highest aim of humans and will lead to happiness. The good person is indifferent to surrounding conditions, because only conformity to the reason of the universe is important. The purpose of reason is to bring the world to perfection. The Stoics maintained a conception of God that made it clear that all things happened by Fate. For the Stoic, virtue and obedience to God's will (Fate) are the same thing.

Categories of Discourse and Religion

To return to religious belief and practice: it has been noted that there were three basic categories in Hellenistic religious thought: piety, mystery, and gnosis.

"Piety" dealt with one's place in society. It signified reverence, honor, or esteem, especially in legal or social relationships. Piety was the traditional system of conventional practices that were part of being at home in the world under the rule of a family or the gods. As a category, it bridged the social and religious spheres of life. "Mystery," on the other hand, dealt with ritual practice. It occurred in the classical Greek cults as well as in the newer Eastern religions. From the Greek verb *myeo,* "to shut the eyes or to keep the mouth shut," the "mysteries" suggest an element of fear or danger in the experience of religious awe. Technically, *gnosis* was any teaching in which salvation depended upon knowledge rather than upon ritual practice. We shall see these three categories in evidence in the four families of religions that existed in the Greco-Roman world: Magna Mater religions, mystery religions, emperor worship, and gnosticism.

Magna Mater, or great mother, religions were the first oriental religions to be accepted by Rome. Their roots were very ancient and were usually associated with fertility, dying gods and mourning goddesses. The death of the gods was represented by the decay of vegetation and the gods' return in spring by the return of natural fertility. This return of fertility also represented the soul's immortality. Each goddess mourned her lost spouse and, by her intervention, returned him to life; thus the goddess was more powerful than the god. Because their cults usually ritualized sexual behavior, none of these religions had high standards of morality by monotheistic terms. Examples of Magna Mater religions were the cults of Cybele and Attis, Isis and Osiris, and the Syrian deities Atargatis, Astarte, and Aphrodite.

Mystery religions focused around ritual initiations, with great secrecy surrounding the ceremonies. Entrance into these religions involved intense periods of purification and preparation followed by initiation in a sacred drama. Through acting out the adventures in the life of the gods, the initiate was in spiritual fellowship with them and felt mastery over the twin enemies of the Hellenistic world: fate and death. Feminine images and goddesses also figure highly in mystery religions such as the worship of Dionysus, the Orphic mysteries, and the Eleusinian mysteries.

While influenced by oriental, especially Egyptian, religions in which the king is a god, emperor worship primarily worked toward unity in the empire. The imperial myth involves the idea that a man is commissioned by the gods to overcome the curse of history. He gains power to effect salvation. All of history is concentrated in the emperor, who brings peace and prosperity to the world. The power of this myth can be seen in the Sibylline Oracles, Virgil's Fourth Eclogue, and Horace's *Carmen Saeculare*. The term *son of man* as applied to Jesus has parallels with myths in the imperial cults in which the man of heaven determines the man of earth's fate. It was Roman politicians, however, who encouraged emperor worship for reasons of expediency.

Gnostic religions, too, often involved a redeemer myth. In these systems salvation comes through knowledge of secret lore that leads to mystic contemplations or visions. This self-realized spiritual knowledge was believed to be deeper than that of the intellect or philosophy. Unfortunately, much of what is known of gnosticism comes from second-century church writings, which viewed it as heresy. Whether it originated in a redeemer myth from Iran or from speculative and syncretistic Judaism of the Hellenistic period is an open question.

Mithraism should be mentioned as a hybrid of these four types of religions. It originated in Persia, where Mythra was the god of light. His chariot drawn across the sky brought light and warmth and caused seeds to sprout. All creatures sprang from the bull which Mithras overcame and sacrificed before he granted immortality to those initiated into his mysteries. A follower was "born again" when he passed under a platform and was drenched in the blood of the sacrificed bull it held. Only males were initiated into Mithraism, and it was made an imperial cult at Rome and was tied to astrology. Mithraism displayed many parallels with early Christianity, which was one of its chief rivals.

The Images and Piety
of Hellenistic Religions

Three ideas dominate the thought of Hellenistic religions: fate, wandering, and salvation. The term *fate* is derived from the Greek *meiromai,* "to receive one's portion," which is also the root of the Homeric term *moira,* "lot" or "fate." Classical tragedy had spoken of necessity, the powerful mystery of human life that is contrary to the movement of free choice. The idea was rooted in the Greek Fates, the three maidens who spun out a life thread for each person. What you got was what you got!

By the time of the Hellenistic period, the idea of fate was tied to astrology. There was no room for individual freedom, because astrology delivered one into the hands of fate. The best that one could hope for was to consult the heavens and arrange plans accordingly. No doubt this contributed to the general pessimism of the period.

The images of wandering and of home reflect the movement of religion from the social conventions of the city-state to the individual. (Recall the previous discussion of the shift of worldviews.) This is seen in literature in which characters are depicted as wandering in a greatly expanded world moved by large forces over which they had little control and less understanding. In this situation it is not surprising that the governing metaphor for habitation in the world became aimless wandering. As a result, "home" became an image of religious significance. Home was a sanctuary against evil, both human and spiritual. It was not simply protection from alien forces but a metaphor for existence in harmony with the cosmic order, and probably could be traced to earlier Greek ideas about hearth (*hestia*).

With these two images in mind, we can easily see why salvation was a sought-after commodity. In the Hellenistic world few principles of order existed apart from that of *sōtēr* ("savior"). The Greek world designated extraordinary personalities, divine and human, who were active in world affairs and who transformed situations for the better. (At this point we have a similarity between the imperial cults and the messianic hopes of Judaism.) "Salvation meant transformation."[8]

What did people actually do to practice their religion in the Hellenistic world? In simple terms, they engaged in divination and healing.

Divination was tied to what we would know as astrology. As Hellenism advanced, it met the sciences in Egypt and Babylon. In Alexandria, Greek science made stunning advances. "Astrology, appearing from the beginning as a consistent scientific system, was successful because it provided the framework for a new philosophico-religious interpretation of the world."[9] The most important Roman work on divination is Cicero's *De divinatione*.

Divination assumes a finite and rational cosmos (thus it is not inconsistent with Greek philosophy) in which all things are subject to the same sympathetic forces. Divination was not so much the prediction of the future as the conquest of ignorance concerning the cosmic order. Two forms of divination were practiced: artificial and natural.

In artificial divination, natural processes and patterns were observed and interpreted as signals of cosmic order. Theriomancy (divination by animals), pyromancy (by fire), and hydromancy (by water) were practiced, but astrology was the most characteristic Greco-Roman form of divination, probably because of its "scientific" roots and its consistency with religious internationalism. Alchemy was also practiced.

Under the influence of mental excitement, natural divination purported to provide information about life and the future unaided by reason or deduction. Cledonomancy was divination by observing acts of speech. Interpreters provided the meaning of what was essentially a kind of glossolalia, spontaneous religious utterances. The practice developed in the context of the great Greek oracles, the most famous of which was the Delphic. Natural divination also involved interpreting dreams, because dreams were understood to be beyond rational control of the intellect.

Hellenistic medicine was "holistic," that is, religion and healing went hand in hand. Illness was viewed as the effect of capricious fortune, and one could appeal to the gods for reversals of that fortune. The most pervasive "healing spirituality" was the cult of Asclepius, centered in Epidaurus, but by the fourth century B.C.E. there were more than four hundred sanctuaries throughout the Hellenistic world. The sick were admitted to these sanctuaries for initial purification, sacrifices, divination, and the announcement of cures which sometimes came in dreams or visions.

For those who wish to enter painlessly into the ethos of the Greco-Roman religious world, two fictionalized accounts, one ancient and one modern, give great insight. *Metamorphoses*, better known as *The Golden Ass,* by Lucius Apuleius (ca. 123 C.E.), depicts religious life in the Hellenistic world with erotic exuberance. *The Ides of March,* by Thornton Wilder, is an epistolary novel of our own day which is set in Rome and depicts the prevalence of religious cult in daily life, especially the daily lives of Roman women, whom many scholars consider to have been the mainstays of religion in that period.[10]

Conclusions

This sketch of Judaism and some of the Hellenistic religions can, I hope, give some sense of the emotional climate and pluralistic environment of early Christian spirituality. In the Greco-Roman world, the old gods and their cults included the oracles, Asclepius, the Mysteries (especially at Eleusis and Samothrace), and Dionysus. Among the new, oriental imports were Serapis and Isis from Egypt, Magna Mater and Attis and Sabazius and others. The Roman world not only was open to new religions but had not found answers to the twin problems of fate and death in its known religions and philosophies. As W. D. Davies remarked, Rome was in search of a spiritual foundation for its political unity.

Judaism, on the other hand, labored under Roman occupation. In its recent memory were the triumphs of the Maccabees and the restoration of the kingdom. Its hopes were for a deliverer to restore that kingdom and God's rule. But within Judaism itself, a variety of understandings of the means to that end were espoused.

The religious world of early Christianity was marked by diversity as people sought meaning and salvation. For both Greco-Romans and Jews it was a time of skepticism and pessimism in contradistinction to the confidence of their earlier histories. People did not feel at home in the universe. They sought a sense of belonging in the midst of philosophic and religious syncretism. Christianity and its spiritual life met many of these needs, and this fact helps to explain its popularity and rapid spread.

Select Bibliography for Chapter 2

General Works

Barrett, C. K., ed. *The New Testament Background: Selected Documents*. London: SPCK, 1961.

Bouyer, Louis. *A History of Christian Spirituality*. Vol. 1. New York: Seabury Press, 1963.

Bruce, F. F. *New Testament History*. New York: Doubleday & Co., 1969.

Bultmann, Rudolf. *Primitive Christianity in Its Contemporary Setting*. New York: Meridian Books, 1956.

Gager, J. G. *Kingdom and Community: The Social World of Early Christianity*. Englewood Cliffs, N.J.: Prentice-Hall, 1975.

Hengel, Martin. *Judaism and Hellenism*. Philadelphia: Fortress Press, 1974, 1991.

Kee, Howard Clark. *Christian Origins in Sociological Perspective*. Philadelphia: Westminster Press, 1980.

————. *The New Testament in Context*. Englewood Cliffs, N.J.: Prentice-Hall, 1984.

Koester, Helmut. *Introduction to the New Testament*. Vols. 1 and 2. Philadelphia: Fortress Press, 1982.

Lohse, Eduard. *The New Testament Environment*. Nashville: Abingdon Press, 1986.

Malherbe, Abraham J. *Social Aspects of Early Christianity*. Baton Rouge: Louisiana State University Press, 1977.

McGinn, B., and J. Meyendorff., eds. *Christian Spirituality: Origins to Twelfth Century*. New York: Crossroad, 1985.

Pfeiffer, R. H. *History of New Testament Times*. New York: Harper & Brothers, 1949.

Judaism

Beckwith, Roger T. "The Daily and Weekly Worship of the Primitive Church in Relation to Its Jewish Antecedents." *Evangelical Quarterly* 56 (1984): 65–80, 139–58.

Black, Matthew. *The Scrolls and Christian Origins*. New York: Thomas Nelson & Sons, 1961.

Burns, Sharon. "The Roots of Christian Prayer and Spirituality in Judaism," in *The Journey of Western Spirituality,* ed. A. W. Sadler. Chico, Calif.: Scholars Press, 1981, 29–48.

Cohen, Shaye J. D. *From the Maccabees to the Mishnah*. Philadelphia: Westminster Press, 1987.

Davies, W. D. *Christian Origins and Judaism*. London: Darton, Longman & Todd, 1962.

Fitzmyer, Joseph A. *Essays on the Semitic Background of the New Testament*. Sources for Biblical Study 5. Missoula, Mont.: Society of Biblical Literature, 1974.

Foerster, Werner. *From the Exile to Christ*. Philadelphia: Fortress Press, 1964.

Gavin. F. *The Jewish Antecedents of the Christian Sacraments*. New York: KTAV, 1969.

Gowan, Donald. *Bridge Between the Testaments*. Pittsburgh, Pa.: Pickwick Press, 1976.

Guignebert, Charles. *The Jewish World in the Time of Jesus*. London: Routledge & Kegan Paul, 1951.

Jeremias, Joachim. *Jerusalem in the Time of Jesus*. Philadelphia: Fortress Press, 1969.

Leon, Harry J. *The Jews of Ancient Rome*. Philadelphia: Jewish Publication Society, 1960.

Meek, Theophile J. *Hebrew Origins*. New York: Harper & Brothers, Harper Torchbook, 1960.

Moore, G. F. *Judaism in the First Centuries of the Christian Era*. 3 vols. Cambridge: Harvard University Press, 1950–1954. Vols. 1 and 2.

Osterley, W. O. E. *The Jewish Background of the Christian Liturgy*. Oxford: Clarendon Press, 1925.

Russell, D. S. *Between the Testaments*. Philadelphia: Fortress Press, 1974.

Sandmel, Samuel. *Judaism and Christian Beginnings*. New York: Oxford University Press, 1978.

Safrai, S., and M. Stern eds. *The Jewish People in the First Century*. 2 vols. Philadelphia: Fortress Press, 1974–1976.

Hellenism

Cochrane, C. N. *Christianity and Classical Culture*. New York: Oxford University Press, 1957.

Cumont, Franz. *The Oriental Religions in Roman Paganism*. New York: Dover, 1956.

Festugiere, A. J. *Personal Religion Among the Greeks*. Berkeley and Los Angeles: University of California Press, 1954.

Grant, Frederick C. *Hellenistic Religions: The Age of Syncretism*. New York: Liberal Arts Press, 1953.

Grant, Robert M. *Gods and the One God*. Philadelphia: Westminster Press, 1986.

Guthrie, W. K. C. *The Greeks and Their Gods*. London: Methuen & Co., 1954.

Hatch, Edwin. *The Influence of Greek Ideas on Christianity*. New York: Harper & Brothers, 1957.

Jaeger, Werner. *Early Christianity and Greek Paideia*. Cambridge: Harvard University Press, Belknap Press, 1965.

————. *Paideia: The Ideals of Greek Culture*. Vols. 1, 2, and 3. Oxford: Basil Blackwell, 1954.

Keronyi, C. *The Religion of the Greeks and Romans*. London: Thames and Hudson, 1962.

Marshall, Frank H. *The Religious Background of Early Christianity*. St. Louis: Bethany Press, 1931.

Martin, Luther H. *Hellenistic Religions: An Introduction*. Oxford: Oxford University Press, 1987.

Nilson, Martin. *Greek Folk Religion*. New York: Harper & Row, 1961.

————. *Greek Piety*. Oxford: Clarendon Press, 1948.

————. *A History of Greek Religion*. Oxford: Clarendon Press, 1949.

Nock, A. D. *Early Gentile Christianity and Its Hellenistic Backgrounds*. New York: Harper & Row, 1964.

Reitzenstein, R. *Hellenistic Mystery Religions*. Pittsburgh, Pa.: Pickwick Press, 1978.

Rose, H. J. *Religion in Greece and Rome*. New York: Harper & Brothers, 1959.

Rostovtzeff, M. *The Social and Economic History of the Hellenistic World*. Vols. 1, 2, and 3. Oxford: Clarendon Press, 1941.

3

The Spiritual Life
of the Early Church
in Acts

We have sampled some aspects of the spiritual environment of early Christianity. We turn now to the early church itself, specifically to the spiritual life of the earliest Christian community as Luke has described it. The focus is on the church in Jerusalem as depicted in Acts 1:1—8:3, but references from the early missionary activity to the commissioning of Paul and Barnabas in Acts 13 will be included as well.

The well-known phrase of Pius XI that "spiritually we are all Semites" is perhaps nowhere better demonstrated than in Luke's picture of the spiritual life of the church in Jerusalem in its early days. This is not the place to rehearse the issue of whether or not Luke's information in Acts is "historical," although we shall discuss the issue briefly in chapter 6 below. The writings of earlier scholars such as C. K. Barrett and more recent summary works like those of David Aune and Mark A. Powell have treated these questions.[1]

From a theological perspective it is clear that, for Luke, Christian community is the locus of divine activity; God directs the church as God directed Israel. This understanding will be our starting point.

F. F. Bruce notes that when Luke speaks of "the church" without qualification he refers to the church in Jerusalem; the word is not used of other followers of Jesus until chapter 13 of Acts.[2] Insofar as it received the Spirit then, the church was born at Pentecost, a Jewish festival. As an "organization," the church grew gradually and unself-consciously. In the New Testament we see little evidence of church order until the late letters of Paul and the pseudonymous works of the second century. The word *church* is frequently used to translate the Hebrew *qahal*, a congregation for religious purposes.[3] When Luke speaks of the church in Jerusalem, then, he means the assembly or meeting of the followers of Christ. Their devotion to the Temple and to participation in Jewish

21

piety suggests that, initially at least, they retained status in the Jewish community.

The mood of these believers was one of anticipation; they expected the immediate return of the Christ. In those early days there was apparently little sense that the return would be delayed. Delay, as Hans Conzelmann has argued, is Luke's contribution to the early church's understanding of the parousia. At this initial stage of the Jerusalem church there was no officialdom to sanction leadership and no fixed organizational pattern. "Though indications are given of a small nucleus in the early community which has authority and shapes the group, nevertheless they are not such as to reveal the community as a well-defined organization."[4] The apostles had authority by virtue of their association with Jesus, and it was their teaching that shaped the community. James, the brother of Jesus, and John led the Jerusalem church until their martyrdoms. Peter also seems to have had a special leadership role; all members of the church, however, were apparently on equal footing and spoke freely in their assemblies. There was no authority but that of the Spirit and no creed but "Jesus is Lord."

As Acts depicts it, the spirituality of the early church was not "the flight of the alone to the Alone," but communal: "They all joined together constantly in prayer" (Acts 1:14 NIV). The word *homothymadon* ("with one mind") is a favorite adjective of Luke, who uses it ten times in Acts. Perhaps, as William Neil and others have suggested, the early church followed an Essene model with regard to the communal nature of its spiritual life.[5] Primitive Christian worship was a matter of fellowship in contradistinction to pagan worship of the time, which was often a matter of private practice.[6] "The corporate character of the Jewish Christians is formulated for the first time in the word koinonia (2:42)."[7] We shall examine some of the implications of that term shortly.

Luke provides summaries of the life of the early Christian community in Acts 2:42-47; 4:32-35; and 5:12-16. "The picture of the church in Jerusalem in the first five chapters of Acts is that of a community of enthusiastic followers of Jesus, growing by leaps and bounds, and enjoying the good will of its neighbours."[8] Acts 2:42 gives an outline of the spiritual practices of this church: "They devoted themselves to the apostles' teaching and fellowship, to the breaking of bread and the prayers." It has been noted that the definite articles before the nouns in the Greek suggest that these are semitechnical terms that denote Christian liturgical custom.[9] Whether or not this is the case, the activities described here have Jewish backgrounds,[10] and all are found in the active life and ministry of Jesus to which Luke wishes to draw a parallel. That is, Luke's design in Acts is to show how the early church followed the model of the Lord's life. Carl Holladay has pointed out that this portrait emphasizes aspects of religious community valued in both Jewish and Greco-Roman society, namely, daily devotion, respect in the presence of divine power, internal harmony and community solidarity expressed in concern for each other, and generosity.[11]

Instruction of the Apostles

The "apostles' teachings" seem to have been presented in two basic forms: *kērygma*, preaching or proclamation to those not yet followers of Jesus with the intent of bringing them to belief, and *didachē*, or teaching for those already converted, which was intended to deepen their understanding of what commitment to Jesus meant. Many of the early sermons preached by Peter and Paul as written by Luke in Acts summarize the kerygma. As exemplified by Peter's Pentecost sermon in Acts 2, it had three basic points. First, the Hebrew Scriptures predicted Jesus (Acts 2:16-22), and thus there was continuity with the past. Second, Jesus is the Messiah (Acts 2:22-32), and thus there is a ful-fillment of a long-held expectation. Third, Jesus is exalted and sends the Holy Spirit (Acts 2:33-36), so there is a connection (not yet fully worked out) among Jesus, God, and the Spirit. Such preaching was understood to call for a response: repentance and baptism (Acts 2:38).

Didache, on the other hand, is worked out in Acts in the narrative (e.g., in the instructive story of Ananias and Sapphira in Acts 5) rather than in parenetic sections like those that usually occur in the latter chapters of the letters of Paul.

Unity of the Members

Fellowship not only meant the assembling of believers (as the term is used today) but also in the early days had certain economic implications, as shown in Acts 2:44-45. These two verses occur in the context of Pentecost and the great baptismal act. They describe the inner life of the Christian community: "all who believed," not "all" or even "all who needed."[12] Verse 44 seems intended to recall Acts 1:14 and the one-mindedness of believers.

It is not surprising that the believers held all things in common, as it was another of the customs carried over from the days when Jesus was among them, and Judas kept the common purse (see John 12:16; 13:29). Common ownership and distribution, though of a different kind, were also practiced by the Essenes.[13] The early Christians were, however, in a different psychological state. They awaited the return of Jesus and the fullness of the new age. Because of such expectation, there is in Acts seemingly less concern with daily routine. (Witness how much time was spent in the Temple in prayer.) They felt no need to change or to continue the existing social order. It was soon to come to an end.

The selling and division of property mentioned in Acts was a voluntary expression of *koinōnia*. Peter's comment to Ananias in Acts 5:4 suggests that this giving up of property was not the universal rule. In any case, provision for the poor was a logical end of the Jewish law, which still exerted moral influence on the church in Jerusalem. One theory about the Christian practice is that it was an organized charity in which alms were not given directly to the poor but collected in a basket. No one who had as much as a week's supply of food at home could make a claim on this *kuppah*. Christians simply had an independent collection in which the expenses of life were covered by periodic sale of property, the proceeds of which were distributed.[14] The criterion for receiving help was need, suggesting a supplement to, not a substitution for, individual responsibility. This is probably not a new economic system. Johannes Munck, in fact, suggests that Acts 4:36-37 stresses Barnabas's action because it was the exception rather than the rule.[15] Historically, there might well have been a need for such a "dole" because there occurred a general famine for which Paul collected money from the Greek churches for the Judean believers (see the Corinthian correspondence and Romans).

Acts 4:32-37 reports that the inner life of the Jerusalem church was beginning to be noticed and persecuted by the Temple authorities. Again, the theme of "one heart and soul" appears in connection with communal property. Again, power comes through witness to the resurrection, and grace and favor are upon believers, in part because they fulfill the condition of Deuteronomy 15:4: "There will, however, be no one in need among you, because the Lord is sure to bless you in the land that the Lord your God is giving you as a possession to occupy." When the promise of land was lost, God offered a more universal means of blessing: Jesus Christ, to whom the actions of the early believers bore witness.

As in Acts 2:45, the "sale and distribution" here described was periodic, an expression of gratitude, a response to the gift by God of Jesus. The spiritually needy had been fed by Jesus, and, being fed, they responded in care for others, not as a general welfare program, but as an act of fellowship within the new community that had a share in the life of the Spirit given by God.

It is true, as Kirsopp Lake has pointed out, that "communism" might seem to be a result of Jesus' teaching. But if it was widely practiced, why does it seem to disappear early in Acts and receive no mention in Paul? Lake states, "Luke is not thinking of 'communism' of production or possession."[16] The experiment with this form of distribution of wealth broke down in the community for three reasons. First, dissension grew between Hellenists and Hebrews (see Acts 6). Second, the church quickly grew to an unmanageable size for such distribution, especially when, by missionary action, it moved beyond the confines of the city of Jerusalem. Finally, flight under persecution from Jerusalem (and later the destruction of the city) dispersed those charged with the distribution. Economic fellowship was an important but brief stage in the spirituality of the early church.[17]

The Breaking of Bread

"The breaking of bread" was the Lord's Supper, which has become Christianity's most important act of worship. In chapter 5 I will treat the subject in some detail. The following brief remarks are intended as preface to that discussion.

Breaking bread was a characteristic act of Jesus, the action by which the early church recognized and remembered him (see, e.g., Mark 6:30-44 and parallels; Luke 24:13-35; John 21:13). The actual breaking was so important that the rite went by that name. Early celebrations were probably like the Jewish *chaburah,* fellowship meals of a teacher and his disciples. They were certainly in the context of a real meal (see 1 Cor. 11), part of which was eaten as an act of remembrance of and in thanksgiving for Jesus the Christ. The occasion was probably the evening meal, following the example of Jesus and of Jewish precedent.

In the Jewish community of the early church in Jerusalem, the connection was probably not the blood and death of Jesus but the fact that he appeared to his friends at meals after the resurrection (see Luke 24:36; John 21:12ff.). As Oscar Cullmann suggests, "The first Eucharistic feasts of the community look back to the Easter meals, in which the Messianic meal promised by Jesus at the Last Supper was already partly anticipated."[18] The association with Passover (and passion) came later.[19] The idea of fellowship was realized in the presence of Christ "with them."

When we come to the matter of prayer, we arrive at what many consider the heart of the spiritual life. Scholars have noted that prayer is a special Lukan concern.[20] Then as now, religious groups were distinguished by their manner of prayer. "Teach us how to pray" can be seen as a request for a distinguishing formula.[21] It is clear from the first six chapters of Acts that prayer sets the tone for the Jerusalem congregation. The power of that body of believers came not just from its location near the events of Jesus' passion but from remaining open to that power through prayer. Most of the remainder of this chapter will consider the prayer life of the Jerusalem church, its Jewish backgrounds, its basic attitudes, and the situations in which the church raised its voice in prayer. Chapter 6 will examine in detail a specific example of the prayer of the Jerusalem community. First, however, a brief digression on the terminology for prayer in Acts is in order.

Prayer Life in
the Jerusalem Church

There are eleven principal occurrences of variations of the English word *pray* in Acts 1–10. Two Greek words, *proseuchē* and *deēsis*, the former of which is prevalent, have been translated by the English word *pray*. In Hellenistic Greek, *proseuchē* means "prayer addressed to God" and has the derived meaning of a place set apart for prayer. It sometimes occurs as the equivalent of "synagogue." Luke prefers it in its verbal meaning, "to offer prayer" (see Acts 1:24; 2:42; 3:1; 4:24; 6:4; 9:11; 10:9, 30, 31).

Luke chooses *deēsis* for the Simon story in chapter 8 (Acts 8:22, 24) because it is a strong word implying not just prayer, or even petition, but "entreaty" or "supplication." "The noun and its original verb . . . retain connection with the idea of 'need'; and . . . was thus ready for its special NT use of 'entreaty' towards God."[22] The word *deēsis* may be used of a request to God or humans that expresses personal need, in contrast to *proseuchē*, which connotes devotion and is limited to prayer to God. The Vulgate translates the former by *deprecatio* and the latter by *oratio*. While the distinction is not entirely satisfactory, one might conclude that *deēsis* denotes the imploring of grace for any necessity, while *proseuchē* is used to offer wishes and desires to God. In any case, in Acts, Luke clearly prefers forms of *proseuchē* to denote prayer, thus choosing the term that seems usually to be restricted to sacred use.[23]

The Jewish antecedents of the church's prayer life have been treated in detail, and we shall not cover that ground again here.[24] We simply note the influence of the Temple and Jewish times and forms of prayer. In Acts, Luke reports that "every day they continued to meet together in the temple courts" (2:46, NIV). Early Christians prayed in the Temple where, according to Malachi 3:1, the Messiah would appear.[25] It is interesting that the gentile writer Luke stresses the Temple. "Jesus establishes himself in the temple in order that the early church may also operate from this base. Thereby Luke seeks to show how the new faith in Jesus is the true Israel and the authentic extension of the dominant religious institution of Israel."[26] The reader is to understand that in the church's earliest days the first believers had no wish to break with national worship and venerated the Temple.[27]

Apparently the church also followed the Jewish times of daily prayer: "Peter and John were going up to the temple at the time of prayer" (Acts 3:1, NIV). While the members of the church met daily in Solomon's colonnade on the east side of the Temple, the apostles attended the Temple at customary times of prayer and preached in the outer court as Jesus had done (see Acts 3:1, 11; 5:12-21).[28] The standard pattern of first-century Jewish worship was apparently followed: use of the Shema (see Deut. 6:4-9) twice daily, in the morning and evening, and of the Tephillah (petitionary prayers) three times daily, morning, afternoon, and evening. Based on the regulations of the Mosaic law, Temple worship was primarily sacrificial, and only in the Temple where the daily sacrifices were offered did the Jews of the locality usually pray together.[29] When Luke describes the early Christians as meeting daily at the Temple and at the hours of prayer, the reader is meant to see it as extraordinary piety.

Acts 1–6 also gives many occasions when the early Christians prayed together apart from the Temple (see, for example, Acts 1:24; 4:23-31; 6:1-7). Luke provides an example of the pattern of such prayer in Acts 4:24-30 (see chapter 6 below). Luke uses the prayers in Acts much as he uses the speeches: to emphasize the theological meaning of the history he narrates. This prayer demonstrates both Luke's theological presuppositions and the church's Jewish roots. In good Lukan style, its literary form is apparently taken from 2 Kings 19:15-19 (parallel, Isa. 37:15-20). We see in the text Luke's interest in the Holy Spirit, God's control of history, signs and wonders, and church unity. The prayer's manner of reference to God and messianic allusions are characteristic of first-century Judaism. The episode closes with a theophany reminiscent of the Old Testament. Examination of the text of the prayer shows that it follows many of the fixed forms of prayer in the Jewish tradition.

We have already noted the characteristic attitude in the sense of manner or disposition of the prayer of the Jerusalem church. It is fervent, focused on the power of the Spirit and the parousia, and communal. Luke takes considerable pains to show the unity of the church in all things: "All the believers were one in heart and mind" (Acts 4:32, NIV). The matter of prayer is no exception. At prayer, the Jerusalem church is one-minded (Acts 1:12–14; 4:24).

The characteristic attitude in the sense of bodily posture of prayer of the Jerusalem church is more difficult to discern. Gerhard Delling has noted two characteristic positions of prayer, standing or kneeling (which might include prostration), and notes that the direction of prayer was east, to face the coming Christ.[30] Standing would follow Jewish custom. Standing with the arms outstretched and raised, palms upward, is the position of prayer described by the early church fathers.[31] In catacomb paintings of the early Christians, standing with elevated hands seems to be the posture for prayer. We may assume that the Jerusalem church followed Jewish custom in the matter of prayer position and that several forms were employed and accepted.

In what situations, then, does Luke describe the Jerusalem church at prayer? They pray "constantly" (Acts 1:14; 2:42), when the need to choose leadership arises (Acts 1:24-25; 6:4), to commission those leaders (Acts 6:6), and in times of crisis (Acts 4:23-31).

We have already noted the constancy of the early Christians' prayers. Christians gathered in the Temple in accordance with Jewish custom and met in private homes for the specifically Christian side of their worship. No doubt the question of leadership arose in this latter context. When Luke describes the selection of Matthias (Acts 1:12-26) as directed by prayer (Acts 1:24-25), he expects us to remember that Jesus was at prayer before selecting the original Twelve (Luke 6:12-13). The church is following the Lord's example. The word *kardiognōstēs* ("heart knower") in v. 24 is suggestive, since elsewhere it occurs chiefly in Christian liturgical literature.[32] Whether or not the prayer follows some set formula, it is addressed to the "Lord" (*kyrios*, from the Greek text), which refers either to God or to Jesus, who was called "Our Lord," *maran*, by many in the primitive church.[33] Luke may include the story of the selection of Matthias to indicate that the infant church had the power both of organization and of continuance.[34] Certainly it gives an opportunity to provide one definition of "apostle" (Acts 1:21-22) and thus is linked to Acts 6:1-6, in which leadership roles are further delineated.

There is no indication of how much time has elapsed between Acts 5 and 6, but it was long enough for two groups of believers to have developed, the original followers and those of Hellenistic cultural heritage. There was time also for the church to have grown sufficiently to diversify its ministry to include two spheres of activity, one of preaching and teaching, and one of administration or of "practical benevolence."[35] It is noteworthy that the Twelve have authority to call together all the disciples and that they understand that a special responsibility of their leadership is to have time for prayer.

Both the calling and the commissioning of leaders in the Jerusalem church began with prayer. The disciples presented their choices to the apostles, "who prayed and laid their hands on them" (Acts 6:6). As in Acts 13:1-3 (to which this passage is parallel in the selection and commissioning of leadership), prayer and the laying on of hands invests the recipient with a particular authority or communicates some power that the agent in laying on of hands possesses. In Acts it is inevitably associated with the gift of the Holy Spirit (Acts 8:17; 19:6), but here, since they already have the Spirit, the seven Greek "deacons" receive special status,[36] or are set apart for a special ministry.

Laying on of hands, not surprisingly, has Jewish roots. In Numbers 8:10 it is used in the mass commissioning of officers. Termed the *seminkha* (from "laying on," *samakh*), laying on of hands was used at the ordination of a rabbi and implied the passing of power, physical or spiritual, from one person to another.[37] According to the Mishnah, members of the Sanhedrin were also admitted to that body by the laying on of hands. So the early church is again following the spiritual precedents of Judaism.

Prayer in the selection and setting apart for service of leaders is prayer that occurred in a "normal, ecclesiological" setting. The early church also had ample opportunity for prayer in crisis. Acts 4:23-31 provides an example of this. The pericope concludes the narrative of Peter and John's encounter at the Beautiful Gate, their arrest, cross-examination, and release by the Sanhedrin (Acts 3:1—4:22). Whether or not Acts 3 and 4 are taken from an earlier source than Acts 2 and are another account of how the disciples received the Holy Spirit will not concern us here. What is most interesting in terms of the spirituality of the church is the substance of the prayer itself. (Full exposition will be given in chapter 6 below.)

Having been commanded by the Sanhedrin to stop speaking or teaching in the name of Jesus (Acts 4:18), Peter and John are released and immediately return to "their own people" (Acts 4:23, NIV). (They knew exactly where they would be found. Perhaps they were in the upper room of 1:13 praying for the release of the brothers.) The reunited believers turn to God in prayer, not for deliverance from trial, but for the ability "to speak your word with great boldness" and "to heal and perform miraculous signs and wonders through the name of your holy servant Jesus" (Acts 4:29-30, NIV).

The text of the prayer (Acts 4:24-30) suggests that Psalm 2:2, which is quoted in vv. 25-26, has been fulfilled in Jesus' passion, in which Gentiles, Jews, kings (Herod Antipas), and rulers (Pilate) had opposed Jesus. The Christians now face the same situation as had Jesus when threatened by the authorities.[38] The primary subject of the prayer is God, who, as sovereign, foretold these events. Thus the "enemy action" against Jesus is under God's control. The church is reassured that its experience is analogous to that of Jesus, and it can expect to be vindicated by God.[39] The earthquake in v. 31 is certainly to be seen as a mark of supernatural assent to prayer and also, perhaps, as a renewal of the church's Pentecostal experience. The imperfect indicative *elaloun* ("spoke") indicates that they went on preaching without regard to the threats made against them.

The spiritual message of the text is clear: the church cannot expect to be exempt from the trials its Lord faced. But God is sovereign and will direct and empower the church as Jesus was directed and empowered. The vehicle of communication and empowerment is to be prayer.

Fasting, Singing, and Devotion
to the Name

Alongside of the four spiritual activities that Acts 2:42 mentions as habitual for the early church, we should note three other aspects of spiritual practice: fasting, singing of hymns, and devotion to the name of Jesus.

Fasting was almost certainly practiced by the church in Jerusalem. The first mention of it, however, occurs in connection with the commissioning of Barnabas and Paul (13:2, 3) and with the elders in congregations established by them on their first missionary journey (14:23). Again, fasting in the New Testament church seems to have had its antecedents in Judaism, although it was practiced in other ancient religions for a variety of reasons (including as a way to prepare for intercourse with the deity).

Definite references to fasting before the exile are not numerous, but thereafter public fasts were called (see Zech. 7:3, 5; 8:19), the most prominent of which was the Day of Atonement (see Lev. 16:29, 31; Num. 29:7). Private fasting in Judaism was usually associated with mourning, penitence, or urgent supplication. Fasting held so high a place in Jewish practice at the time of the New Testament that, for Gentiles, it was one of the marks of a Jew.[40] It was, as well, characteristic of the piety of the disciples of John the Baptist.

Jesus seems to have taken fasting for granted as a pious practice, but he insisted it be done in sincerity and for the glory of God, not for the purpose of being admired by other persons as "deeply religious" (see Matt. 6:16-18). Apparently, for Jesus, the worth of fasting rested in the disposition of the heart. He laid down few specific regulations for fasting, although he, himself, fasted and probably kept the fasts of Judaism.[41] Johannes Behm argued that Jesus' wilderness fast equipped him to confirm the messianic dignity and power, and was not for penitential reasons.[42] Jesus' disciples apparently did not fast until after his departure from them, because fasting marked sorrowful occasions, and Jesus' presence was a source of joy. After Jesus' death and ascension, the circumstances of his disciples were again anticipatory; vigilance, therefore, marked by fasting, was again in order.

Outside the Gospels, the only clear New Testament references to fasting as a specifically religious practice are the two in Acts, mentioned above. Both occur in the context of solemn prayer and commissioning for service and mark serious preparation for spiritual responsibility. From Acts, one might conclude that the early church did not fast regularly, but references to fasting in the Gospels suggest otherwise,[43] as does the *Didache*, which enjoins fasting on Wednesdays and Fridays (in contradistinction to the Jewish community, which fasted on Mondays and Thursdays).[44]

The reference in Acts 2:47 to "praising God" is sometimes taken to refer to the singing of hymns. The earliest clear reference to the practice in Acts, however, is at 16:25, where Paul and Silas sing while imprisoned in Philippi. In any case, the use of hymns was apparently widespread in early Christianity, as the letters of Paul and the Revelation to John attest. Once again, early Christianity received from Judaism the use of hymns and religious songs for public and private devotion. The songs are of several types: baptismal hymns, creedal or confessional songs, and paraphrases from the psalms and earlier literature. Not only of devotional value, metrical hymns were excellent for catechetical purposes because they were easy to remember.[45]

Hymns of the early church reflected not only its beliefs but how it worshiped. Unfortunately there is virtually no clear and unambiguous quotation of hymns in the New Testament outside the Revelation to John (Rev. 5:9-10; 15:3-4), although both Colossians and Ephesians refer to the singing of hymns and seem to contain poetic material. Eduard Norden has suggested that fragments of New Testament hymns share common formal elements with Hellenistic hymnody,[46] and Leonard Thompson has argued that in the hymnic material in the New Testament, christological themes predominate.[47] What is evident is that the early Christians sang hymns to God as part of their worship.

Finally, it is clear from the early chapters of Acts that the church had a special devotion to the name of Jesus as a source of knowledge, protection, and power. The next chapter presents an extended study of "The Name."

Conclusion

The spiritual life of the early church as it is depicted by Luke in the early chapters of Acts may well be idealized (although, as chapter 6 below will suggest, not all scholars agree on this point). Be that as it may, the customs of these early Christians would have caused little surprise in the larger Jewish community of their time. Their spirituality was characterized by the instruction given by the apostles who had known Jesus, by the unity of the members and their charity to one another, by the breaking of bread in fellowship meals, and by prayer both in the Temple and in their own meetings. The rapid increase of the fellowship as described by Luke is certainly intended to indicate the favor in which the early church was held both by God and by its society. Luke indicates that they enjoyed "the favor of all the people" (Acts 2:47, NIV) and that "they were highly regarded by the people" (Acts 5:13, NIV). The view of official Judaism, as we know, is depicted somewhat differently, probably for reasons of Luke's appeal to his Hellenistic audience.

The early Christians had a quality of life that others both noticed and wanted to share. That "quality" arose from their spiritual life, a life begun and nourished in prayer. "Prayer marks not only the ministry of Jesus and his first disciples, but also every stage in the outreach of the gospel to the Gentile world. It is one of the principal methods by which God has taught and strengthened his people, empowering them by his Spirit for service and ministry in the world."[48] Accordingly, we shall return later in this study to the matter of prayer in Acts and in the letter to the Ephesians.

4

"The Name"
in Acts 1–10

Even a cursory reading of Acts 1–10 reveals the prevalence of the phrases "in the name" and "the name of Jesus Christ." The frequency alone (about twenty significant references) suggests the importance of the name of Jesus. The use the early church made of the name of Jesus provides us with a specific example of the spirituality of that church as Luke understood it.

Again, scholarship suggests that Luke may not be used uncritically as a source of historical information about the church in Jerusalem.[1] The questions governing this inquiry may, however, be framed in such a way that the Lukan material can be taken with appropriate seriousness. Two questions suggest themselves. First, why did Luke as a writer make extensive reference to the name, and, second, what did the early church mean by its use of the name?

Uses of the Term in Acts 1–10

In Acts 1–10, the phrase "in the name," referring to the name of Jesus, occurs in eight contexts. The occurrences are grouped by frequency of use as follows:

1. To speak or teach in the name (of Jesus) or to invoke the name (4:17, 18; 5:28, 42; 9:28, 29—six occurrences);
2. To heal by the power of the name (3:6, 16; 4:7, 10, 30—five occurrences);
3. To be baptized in the name (2:38; 8:16; 10:46—three occurrences);
4. The name as a means of awakening faith, as a means of salvation, and as a means of forgiveness of sin (2:21; 4:12; 10:43—three occurrences);
5. The name as a synonym for Christians (9:14, 21—twice);
6. The name as the substance of the preaching of Philip (8:12);
7. The name as the cause of persecution (5:42);
8. The name in a quotation from Joel (2:21).

Luke understood "the name" to be of crucial significance to the early Christians. In his writing in Acts it is depicted as the substance of their proclamation, the source of their power, the ownership by which they were claimed in baptism, the means of their forgiveness and salvation, and the reason for which they were persecuted. It was, in fact, the name of Jesus that the opponents of the Way seemed to fear. It is the main bone of contention in the early conflicts with religious authority in Jerusalem that Luke describes.

Consistent with most of the material in the early chapters of Acts, "the name" appears there primarily in connection with the Petrine ministry (the Pentecost sermon, the healing of the lame man and subsequent interrogations by the Sanhedrin, and the mission to Cornelius), but it is foundational in Philip's mission to Samaria and figures in the story of Saul's conversion as he went from being a persecutor of those who invoked the name (9:21) to one who spoke boldly in it himself (9:28-29).

In these various accounts, the Greek prepositions chosen by Luke— *epi, en, hyper, eis,* and *dia*—are all translated into English by "in." I have been unable to observe any correspondence between the contextual occurrence of the phrase "in the name" and the Greek preposition chosen. For example, the Greek of the expression to be baptized "in the name" variously employs the prepositions *epi, eis,* and *en.* A student of Greek recognizes the different shades of meaning expressed by prepositions in various cases, but the student is not at an advantage here, because Luke apparently does not give us consistent theological information by the use of the prepositions connected with "the name." That is, no consistent use of a particular Greek preposition with a particular use of "the name" (for example, as a means of salvation or in the context of a healing) can be discerned.

Moreover, to complicate matters, various textual traditions prefer different prepositions. For example, in 2:38 the preposition is variously *epi* and *en.* We should be wary, then, of placing too much significance on linguistic formulations. If one wishes to make use of this information, it is best done in connection with individual verses in which the text is free, or relatively free, of variant readings. (This procedure is carried out in the material that follows.)

Naming in the Ancient World

A great deal of scholarly material is available on naming in the ancient world.[2] The following brief review of that material provides a framework in which to view the use of the name in Acts.

For the ancients (and in many traditional religions today), names were more than labels of identification; they were expressions of the essential nature of the bearer, indispensable parts of personality.[3] Most ancient Semitic names had understandable meanings. Children's names, for example, often expressed the parents' recognition of divine assistance (as in Nathanael, "God has given") or the circumstances of the birth (as in Isaac, "he laughs"). As in the first instance, names themselves give cultural clues about which deities were important in which societies, and they serve as a guide to the qualities associated with those deities.[4]

The name denoted the character, fame, and authority of the one indicated.[5] As Johannes Pedersen puts it, "The soul in its entirety . . . finds expression in the name, *shēm*."[6] Furthermore, on the level of spiritual experience, G. van der Leeuw suggests that humans limit experiences of power by giving them names. In the name, the power is experienced. "It is, then, the name that makes the actual 'special god.' "[7]

This observation is borne out by the important value given to the name of God by the Hebrews. In Hebrew Scripture, God reveals God's self by the disclosing of a name. "Moses said to God, 'If I come to the Israelites and say to them, "The God of your ancestors has sent me to you," and they ask me, "What is his name?" what shall I say to them?' God said to Moses, 'I AM WHO I AM.' He said further, 'Thus you shall say to the Israelites, "I AM has sent me to you" ' " (Exod. 3:13-14). The name of God is not an instrument of magic (more about this later) but a gift of revelation and relationship.[8] To know a name of God is to be granted fellowship with God. In the works of the Deuteronomist the *shēm* concept answers the question of how Israel may be sure of the presence of its God. Israel can commune with God because God will choose a place and cause God's name to dwell there.[9] God declares, "In every place where I cause my name to be remembered I will come to you and bless you" (Exod. 20:24).

It is a relatively small step to the hypostatization (the "making substantive") of the *shēm*. Shem becomes a transcendent entity at work in the world. The name of God itself carried the creative power and activity of God. "Pronouncement or invocation of the name sets in operation the energy potentially contained in him."[10] The postexilic tendency to heighten the sense of God's transcendence results in the name becoming an almost independent force. Already this is reflected in Jeremiah: "There is none like you, O Lord; you are great, and your name is great in might" (Jer. 10:6). Belief in the wonder-working power of the name of God is evident at many points in the Jewish tradition, but especially in later Judaism, which was influenced by contact with Hellenism.[11]

In the Greek world, then, "name" is also used in the sense of "repute." The Greeks sought to learn the nature and essence of the gods from their names. Like the ancient Semitic religions, Roman religion emphasized the names of gods. Deities who would otherwise remain disembodied, pure abstractions, were personalized by naming, which is evidenced by the great number of divine names in Roman religion.

We also see this tendency to proliferate the names of gods in the magical papyri. Those "who practiced magic were willing to adopt from any source names and formulas which sounded impressive and effective."[12] Notice the number of names used in this selection from an exorcism "for those possessed by daemons."

> Take oil made from unripe olives, together with the plant mastigia and lotus pith, and boil it with marjoram (very colourless), saying: "Joel, Ossarthiomi, Emori, Theochipsoith, Sithemeoch, Sothe, Joe, Mimipsothiooph, Phersothi, Aeeioyo, Joe, Eochariphtha: come out of such an one (and the other usual formulae)."

> But write this phylactery upon a little sheet of tin: "Jaeo, Abraothioch, Phtha, Mesentiniao, Pheoch, Jaeo, Charsoc," and hang it round the sufferer: it is of every demon a thing to be trembled at, which he fears. Standing opposite, adjure him. The adjuration is this: "I adjure thee by the god of the Hebrews Jesu, Jaba, Jae, Abraoth, Aia, Thoth, Ele, Elo, Aeo, Eu, Jiibaech, Abarmas, Jabarau, Abelbel, Lona, Abra, Maroia, Arm, thou that appearest in fire, thou that art in the midst of earth and snow and vapour, Tannetis: let thy angel descend, the implacable one, and let him draw into captivity the daemon as he flieth around this creature which God formed in his holy paradise."[13]

The repetition of a number of gods' names and the use of many words in general were rejected by Christian teaching and, for example, are criticized by Jesus in Matthew's Gospel when he says, "And when you pray, do not keep on babbling like pagans, for they think they will be heard because of their many words" (Matt. 6:7, NIV).

Greco-Roman thought, then, shared with Semitic the belief in the significance of the name, but it went on to raise the philosophical question of whether human speech and its names for things is a true reflection of reality (see, e.g., the Dialogues of Plato).[14]

The names of gods and magical incantations are often connected in Hellenistic religion. As the previous example demonstrates, the magical papyri are full of expressions that show belief in the power and efficacy of names. As in Semitic traditions, knowledge of names gives power over their bearers. If a person asks for something in the name of the deity, it will be fulfilled because the asker knows the god's name.[15]

Use of "the name" as it is reflected in Acts is derived to some degree from both the Hellenistic and Semitic traditions. In both, a name is essential to a person, a connection to the power and authority of the one named. The New Testament does not view the name as a theurgic formula or magical incantation, however, as Acts 19 illustrates.[16] In that account, in Ephesus when the sons of Sceva (who were not followers of Jesus) tried to use the name of Jesus in an exorcism, "the man with the evil spirit leaped on them, mastered them all, and so overpowered them that they fled out of the house naked and wounded" (Acts 19:16). Luke begins the pericope (Acts 19:11-20) with the remark, "God did extraordinary miracles through Paul " (19:11) to make the point clear that God is the one who acts.

In the New Testament, power and name are parallel concepts. As the words of Peter in Acts 9:34 ("Aeneas, Jesus Christ heals you") demonstrate, it is not magical formulas that heal, but Jesus himself. The name of Jesus shows its power only where one joins Jesus in faith and obedience. (Compare these accounts in Acts with Mark 9:38-41.) "Healing does not take place by pronouncing a set formula, but through the Lord in answer to the prayer which calls upon Him in faith."[17]

"The Name" in Acts 1-10

With this general material as background, let us turn to the text of Acts and examine four uses of the name: the Joel quotation, being baptized in the name, healing by the power of the name, and speaking in the name.

The first use of "the name of the Lord" occurs in Acts 2:21, in the quotation from Joel that is chosen for Peter as the text for his Pentecost sermon (see Joel 2:28-32). Here "the name" refers to God. In Joel, the text occurs in a section in which a plague of locusts is understood as God's judgment on Israel. The prophet offers a cry of alarm (Joel 2:1), a call for repentance (Joel 2:15-17), and an announcement of God's recompense and mercy after judgment (Joel 2:18-32 and continuing into Joel 3). On the "day of the Lord," which is described in Joel 2:30-31 in vivid, apocalyptic imagery, those who worship God, who call upon God's name, will be saved (Joel 2:32). In Joel, God's name is "the guarantee of his will to save; to it and it only Israel has to hold fast."[18]

The quotation from Joel in Acts 2:21 is, in a sense, programmatic for the use of the name in the next ten chapters of Acts. By the words and actions that Luke uses to report of him, Peter is depicted as viewing his own time as "the last days." To call upon the name of God in this time is to invoke God's presence, protection, and power. In Peter's thought, insofar as it is represented in Acts, salvation, rescue, and deliverance can be had only in God's name: "There is salvation in no one else, for there is no other name under heaven given among mortals by which we must be saved" (Acts 4:12).

God's name functions as God's power. Those who invoke the name, invoke the power of God, the power that raised Jesus from the dead. Insofar as the connection between God and Jesus the Christ were made at this point, the name of Jesus would carry the same weight to believers as the name of God. It is doubtful that the christological questions of the great councils are in evidence here. The connection between God's salvation and the Son is alluded to in *Enoch* 48:7, however, which says of the Son of man, "In his name they are saved." Bearing in mind that "to save" and "to heal" can be the same word in Greek, we see in subsequent occurrences of the name in Acts 1–10 specific instances of the Name's ability to effect healing and salvation.

At the end of the Pentecost sermon, Peter explains that to have salvation and deliverance one must be "baptized . . . in the name of Jesus Christ" (Acts 2:38). In Acts 8:16 the Samaritans as well are "baptized in the name of the Lord Jesus," as were Cornelius and his household (Acts 10:48). These three references to baptism in the name serve to summarize Luke's understanding of the spread of the church. From Jewish Jerusalem the message was carried into "half-breed" Samaria, and finally to the gentile "ends of the earth" (see Acts 1:8).

Some commentators think that "baptized in the name of the Lord Jesus" in 8:16, which is paralleled in 10:48 and 19:5, is the oldest baptismal formula of the church, and only later was it replaced by the trinitarian formula of Matthew 28:19.[19] In 8:16 one is baptized *eis to onoma* ("into the name"). The same phrase is frequent in the papyri with reference to payments made to the account of someone. Thus its meaning would seem to be "baptized into the possession of."[20] The expression is common in the commercial context in usages where some property is transferred "into the name" of some person or account. The person baptized into Christ, then, "bears public testimony that he has become Christ's property."[21] As in 1 Corinthians 1:13-15, "the intimate relation between soul and property is expressed by its being called after the name of the owner."[22] As Jesus' possessions, those baptized in his name became his servants, those who could be sent out to do his bidding by means of the authority that his name conferred.[23]

When the disciples were sent out in Luke, they were charged, in part, with the ministry of healing. Most of the occurrences of healing in the name in Acts 1–10 occur in the context of Peter and John's healing of the lame man at the Beautiful Gate and their subsequent conflicts with the Temple authorities as a result of that healing (see 3:6, 16; 4:7, 10-11, 30). Three of the five instances (3:3; 4:7, 10) use the preposition *en* with the dative. In the New Testament, *en* with the dative may express instrument, that is, the sense "by the power and/or authority of."[24] "The most general meaning of *en (tō) onomati* is 'with invocation of.' . . . He who says or does something in the name of someone appeals to this one, claims his authority."[25] (See, e.g., this dramatic usage in 1 Sam. 17:45, where David announces to Goliath, "You come to me with sword and spear and javelin; but I come to you in the name of the Lord of hosts.")

The use of the name in religious formulas and practices springs, as we noted above, from identification of the name with the god to whom it belongs and the belief that the qualities and powers of that god are inherent in the god's name. By invoking the name, the power and authority are called into operation.[26] For example, in Josephus's *Antiquities of the Jews* (18.2.5), Eleazar heals demoniacs by drawing the devil out through their noses using a ring, an herb, and Solomon's name.

Recall that in Luke's Gospel when Jesus sends forth the disciples, "the power which he gives them is exercised through the use of his name."[27] When they return from their mission, the seventy report that in Jesus' name "even the demons submit to us!" (Luke 10:17). In Mark 9:38-41 there is a discussion of exorcism in the name of Jesus, and Matthew 7:22 speaks of doing deeds of power in Jesus' name.

In Acts, by healing with the power and authority of Jesus, Peter and John are doing what they earlier were commissioned by Jesus to do. As Acts 3:16 makes clear, the lame person is cured, not by the magic power of the name, but through his faith in the power of Jesus.[28] Jesus' name, in effect, makes Jesus present in action (which, incidentally, provided the early Jewish-Christian community with another reason for taking seriously the command not to take the Lord's name in vain). To act in one's name is "the same as if the person in question had done it himself."[29] Peter and John bring Jesus to bear on the lame man. The name of Jesus made manifest the power of Jesus. Luke gives an example in Peter and John of exactly what the psalmist had asserted when he wrote, "He saved them for his name's sake, so that he might make known his mighty power" (Ps. 106:8). This use of "the name of" to equal "the power of" is very Jewish and certainly serves Luke's design to tie the early church with its Jewish antecedents.

As the disciples attributed their power to God working through them as they restored persons to wholeness in the name of Jesus,[30] they attributed to the same source their authority to speak (Acts 4:10, 30; 5:28-29). To speak in someone's name, as the disciples are charged with doing in 4:17, 18; 5:28, 41; and 9:28, is to act as representative of that person and to participate in his authority. The precedents for this in Hebrew Scripture are numerous (see, e.g., 1 Sam. 25:5). No doubt this is why in Acts 1–10 the context of speaking the name is often that of conflict with the Jewish authorities: the name of Jesus represents an authority they did not sanction.

When the disciples teach in the name of Jesus, they are teaching with his authority. In the Synoptic tradition the disciples are told that they will face persecution for just this activity (see Luke 6:22-23 and Matt. 10:22a). Speaking in the name is the cause of persecution of the Christians, because it represented an authority not recognized or conferred by the religious establishment in Jerusalem. In three of the five instances when they are charged not to speak in the name (Acts 4:17, 18; 5:29), the preposition chosen by Luke is *epi* with the dative, implying "on account of" and "with the authority of." In these contexts, too, the personal name is avoided and speech about Jesus is indirect, as is frequently the case in later Jewish references to him.[31]

To describe the disciples as being charged by the Jewish officials not to speak in the name suits Luke's purposes. It is a way he can address another of his aims, namely, to demonstrate that Christianity's conflicts were with Judaism and not with Roman officialdom and the gentile world from which the majority of his audience was probably drawn. In Luke's mind the name of Jesus was both the reason why the Christians were persecuted and the source of their protection and power under persecution.

Conclusion

We are now in a position to answer the two questions with which this chapter began.

Why did Luke as a writer and theologian make such extensive use of the name of Jesus? First, it provided him with an important link to both the Hebrew and Hellenistic worlds. Recent scholarship on Luke has noted the "Jewishness" of his backgrounds.[32] Study of the name in Acts bears out this assertion. Use of the name in Acts 1–10 shows continuity with contemporary Jewish understanding of the name of God and also provides links to the practice of Hellenistic religions (even if those practices were now forbidden to Christians).

Second, the name ties Acts to the Jesus traditions of the Synoptic Gospels. Jesus shared his power and authority by giving his disciples his name, and he foresaw that because of its use, they would be persecuted. We observe the fulfillment of the acts and predictions of Jesus in the Acts of the Apostles; it is theologically of a piece with the Gospel of Luke.

Third, the name furthers the apologetic appeal that Luke is making to his gentile audience. Through its use he can show how Christianity's early conflicts were with Judaism, not with Rome. Perhaps the suggestion is too speculative, but it may be that the name also provides a link with Pauline traditions, especially in connection with baptism in the Corinthian correspondence. If it could be demonstrated that Luke was an associate of Paul's, and if Luke did write from Corinth, then use of the name could be explored in Lukan/Pauline theology. But such speculations are outside the scope of this work.

Finally, then, Luke used the name because the early church used the name. That is, in Acts, Luke is reflecting a historical reality in the life of the early church.

This brings us to the second question: What did the early church mean by its use of the name? Whether chosen by Peter or by Luke, the quotation from Joel set the terms of the engagement. At an early stage of the church the name of Jesus was a source of its salvation and thus its authority and power. In Acts 1–10 Peter, John, Philip, Paul, and others are shown doing what Jesus did, and what he had charged them to do, by means of the name.

The disciples would certainly have been aware of the tradition of the name as it was used of Yahweh's self-manifestation, to designate God's ineffable reality, the power by which God accomplished God's work, and as the place where God "dwells."[33] Thus, in very real terms, the name was a means by which the risen Jesus remained with them. "As name and renown belong together, so do also life and memory. He who lives acts upon other souls; as long as he acts, he is not dead."[34]

To call upon the name of Jesus, however, was to acknowledge Jesus as alive and potent.

It would significantly increase the subtlety of this point if it were possible to connect Matthew's quotation that Mary's son was called Jesus, "Emmanuel, which means 'God with us' " (Matt. 1:23), to the accounts in Acts (cf. Heb. 1:4; Eph. 1:21). But the name "Jesus" is itself evocative. "Jesus" is the Greek form of the Hebrew "Joshua" or "Yehoshuah," which means "YHWH is salvation" or "YHWH saves" or "YHWH will save."[35] The etymological meaning of the name of Jesus reflects its agency. As far as the early Christians were concerned, what it said, it did. The unity of name and nature reflected in the Johannine writings ("the Word was God," for example) is, to some degree, also evident in Acts. At an early stage of the church's life the name of Jesus not only "embraces the whole content of the saving acts revealed in Jesus, but it makes them present again to the community."[36] For the early church, the name of Jesus literally represented the Christ. It set forth his identity, revealed his essence, and continued his function in the world. This is why the name of Jesus was used extensively in the early church and continues to be used as a special form of prayer in many Christian communities, especially in the Orthodox tradition.[37]

Finally, the use of the name of Jesus in Acts 1–10 sets us out on the path that did, eventually, result in the Christology of Nicaea and Chalcedon because the name "seems to designate Christ's divine nature, that which He has in common with the Father and the Holy Ghost."[38] Furthermore, from an embodiment of the presence and power of the risen Lord as understood in a Jewish environment, the name of Jesus reflected the spread of Christianity into the Hellenistic world where Greek and Latin proper names included two words.[39] Jesus from Nazareth became Jesus Christ: "God saves" and "anointed." But that move into systematic Christology goes beyond the use of the name in Acts and our focus on its meaning with regard to early Christian spirituality.

5

The Breaking
of Bread

No act of our worship is more distinctively Christian than the breaking of bread—the Eucharist or the Lord's Supper, as it is variously called. Perhaps no Christian institution is more difficult to write about, in part because it has been so extensively treated by ecclesiastics and scholars and in part because the Christian writer is so conditioned by the traditions and doctrines of his or her own particular branch of Christendom. It may not be possible objectively to answer the questions: What did the early church do in its celebration of the breaking of the bread, and what did it understand the meaning of those actions to be?

Nevertheless, this chapter proposes, first, to review some information that can be gleaned from the oldest New Testament text that discusses the Eucharist directly (making no pretense of contributing new information), and, second, to suggest three avenues of approach to the meaning of the ordinance for the early Christians: that of ritual action, of table fellowship, and of the understanding of time presented in the act itself.

The most important texts of the New Testament for a study of the Lord's Supper occur in the Synoptic Gospels (Matt. 26:26-29; Mark 14:22-25; Luke 22:15-20) and in 1 Corinthians 11:23-25.[1] The Gospel of John is theologically important to our understanding of the Lord's Supper but does not record its institution. Significant texts on the subject would include John 2:1-11; 6; 13:1-20; 13:31—17:26, and 19:34. Paul's account, probably written not later than the early 50s, provides the oldest literary record, although some scholars have suggested that Mark with its Aramaisms may contain the more primitive account.[2] The Synoptics identify the Last Supper as a Passover meal, but, again, there is debate on this point.[3] In that meal, Jesus broke the bread and handled the cup differently from what was the custom. His actions in the Synoptics are understood as part of the passion narrative, and their meaning is projected in the direction of the passion in all three accounts. (More on this shortly.)

In the discussion that follows, I have chosen the Pauline text 1 Corinthians 11:23-26 to exemplify the events that took place when the early church broke bread.

> For I received from the Lord what I also handed on to you, that the Lord Jesus on the night when he was betrayed took a loaf of bread, and when he had given thanks, he broke it and said, "This is my body that is for you. Do this in remembrance of me." In the same way he took the cup also, after supper, saying, "This cup is the new covenant in my blood. Do this, as often as you drink it, in remembrance of me." For as often as you eat this bread and drink the cup, you proclaim the Lord's death until he comes.

This text occurs in the section of the letter that deals with worship in general, and, specifically, it occurs in the context of abuses of the Lord's Supper. The details of the abuses are found in 1 Corinthians 11:17-22. Paul records the formulas concerning bread and wine and an eschatological saying in 11:23-26, and he suggests correctives to the abuses in 11:27-34.

We begin by noting that Paul did not make up the account. Like the Gospel writers, he had sources: information gleaned from the other apostles on his Jerusalem visits, contact with other missionaries, knowledge of Hebrew Scripture, and perhaps even direct revelation from Jesus ("I received from the Lord"). The phrase "For I received from the Lord what I also handed on to you" contains technical terms for transmitting tradition. Describing this process, Paul begins with the verb *paralambanō*, which means "receive" and corresponds to the term in rabbinic literature, *qibbel*, to receive tradition that has been passed on. Paul then employs the verb *paradidōmi*, which means "to pass on," "to hand down." "The word corresponds to the rabbinical technical term *masar* indicating the passing down of tradition. The words mean the chain of historical tradition that Paul received goes back unbroken to the words of Jesus Himself."[4] In the Pauline corpus this tradition includes both doctrinal and ethical materials, and "it always issues from 'the Lord' who authorizes it."[5] With this in mind, what does the text itself tell us about the Lord's Supper?

First, in Paul's day, the Lord's Supper still occurred as part of a full meal. Since the Jews had their main meal of the day in the evening, and Greeks and Romans in the afternoon or evening, it was natural for the meal to be carried out in the evening, as it had been at its institution.

Luke's account in Acts 20:7 corroborates the practice. There, "on the first day of the week" the Christians "met to break bread," and Paul's discussion with them "continued . . . until midnight" (see Acts 20:11).

The word for the bread that Jesus took and broke, *artos* in Greek, means simply "bread" or "loaf." It is the common and only word for bread. Greek has a special word for the unleavened bread used in Passover, *azyma*. Whatever the loaf was, it was large enough to be broken and divided among those present.

To "give thanks" (*eucharistein*) originally meant to "do a good turn to"; later, "to oblige"; and in late Greek, "be thankful." To "give thanks to god" is a common formula in votive inscriptions and recalls Paul's frequent use of "I give thanks to my God." It is a term associated with liturgical usage in 1 *Clement* 38.2; Ignatius's *Epistle to the Ephesians* 21.1; and the *Didache* 9. Paul's account of the Lord's Supper reports what was delivered to him, so he reports what Jesus "said." This accounts for the aorist form of the verb *take* in the Greek text.

In considering what is reported as the interpretation of the blessed and broken bread in v. 24, one must treat the verb *is* with special caution. The language that Jesus spoke was probably not Greek but Aramaic, so the "is" would not have been expressed. This would also be the case if Jesus spoke the blessing in Hebrew, since Hebrew does not require the use of the verb "to be." The point is that, in English, "is" frequently functions as an equals mark, implying "means," "represents," or "stands for."[6] Given the cultural background of the first Jewish disciples of Jesus, the eucharistic words about flesh and blood are shocking enough in themselves. (Recall the reaction to Jesus' statement, "The bread that I will give for the life of the world is my flesh," in John 6:41-71: "Because of this many of his disciples turned back and no longer went about with him" [v. 66].) One questions the heightening that would have occurred had Jesus used the *lingua sacra*.

We turn now to the verses devoted to the cup. The word in v. 25 translated "supper" can also be rendered "feast," occurring as it does in the papyri in connection with wedding festivities. Many passages in the Fathers use this term for the Lord's Supper, and the banquet idea should not be underestimated. "The Eucharist is primarily the *Banquet*. It is a real meal and it is a joyous meal."[7] It is likely that the early Christians associated the Lord's Supper as much with the messianic banquet as with the passion of Jesus, which was the context in the evangelist's accounts.

The word *potērion* means a drinking cup or bowl and appears metaphorically in the New Testament as a reference to the "cup of sorrow" (Matt. 20:22) and in the Fathers as a reference to martyrdom as well as in connection with the Supper. No mention is made of what was in the cup, but it was certainly wine. If the meal was Passover, wine was the required drink. Unless specified "unmixed," in early Christian celebrations it would have been wine mixed with water. Justin Martyr's term in his eucharistic text is literally "mixture."[8]

In Paul's account, Jesus blesses the cup as well as the bread, and Paul reports that Jesus spoke of it as the "new covenant in my blood," recalling the Hebrew notion of covenant which was sealed in blood (see Exod. 24:8; Jer. 31:31; and Zech. 9:11). Blood indicated a life given up in death which was the penalty for breaking the covenant.[9] The suggestion of deliverance from captivity is implicit. Paul's report treats the supper as meant to be recurrent ("as often as you drink"), stressing the idea of this new covenant in blood as a preparation for the kingdom. "The cup is the sign and pledge of a share in the new covenant, and so in the kingdom."[10]

> The Eucharist is therefore a proclamation and a remembrance of what has taken place—or, rather, of what God has done—just like the Passover. What is to be emphasized is not the eucharistic elements themselves, but the sacrificial act they call to mind.[11]

Ritual Action

This leads us to the first of the three suggestions about ways the early church might have understood and interpreted the Supper. They understood it to be what in modern parlance we would call "ritual action." The institution of the Lord's Supper as presented by Paul points clearly to the fact that it is something done. As William Robinson wrote with such precision, "This is a service of *action*. It is not hortatory, but dramatic."[12]

The language tells us that Jesus acted in the meal: he took, blessed, broke, gave thanks, said. The crucial verbs are all aorists, either active participles, indicatives, or imperatives—doing verbs. The manual acts of Jesus were important enough to be specified.

The questions raised at the Reformation were not those of the earliest Christians. For them, thanksgiving, memorial action, fellowship, and eschatological hope were the key associations of the Lord's Supper.[13] The symbolism was not so much in the elements as in the action. "It was the *action* that was symbolical, the breaking rather than the bread, the outpouring rather than the wine."[14] As the church moved through its history, the Supper shifted from an actual meal to a special rite. By 150 C.E. this shift was nearly universal (see, e.g., Justin Martyr, *First Apology* 67). It is not surprising, then, that the focus of ritual shifted from act to elements. But for the early church the action done to the elements was as important as, if not more important than, the elements of bread and wine themselves.

The actual breaking of the bread was so important that the rite went by this name in the early church (cf. Luke 24:30, 35; Acts 2:42, 46; 20:7, 11). The formula "took, blessed, broke, gave" was echoed by three of the four evangelists in the only miracle story common to the Gospels, the feeding of the five thousand, the symbol of the messianic banquet that the Jewish believers expected to inaugurate the Messiah's reign. The physical breaking represented the passion of Jesus; the physical pouring, the outpouring of Christ's blood. Both were understood to usher in the anticipated kingdom with its grand consummation feast.

We are out of touch with a culture in which symbolic action meant far more than it does today. Jesus speaks from the tradition of the prophets and their sign acts. Isaiah went about naked and barefoot (Isaiah 20), and Jeremiah shattered a clay flask (Jeremiah 19). Ezekiel lay on his side, fasted, and cut off his hair (Ezekiel 4–5). These signs showed what God was about to do. Indeed, there was a causal connection between sign act and event. "The ability to see signs is . . . characteristic of Israel's faith, a vivid sense of divine activity in the realm of human affairs. God is *with us* . . . not only can his word be *heard* . . . but his action can be *seen*."[15] And so it was with the meaning of Jesus' actions in the Lord's Supper. "It is . . . important to see the sacraments as distinctly nonverbal, as sacred acts."[16]

Table Fellowship

Second, in addition to a symbolism understood to reside importantly in the action as well as in the elements of the Supper, the early church must have coveted the idea that individual Christians were united as the body of Christ in the eucharistic feast. It has been suggested that "This is my body" refers not just to the bread of the Lord's Supper but to the disciples who shared table fellowship.[17] This suggestion is borne out by Paul's use of the body metaphor in the Corinthian correspondence (see, e.g., 1 Corinthians 12). "The death of Jesus is a valid action into which those who partake of the Meal are drawn: thereby they are united with Him for ever, also . . . beyond death, in a real and decisive event."[18]

As the elements were shared, the early Christians became one with Christ in taking him in, but also one with each other by sharing common elements.

> The cup of blessing that we bless, is it not a sharing in the blood of Christ? The bread that we break, is it not a sharing in the body of Christ? Because there is one bread, we who are many are one body, for we all partake of the one bread (1 Cor. 10:16-17).

Breaking and eating a common loaf, sharing a cup of wine, was a means of fellowship with one's brethren in Christ.

> Since to Paul . . . Christ is not only the individual Jesus Christ, but a corporate personality whose visible, material manifestation is the Church which is his body, union with Christ finds its expression in this societary way in membership in the body of Christ.[19]

As we have forgotten or neglected the visual and theological impact of ritual action, we have a tendency to forget how important the issue of table fellowship was in the world from which Jesus came. When Jesus shared table fellowship with outcasts and the unacceptable, he called into question what Marcus Borg has termed the "politics of holiness." In eating and drinking with all kinds of people, tax collectors and sinners, Pharisees and women, Jesus was showing in dramatic form that all people are acceptable to God. Scholars like Norman Perrin and W. R. Farmer have argued that Jesus' acceptance of outcasts was the primary source of hostility to his ministry.

The act of sharing a meal had religious and social significance in Jesus' time. "It became a vehicle of cultural protest, challenging the ethos and politics of holiness, even as it also painted a different picture of what Israel was to be, an inclusive community reflecting the compassion of God."[20] Jesus' willingness to share table fellowship with a variety of people was a way of demonstrating his love. As noted above, in a setting in which symbolic action meant far more than it does in our world, acceptance of outcasts at table fellowship was of great significance.[21]

The table fellowship of the Lord's Supper was a visible manifestation of what the church, as preface to the kingdom, was to be. Here was enacted the original intention of the covenant as spelled out by the Torah, that Israel would be a community of equals under God. In the early church's thinking, the conventional barriers between people had been broken down by Jesus. As Paul wrote to the Galatians, "There is no longer Jew or Greek, there is no longer slave or free, there is no longer male and female; for all of you are one in Christ Jesus" (Gal. 3:28). To sit down together at their Lord's Table was to live out that fellowship, to express *koinōnia* in spite of economic, social, and cultural differences. To partake in the Lord's Supper was to be at one with Christ in his sacrifice and to share by anticipation the fruits of his passion in the messianic meal in the kingdom.[22] But it was also to be brought into wholeness with those who would come to share that final, eschatological banquet. At his table, the Lord's people were "re-membered," brought together in a visible symbol of equality and oneness.

This leads to the final aspect of the Lord's Supper as it may have been understood by the early church: its radical reordering of time.

Time

As noted, the New Testament was produced by those whose defining religious practice was the Lord's Supper. They believed in the continuance of their risen Christ with them. For those early Christians, there was no break between the forty days of his risen life with them and their eucharistic celebration.[23] They were more interested in a living Lord who was present in their midst and about to return to judge the living and the dead than they were in Jesus of Nazareth. The power and energy of that living Lord is attested throughout the New Testament. From that record, we reconstruct that the early church thought about Jesus in three "tenses."

Early Christians remembered a Jesus from the past: Jesus of Nazareth who had lived among them and proclaimed a message of repentance and kingdom as he traveled about in Galilee and Judea. In the present, they proclaimed him as risen and living with the Christian community, still conducting his ministry in and through them. In the future (which, in the early days, they thought of as imminent), they looked for this risen Lord to appear in his full glory to judge, redeem, rectify, and destroy.

The Lord's Supper was the weekly reminder that Jesus Christ was the living Lord of all time: past, present, and future. In sharing the Supper, all of time was collapsed into a moment of time. Theologically, the point is this: all of history was understood to be the record of salvation from the hand of God. That whole record was contained in the Lord's Supper, a memorial of the past, an action in the present, and an anticipation of the future. What follows, then, is a partial exposition of the "three tenses" of the breaking of the bread.

Past

As noted earlier, the Synoptic Gospels and John do not seem to be in harmony on the question of whether or not the Last Supper was a Passover meal. Whether or not it was that meal itself, there is little disagreement that the event occurred in the context of the Jewish Passover festival in which remembrance is central. "This day shall be a day of remembrance for you. You shall celebrate it as a festival to the Lord; throughout your generations you shall observe it as a perpetual ordinance" (Exod. 12:14).

In the text noted above, Paul reports Jesus as saying, "Do this in remembrance of me." The Lord's Supper is "a proclamation and a remembrance of what has taken place—or, rather, of what God has done—just like the Passover. What is to be emphasized is not the eucharistic elements themselves, but the sacrificial act they call to mind."[24]

For the early Christians the connection was probably not blood and death but that Jesus appeared after the resurrection to his friends at meals. The Gospel literature of the New Testament places the extended resurrection appearances of Jesus in the context of eating. In the Emmaus road account in Luke 24:13-35, Jesus was "made known to them in the breaking of the bread." At his appearance in Jerusalem, the disciples have been eating, for, when asked whether they have anything to eat, they give Jesus a piece of broiled fish which he eats (Luke 24:41-43). In John's Gospel when Jesus prepares breakfast on the beach for the disciples, "none of the disciples dared to ask him, 'Who are you?' because they knew it was the Lord" (John 21:1-14).[25] Cullmann correctly notes that "the first eucharistic feasts of the community look back to the Easter meals, in which the Messianic Meal promised by Jesus at the Last Supper was already partly anticipated."[26]

"The Lord's Supper looks back at that which has already happened. It is a proclamation of the death of Jesus."[27] But, as with Passover, the Lord's Supper was not a matter of passive memory. The Greek word rendered in English by "remembrance," *anamnēsis*, implies bringing the past into the present. Johannes Behm maintains that it is to be philosophically distinguished from *mnēmē* ("memory"). In commenting on 1 Corinthians 11:24, he suggests that the whole action of the Lord's Supper is in memory of Jesus. "The making present of the later community of the Lord who instituted the Supper . . . is the goal and content of their action.[28] The early Christians were "recalling or re-presenting before God an event in the past so that it becomes living, powerful, operative."[29]

Present

The present aspect of the Lord's Supper is contained in the opening and closing verses of Paul's text: "I received from the Lord what I also handed on" and "you proclaim the Lord's death" (1 Cor. 11:23, 26). As noted above, to receive and deliver echoes the technical terminology of rabbinic teaching for passing on tradition. In the present tense of the Lord's Supper, the early Christians were receiving what was delivered to them and were passing it on. The point is that the Lord's Supper is proclamation. Proclamation (from *katangellein*) is public narrative of the events of the death of Jesus and their consequences.[30] What "goes on" in the present at the Supper is the "showing forth" of the central event of Christianity. This, of course, is why the notion of ritual action was of such importance.

In Paul's Greek text, with its insertion of the "to be" verbs, there is an insistence on the presence of Jesus at the present moment of the Supper: "This *is* my body"; "This cup *is* the new covenant in my blood" (emphasis added). Christ was understood to be present at the Supper if for no other reason than his promise: "For where two or three are gathered in my name, I am there among them" (Matt. 18:20). It is a mistake to be sidetracked by the questions of the Reformation. What "happens" to the bread and wine was not the point for the early Christians. For them the memory of Jesus' Aramaic, "This is my body" meant "This is I, myself." The saying assured the church "that the risen Lord himself is present at the Supper."[31] To apply the words of John's Gospel, Jesus is, and continues to be, the living bread (John 6:51).

The Lord's Supper, then, was an event in the present tense, an event of proclamation of the fundamental truths of the faith, and an occasion when Jesus was present with his church. In Eduard Schweizer's words, "The Lord's Supper may be thought of as a continuation of this fellowship of the Lord at table with his disciples."[32] But the final goal of full fellowship with the Lord was not yet completed.

Future

Paul's text enjoins repetition of the eucharistic meal until the Lord comes. Anticipation of the parousia, of the return of Jesus the Christ, was basic to the early church. As Hans Conzelmann has argued in his classic study, at least until the time of Luke's writings the expectation was that the return of Jesus was imminent.[33] Jesus was with them in presence and power and was soon to return to be with them in fullness of glory.

During Jesus' days with the disciples, he had hosted a messianic banquet that no Jew of the day would have misunderstood. In the feeding of the five thousand they would have seen the great feast that only the Messiah could host and that was promised to inaugurate the reign of God. As noted, it was the only miracle recorded by all four evangelists, and it contained explicitly eucharistic language (see Mark 6:30-44 and parallels). "The Messianic Banquet is an eschatological Banquet; it is a meal toward the future; it is a meal which, while celebrated now, points toward the future."[34]

One of the earliest accounts we have of eucharistic liturgy, the *Didache*, a teaching manual of the church of the second century, stresses the forward-looking character of the Lord's Supper. In its thanksgiving prayer after the supper, the *Didache* asks God to remember the church, "gather it together in its holiness from the four winds to thy kingdom which thou hast prepared for it" (*Didache* 10:5-6).

From one point of view, then, the Lord's Supper was understood to be memorial action. From another, it was an act of anticipation of the future. At the Lord's Table "the partition between here and hereafter became transparent; the parousia came as near as possible to being realized." The eating and drinking were prophetic action "helping to ensure the fulfillment of the prayer, Maran atha."[35] This is the element that gave the meal "its primary character of an anticipatory meal pointing toward the future."[36] The "future tense" of the Lord's Supper "is the anticipation of the messianic banquet which is to come."[37]

The text of 1 Corinthians 11:23-26 points clearly toward the three "tenses" in which the early church understood the Lord's Supper. For those believers, all of time was mystically present in the moment of time in which the bread was broken and shared and the wine poured and passed. The Lord's Supper made dramatic and visible the fact that the past was for remembrance, the present for action, and the future for hope. The early Christians, who were rooted in the past of their Lord's earthly life with them and expectant of his return, feasted between resurrection and Parousia.[38]

Conclusion

From the institution of the Lord's Supper as recorded by Paul in 1 Corinthians, it is possible to see three trajectories along which the meaning of the event as the early Christians understood it runs. First, their focus was not on the elements of bread and wine but on the action of breaking and pouring, which were understood to be sign acts not unlike those of the prophets. Second, participation in the Lord's Supper was itself a symbol of the unified community. The table fellowship of the meal unified the believers with Christ and with each other and showed forth the Lord's death and its practical consequences for the community. Finally, in the Lord's Supper, time collapsed in on itself. That is, in the Lord's Supper, past, present, and future coalesced and in what was happening, what had happened, and what would happen united so that all of time was present in those moments of time. Little wonder that Luke records that "they broke bread . . . with glad and generous hearts, praising God" (Acts 2:46-47).

6

The Prayer
in Acts 4:23-31

After they were released, they went to their friends and reported what the chief priests and the elders had said to them. When they heard it, they raised their voices together to God and said, "Sovereign Lord, who made the heaven and the earth, the sea, and everything in them, it is you who said by the Holy Spirit through our ancestor David, your servant: 'Why did the Gentiles rage, and the peoples imagine vain things? The kings of the earth took their stand, and the rulers have gathered together against the Lord and against his Messiah.' For in this city, in fact, both Herod and Pontius Pilate, with the Gentiles and the peoples of Israel, gathered together against your holy servant Jesus, whom you anointed, to do whatever your hand and your plan had predestined to take place. And now, Lord, look at their threats, and grant to your servants to speak your word with all boldness, while you stretch out your hand to heal, and signs and wonders are performed through the name of your holy servant Jesus." When they had prayed, the place in which they were gathered together was shaken; and they were all filled with the Holy Spirit and spoke the word of God with boldness.

Acts 4:23-31

Up to this point we have surveyed the general spiritual life of the church in Jerusalem, its devotion to the name of Jesus, and its practice of the Lord's Supper. When we turn our attention to the church's life of intercessory prayer, we both focus on the essential element of the church's spirituality and come face to face with the issues connected with Luke as the writer and theologian of Acts.

It frequently has been noted that prayer is of particular theological concern to Luke.[1] Luke's Gospel has much material on prayer that does not occur in the parallels (see, e.g., 11:5-8 or 18:1-14), and Luke frequently depicts Jesus in prayer at crucial junctures in his life (see Luke 3:21; 5:16; 6:12ff.; 9:18, 28-29; 23:34). "The gospel of Luke apparently seeks to establish the practice of prayer as the basis for the continuing life of the church."[2] This focus on prayer carries over into

Luke's second volume, in which the church "after the example and precept of her Lord, is diligent in prayer. It is a characteristic element of its life."[3] There are at least twenty-five significant instances of prayer in the book of Acts.

In the first chapters of Acts, the early church is depicted by Luke as engaged in the same activities that had characterized the ministry and life of Jesus. This is particularly true of its life of prayer. Prayer is the prominent characteristic of the spiritual leadership of the early church as described in Acts. It is the manner by which the power that empowered Jesus was transmitted to his followers.[4]

This assertion is seen most clearly in Luke's description of the Jerusalem congregation, that "all joined together constantly in prayer" (Acts 1:14, NIV; cf. 2:42). They prayed together when the need arose to choose leadership (1:15-26; 6:1-7) and to commission those leaders (6:1). They prayed at the Temple at regular hours (3:1) and in times of crisis (4:23-32), and thanksgiving (2:46-47).

F. J. Foakes-Jackson has noted that the description of the Jerusalem church is ideal rather than historical.[5] This may or may not be the case. The prologue to the Gospel of Luke (Luke 1:1-4) suggests that Luke's methodology is historical and that he intends to deal responsibly with the materials available to him so that Theophilus "may know the truth concerning the things about which [he has] been instructed" (Luke 1:4). Allison Trites notes, "The fact that Luke uses the word *asphaleia* ("accurate information," "full truth") indicates how seriously he takes his task. He purposes to give his readers 'reliability' by providing accurate information on the origins of the Christian movement." Trites believes that only if internal evidence suggests that Luke has departed from his own methodology can we assert that his portrait is idealized.[6] Furthermore, Luke is found to be accurate when other information allows us to corroborate his historical assertions.[7] Luke's perspective may be influenced by his theological interests, but his presentation of material would seem to be historical in the Hellenistic sense.

Theologically, then, for Luke prayer sets the tone of the Jerusalem congregation. The energy of that church comes not just from remaining near to the scenes of Jesus' passion but, through prayer, from remaining open to the power that raised him from the dead.

In the now dated but classic work, *Luke the Historian in Recent Study*, C. K. Barrett notes that ancient historians used speeches not as verbatim reports but to convey to the reader insights into aspects of their subject. These insights may have been into the total situation, into the meaning of the historical moment beyond the facts of history, into the character of the speaker, or into general ideas that explain the situation.[8]

My suggestion is that Luke uses prayers in the Acts of the Apostles in much the same way. If, as Barrett noted, the "speeches are the means Luke uses to bring out the meaning of the history he narrates,"[9] then the prayers are the means he uses to reinforce the church's Jewish heritage. This is particularly important since, as a biblical historian, Luke's concern is to link Israel's history with that of the church. Jerusalem, then, becomes the bridge between the two, so the events, speeches, and prayers located there are especially significant.[10] Secondarily, the prayers in Acts serve to summarize Luke's theological concerns. Both uses of prayer are evident in Acts 4:23-31, the prayer of believers when Peter and John are released from prison.

Narrative Context

Acts 4:23-31 concludes the story of Peter and John's healing of the blind beggar at the Beautiful Gate, their subsequent arrest, and their cross-examination by the Sanhedrin (3:1—4:22). Foakes-Jackson suggests the story may have derived from some double narrative of the pentecostal bestowal of the Spirit first seen in Acts 2 and that Acts 3–4 is sometimes taken to be from a source earlier than the second chapter and is another account of how the disciples received the Holy Spirit.[11] These textual issues will not concern us at this point.

The whole episode is framed by the two frequently discussed summaries of the inner life of the Jerusalem congregation, 2:42-47 and 4:32-35.[12] "The picture of the church of Jerusalem in the first five chapters of Acts is that of a community of enthusiastic followers of Jesus, growing by leaps and bounds, and enjoying the good will of its neighbors. Its members practice community of goods voluntarily . . . to manifest their conscious unity and charity."[13] As was noted in chapter 3 above, this portrait emphasizes aspects of religious community valued in both Jewish and Greco-Roman society: daily devotion to public and private religious activity; awesome respect in the presence of divine power; internal harmony and community solidarity expressed in concern for each other; and generosity.[14]

This is the atmosphere in which Luke places the text. Without arguing for or against Conzelmann, I believe that architecturally, Luke, in the overlap between his two volumes, is building a bridge between two periods of history, between Israel and the church.[15] The text of this prayer, then, exemplifies both elements of the Jewish tradition from which Christianity grew and Luke's theology of the church as it moves forward in Acts. As noted above, it also suggests elements of spiritual practice familiar to and approved by Hellenistic society.

The following is the text of the prayer from the NRSV:

> "Sovereign Lord, who made the heaven and the earth, the sea, and everything in them, it is you who said by the Holy Spirit through our ancestor David, your servant: 'Why did the Gentiles rage, and the peoples imagine vain things? The kings of the earth took their stand, and the rulers have gathered together against the Lord and against his Messiah.' For in this city, in fact, both Herod and Pontius Pilate, with the Gentiles and the peoples of Israel, gathered together against your holy servant Jesus, whom you anointed, to do whatever your hand and your plan had predestined to take place. And now, Lord, look at their threats, and grant to your servants to speak your word with all boldness, while you stretch out your hand to heal, and signs and wonders are performed through the name of your holy servant Jesus."

Jewish Elements in the Prayer

The current consensus on the genre of Luke-Acts seems to be that Luke has written a historical monograph shaped by theological concerns, not the least of which is to continue the biblical story where the Hebrew canon left off.[16] Bertil Gärtner has argued that Jewish, and not Greek, historiography is the proper background for Luke.[17] (Recall that C. C. Torrey argued that Acts 1–5 was translated from an Aramaic original.) Barrett suggests that we might see Luke as a Jewish historian like the writer of 1 Maccabees.[18]

More recent scholarship has given attention to Luke's concern for Israel, some scholars arguing that in Luke's milieu Jewish Christians had formidable influence.[19] Several studies have noted the positive attitude in Acts to the Jewish people and the law.[20] Roger Beckwith has noted that while "apparent echoes of *wording* from Jewish prayers to Christian must be treated with caution," the structure and themes of traditional Jewish prayers "show remarkable stability" and "some formulas and linguistic conventions are so regular in Jewish prayers that they had probably been habitual . . . and can therefore be compared with the corresponding formulas and linguistic conventions in Christian prayers."[21] Certainly this text manifests numerous Jewish elements. Singled out for comment are literary antecedents, manner of reference to God, messianic allusions, and allusions to figures and theophanies in Hebrew Scripture.

Literary Antecedents

It is a commonplace that Luke's style follows that of the Greek text, and the observation is borne out here. Psalm 2, quoted in Acts 4:25-26, is an exact quotation from the Greek text, and "who made the heaven" in v. 24 reflects the Greek text in Exodus 20:11; Nehemiah 9:6; and Psalm 146:6.

Furthermore, Luke continues to use a device that first appeared in the early chapters of his Gospel; he patterns a speech (in this case a prayer) on a Hebrew scriptural model. The prayer of the faithful here in Acts 4:24-30 seems to follow that of Hezekiah in 2 Kings 19:15-19 (parallel Isa. 37:15-20). In each, God is addressed as sovereign creator (Acts 4:24-26; 2 Kings 19:15); the present circumstances of the speaker are reviewed (Acts 4:27-28; 2 Kings 19:16-18); and God's help is requested so that God's cause may be advanced (Acts 4:29-30; 2 Kings 19:19).

In literary terms, then, our text is in the style of the Greek text which it quotes, and it follows models found in the earlier Scripture of Israel. The text has a strong Hebrew flavor, recalls the prayers of Luke 1 and 2 with their antecedents, and echoes early Christian liturgical forms (which themselves were borrowed from Temple and synagogue).[22]

Manner of Reference to God

The manner of reference to God is thoroughly Hebraic. God is the creator who has communicated through history and through chosen leaders. "The invocation of God as Creator here and elsewhere has been considered liturgical, from the stereotyped character of the wording."[23] The primary subject of the prayer is God who foretold the events narrated.[24]

The reference to *despotēs* ("lord," "master") in v. 24 seems particularly Lukan. The term is used of God by Luke only here and in Luke 2:29 (in Simeon's speech, which is also based on an Old Testament model). In both instances the term is antithetical to *doulos* ("slave").[25]

Messianic Allusions

The messianic allusions in the text are focused in the quotation from Psalm 2, which is the centerpiece of the prayer, and in the reference in v. 27 to "holy servant Jesus" whom God anointed. (Recall the large part that Old Testament quotation plays in the early speeches in Acts.)

The difficult textual and translation problems in v. 25 are well known, and since they do not bear directly on our inquiry, there is no need to rehearse them here.[26] The point for us is that Psalm 2 is one of the principal New Testament sources for the concept of the Messiah and his divine sonship. The first record of its messianic interpretation is found in *Psalms of Solomon* 17:26, where the messianic king will dash in pieces the pride of the sinner like a potter's vessel and break all their substance with a rod of iron.[27] The psalm is used with messianic connotations in Acts 13:33 and Hebrews 1:5 and 5:5.

In v. 27 Jesus is referred to as "your holy servant." It is true that *pais* may mean "child" or "son" or "servant." (In *Didache* 9.2ff. and 10.2, there also occur formulas in which David and Jesus are called "child.") In this context, the allusion surely must be to v. 25. "David and Jesus are both *paides* of God."[28] Behind the suggestion, I think we are to hear the words of Isaiah 52:13: "See, my servant shall prosper; he shall be exalted and lifted up, and shall be very high." Of course, to anoint was to "make Messiah."

The prayer is drawing on the Jewish understanding of Messiah to show how Psalm 2:2 has been fulfilled in Jesus' passion in which Gentiles (*ethnē*), Jews (*laoi*), kings (Herod Antipas), and rulers (Pilate) had opposed Jesus.[29] As v. 28 makes clear, Jesus is to be seen as Messiah, the fulfillment of prophecy in God's plan of salvation.[30]

Allusion to Figures and Theophanies in Hebrew Scripture

While it is admittedly a less significant point in this argument, it seems that in v. 30 allusion is being made to Moses and perhaps to the theophanies of Hebrew Scripture; in v. 30 Moses' characteristic gesture was to stretch out the hand (see, e.g., Exod. 4:4; 14:21; 17:11-13). In view of the similarity of vocabulary between the Moses episodes in the Greek text and Acts 4:30, and in view of Luke's interest in "religious personalities,"[31] the suggestion does not seem without merit. Moses the deliverer is alluded to in the context of David the king and Jesus the Messiah. We have a summary of the "major players" in salvation history.

Second, an earthquake is a typical feature of the theophanies of Hebrew Scripture (e.g., Exodus 19 and Isa. 6:4). It becomes a symbol of the presence and the power of God (in Acts 2:2-3 all of the imagery from the giving of the law at Mount Sinai is employed). For Luke to note it here in this second or renewed pentecostal experience is for him to place the experience of the early church squarely in the context of its Jewish heritage.

Luke's Theological
Preoccupations

Having established the Jewishness of the prayer and its context, we must now examine how it reflects Luke's characteristic theological emphases.

In writing about the speeches in Acts, many scholars have noted how they summarize the early Christian kerygma as well as Lukan theology.[32] This is also true of the prayers in Acts. Luke employs the prayers for a theological purpose. He believes that these early congregations originated by God's activity. He shows the appointment and commissioning of their leaders as related to petitionary prayer. The continuation of the congregations was due, according to Luke, to God's gracious help given in answer to petition. Thus the prayers in Acts are to demonstrate how God had continued to guide God's people.[33] Theologically, Luke makes this clear by depicting God and the Holy Spirit as "characters in the story," by noting God's control of history and God's power present in "signs and wonders" done through the power of Jesus' name.

God and the Holy Spirit

Acts 4:24-30 focuses on God as a "player" in the drama. As noted, the prayer opens by addressing the creator God. It continues by reminding that God speaks through the Holy Spirit (v. 25; cf. 1:16). Throughout Acts, the role of the Holy Spirit in redemptive history is stressed (see the references in the opening chapters alone: 1:2, 8, 16; 2:4, 16-18, 33, 38). The Spirit is a "main character" in Acts, no less important than Peter or Paul.

God's Control of History

In these early chapters of Acts, reference to the Holy Spirit has frequently illustrated how God prepared and directed the events of history. Luke's theme of salvation history is present in the text of the prayer in v. 28: God had decided beforehand what should happen. The word *proorizō* means, literally, "to see beforehand." In at least one earlier reference (Peter's Pentecost sermon at 2:23), Luke has stressed the foreordained character of the death of Jesus. Acts 2:31-35 suggests that David foreknew these events. Here, the theological point for Luke is that Jesus is under God's sovereignty (cf. Luke 22:22). The church, thus reassured that its experience is analogous to Jesus', can expect to be vindicated by God as, in being raised from the dead, Jesus was vindicated.[34]

The idea is alluded to again in 4:29 as God is asked to "look upon" or consider their threats. According to J. Rawson Lumby, the word *epide* ("concern oneself with," "take notice of") is used in parallel writings of the oversight and notice of the gods, and it is common in the Greek text for God's providential care (Job 22:12; Ps. 112:6; Ezek. 8:12).[35] The pentecostal experience, with which the passage closes, serves to confirm God's presence and care, as, for example, does the earthquake in the Philippian prison after Paul and Silas prayed in Acts 16:26. The imperfect *elaloun* ("speak") indicates that the church went on preaching without regard to the threats.[36]

Signs and Wonders in the Name

The earthquake highlights another Lukan preoccupation evident in the text of the prayer, "signs and wonders." In v. 30 it is noted that "through the name of your holy servant Jesus" there are healings and "signs and wonders are performed." The quotation from Joel in Peter's sermon (2:19) introduced the theme of signs and wonders which is continued in the reference to Jesus (2:22) and in numerous references to the life of the early church in Jerusalem (2:43; 4:30; 5:12; 6:8).

It will be recalled that in the Hebrew tradition a sign (*sēmeion*) was more than a miracle, a disruption of natural law or cause and effect. A sign was "a visible evidence of the presence and purpose of God."[37] A sign could be as ordinary as a plague of locusts or as unusual as the death of the firstborn of Egypt, but it signaled that God was not aloof from day-to-day life but was actively engaged "in the midst."

"Signs and wonders" as a standard New Testament phrase provides another instance of continuity with Jewish backgrounds. Signs and wonders necessarily precede all missionary advances of the church in Acts and link the prior activity of God with that of Jesus, and that of Jesus to that of the early church. Signs and wonders are evidence of God's power and a sign of the inbreaking kingdom. As in 3:12-16, the power that generated them is attributed to God working through the name of Jesus.[38]

As noted in chapter 4 above, reference to the name of Jesus appears repeatedly in the early chapters of Acts. As we recalled from Genesis 32:29 and Exodus 3:13-14, the name of God contains the essence and power of God, thus the potent character of the name of Jesus for the early church. Use of the name represents confidence in God who bestows gifts through Jesus.[39] For Luke, the name of Jesus is a channel of the power of the risen Christ to the church, and thus reinforces his theological emphasis on continuity in salvation history.

Two final Lukan interests appear in the text. In contrast to the emphases heretofore mentioned, they serve to make a distinction between the early church and its Hebrew ancestors.

Unity of the Church

In contradistinction to his depiction of the Judaism of his time (for example, in Acts 5:17-40 when the Sadducees and the Pharisees disagree), Luke depicts the early church as unified, "of one mind." In fact, *homothymadon* ("with one mind") is a favorite Lukan word, occurring ten times in Acts. We are told that the members of the church "were constantly devoting themselves to prayer" (1:14), "they spent much time together in the temple" (2:46), and "the whole group of those who believed were of one heart and soul" (4:32). This unity is an important factor in Luke's portrait of the community. Internal harmony and unity in a religious community was a characteristic valued by Greco-Roman society.

The theme of unity in prayer is of particular importance, because pagan criticism of prayer at the time assumed that prayer was to multiple gods and for various external "things." Joachim Jeremias, in *The Prayers of Jesus,* noted that parodies of prayers became a stock convention for comedians (consider, e.g., the works of Aristophanes). The Stoics and the Epicureans taught the futility of prayer on the basis that people pray for contradictory things; they asked how a god could hear, much less respond, to each different request. The numerous names of gods in the magical papyri attest to the "acute crisis into which prayer has fallen."[40]

In contrast to this state of affairs, early Christian prayer freed from isolation and egocentricity. The Christians prayed for, and in community were understood to be united with, all praying at that same time.[41] In this emphasis on unity in prayer, Luke is appealing to his Greco-Roman audience. We see in this prayer text both a feature of Luke's characteristic depiction of the early church and a reflection of the Roman audience that has traditionally been associated with Luke. Prayer is shown to be efficacious and powerful when directed to the God of Jesus and the Christians.

Jewish Antagonists

In this regard it has often been noted that, in Luke-Acts, the Romans appear in a favorable light; antagonists of Jesus and opponents of the Christians are usually understood to be Jewish officials. In 4:23 it is clear that the chief priests and elders had opposed Peter and John. In the text of the prayer itself, exact identification of the adversaries is more difficult. Certainly the nations (*ethnē*) of v. 25 are Gentiles. The peoples (*laoi*) would have been commonly understood to be the people of Israel; the kings (*basileis*) are represented by Herod[42] and the rulers (*archontes*) by Pilate.[43] The quotation in vv. 25-26 and its interpretation in v. 27 are consistent with Luke's picture of the Jews as active conspirators against Jesus and the Christians (Luke 23:13; Acts 2:23; 3:13-14).[44]

In Acts 4:23-32, then, we see not only Luke's interest in maintaining a sense of continuity with the church's Jewish past but ample evidence of his own theological interests and presuppositions: in vv. 23 and 27 his concern with Jewish antagonists; in v. 24 the unity of the church; in v. 25 the Holy Spirit as a "main character" in the church's story; in v. 28 God's control and direction of history; in v. 30 signs and wonders done in Jesus' name as evidence of God's power present in the church; and in v. 31 a pentecostal experience to confirm that power and presence.

Conclusion

The prayer life of the church in Jerusalem as Luke depicts it in the early chapters of the Acts of the Apostles reinforces the theology of his history. Christian community is the locus of divine activity. Luke's ecclesiology is charismatic: through the Holy Spirit, God directs the church as God directed Israel.[45] In Acts 4:23-31 this is dramatically shown as God answers prayer with visible signs. What was requested in prayer comes to pass, thus providing an instance of promise fulfillment within the pericope itself.[46] The word for prayer in v. 31 (*deēthentōn*) originally meant to have a need and to express it. Luke shows that, in the early church, need expressed is need answered by God.

Writing to complete the story of what God was doing in Jesus, Luke understands the events he narrates as the work of God, not of human ingenuity. As Acts 4:23-31 demonstrates, he uses the text of the prayer as he has used speeches, to give insight into the meaning of the history he narrates and into the character of the early church. (In the light of the many similarities between the two, I wonder, for example, whether

Luke has not written this prayer to highlight the major themes of Peter's Pentecost sermon.)

In theology and practice, much of the character of the church comes from the Hebrew tradition. It has been a commonplace of Lukan studies that the Jews oppose Jesus and the Christians and that Luke directs the message of Jesus to Gentiles, especially Romans, who are willing to listen. The evidence here, however, suggests that Luke's thinking is more complex. Not only is Luke stressing continuity with the Jewish backgrounds of Christianity (events in Jerusalem forming the bridge between Israel and the church), but his own theological interests have strong connections to that very background.[47] Luke's work bears out many suggestions in historical studies about the "Jewishness" of Christianity in its earliest days. But to assert anything about the "Jewishness" of Luke would require much more evidence than has been presented here and is, in fact, outside the scope of this study.

Finally, looking at 4:23-31 in its context in Acts, we see the church's life of prayer as summarized in 2:42 and 4:33 vividly exemplified. "Prayer . . . according to Luke, has a direct bearing on the out-working of God's purposes and the bringing of his sovereignty to its final and ultimate expression."[48] In this prayer text Luke is giving a concrete example of his generalizations. This, it seems to me, is the genius of the Acts of the Apostles: ecclesiology is incarnate; what Luke wants us to know and to do, Luke makes it possible for us to see.[49]

7

Acts,
Ephesians, and the
Hellenistic Environment

It may seem anomalous that Acts and Ephesians should appear together in a study of the spirituality of the early church. Why study Acts, which is a narrative, with Ephesians, an epistle whose language is marked by the rhythms of prayer? The most superficial answer would be to say that Acts 1–10 provides a picture of the spirituality of Jewish Christianity and that Ephesians provides an introduction to the gentile Christian environment. The facts of the matter are more complex and interesting than that. Acts 1–10 is probably written by a gentile Christian but set in a Jewish environment, and Ephesians is probably written by a Jewish Christian but addressed to a gentile community. In the simplest terms, that is why the two are included. They provide us with a look at the different environments of the early church, and the two books represent early Christian writers from two different cultural-religious backgrounds.

The literary relationship between Acts and Ephesians has attracted attention as well, but it has not recently been in the forefront of New Testament study. After examining the external issue of the Ephesian church's cultural background as a case in point of the general discussion of gentile backgrounds of early Christianity presented in chapter 2 above, we shall examine the more complex and as yet unresolved issues of the literary and theological relationships between Acts and Ephesians. Finally, we shall suggest similarities that the two exhibit in their depiction of the spiritual life of the early church and point out some features of the spirituality of those to whom the letter is addressed.

As we noted above, the piety of Acts and that of Ephesians are very different. Ephesians belongs to the eastern and Acts to the western part of the Pauline mission field. Ephesians is rooted in the world of Hellenistic mystery-religion piety and Acts in the world of Hellenistic Judaism.[1]

Before we describe the city of Ephesus, we must raise the question of the destination of the epistle to the Ephesians. As is commonly known, the earliest manuscripts of the letter lack "in Ephesus" in 1:1. A great many theories have sprung up to solve the problem, and they vary in credibility.[2] No less monumental a work than Marcus Barth's two-volume commentary in the Anchor Bible puts forth as its thesis that Paul wrote the letter from Rome at the end of his life and addressed it to gentile Christians in Ephesus.[3] Even if scholarship does not agree on the Ephesian destination, there is consensus that the letter was probably addressed to a church in western Asia Minor. Since Ephesus was the leading city in that area, there is a strong likelihood of Ephesian readership whether or not the author addressed the letter to that city. I shall assume at least that much in what follows.

The City of Ephesus

According to Greek legend, Ephesus I was originally founded by the Amazons. (The location of the city has been moved about five times through the centuries, largely due to the silting up of the harbor. Successive cities are designated by Roman numerals.) Another legend reports that about 1100 B.C.E. the Greek prince Androclus received information from a soothsayer about where he and his group of a thousand colonists from Argos would build a city.

A more historical source, Strabo's *Geography* (14.1.24), reports that Ephesus was "the largest emporium in Asia this side of the Taurus." In the first century, the city of Ephesus had a quarter of a million inhabitants and was ranked with Antioch in Syria and Alexandria in Egypt as one of the three great cities of the Eastern Mediterranean. It was probably first colonized by Ionian Greeks. Croesus of Lydia attacked Ephesus in 560 B.C.E. and dedicated the conquered city to Artemis. Cyrus defeated the city in 547 B.C.E. and it came under Macedonian power in 334 B.C.E., after which time Alexander's general, Lysimachus, moved the city to higher ground. In 133 B.C.E., Ephesus was added to the Roman Empire.[4]

At the height of its prosperity in the first and second centuries of our era, Ephesus III, at the mouth of the Caÿster River, was important as a center of reshipment and was the terminal of an important trade route from inland areas.[5] As it was the residence of the Roman proconsul and the capital of the Roman province of Asia, it was, as well, a city of political importance. At the time of Paul's residence (ca. 57 C.E.?), the city was laid out according to a Hellenistic plan. The stadium would have been a focus of special interest at the time as it was rebuilt under Nero (54–68 C.E.). The theater (which is said to have had perfect acoustics), where, Acts records, there was a riot against Paul instigated by one Demetrius (Acts 19), seated twenty-four thousand spectators. The main street running from this theater to the harbor, the Arcadian Way, was thirty-five feet wide and half a mile long, lined with columns.[6]

The luxury of the city in Paul's time is attested to by the remnants of marble streets with statues of prominent citizens and canopied colonnades that shielded shoppers from the weather. The city contained public buildings and temples as well as restaurants, a brothel, and patrician homes. The city had six public baths with provision for both hot and cold water. The most imposing part of the present-day ruins, the Library of Celsus, was not built until 135 C.E., but indicates the continuing prominence of the city in Christian antiquity.

Excavations at Ephesus began under J. T. Wood with the support of the British Museum in the nineteenth century and have been carried on with great care by the Austrians, who have contributed greatly to the literature on Ephesus.[7] Still, only about 20 percent of the Ephesian sites have been excavated, primarily in the area of Ephesus III.

Religious Life in Ephesus

For our purposes Ephesus must also be regarded as a great religious center. Before Ionian colonization, there seems to have existed in the area a cult of a goddess whom the Greeks associated with Artemis.[8] As examples of the gentile religious background of the city, the cult of Artemis and its linkage to Hellenistic magic and astrology will be surveyed, and emperor worship, gnosticism, and Judaism will receive brief mention.

Artemis was worshiped more widely than any other female deity in the Greek world. The sister of Apollo and daughter of Leto and Zeus, Artemis was the virgin hunter, the moon goddess and patroness of maidens, helper of women in childbirth and giver of gentle death to women. The Ephesian Artemis, however, was different in character. She was more nearly a form of the Asian mother goddess. Ephesian Artemis is depicted as a female figure with multiple breasts which, it has been suggested, signified her nourishing power, fertility, and fruitfulness.

> In lonely majesty, and under various names . . . the goddess of blessing and fertility united virginity, motherhood and queenship in one person.

At the latest after the Egyptian Isis enriched her functions, she became a symbol of Women's Liberation: fulfilment of womanhood by motherhood without male assistance. A novel interpretation . . . of the many so-called "breasts" that were fixed to the deity's festival garment, suggests that she represented woman's glory at the price of the castration of males (which indeed was a prerequisite of her priests).[9]

Ephesus was famous for its Artemision. The Hellenistic Temple of Artemis (who was called Diana by the Romans) was one of the wonders of the ancient world. Apparently the first Artemision dated back to an eighth-century B.C.E. shrine. The larger temple was begun about 550 B.C.E. (and sported columns given by Croesus). Its final dedication was about 430 B.C.E. This temple was mentioned by Herodotus, and tradition says it burned on the night Alexander the Great was born in 356 B.C.E. The Hellenistic temple of Paul's time was probably begun before 350 B.C.E. It was roughly 160 by 340 feet, with 100 columns 55 feet high. It lasted until 262 C.E., when it was sacked by the Goths.[10] The temple was a landholding corporation served by eunuch priests, attendants, and thousands of female slaves (who may or may not have been prostitutes). The worship of Artemis (Diana) was practiced not only in Ephesus but in nearly all the cities of Asia, on the Greek mainland, and in Rome.

Magic was an integral aspect of the religion of Artemis. This made Ephesus a center for magical practices. Clinton E. Arnold's very helpful book, *Ephesians, Power, and Magic*, quotes B. M. Metzger as saying "of all ancient Greco-Roman cities, Ephesus . . . was by far the most hospitable to magicians, sorcerers, and charlatans of all sorts."[11] Ephesus proliferated in magical practice, the aim of which was to gain power over the spirit world (which, it was believed, exercised influence over all aspects of human life). Followers of Artemis saw her as more powerful than this demonic realm, and Arnold believes one purpose of the Ephesian letter was to address the Christians' relations to "the powers."[12]

The worship of Artemis was also associated with astrology. As Helmut Koester has pointed out, "At the beginning of [the first century C.E.] everybody was acquainted with astrology. . . . Astrological symbols appeared widely in everyday life."[13] The traditional gods and goddesses began to be understood according to astrological concepts. An example of this is the fact that a copy of Artemis of the Ephesians "shows the goddess with a necklace made of the twelve signs of the zodiac."[14]

While the religious environment of Ephesus may have been dominated by Artemis, it was not limited to her cult. Emperor worship was also active in Ephesus, as is witnessed by a temple erected in Ephesus by the province of Asia for the worship of the Emperor Domitian (81-96 C.E.). While slightly beyond the period of time we have in view, this was significant for Christians in Ephesus (and throughout the empire) for whom Domitian was an enemy. It was the Domitian persecution that probably occasioned the Revelation to John, which also has ties to the city of Ephesus.

Again, while Artemis and magic are probably more significant as backgrounds to the Ephesian letter, gnosticism is not absent. In his *History and Literature of Early Christianity*, Koester entitles his discussion of Ephesians "The Struggle Against Gnosticism." He argues that the Pauline mission had been deeply affected by syncretistic gnosticism and that the author's universalism is possible because he draws his theological categories from gnosticism.[15] On the other hand, Barth states that Ephesians is not dependent upon classical Christian-heretic gnostic systems.[16] Elsewhere Barth points out that scholars in the field of history of religions have questioned, not confirmed, gnostic influence on the New Testament, and thus "it does not make sense to discover the complete Gnostic myth in Ephesians."[17]

The point for our purposes is not to come down on one or the other side of the debate. We need to note that gnostic ideas are at least evident enough in Ephesians to have sparked the discussion. The Ephesian letter does share with gnostic literature the head/body imagery (which also appears in the Corinthian correspondence). Terms such as "mystery," "revelation," "fullness," and "principalities and powers" at the very least suggest the need for sensitivity to the issue of gnosticism in Ephesus.

Finally, while the religions of the Hellenistic world dominate the background of the Ephesian letter, Judaism is not absent. Acts 19:8 reports that Paul preached in the Ephesian synagogue for three months. Acts 19 also tells of "Jewish exorcists," suggesting that the Judaism of Ephesus had been influenced by the prevalence of magical practice in that city. The text of the letter itself reflects clear uses of Hebrew Scripture in every chapter except chapter 3, and the theology of Hebrew Scripture clearly plays a formative role in the author's understanding of the Christian gospel.[18] This is to be expected if the author is understood to have been a Jewish Christian.

While this picture of the religious life in Ephesus is more in the nature of a panorama than a detailed portrait, it at least suggests something of the difference between the setting of the material in Acts and that in Ephesians. The spirituality of Acts 1–10 is dominated by the center of Judaism, the Temple in Jerusalem and its practices. That of the Ephesian letter finds itself under the shadow of the Artemision and the religious life of the pagan Hellenistic world. Before noting how, in spite of this fact, Acts and Ephesians show many likenesses in their depiction of Christian spirituality, we must examine the literary and theological relations between the two books.

The Literary Relationship Between Acts and Ephesians

The traditions that influence and, indeed, make up the Ephesian letter are varied and have attracted significant scholarly attention. The Jewish Christian who wrote Ephesians (note the use of "you" when speaking to the Gentiles in Eph. 2:11, 17)[19] was, as we shall see in the next chapter, aware of and used Hebrew Scripture.[20] Ephesians also exhibits a hymnic and liturgical heritage.[21] Barth notes that since "a large part of the content is public prayer to God, the diction of the epistle resembles that of contemporary Jewish and some pagan prayers and . . . the extant examples of the prayers of Paul."[22] What of a relationship with the Acts of the Apostles?

The question of the literary relationship between Acts and Ephesians has been treated most extensively in C. Leslie Mitton's classic study, *The Epistle to the Ephesians: Its Authorship, Origin, and Purpose.*[23] Much of the discussion that follows is indebted to chapter 13 of that work.

Scholarly consensus on the date of Acts and Ephesians would place the origins of the two works in the same decade. Luke-Acts is generally dated from 85 to 90 C.E., and Ephesians cannot be earlier than 58 C.E. or later than 115 C.E., with a date of 90 C.E. often suggested. Obviously, proximity of origin does not establish literary relationship, especially since scholars generally agree that the author of Acts did not know the letters of Paul. Acts itself does not seem to reflect any awareness of them. J. Moffatt, however, noted that there are about a dozen words that are peculiar to the vocabulary of both Luke and Ephesians. Most of the similarities he notes occur in Paul's address to the Ephesian elders at Miletus.[24]

Mitton examines the linguistic correspondence between Luke-Acts and Ephesians in detail. He notes that of the fifty or so words in Ephesians that are not used elsewhere in the Pauline corpus, ten appear in Luke-Acts but in no other New Testament writing. Some occur only in Luke and some with a different sense in Acts than in Ephesians; direct dependence, therefore, cannot be argued from vocabulary alone.

Mitton examines the Ephesian-Lukan parallels and concludes that there is nothing "which cannot be accepted as due to coincidence, or at most to a common atmosphere of Christian thought."[25]

Mitton proceeds to analyze the parallels between Acts and Ephesians, noting that six passages from Ephesians have agreements in vocabulary with the twenty verses in Acts that report Paul's farewell address to the Ephesian elders at Miletus (Acts 20:17-38). He believes that these points of correspondence between Acts and Ephesians cannot be dismissed as mere coincidence, since no other Pauline epistle has so many or is so closely related to Acts. The most likely explanation for the literary correspondence is that Ephesians was written later than Acts and that its author knew the work. If, Mitton speculates, the author of Ephesians lived in the area of Ephesus and wrote for his fellow Christians with both Paul's letters and Acts available to him, it would make sense that Acts 20 would be of the most interest to his audience.[26]

A study that has as its focus the spiritual life of the early church is not the place to engage in an argument about literary interdependence. Recent scholarship seems not to have taken up the issue; perhaps a reader of this work will choose to pursue it. The possibility of such a relationship, however, is of interest because of the theological similarities that are evident between Acts and Ephesians.

The Theological Similarity of
Acts and Ephesians

Both the Acts of the Apostles and the Ephesian letter presuppose a church that has expanded across the world and that evinces a church order that has developed beyond that which existed at the time of the apostles. As Ernst Käsemann has pointed out, in the New Testament "it is Ephesians that most clearly marks the transition from the Pauline tradition to the perspectives of the early Catholic era."[27] But the Acts of the Apostles, as well, marks this moment of transition. "Both still know the gospel only in the form of tradition, nourish their proclamation either meditatively (Eph.) or narratively (Acts) out of the material of the tradition, and conversely by means of this same tradition make their message normative."[28]

A central theme of Ephesians is the divine plan of salvation "from before the foundation of the world" (1:4) "unto all generations for ever and ever" (Eph. 3:21).[29] In Acts we see the physical working out of this plan as the gospel is carried from Jerusalem to Rome. Again, Ephesians stresses the unity in Christ of the church. The early chapters of

Acts are not primarily concerned with the unity in Christ of Jew and Gentile that dominates the doctrinal section of Ephesians. That issue appears in Acts 10 and 11 in the narrative of Peter and Cornelius and is treated again in Acts 15, the Jerusalem Council. The other two major themes of the Ephesian letter, however, the world mission of the church and the necessity of a moral life-style, both appear in Acts, which also shares with Ephesians an interest in the resurrection and ascension of Christ to God's right hand.[30]

Luke's purpose in writing Acts is to portray the Palestinian origins of the church and the Jewish milieu of its birth and to show how it spread to Rome and into the empire. He is concerned that his gentile audience understand that Christianity is not a danger to the empire. Likewise, the church in Ephesus is predominantly gentile. Its Jewish author counsels his readers against their pre-Christian moral standard and puts them on guard against a pagan teacher who would undermine the Christian ethic. He also reminds them that Jewish Christians are fellow believers with them.[31]

R. P. Martin believes that the situation in the Ephesian letter is one in which antinomian tendencies were felt in a church in Asia Minor, a church in which Gentiles entered boasting of their independence of Israel and showing a lack of tolerance for Jewish Christians. Luke-Acts resonates with this problem.[32]

Both Luke and the author of Ephesians understand that there are those in their audiences who see themselves as members of the body of Christ and, having received the Spirit, they are in danger of forgetting the origins and history of the gospel.

> It is a chief concern of Ephesians to bring this history to remembrance and to make the acknowledgment of it obligatory for the sake of the unity of the church. In this regard also it coincides with the intention of Acts. Just as the astonishment over the acceptance of the Gentiles in Eph. 1:13-14 has its closest parallel in the conclusion of the Cornelius pericope, so the redemptive-historical aspect dominates the work of Luke as a whole and also its ecclesiology. To both of them the "center of time" is inconceivable without the holy beginnings and without a backward look toward the promise and the anticipation of the saving event given in the Old Testament. The church stands in continuity with the people of the old covenant."[33]

In short, both Acts and Ephesians have as one common purpose that of reminding the church of its Jewish origins.

The continuity observable in the theology of the two books is also seen in the similarities of spiritual practice observable in Acts and Ephesians.

The Depiction of Spirituality in
Acts and Ephesians

A number of the spiritual practices that we noted in Acts also appear in the Ephesian letter. Both are interested in prayer and contain prayers composed by the authors (Eph. 1:16-17; 3:14-20; 6:18). (We shall return to this in the next chapter.) Both depict devotion to the name of Jesus (Eph. 1:21; 3:15; 5:20). In Ephesians this is reflected in part in the number of times the phrases "in Christ Jesus" and "in him" appear. Both reflect the power, presence, and animation of the Holy Spirit in the church. While Acts only alludes to the singing of hymns, Ephesians enjoins the singing of psalms, hymns, and spiritual songs (Eph. 5:19). Both focus on thanksgiving to God. Also, the charisms of ministry that Ephesians lists (apostles, prophets, evangelists, pastors, and teachers, Eph. 4:11) are the same as those operative in the narrative in Acts.

While Acts and Ephesians share common elements of spirituality, several aspects of the Ephesian letter are specifically reflective of its setting in the Hellenistic community. The prayerful—even liturgical—style of the letter has already been noted. The "doxological" style of Ephesians has been likened to ancient panegyric or festal address in praise of someone. In Ephesians the object of the praise is God.[34] One wonders whether this panegyric style was chosen in part for its familiarity to the audience who would have heard such in praise of Artemis (it is alluded to in Acts 19:28, "Great is Artemis of the Ephesians!").

Marcus Barth raises the issue of references to Artemis in Ephesians. He notes that no other New Testament epistle is so positive about marriage, suggesting as it does mutuality and self-giving love with no hint that fertility is the main purpose of marriage. Ephesians 5:21-33 may reflect a critical dialogue with the Artemis tradition in which the church as Christ's bride gives Christian women a more esteemed position than does the cult of Artemis. Barth even suggests that the spiritual temple in 2:20-22 may be an alternative not only to the Jerusalem Temple but also to the Artemision. (Later church traditions of popular piety associated with Ephesus made Mary the true counterpart to Artemis.)[35] These connections are not explicit, but in the cultural context of the letter they cannot be ignored.

A similar circumstance exists with regard to the attitude toward prayer on the part of the letter's author and to the language of gnosticism observable in his work. In 3:14-15 the author says, "I bow my knees before the Father, from whom every family in heaven and on earth takes its name." As noted in chapter 3 above, standing was the customary position for prayer in the Jewish tradition. The reference to God "the Father of all families" and to kneeling before him may be an allusion to *Zeus patēr*. Kneeling for prayer was, at the time, characteristic of pagan worship, and the omnipotence formula sounds more like Heraclitus the Ephesian's praise of Reason than Hebrew or Aramaic descriptions of God.[36] Likewise, five times in Ephesians the term *mystery* "signifies a secret that is now revealed, and that is to be communicated to all the world."[37] It is probable that mystery religions and cults (and conflict with them) have influenced the language and theology of the letter.

Perhaps the most convincing effort to link the Ephesian letter and its religious environment is Arnold's *Ephesians—Power and Magic* (mentioned above). Arnold notes that the greatest percentage of power terminology in the New Testament occurs in Ephesians. Ephesus was a center of magic, and knowledge of Hellenistic magic provides the most important background for understanding the "powers" in Ephesians; the epistle concludes by telling its readers they must prepare for spiritual warfare (6:10-17). At least some, if not a majority, of the converts entering the Ephesian church were formerly associated with the worship of Artemis and the practice of magic. For them, the powers were demonic and threatening. The writer of Ephesians has as his task to convince them that no "power" is outside the realm of God's sovereignty or Christ's supremacy. Through Christ, in fact, they have a means of access to the power of God.[38] The argument is convincing and does much to help us understand the personal and psychological situation of the Christians to whom the letter is addressed.

Finally, the spirituality of the Ephesian community may be seen most clearly in the practical and parenetic material in chapters 4–6 of the letter. Primarily Gentiles, the Ephesian Christians do not have the monotheistic or moral background assumed in Jewish Christianity. They must be taught how "to lead a life worthy of the calling to which [they] have been called" (4:1). The writer does this by making explicit the connection between belief and practice (4:1-6), by telling them not to live like the Gentiles, and then describing what that means (4:17—6:9).

Specific instructions on how not to "live as the Gentiles live, in the futility of their minds" (4:17) are given in 4:17—5:20. Because of repeated licentiousness, they have lost spiritual sensitivity. In 4:19-24 and 5:3-5 the author singles out sexual laxity as a major factor contributing to this loss. In contrast to this sexual immorality, Christians are to imitate Christ who gave himself up for us, "a fragrant offering and sacrifice to God" (5:2). The image is drawn from the practice of offering incense to the gods.

The importance of honest and upbuilding conversation as part of the larger issue of how Christians should live together in community is stressed in 4:25-32 and 5:6. One wonders whether the "empty words" mentioned in 5:6 might reflect a situation not unlike that in the Pastoral Epistles, in which pagan philosophers or false Christian teachers are infiltrating the community.

It is the *Haustafel* of 5:21—6:9 that most clearly reflects a "Christianization" of Hellenistic teaching. Barth notes that Stoic writings of the period "bristle with charming legendary examples of great love or majestic rule over a house."[39] Much recent scholarship has been devoted to the way Christian writers employed the household codes of pagan antiquity to show how the Christian household should be organized.[40] In the Christian household, mutual submission "out of reverence for Christ" (5:21) is to be the rule.

Finally, the well-known "armor of God" passage in 6:10-17 reflects a struggle not just in human but in cosmic terms. When the writer asserts that "our struggle is not against enemies of blood and flesh, but against . . . the cosmic powers of this present darkness, against the spiritual forces of evil in the heavenly places" (6:12), he speaks out of a context of a lively belief in the unseen world and its power to affect human life for good or ill. Christ has come to provide victory in this warfare.

Conclusion

For reasons both of their likenesses and their differences, Acts and Ephesians may be fruitfully studied together in an inquiry into the spirituality of the early church.

Whether or not there is a literary relationship between the two books, both mark transition points in the thinking of the early church about its mission. Both reflect a universalizing of the Christian gospel, its applicability to Jew and Gentile alike. Both seek to remind the gentile

Christians of their roots in Jewish life and piety, and a number of spiritual practices appear in both books.

But just as the first chapters of the Acts of the Apostles reflect their Jewish environment, Ephesians bears the mark of the spiritual life of Asia Minor. Its theological formulations and practical advice are directed to those who have lived in the shadow of Artemis of the Ephesians, mystery religions, and, if not full-blown, at least incipient gnosticism.

How Hebrew and Hellenistic traditions converge in the prayers of the Ephesian letter is the subject of the next chapter.

8

The Prayer
in Ephesians 3:14-21

For this reason I bow my knees before the Father, from whom every family in heaven and on earth takes its name. I pray that, according to the riches of his glory, he may grant that you may be strengthened in your inner being with power through his Spirit, and that Christ may dwell in your hearts through faith, as you are being rooted and grounded in love. I pray that you may have the power to comprehend, with all the saints, what is the breadth and length and height and depth, and to know the love of Christ that surpasses knowledge, so that you may be filled with all the fullness of God. Now to him who by the power at work within us is able to accomplish abundantly far more than all we can ask or imagine, to him be glory in the church and Christ Jesus to all generations, forever and ever. Amen.

Ephesians 3:14-21

Both Acts and Ephesians reflect their authors' interests in prayer. Having in the previous chapter introduced the Hellenistic religious environment of Ephesus and examined some aspects of the relationship between Acts and Ephesians, we turn to the text of the Ephesian letter. The methodology here will parallel that in chapter 6 above. After discussing Ephesians 3:14-21 in its context in the letter, we will examine some of the Jewish and Hellenistic elements in the prayer and will note its purposes in the text.

The following assessment of Ephesians by Marcus Barth sets the theological context for this chapter:

Because more often than any other New Testament epistle the doctrinal and hortatory statements are phrased in the form of prayer, Ephesians occupies a unique place among the epistles. Both its possible strength and weakness are directly related to the fact that its author aims at doing the best he can for Christians he does not know. He prays for them; no wonder then that the peculiar content and purpose of Ephesians has found its expression in a peculiar form, the language of prayer.[1]

Many have noted that the first half of Ephesians, (chaps. 1–3), which is sometimes called the "doctrinal section," is dominated by prayers and the language of prayer.[2] The "first three chapters of Ephesians are almost continual prayer."[3]

The first section of Ephesians, in which God's mysterious plan of salvation is revealed and discussed, culminates in the prayer of 3:14-21, which recapitulates the main ideas of the first half of the letter and provides the transition to the parenesis in chapters 4–6. Before we examine the text of the prayer, however, some general remarks and reminders about the Ephesian letter are in order.

The Letter:
General Considerations

None of the questions connected with the origin, genre, author, or recipients of Ephesians have simple answers, and this chapter will probably not add anything new to the discussion of those issues.[4] The focus of our interest is the function of the prayer within the text as we have it and what it tells us about the spirituality of its author and his intended audience.

For these purposes, the following "lowest common denominator" of scholarly consensus is assumed. First, Ephesians is a Christian document of the late first century that was addressed to a predominantly gentile church or churches in Asia Minor. In spite of the textual difficulty in 1:1, I think the letter was at least read by the Christians in Ephesus, the leading city and transportation hub of Asia Minor at the time. The issues raised in the letter itself are too close to the situation of the church in Ephesus for all connections to be ruled out.[5] Second, the author, if not Paul himself, was a Jewish Christian highly influenced by and knowledgeable of Pauline thinking. He apparently did not know well the church he addressed.

Scholars who address the issue of origin usually find a pastoral reason for the letter's composition. Chadwick believes it was written to remind a gentile church of its Jewish origin (this is Käsemann's position as well) and to convince a world where "nothing new was true" that Christianity's roots were ancient.[6] Several scholars have argued that Ephesians is a liturgical document used in a baptismal connection.[7] Arnold has suggested that the most pressing question of converts in Ephesus and Asia Minor was the position of Christ in relation to hostile "powers." Arnold presents a strong case that Ephesians was written to affirm the supremacy of Christ over "the powers."[8]

In the previous chapter, I suggested that Ephesians was written, in part, to remind a gentile church of its Jewish predecessors. Consistent with that, I assume that the main theme of the letter is the divine plan of God, accomplished through the death and resurrection of Jesus, to reconcile to himself Jews and Gentiles. "He has made known to us the mystery of his will, according to his good pleasure that he set forth in Christ, as a plan for the fullness of time, to gather up all things in him, things in heaven and things on earth" (1:9-10; cf. 3:9-11). The church, with Christ as its head, is to be involved in the full accomplishment of God's plan.[9] Chapters 1–3 set forth this central theme, the divine plan of salvation that begins "before the foundation of the world" (1:4) and continues "to all generations, forever and ever" (3:21).[10] This observation introduces the issue of the text in its context.

The Text in Its Context

As previously noted, unlike the undisputed letters of Paul, the language and substance of the first half of Ephesians bears the character of prayer. Paul's usual sequence of kerygma-parenesis is replaced by prayer-parenesis.[11] The thanksgiving of the letter (1:3-14) is followed by a prayer for the enlightenment of the readers (1:15-23). The exposition of the gospel of the unity of all creation in Christ (2:1—3:13) is concluded by a prayer that the believers may comprehend God's great design.[12]

Some scholars have seen the entire first half of the letter as a series of different kinds of prayer. These chapters are made up of a sort of catalog of the types of prayers used by the early church. They include blessing (1:3-14), thanksgiving (1:15-16), intercession (1:17—2:22; 3:1-19), and doxology (3:20-21). In these prayer forms the liturgical origin of the work is seen.[13] "Those who believe that the basis of this work lies in early Christian liturgical material see in our passage an intrusion by the writer made when he put this material into letter form, presumably in order to circulate it."[14] In the liturgical view of Ephesians, these verses, 3:14-21, are "a prayer that those newly baptized shall bring forth the fruits of their Christian profession."[15]

It is certainly the case that the first section of the Ephesian letter begins and ends with prayer. Ephesians 3:14-21 resumes the intercessory prayer begun in 1:15-20 which was taken up again at 3:1 and interrupted by a digression on the author's role in the revelation of God's mystery.[16] Ephesians 3:14 ("For this reason I bow my knees before the Father") follows more naturally from 2:22 ("in whom you also are built together spiritually into a dwelling place for God") than from 3:13 ("I pray therefore that you may not lose heart over my sufferings for you; they are your glory"). That is, the author "bows his knees" because of the unity of Jew and Gentile, the end of hostility between those communities and the peace that comes from "access in one Spirit to the Father" (2:18). Both 3:1 and 3:14 refer to the salvation outlined in 2:11-22 (esp. vv. 19-22). Our text occurs between the author's explanation of God's plan (chaps. 1–3) and the way of life it calls forth (chaps. 4–6) and provides the logical transition between the two.

The Structure of the Prayer
in 3:14-21

The prayer itself falls into three parts: vv. 14-15 describe God's majesty, vv. 16-19 contain the three intercessory petitions of the prayer itself, and vv. 20-21 praise God in a doxology.[17]

> For this reason I bow my knees before the Father, from whom every family in heaven and on earth takes its name. I pray that, according to the riches of his glory, he may grant that you may be strengthened in your inner being with power through his Spirit, and that Christ may dwell in your hearts through faith, as you are being rooted and grounded in love. I pray that you may have the power to comprehend, with all the saints, what is the breadth and length and height and depth, and to know the love of Christ that surpasses knowledge, so that you may be filled with all the fullness of God.
> Now to him who by the power at work within us is able to accomplish abundantly far more than all we can ask or imagine, to him be glory in the church and in Christ Jesus to all generations, forever and ever. Amen.

Form-critical research to date has not uncovered hymns or traditional *Vorlage* behind the prayer.[18] However, before a final doxology, Jewish blessings commonly ended with a prayer that God's gifts might be rightly received (Psalm 106, for example).[19] So, while the prayer is apparently composed by the author, it follows a customary pattern.[20]

In the Greek text, the three petitions of the intercession are formed by *hina* ("that") clauses, the first two of which are followed by parallel infinitives. In English, the prayer may be outlined as follows: The author prays:

1. that
   a. they may be strengthened in the inner man through God's spirit, and that

   b. Christ may dwell in their hearts through faith;
2. that
   a. they may comprehend the love of Christ,
   b. they may know the love of Christ;
3. that
   a. they may be filled with the fullness of God.

The author prays for inner strengthening of his hearers and for their understanding of the love of Christ. Possessing these, they will "be filled with all the fullness of God" (v. 19b). "Whereas the prayer of Ephesians 1 sought for the readers an increased knowledge of the vastness of the divine power working on their behalf, the prayer of chapter 3 goes beyond knowledge to the experience of actual inner divine strengthening."[21]

Two other aspects of the structure of the prayer are noteworthy. First, it is possible to see an implicit trinitarian pattern at work with reference to the Father in vv. 14-15 and 20-21, the Spirit in v. 16, and the Son in vv. 17-19 and 21.[22] Second, it should be noted that, in cosmic terms, the prayer comes full circle from God as the source of life in v. 15 to God as the goal of humanity in vv. 19 and 21.[23] The overall movement of chapters 1 to 3 (from the "foundation of the world" in 1:4 to "forever and ever" in 3:21) is replicated in the passage. The historic scope of the ideas in Ephesians 1–3 is reflected in its concluding prayer. Both Jewish and Hellenistic traditions lie behind the author's thought.

Hebrew Traditions in the Prayer

A. T. Lincoln has argued that the use of Hebrew Scripture in Ephesians is supportive rather than formative. There are few actual quotations from Hebrew Scripture in Ephesians and none in chapter 3. (This is undoubtedly due to the predominantly gentile character of the audience addressed; see, e.g., 2:11 and 3:1.) With Chadwick and Käsemann, Lincoln believes that the use made of Hebrew Scripture is intended to remind gentile Christians that they have come into the heritage of Israel. It is the theology of Hebrew Scripture that played the formative role in the author's understanding of the Christian gospel.[24]

For example, the notion in v. 15 of the families of earth receiving their name from the Father clearly comes from the traditions of Israel. In Hebrew Scripture, God is the prototype of all fatherhood. He gives names to his families (Gen. 17:5; 32:28). As noted in chapter 4 above, the name stands for the identity or character of the one named.[25] To receive a name from God is to receive a portion of God's power and presence.[26] The writer of the letter uses the Hebrew idea to extend the power and presence of God to "every family" (v. 15). The reference serves as a way of emphasizing the unity of Jew and Gentile now found in God's fatherhood and in Jesus Christ.

Another example of Hebrew thought is evident in the author's use of the Jewish tradition of the immeasurable vastness of the world, which is illustrated by the limits of human understanding (Job 11:7-10).[27] In using the "dimensions" of the universe as rhetorical preamble to prepare for the climax of the prayer in v. 18, the author reinforces the need expressed for divine comprehension and "knowledge."

Another aspect of Hebrew tradition in the prayer has already been mentioned in connection with the prayer's structure, which is firmly in the tradition of *berakah*. The doxology at the end makes use of a liturgical pattern not of the author's own creation.[28] Being Jewish in form and Christian in content, it provides a Hebrew solemn ending to the first half of the letter.[29] Thus it is perhaps Jewish worship which has left its liturgical mark most clearly in our text.

Finally, Barth has noted that the special concerns of Qumran emerge when Ephesians speaks of angels, powers, the devil, the heritage of the saints, mystery, and the role of knowledge in the life of the believer.[30] Although they are on the periphery of this study, it would be fruitful to pursue the concepts of "inner man," "power," "knowledge," and the dimensions of the universe in connection with the Qumran literature, bearing in mind that Jerome Murphy-O'Connor has suggested that Ephesians was written by an amanuensis of Paul's from the ranks of the Essenes.[31]

Hellenistic Traditions in the Prayer

Discussion of the Hellenistic backgrounds of the text naturally focuses on vv. 16 and 18-19 and the terms "power," "know," "knowledge," "filled," and "fullness."

In *Ephesians, Power and Magic,* Arnold argues that when the author of the letter spoke of "powers," his readers would naturally think of the demonic powers they feared. In Arnold's view, this prayer is inserted to assure the hearers that no conceivable power is outside the parameters of God's sovereignty. The author describes where Christ stands in relation to "the powers"; he asserts Christ's supremacy over them. The form *exischysēte* ("you may have the power") in v. 18 is a *hapax legomenon* in the New Testament, seemingly employed "to emphasize the difficulty of comprehending the vastness and magnitude of the intended object."[32] The writer's point is that God's power empowers believers to overcome "the powers."

Second, the terms *to know* and *knowledge* are, as usual, red flags for those looking for gnosticism. I agree with Barth, who holds that Ephesians is not dependent upon classical Christian-heretic gnostic systems.[33] Gnosticism was a second-century phenomenon, and Ephesians seems to be a late-first-century document. Likewise, discussion of formulas from mystery cults and Hermetic literature, which are similar to v. 18, sometimes fails to note the Christian context in which "love . . . surpasses knowledge." That is, Christians have a source of knowledge greater than that of the mysteries or even of gnosis (more about this shortly).

Finally, the phrase "the fullness of God" was certainly chosen by the author with the Hellenistic religious environment in mind. It possesses impressive spiritual associations as a term that was variously used in the religiously syncretistic atmosphere of late antiquity. For example, in the Christian gnosticism of the second century, it signified the uppermost spirit world, that closest to God, thus implying a hierarchy of heavenly powers.[34] (It might also reflect a Hebrew background if it is an allusion to Jer. 23:24: "Do I not fill heaven and earth? says the Lord.")[35] Eduard Lohse has pointed out that the Christian community took the term *fullness* from Hellenistic religion but transferred it from the realm of cosmology to soteriology.[36] Here and elsewhere, it is "through Christ" that the fullness of God is available.

The Purpose of the Prayer in the Text of Ephesians

Other aspects of the traditions behind Ephesians 3:14-21 could be examined; for example, the issue of addressing God as Father, the "Abba tradition,"[37] and the connections and parallels to other New Testament works. My comments about the religious traditions behind the text are intended to recall the richness of the thought of the letter and to prepare for the central issue to be examined. Recall that Luke also drew on traditional material in the composition of the prayer in Acts 4:23-31, a text that also served a narrative purpose in that work (see chapter 6 above).

There is no reason to suppose that the prayer in Ephesians 3:14-21 is not really a prayer. That is, the primary purpose of the text is to intercede for the inner fortification of the saints, their perception of all the dimensions of God's will, and for their perfection in line with God's perfection.[38] Like the prayer in John 17, to which Mitton so favorably compares this text, it is a prayer directed to God but now read to the hearers of the letter in a communal setting. The "overheard" aspect of the prayer suggests two additional functions it may have performed in the Ephesian letter.

As was the case in Acts 4:23-31, the first function of the language of the prayer seems calculated to summarize the major ideas of chapters 1–3. The writer's technique is to remind the hearer of earlier ideas by repeating or paraphrasing key terms from the earlier part of the letter in the prayer itself. The prayer begins by referring back to the previous chapter ("for this reason," 3:1, 14). The developmental linking of ideas in the progression of thought intended by this transitional phrase is obvious. In 3:15 the phrase "from whom every family in heaven and on earth takes its name," is surely meant to recall and reinforce the point of 2:19, "You are no longer strangers and aliens, but you are citizens with the saints and also members of the household of God." As descendants from a common Father, the Christians in Ephesus are literally "members of the household of God." The repetition of "in heaven and on earth" links this prayer to the opening verses of the letter and to the idea of God's plan of cosmic unification in Christ, which unites "things in heaven and things on earth" (cf. 1:10).

Four key ideas from the earlier chapters are reiterated in the petitionary section of the prayer (vv. 16-19). First, the "riches of his glory" echoes earlier uses in the letter of forms of the word *riches*. The hearer is reminded of God's rich grace (1:7; 2:7) and of the "unsearchable riches of Christ" (3:8 NIV). Further, the hearer is to recall the prayer in 1:15-23 where the author also prays that they may know "what are the riches of his glorious inheritance among the saints" (1:18). The author wishes to stress the superabundant generosity of God to God's people. In both prayers the power (*dynamei*; cf. 1:19 and 3:16) of God is associated with this strength and abundant wealth. In fact, it was the "power at work within us" (3:20) which was the subject of the prayer in Ephesians 1.

Second, commentators have puzzled over the mixed metaphor "rooted and grounded" (v. 17).[39] The difficulty is resolved when it is realized that the author is recalling the images he has used earlier of the church or the household of God which is "built upon the foundation of the apostles and prophets" and "is joined together and grows into a holy temple" "for a dwelling place for God" (2:20-22). The metaphors of building (grounded, foundation), agriculture (rooted, grows), and permanent dwelling are used together again at the end of Ephesians 3, as they were at the end of Ephesians 2, to reinforce the hearers' understanding of their relationship to the Trinity which appears with this constellation of images in both passages. (Note that Paul himself was fond of conjoining the building/agriculture metaphor; see 1 Cor. 3:6-15 and, perhaps, Col. 2:6-7. The unusual combination suggests, if not Pauline authorship, at least intimate knowledge of Pauline writings.)

Third, the much discussed set of "dimensions" of the love of Christ in v. 18 echo and expand the extent of God's power as depicted in the earlier prayer in 1:21.[40] It may also shed light on Christ's destruction of the "dividing wall, that is, the hostility between us" (2:14). Many commentators have assumed that the "dividing wall" was a reference to a low barrier around the outer court of the Jerusalem Temple on which notices were posted in Greek and Latin warning Gentiles against entry. G. B. Caird argues instead that the metaphor comes from biblical and rabbinic theology. The word *phragmos* ("fence, partition") is used in the Greek text (Isa. 5:2) and in Mark 12:1 for the hedge God planted around his vineyard, Israel. Caird thinks the author of Ephesians believes that God's protective hedge has been turned by Jewish nationalism into a rigid legal system that has led to hostility with Gentiles.[41] The "breadth and length and height and depth" of Christ's love has overcome even that barrier.

Finally, "the 'fullness of him who fills all in all" closes the prayer of 1:15-23 and is, again, the goal for which the author prays in 3:19. In both instances, the term reinforces the claim in 1:10 of Christ's authority over the cosmos and does so, in part, by relying on the Hellenistic associations of the term. Later, in the parenetic section of Ephesians, it will be the "fullness of Christ" that earmarks mature Christianity (see 4:13). Thus the phrase serves to foreshadow what is to follow in the letter.

The first function of the prayer of 3:14-21 in the text of Ephesians, then, is to summarize and reinforce the three major ideas presented in chapters 1–3 of the epistle. First, the abundance and power of God and its cosmic extent, which planned and effected the unity of all persons in Christ; second, the foundation and growth of the individual Christian in Christ; and, third, the fullness of God—these have been the main themes of Ephesians to this point and are the substantive concepts in this prayer. Careful examination reveals that these ideas, and the specific words and phrases that carry their weight, are paralleled in the prayers in 1:15-23 and 3:14-21. The author may well be using the prayers to effect literary inclusion, to mark for the hearers the end of one section of the letter and the beginning of another.

The second function of the prayer in 3:14-21 is to provide the transition between the "doctrine" in the first half of the letter and the "practical admonition" in the second. "Love" is the idea that links the two halves of the epistle.

The heart of the prayer is "emphasis on love as better than knowledge."[42] Appearing in some form nineteen times in the letter, love (*agape*) is an important concept in Ephesians.[43] Mitton entitles the prayer of 3:14-21 "The Love of Christ."[44] The prayer contrasts love and knowledge and implies a challenge to Hellenistic teaching, which required some form of knowledge as necessary for a relationship with God.[45] Here the author sets forth "a Christian gnosis which recognizes love as supreme rather than knowledge" (see 1 Cor. 8:1, 13).[46] In this view, love surpasses knowledge, because action and practical benevolence necessarily proceed from love but not from knowledge.

The author's prayer for the indwelling of Christ by faith and firm establishment of their lives in love expresses the desire that the hearers may progress to a deep understanding of God and may come to act as God has acted. The danger in the Greek world was a faith built simply on some form of intellectual knowledge. (Recall that this issue is important in both the Corinthian correspondence and Colossians; see 1 Cor. 1:22, Col. 2:18, 23.) If there is no love, the Spirit of Christ is not present and there can be no progression in "understanding."[47] The author wants his readers not just to comprehend (*katalabesthai*, v. 18), which implies grasping something mentally, but to know (*ginōskō*, v. 19), which implies practical apprehension through personal experience. "To know" in this sense is to make personal application.[48] The content of the "knowledge" to be applied is God's love, the "love of Christ which surpasses knowledge." In the Christian sense of the term, to know is to love, to be an "imitator of God" (5:1), to "live in love, as Christ loved us and gave himself up for us" (5:2).

To know and to love in this way requires a community. As Barth noted, in 3:16-19 increase of knowledge is a social, not a private, event because of chapters 2–3; the mode of knowledge is determined by what is to be known.[49] The "love of Christ" cannot be apprehended fully by an individual but can be "with all the saints" (3:18).[50] One cannot "know love" without loving, without giving up the self for the other.

The place where the full knowledge, that is application, of love is attained is the church, to which the author turns in chapters 4–6 with practical advice. For example, the goal of the "gifts" is that the church may build "itself up in love" (4:16). The new life is to be lived "according to the likeness of God" (4:24), which is love. The relationship between husband and wife is to be modeled on Christ's love for the church (5:25). "The second section . . . contains a series of instructions to love (4:2, 15; 5:2, 25, 28, 33; 6:24) summarized best by the statement of 5:2."[51]

It is from the "love of Christ," which the prayer in 3:14-19 asks that they understand fully, that the "new life" described in practical terms in chapters 4–6 proceeds. No commands to love appear in the first three chapters, which instead speak of the great love of the Father for the Son (1:6) and for believers (1:4; 2:4; 3:17, 19).[52] The second section of the letter presents the imperatives. It is as though the author is providing an essential definition of love in chapters 1–3 (what it is) and a functional definition in chapters 4–6 (what it does). Without a profound, internal (4:16, 17) understanding of the nature of love, the actual living or "putting on" of this new life would be impossible. Full realization of the Christian life is possible only through the power of God, which can do "far more abundantly than all that we ask or think" (v. 20, RSV). Thus the prayer in 3:14-21.

Chapters 1–3 of Ephesians demonstrate the meaning of God's love, and chapters 4–6 provide practical instructions on "how to do it." The author's prayer "is that his readers should become what they already are in virtue of the Christ-event (vv. 16-19)."[53] This blessing, and the intercession for their empowerment for the life of love, can be granted only by God. Thus we have the "strategic positioning" of the prayer in the text of Ephesians.

Conclusion

Dominated by the language of prayer, the Ephesian letter is a rich source of information on the early church's spiritual life and attitudes. By examining the prayer at the center of the letter, we learn something of the Hebrew and Hellenistic backgrounds on which the author drew, but, more important, we see his summary of the first half of the letter and his understanding of the connection between doctrine and practice. "It is by prayer that the faithful open themselves to Christ's power and so participate in God's saving love for the universe."[54]

In the light of the relationship between Acts and Ephesians, which was noted in chapter 7 above, it is interesting to discover that the authors of both works use prayer texts in similar ways. As chapter 6 above explained, Luke uses the texts of prayers as he does speeches: first, to reinforce the church's Jewish heritage and, second, to provide theological commentary on the narrative. As is evident from the above, the author of Ephesians draws on Hebrew traditions and forms in composing his prayer. Implicitly he too is reminding his readers and hearers of their heritage among the people of Israel. And, like the prayer in Acts, the prayer in Ephesians 3:14-21 summarizes the theological discussion that preceded it.

The authors of the Acts of the Apostles and the Letter to the Ephesians not only share literary antecedents and forms from the Greek text and allude to Jewish theological concepts, but they also both focus on Christian community. In both books in the examples discussed (Acts 4:23-31 and Eph. 3:14-21), the prayers are for the empowering of the Christian community, that the church may declare God's word with boldness and live lives reflective of God's love. The spiritual locus of the prayers is not individual persons but the community of believers.

The early church was especially noted for its life of prayer. The literature of the New Testament not only records that the early Christians prayed, but it provides examples of those prayers. At least two authors recorded or wrote prayers and used those prayers for literary and theological purposes within the longer works in which they appear. For them, prayer was theology, and theology, prayer.

9

Conclusion

We now return to the question raised at the outset of this study: How did the early Christians set out and journey in God's direction? In other words, what characterized the spirituality of the early church as it has been reflected in the Acts of the Apostles and the Ephesian letter?

Anyone familiar with the text of the New Testament will find that the answers given here seem obvious. Indeed, they belabor the obvious. Yet it is remarkable how far the modern church has wandered from its roots and neglected the fundamentals of its spiritual heritage. This is all the more startling in view of the fact that the world of the first century and of our own age have several things in common.

People of the first century of our era searched as we, poised on the verge of the twenty-first century, search for moral and religious grounding. Traditional answers no longer seem to provide sufficiently for the questions of the day. The need is for spiritual empowerment in a world that seems to many to be, at best, indifferent and, at worst, hostile. Both our Christian ancestors and we ourselves live in a religiously pluralistic environment. Even small towns, which once offered several Christian denominations and perhaps a synagogue, now face challenges from world religions such as Hinduism and Islam as well as from a variety of cults and esoteric practices that seem to scholars of religion like nothing so much as Hellenistic mysteries, magic, and gnosis.

Finally, like those early Christians, we modern Christians are in the minority. In the introduction to this study I argued that the Christian worldview is countercultural, that it does not share the assumptions of our age. We live in post-Constantinian times. Christian assumptions are no longer the norm. Christian values are no longer foundational in our societies. We, in America, pay lip service to being "one nation under God," but we live as if we are alone on the planet and in the universe. Christians today face the same practical issues that their first-century counterparts did. We must live the Christian life in an indifferent, even hostile environment. We must be salt, light, and leaven even when the world does not know they are lacking.

What have we learned from this study of the early church that will aid us in this task? We can approach the answer in two ways: first, by commenting on the general characteristics of the early church's spirituality, and, second, by noting specific practices of special importance that it engaged in.

Four general characteristics of the early church's spiritual life are important for us to note. Its spirituality was holistic, communal, pluralistic, and open to and enlivened by the Holy Spirit.

When I say that the spirituality of the early church was holistic, I mean that the implications of the Christian calling embraced the whole of life. To become a Christian was to enter a radically new mode of being. In the metaphor of the Ephesian letter, it was to "put off" one mode of being and to "put on" another (Eph. 4:22-24). To become Christ's in baptism was to be changed radically. Because life in Christ destroyed the ethnic, sexual, and economic categories of society (cf. Gal. 3:28), Christianity made claims on every aspect of an individual's life.

Perhaps the most dramatic example of the totality of the Christian commitment is represented by the economic experiments depicted in Acts and discussed in chapter 3 above. To be a Christian in the first century in Jerusalem meant to have economic responsibility for all other Christians, not just for members of one's own biological family. And, by extension, Paul's collection suggested that richer gentile Christians had responsibility for their poorer Judean brothers and sisters (see 2 Cor. 8:13-14). What was called for was not just a confession of faith but a commitment of resources.

We have a great deal to learn from the totality of the commitment of the early Christians to Christ. We must recover a spirituality that not only understands that Christ's claim is on every aspect of our lives but willingly commits every aspect of life, time, talents, resources, and possessions to Christ and his cause.

Second, and related to the first characteristic, the spirituality of the early church was communal. The "rugged individualism" of America in the twentieth century is a far cry from the communal responsibility of Christians in the first. Perhaps the most potent indication of how much interrelatedness the early Christians felt with one another is the pervasiveness of the image of the body in the New Testament. Christians understood themselves to be organically related to one another. Their prayers were for the sustenance and empowerment of the community. The focus of religious life in both Acts and Ephesians (and for Paul and the churches to which he wrote) was the community, its upbuilding and its sanctity.

Early Christian writings reflect an understanding that Christ had called believers into relationship not only with him but with one another. It was not possible to be a Christian alone, because Christian love must be perfected in loving. And loving requires an object. Love is a transitive verb. How, indeed, can one love God and not love those whom God has placed in the sphere of one's own life and influence (see 1 John 4:20)?

Over and over again the prayers of the early church moved beyond the realm of private concern into the arena of life in community. Early Christian prayer freed people from the prison of egocentricity and the isolation that it imposes. Even when they prayed alone, the followers of Jesus were taught to pray in the plural, in communion, "*Our* Father." This focus on the community and its needs and mission must be reappropriated by modern Christians both for the good of the kingdom and for our own spiritual health. We are not isolated individuals hermetically sealed within our own skins. We are not alone, not just because the Paraclete has been sent, but because we are, whether we realize it or not, in community with other Christians. We must relearn from the first-century church how to live out the implications of this fact.

Third, the church of the first century was pluralisitic in form. There has never been a monolithic Christianity, one "official" and "approved" way to be Christian, to practice Christianity, or to worship God. We have a tendency to forget this, to look with longing back to a golden age (which never existed) when Christianity was "standardized."

Our study of Acts and Ephesians points to the fact that one of the accomplishments of early Christianity was its ability to adapt existing cultural forms to its own purposes. In Jerusalem, Judea, and Galilee, Christianity used the language and forms of worship of its Jewish parents and neighbors. But when the gentile Christian mission moved into Antioch and beyond, the church was not bound by its origins in Judaism. It adopted the language and forms of the Greco-Roman world. The early missionaries, of whom Paul is our most familiar example, preached the message of the death and resurrection of Jesus the Christ to people in an idiom they could understand. Acts 15 (and Galatians and Romans) is trying to tell us that Judaism was not to be imposed on Christians as a culturally required form. The issue was not to maintain Judaism, but to maintain the unity of the church and its fellowship across cultural lines. Christian unity necessitates pluralism of form and practice in the spiritual life.

Furthermore, if the early church was willing and able to adopt and appropriate new cultural forms to the message and mission of Christianity, should not the modern church be at least as open to diversity? Syncretism of a certain sort has always been part of the Christian tradition. No historic group or denomination in Christendom has ever had a corner on the market on how to be the church, how to worship, how to practice allegiance to Christ. Our modern Christian spirituality must learn from its original spiritualities.

The final general characteristic of the spirituality of the early church of which we would do well to take note is its understanding of the place and potency of the Holy Spirit in its midst. In the Acts of the Apostles, the Holy Spirit is a main character in the narrative. The story begins with Jesus' promise of "power when the Holy Spirit has come upon you" (Acts 1:8) and with the outpouring of that power at Pentecost (Acts 2). Early Christians were open to the Spirit's power; they coveted it, sought it, and were willing to be its instruments in the world.

Our spirituality must again be spiritual, charismatic in the classical sense of that term, open to the reception of gifts for ministry. We can learn from the early church not to fear the power and possession of the Spirit. We are not to "grieve the Holy Spirit of God" (Eph. 4:30) by refusing its gifts, muzzling its word, and restraining its activity. Those who find the experience of Pentecost too enthusiastic and frightening might do well to recall that this is the same Spirit promised by Jesus in the quietness of the farewell discourses in John 14-17.

The spiritual fire, practical pluralism, communal commitment, and holistic understanding of the early Christians were worked out in what they did to manifest their belief. Three practices stand out as definitive of the early church: prayer, the Lord's Supper, and devotion to the name of Jesus.

It seems ludicrous even to mention that prayer was the defining spiritual practice of the early church. Yet the number of Christian gatherings in our day that neither begin nor end with prayer suggest how necessary it is to stress this fact. Prayer preceded every advance in the Christian mission as depicted in Acts. It preceded and followed all significant endeavor. The church prayed for the selection of leadership and to commission that leadership. It prayed in crisis and in triumph. No occasion was too insignificant or of too great import for prayer.

Many modern Christians are apparently interested in the "methodology" or "how to" of prayer. This fact is attested to by the numbers of people who seek instruction in Eastern prayer practices. Study of the early church reveals what may be helpful information about its "method." First, there were many types of prayer in the early church: intercession, petition, thanksgiving, confession, doxology, blessing—to name but a few. Second, several bodily positions were assumed in prayer (standing, often with hands raised; kneeling; prostration), and at least some early Christians faced East when they prayed. While these details are not essentials of faith, they are of interest to and may enrich persons in our day seeking for a deeper life of prayer. Of real significance about the early church's prayers were their spirit, fervency, and expectancy. The early Christians assumed God would act in response to prayer in Jesus' name.

Of related interest is the degree to which the written prayers in the literature of the New Testament were used by their authors to express theology. Written prayers were an important vehicle for the Christian message and were used to summarize that message. Without denigrating extemporaneous prayer, we might do well to examine what our own prayers reflect about our theology. What will the prayers of the church in the literature of the twentieth century say about its theology to readers in future generations? In an age of liturgical experimentation and reform we must not lose sight of the crucial importance of what we say and to whom we say it.

The second special focus of the early church's practice was the Lord's Supper. Our discussion of the Eucharist stressed the necessity of reaching back beyond the questions of the Reformation to the eschatological context of early Jewish Christianity and to the fellowship meals of Hellenistic clubs and religious societies. It is perhaps here that serious historical study is of most benefit to the modern Christian. We would do well to try to recover some of the original context of the early meals of remembrance and expectation so that our focus is not too narrowly on the means and the elements by which those ideas and expectations were (and are) expressed.

Again, in the light of the text of the New Testament, it seems strange to have to stress the devotion of the church to the Lord's Supper and to its weekly celebration. The early church's devotion to the Lord's Supper focused on thanksgiving, appreciation of the presence of Christ with them, and expectation of his final return. Their meals were characterized by an openness and inclusivity of table fellowship that was extraordinary in its day and, if practiced, would be extraordinary in our own. The whole notion of table fellowship is one that we need to rediscover, especially in a world where modern denominational lines are more defined by socioeconomic status and race than by historic questions of theology and practice.

It apparently was also the case that the early church's eucharistic celebrations had a much livelier sense of "re-membering" in the sense of "putting back together" the whole church, living and dead, than we have in the Protestant traditions today. If we confess that we "believe in all things, visible and invisible," what does this mean to our practice of the Lord's Supper, calling together as it does the "great cloud of witnesses"?

Prayer and the Lord's Supper are obvious examples of the early church's spiritual practices that are in evidence today, albeit in altered form. That church's devotion to, reverence for, and empowerment by the name of Jesus is perhaps less well known in Christianity today. For the early church, the name of Jesus was a creative power at work in the world, granting relationship with Christ by the Spirit and setting in motion the energy that was Christ's. The name was a channel of God's power.

Unfortunately, we have lost this sense of the sacredness and potency of the name of Jesus. We have lost the reality expressed by the old hymns such as "All Hail the Power of Jesus' Name," "At the Name of Jesus," "Savior, Again to Thy Dear Name," "Our Father, Thy Dear Name," "How Sweet the Name of Jesus Sounds," and many others that speak of the name of Jesus. We say the words, but we no longer are in touch with the powerful reality they mediate. This is a great loss—and not only in the context of Christian practice. To forget the potency of the name means we lose an important point of ecumenical contact with other religious traditions such as Hinduism, Buddhism, and Islam, which have a long heritage of spiritual practice focused on the name of the divinity or avatar.

Furthermore, our ignorance of the practices surrounding the name of Jesus cuts us off from Eastern Christendom, in which the tradition of hesychasm developed a whole method of prayer focused on repetition of the Name of Jesus and coordinating that repetition with the breath until the prayer "prays itself" spontaneously in the one who prays. For those interested in prayer methodology, then, devotion to the name provides another point of entry to the traditions of mystical prayer within Christianity.

How did the early Christians set out and journey in God's direction? First, they took as magnetic north the person of Jesus Christ, his cross, passion, and resurrection. Everything else was subordinate to their devotion to him. In prayer they continued relationship with the Christ and were empowered by him for service. In the Lord's Supper, they maintained living fellowship with the host and with all those whom he called to the Table as fellow guests. By devotion to the name of Jesus they remained open to the power of God which came to them in the Holy Spirit. The response engendered was not compartmentalized; it pervaded the whole of life and called persons from isolation into communities of concern and self-giving love. These communities were extraordinary. People noticed them ("See how they love one another") and wanted what they had to offer. So the early Christians found ways to present their message that were comprehensible to the spiritually hungry and pluralistic empire in which they lived.

The pages of the New Testament are alive with the spiritual energy of early Christianity. To recover it we can do no better than to turn to those accounts with hearts open to the one whose power they mediate and with lives ready to yield to the demands he will inevitably lay upon us.

Abbreviations

ATR	*Anglican Theological Review*
BJRL	*Bulletin of the John Rylands University Library of Manchester*
EQ	*Evangelical Quarterly*
ET	*Expository Times*
HBC	*Harper's Bible Commentary*
HBD	*Harper's Bible Dictionary*
IB	*The Interpreter's Bible*
IDB	*The Interpreter's Dictionary of the Bible*
JBL	*Journal of Biblical Literature*
JETS	*Journal of the Evangelical Theology Society*
JSNT	*Journal of the Study of the New Testament*
NIV	*New International Version*
NRSV	*New Revised Standard Version*
NT	New Testament
NTS	*New Testament Studies*
OT	Old Testament
RE	*Review and Expositor*
TDNT	*Theological Dictionary of the New Testament*
VGT	*Vocabulary of the Greek Testament*
ZNW	*Zeitschrift für die neutestamentliche Wissenschaft*

Notes

Chapter 1. What Is Spirituality?

1. Marcus J. Borg, *Jesus: A New Vision* (San Francisco: Harper & Row, 1987) 32.

2. Evelyn Underhill, *The Spiritual Life* (New York: Harper & Brothers, n.d.) 36.

Chapter 2. The Spiritual Backgrounds of the New Testament Church

1. For discussion of these groups within Judaism, see the section "Judaism" in the bibliography at the end of this chapter.

2. Roger T. Beckwith, "The Daily and Weekly Worship of the Primitive Church in Relation to Its Jewish Antecedents," *Evangelical Quarterly* 56 (1984): 65–69.

3. Louis Bouyer, *A History of Christian Spirituality,* vol. 1 (New York: Seabury Press, 1963) 20.

4. For a fuller discussion of apocalyptic and its implications see W. G. Kümmel, *Introduction to the New Testament* (Nashville: Abingdon Press, 1975) 452–474; Norman Perrin, *The New Testament: An Introduction* (New York: Harcourt Brace Jovanovich, 1974), chap. 4; and A. N. Wilder, "Eschatological Imagery and Earthly Circumstance," NTS 5 (1958–59): 229–245.

5. For a concise and accessible survey of the view of the Messiah in the period see F. F. Bruce, *New Testament History* (New York: Doubleday & Co., 1969) chap. 10.

6. Urban T. Holmes, *A History of Christian Spirituality: An Analytical Introduction* (New York: Seabury Press, 1981) 14–17.

7. For an excellent overview of the subject, see Luther H. Martin, *Hellenistic Religions* (Oxford: Oxford University Press, 1987). Much of my discussion is indebted to and relies on the categories presented in that work.

8. Martin 24. For a fuller description of these images, see pp. 21–25.

9. Helmut Koester, *Introduction to the New Testament,* 2 vols. (Philadelphia: Fortress Press, 1982) 1:157.

10. See, e.g., Ross S. Kraemer, "Women and the Religions of the Greco-Roman World," *Religious Studies Review* 9 (1983): 127–139.

Chapter 3. The Spiritual Life of the Early Church in Acts

1. See David E. Aune, *The New Testament in Its Literary Environment* (Philadelphia: Westminster Press, 1987); C. K. Barrett, *Luke the Historian in Recent*

Study (London: Epworth Press, 1961); and Mark A. Powell, *What Are They Saying about Luke?* (New York: Paulist Press, 1989) and *What Are They Saying about Acts?* (New York: Paulist Press, 1991).

2. F. F. Bruce, "The Church of Jerusalem in the Acts of the Apostles," *BJRL* 67/2 (1985): 641.

3. I. H. Marshall, "The Biblical Use of the Word ἐκκλησία," *ET* 84 (1973): 359–364.

4. Joseph A. Fitzmyer, *Essays on the Semitic Background of the New Testament,* Sources for Biblical Study 5 (Missoula, Mont.: Society of Biblical Literature, 1974) 276.

5. William Neil, *The Acts of the Apostles* (Grand Rapids: Wm. B. Eerdmans, 1987); see also Joseph A. Fitzmyer, "Jewish Christianity in Acts in the Light of the Qumran Scrolls," in Fitzmyer, *Essays.*

6. Gerhard Delling, *Worship in the New Testament* (Philadelphia: Westminster Press, 1962) 172.

7. Fitzmyer, *Essays* 275.

8. Bruce, "The Church" 643.

9. C. S. C. Williams, *A Commentary on the Acts of the Apostles* (New York: Harper & Brothers, 1957) 71.

10. See Roger T. Beckwith, "The Daily and Weekly Worship of the Primitive Church in Relation to Its Jewish Antecedents," *Evangelical Quarterly* 56 (1984).

11. Carl R. Holladay, "Acts," *HBC*, ed. James L. Mays et.al. (San Francisco: Harper & Row, 1988) 1082.

12. Codex Bezae suggests only the Jerusalem church.

13. See Fitzmyer, *Essays.*

14. F. J. Foakes-Jackson and Kirsopp Lake, eds., *The Beginnings of Christianity* (London: Macmillan & Co., 1933) 5:140, 148–149.

15. Johannes Munck, *The Acts of the Apostles, Anchor Bible* (Garden City, N.Y.: Doubleday & Co., 1967) 22.

16. Foakes-Jackson and Lake 141.

17. See also Martin Hengel, *Property and Riches in the Early Church* (Philadelphia: Fortress Press, 1974); and Bonnie Thurston, " 'Christian Socialism' and Acts 2:44-45 and 4:32-37," *Mission Journal* 17 (1984): 21–23. A whole issue of *Interpretation* (41/4, October 1987) is devoted to "Wealth and Poverty in Biblical Perspective," and the May 12, 1989 issue of *Christianity Today* also has an essay on the New Testament teachings on wealth.

18. Oscar Cullmann, *Early Christian Worship* (London: SCM Press, 1953) 15.

19. See Strack-Billerbeck, *Kommentar,* for the way the Last Supper fits the pattern of Passover meals as set out in the Mishnah, *Pesahim* 10. Associations with the fellowship meals of Greek religion would form another study.

20. H. M. Conn, "Luke's Theology of Prayer," *Christianity Today* 17 (1972): 6–8; and P. T. O'Brien, "Prayer in Luke-Acts," *Tyndale Bulletin* 24 (1973): 111–127.

21. Joachim Jeremias, *The Prayers of Jesus* (Philadelphia: Fortress Press, 1978) 77.

22. James H. Moulton and George Milligan, *VGT* (Grand Rapids: Wm. B. Eerdmans, 1980) 137.

23. For this discussion I am indebted to Burton B. Thurston, Sr., for use of "A Comparative Summary of Terminology for Prayer in the New Testament," October 1956.

24. See Beckwith (n. 10 above); Louis Bouyer, *A History of Christian Spirituality,* vol. 1 (New York: Seabury Press, 1963); and Sharon Burns, "The Roots of Christian Prayer and Spirituality in Judaism," in *The Journey of Western Spirituality,* ed. A. W. Sadler (Chico, Calif.: Scholars Press, 1980).

25. G. H. C. Macgregor, "The Acts of the Apostles," *IB*, vol. 9, ed. G. A. Buttrick et al. (New York: Abingdon-Cokesbury Press, 1954).

26. Robert A. Spivey and D. Moody Smith, *Anatomy of the New Testament* (New York: Macmillan Co., 1982) 155–156.

27. F. J. Foakes-Jackson, *The Acts of the Apostles* (London: Hodder & Stoughton, 1951) 23.

28. Bruce, "The Church" 647.

29. See Beckwith, note 10 above.

30. Delling 104–109.

31. See *Clement* 2.29; Tertullian, *On Prayer*, 23.

32. F. F. Bruce, *The Acts of the Apostles* (London: Tyndale Press, 1952) 80.

33. Williams 61.

34. Foakes-Jackson 9.

35. Foakes-Jackson 51–53.

36. Neil 104.

37. Williams 98.

38. Munck 37.

39. Holladay 1084.

40. Johannes Behm, "νηστις, νηστεύω, νηστεία," *TDNT*, ed. Gerhard Kittel (Grand Rapids: Wm. B. Eerdmans, 1967) 4:929.

41. H. H. Guthrie, Jr., "Fast," *IDB*, ed. G. A. Buttrick et al (Nashville: Abingdon Press, 1962) 2:244.

42. Behm 432.

43. See also Textus Receptus on Matt. 17:21; Mark 9:29; Acts 10:30; and 1 Cor. 7:3.

44. For fuller treatments of fasting in the New Testament, see C. C. Mitchell, "The Practice of Fasting in the NT," *Bibliotheca Sacra* 147 (1990) 455–469, and Joseph A. Wimmer, *Fasting in the New Testament* (New York: Paulist Press, 1982). An excellent practical exposition is found in Arthur Wallis, *God's Chosen Fast* (Ft. Washington, Pa.: Christian Literature Crusade, 1973).

45. M. H. Shepherd, Jr., "Hymns," *IDB* 2:667–668.

46. See Eduard Norden, *Agnostos Theos* (Stuttgart: B. G. Teubner, 1956).

47. Leonard Thompson, "Hymns in Early Christian Worship," *ATR* 55 (1973) 458–472.

48. Allison Trites, "The Prayer Motif in Luke-Acts," in *Perspectives on Luke-Acts,* ed. Charles H. Talbert (Perspectives in Religious Studies, 1978) 181.

Chapter 4. "The Name" in Acts 1–10

1. I assume that Acts does contain historical information; see Gerd Lüdemann, *Early Christianity according to the Traditions in Acts* (Minneapolis: Fortress Press, 1989.)

2. R. Abba, "Name," *IDB*, ed. G. A. Buttrick et al. (Nashville: Abingdon Press, 1962) 3:500–508; Hans Bitenhard, *"onoma," TDNT*, ed. Gehard Kittel (Grand Rapids: Wm. B. Eerdmans, 1967) 5:243-277; Silva New, "The Name, Baptism, and the Laying on of Hands," in *The Beginnings of Christianity,* ed. F. J. Foakes-Jackson and Kirsopp Lake (London: Macmillan & Co., 1933) 5:121-140; Johannes Pedersen, *Israel: Its Life and Culture* (London: Oxford University Press, 1926) 245–259; G. van der Leeuw, *Religion in Essence and Manifestation* (London: Allen & Unwin 1964); and Gerhard von Rad, *Studies in Deuteronomy* (London: SCM Press, 1953) chap. 3.

3. Abba, "Name" 500; Bitenhard, *"onoma"* 243.

4. Dana M. Pike, "Names," HBD (San Francisco: Harper & Row, 1985) 682–683.

5. James H. Moulton and George Milligan, *VGT* (Grand Rapids: Wm. B. Eerdmans, 1980) 451.

6. Pedersen 245.

7. Van der Leeuw 153; and Bitenhard 243–248.

8. Bitenhard 255.

9. Von Rad, chap. 3.

10. Bitenhard 243.

11. Bitenhard 255–269.

12. C. K. Barrett, ed., *The New Testament Background: Selected Documents* (London: SPCK, 1961) 31.

13. Barrett 31–32.

14. Van der Leeuw 153; and Bitenhard 243–248.

15. Bitenhard 250–251.

16. Abba 507.

17. Bitenhard 277–278.

18. Von Rad 39.

19. Foakes-Jackson and Lake, 4:123; and G. H. C. Macgregor, "The Acts of the Apostles," *IB,* ed. G. A. Buttrick et al. (New York: Abingdon-Cokesbury Press, 1954) 9:141.

20. Moulton and Milligan 451. Bitenhard disagrees with this Hellenistic reading and prefers the Semitic roots of the idea. See Bitenhard 275.

21. F. F. Bruce, *The Acts of the Apostles* (London: Tyndale Press, 1952) 187.

22. Pedersen 250. See also the discussion in Markus Barth, *Ephesians 1–3, Anchor Bible* (Garden City, N.Y.: Doubleday & Co., 1974) 382ff.

23. J. W. Packer, ed. *The Acts of the Apostles* (Cambridge: Cambridge University Press, 1966) 85.

24. William Neil, *The Acts of the Apostles* (Grand Rapids: Wm. B. Eerdmans, 1987) 83. Bruce 120.

25. Bitenhard 271.

26. Macgregor 55.

27. New 128.

28. Neil 85.

29. Pedersen 246.

30. Neil 92.

31. Bruce 124. Foakes-Jackson and Lake 4:62–63.

32. For a summary of this discussion see Mark A. Powell, *What Are They Saying About Luke?* (New York: Paulist Press, 1989).

33. Jean Daniélou, *The Theology of Jewish Christianity* (London: Darton, Longman & Todd, 1964) 147–148.

34. Pedersen 256.

35. F. C. Grant, "Jesus Christ," *IDB* 2:869; and G. A. Smith, "Joshua," *Dictionary of the Bible,* ed. James Hastings (New York: Charles Scribners, 1906) 770.

36. Bitenhard 273.

37. Anon., *The Jesus Prayer* (Crestwood, N.Y.: St. Vladimir's Seminary Press, 1987). See also the works on the Orthodox tradition of prayer recorded in the *Philokalia*. Meditation upon and repetition of the sacred name or names is a common spiritual practice in many religions and is of special importance in Hinduism, some branches of Buddhism, and Islam.

38. Daniélou 150.

39. Grant 869.

Chapter 5. The Breaking of Bread

1. Some of the following material derives from my article "Do This: A Study on the Institution of the Lord's Supper," *Restoration Quarterly* 30 (1988): 207–217.

2. See Joachim Jeremias, *The Eucharistic Words of Jesus* (Oxford: Basil Blackwell, 1955).

3. See, e.g., M. Barth, *Das Abendmahl*; G. Dalman, *Jesus-Jeshua*; A. J. B. Higgins, *The Lord's Supper in the New Testament*; and H. Lietzmann, *Messe und Herrenmahl*. See Strack-Billerbeck, *Kommentar,* for an account of how the events of the Last Supper fit the pattern of the Passover meal as set out in the Mishnah.

4. Fritz Rienecker, *A Linguistic Key to the Greek New Testament,* trans. Cleon Rogers, Jr. (Grand Rapids: Zondervan, 1980) 426.

5. Howard Clark Kee et al., *Understanding the New Testament,* 2nd ed. (Englewood Cliffs, N.J.: Prentice-Hall, 1965) 399.

6. A. J. B. Higgins, *The Lord's Supper in the New Testament* (Chicago: Henry Regnery, 1952) 51.

7. Krister Stendahl, "New Testament Background for the Doctrine of the Sacraments," *Oecumenica* (Minneapolis: Augsburg Publishing House, 1970) 56.

8. Everett Ferguson, *Early Christians Speak* (Austin, Tex.: Sweet Publishing Co., 1971) 102.

9. See Cleon Rogers, "The Covenant with Moses and Its Historical Setting," *JETS* 17 (1971) 152.

10. Higgins 30.

11. Higgins 53.

12. William Robinson, *The Administration of the Lord's Supper* (Birmingham, Eng.: Berean Press, 1947) 23.

13. Ferguson 109.

14. P. T. Forsyth, *The Church and the Sacraments,* 2nd ed. (London: Independent Press, 1947) 234.

15. Bernard W. Anderson, *Understanding the Old Testament,* 3rd ed. (Englewood Cliffs, N.J.: Prentice-Hall, 1975) 310–311.

16. Stendahl 44.

17. S. Scott Bartchy, "Table Fellowship with Jesus and the 'Lord's Meal' at Corinth," in *Increase in Learning,* ed. Robert Owens, Jr., and Barbara E. Hamm (Manhattan, Kans.: Manhattan Christian College, 1979) 53.

18. Gerhard Delling, *Worship in the New Testament* (Philadelphia: Westminster Press, 1962) 139.

19. Higgins 69.

20. Marcus J. Borg, *Jesus: A New Vision* (San Francisco: Harper & Row, 1987) 132–133.

21. Bartchy 54–55.

22. Higgins 53.

23. Evelyn Underhill, *Worship* (New York: Harper & Brothers, 1937) 154–155.

24. Higgins 53.

25. Although the remarks are metaphorical and refer to more than physical food, immediately after this breakfast, Jesus commands Peter, "Feed my lambs" and "Feed my sheep." (John 21:15, 17). This could be seen to strengthen the connection between Jesus and meals and eating in the resurrection appearances.

26. Oscar Cullmann, *Early Christian Worship* (London: SCM Press, 1953) 15.

27. Eduard Schweizer, *The Lord's Supper according to the New Testament* (Philadelphia: Fortress Press, 1967) 1.

28. Johannes Behm, "ἀνάμνησις," *TDNT,* ed. Gerhard Kittel (Grand Rapids: Wm. B. Eerdmans, 1965) 1:349.

29. Neville Clark, *An Approach to the Theology of the Sacraments* (Chicago: Alec R. Allenson, 1956) 62.

30. F. F. Bruce, *I and II Corinthians* (Grand Rapids: Wm. B. Eerdmans, 1978) 113–114.

31. Schweizer 17.

32. Schweizer 2.

33. See Hans Conzelmann, *The Theology of St. Luke,* 2nd ed. (London: Faber & Faber, 1960).

34. Stendahl 52.

35. Bruce 114.

36. Stendahl 52.
37. Schweizer 3.
38. Clark 50.

Chapter 6. The Prayer in Acts 4:23-31

1. H. M. Conn, "Luke's Theology of Prayer," *Christianity Today* 17 (1972): 6–8; P. T. O'Brien, "Prayer in Luke-Acts," *Tyndale Bulletin* 24 (1973): 111–127; and Allison Trites, "The Prayer Motif in Luke-Acts," in *Perspectives on Luke-Acts,* ed. Charles H. Talbert (*Perspectives in Religious Studies,* 1978): 168–186.

2. Robert A. Spivey and D. Moody Smith, *Anatomy of the New Testament* (New York: Macmillan Co., 1982) 144.

3. A. Hamman, quoted in O'Brien 123.

4. Trites 185.

5. F. J. Foakes-Jackson, *The Acts of the Apostles* (London: Hodder & Stoughton, 1951) 21.

6. Professor Trites was kind enough to send me extensive commentary on an early draft of this chapter. These reflections are from that letter dated January 16, 1990. Trites has done extensive work on Acts. See note 1 above and "Church Growth in the Book of Acts," *Bibliotheca Sacra* 145 (1988).

7. See e.g., the work of Colin J. Hermer, "Luke the Historian," *BJRL* 60 (1977) 28–51; and *The Book of Acts in the Setting of Hellenistic History* (Tübingen: J. C. B. Mohr [Paul Siebeck], 1989).

8. C. K. Barrett, *Luke the Historian in Recent Study* (London: Epworth Press, 1961) 28–30. On Luke-Acts and ancient historiography see also David E. Aune, *The New Testament in Its Literary Environment* (Philadelphia: Westminster Press, 1987) chaps. 3 and 4.

9. Barrett 60.

10. W. Ward Gasque, "A Fruitful Field: Recent Study of the Acts of the Apostles," *Interpretation* 42/2 (1988): 117–131.

11. Foakes-Jackson, *Acts,* 38, 24.

12. Neil has noted striking parallelism between 2:1—4:22 and 4:31—5:40. William Neil, *The Acts of the Apostles* (Grand Rapids: Wm. B. Erdmans, 1987) 31. For another helpful reading of the passage see chapter 3 of Linda M. Maloney's *"All That God Had Done. . ."* (New York: Peter Lang, 1991) and S. F. Plymale, *The Prayer Texts of Luke-Acts* (New York: Peter Lang) 78–87.

13. F. F. Bruce, "The Church of Jerusalem in the Acts of the Apostles," *BJRL* 67/2 (1985): 643.

14. Carl R. Holladay, "Acts" in *HBC,* ed. James L. Mays et al. (San Francisco: Harper & Row, 1988) 1082.

15. Barrett 55; and Gasque 120, 129.

16. Gasque 129.

17. Bertil Gärtner, *The Areopagus Speech and Natural Revelation* (Upsala: C. W. K. Gleerup, 1955).

18. Barrett 16.

19. See Jacob Jervel, *Luke and the People of God* (Minneapolis: Augsburg Publishing House, 1972); and *The Unknown Paul: Essays on Luke Acts and Early Christian History* (Minneapolis: Augsburg Publishing House, 1984).

20. Gasque (p. 130) refers us to S. G. Wilson, *Luke and the Law, Society for New Testament Studies Monograph Series* 50 (Cambridge: Cambridge University Press, 1983).

21. Roger T. Beckwith, "The Daily and Weekly Worship of the Primitive Church in Relation to Its Jewish Antecedents," *EQ* 56 (1984): 69.

22. Neil 91.

23. F. F. Bruce, *The Acts of the Apostles* (London: Tyndale Press, 1952) 126.

24. Holladay 1084.

25. F. J. Foakes-Jackson and Kirsopp Lake, eds., *The Beginnings of Christianity* (London: Macmillan & Co., 1933) 4:46; and G. H. C. Macgregor, "The Acts of the Apostles," *IB*, ed. G. A. Buttrick et al. (New York: Abingdon-Cokesbury Press, 1954) 9:71.

26. See Foakes-Jackson and Lake, *Beginnings* 4:46; and Bruce Metzger, *A Textual Commentary on the Greek New Testament* (New York: United Bible Societies, 1975) 321–323.

27. Bruce, *Acts* 27.

28. Foakes-Jackson and Lake, *Beginnings* 4:47; and Neil 92.

29. Johannes Munck, *The Acts of the Apostles,* Anchor Bible (Garden City, N.Y.: Doubleday & Co., 1967) 37.

30. Neil 92.

31. Barrett 58.

32. See, e.g., William Barclay, "Great Themes of the New Testament: Acts 2:14-40," *ET* 70/7 (1959): 196–199, and 70/8 (1959): 243–246.

33. O'Brien 126–127.

34. Holladay 1084.

35. J. Rawson Lumby, *The Acts of the Apostles* (Cambridge: Cambridge University Press, 1904) 130.

36. Lumby 130

37. Bernard W. Anderson, *Understanding the Old Testament,* 3rd ed. (Englewood Cliffs, N.J.: Prentice-Hall, 1975) 65.

38. Neil 92.

39. Gerhard Delling, *Worship in the New Testament,* trans. Percy Scott (Philadelphia: Westminster Press, 1962) 116.

40. Joachim Jeremias, *The Prayers of Jesus* (Philadelphia: Fortress Press, 1978) 67.

41. Delling 113–114.

42. Luke alone tells of Jesus' appearance before Herod. See Luke 23:7ff.

43. Bruce, *Acts* 127–128.

44. Holladay 1084.

45. Gasque 126–127.

46. Holladay 185.

47. If Luke were an associate of Paul's, some of his depth of insight into Hebrew tradition would be readily accounted for.

48. Trites 178.

49. I am grateful to Mark Kiley and Allison Trites for their helpful suggestions offered on an early draft of this chapter.

Chapter 7. Acts, Ephesians, and the Hellenistic Environment

1. Ernst Käsemann, "Ephesians and Acts," *Studies in Luke-Acts,* ed. Leander E. Keck and Louis J. Martyn (London: SPCK, 1968) 293.

2. See Richard Batey, "The Destination of Ephesians," *JBL* 82 (1963):101; and R. P. Martin, "An Epistle in Search of a Life Setting," *ET* 79 (1967–68): 296–302.

3. Markus Barth, *Ephesians 1–3*, Anchor Bible (Garden City, N.Y.: Doubleday & Co., 1974) 3–4.

4. For a summary, see Jack Finegan, "Ephesus," *IDB*, ed. G. A. Buttrick et al. (Nashville: Abingdon Press, 1962) 2:114–118.

5. Helmut Koester, *Introduction to the New Testament*, 2 vols. (Philadelphia: Fortress Press, 1982) 1:328.

6. See Finegan, *IDB* and *Light from the Ancient Past* (Princeton: Princeton University Press, 1946) 265–269.

7. See Forschungen en Ephesos, veröffentlicht vom österreichischen archäologischen Institute (5 vols., 1905–1944).

8. Finegan, *IDB* 115.

9. Markus Barth, "Traditions in Ephesians," *NTS* 30 (1984): 16.

10. Finegan, *Light* 267–268.

11. Clinton E. Arnold, *Ephesians, Power and Magic* (Cambridge: Cambridge University Press, 1989) 14.

12. Arnold 27.

13. Koester 1:378.

14. Koester 1:378.

15. Koester 2:267–272.

16. Barth, *Ephesians 1–3* 12–18.

17. Barth, *Traditions* 21.

18. See A. T. Lincoln, "The Use of the Old Testament in Ephesians," *JSOT* 14 (1982) 16–57.

19. Koester 2:270.

20. See Barth, *Ephesians 1–3* 27–31; and note 18 above.

21. See John C. Kirby, *Ephesians, Baptism and Pentecost* (Montreal: McGill University Press, 1968); and J. T. Sanders, "Hymnic Elements in Eph. 1–3," *ZNW* 56 (1965): 214–232.

22. Barth, *Ephesians 1–3* 6.

23. C. Leslie Mitton, *The Epistle to the Ephesians: Its Authorship, Origin, and Purpose* (Oxford: Clarendon Press, 1951).

24. J. Moffatt, *Introduction to the Literature of the New Testament,* 3rd edition (1918) 384. This discussion occurs in A. H. McNeile, *An Introduction to the Study of the New Testament,* 2nd ed. (Oxford: Clarendon Press, 1953) 169–170.

25. Mitton, *Epistle* 203.

26. Mitton, *Epistle* 216–218.

27. Käsemann 288.

28. Käsemann 290.

29. See A. Borland, "God's Eternal Purpose," *EQ* 34 (1962) 29–35.

30. C. Leslie Mitton, *Ephesians* (Grand Rapids: Wm. B. Eerdmans, 1981) 16.

31. Martin 299.

32. Martin 299–300.

33. Käsemann 297.

34. See B. T. Viviano, "The Letter to the Ephesians," *The Bible Today* 102 (1979): 2019–2026.

35. Barth, "Traditions" 16.

36. Barth, "Traditions" 15.

37. Barth, "Traditions" 19.

38. See note 11 above.

39. Barth, "Traditions" 17.

40. For an excellent treatment, see David C. Verner, *The Household of God* (Chico, Calif.: Scholars Press, 1983).

Chapter 8. The Prayer in Ephesians 3:14-21

1. Markus Barth, *Ephesians 1–3,* Anchor Bible (Garden City, N.Y.: Doubleday & Co., 1974) 58-59.

2. Barth, *Ephesians 1–3;* Francis Foulkes, *The Epistle of Paul to the Ephesians* (Grand Rapids: Wm. B. Eerdmans, 1963); John C. Kirby, *Ephesians, Baptism and Pentecost* (Montreal: McGill University Press, 1968); J. T. Sanders, "Hymnic Elements in Eph. 1–3," *ZNW* 56 (1965): 214–232; and Lionel Swain, *Ephesians* (Wilmington, Del.: Michael Glazier, 1980).

3. G. B. Caird, *Paul's Letters from Prison* (Oxford: Oxford University Press, 1981) 17.

4. For classic discussions of the issue, see E. J. Goodspeed, *The Meaning of Ephesians* (1933) and *The Key to Ephesians* (1956); C. Leslie Mitton, *The Epistle to the Ephesians: Its Authorship, Origin, and Purpose* (1951) and "The Authorship of the Epistle to the Ephesians," *Expository Times* 68 (1955–56): 195–198; and Ernst Percy, *Die Probleme der Kolosser und Epheserbriefe* (1946). These are summarized, and more recent material is provided by Kirby (see note 2 above).

5. See Clinton E. Arnold, *Ephesians—Power and Magic* (Cambridge: Cambridge University Press, 1989) 1–40; Richard Batey, "The Destination of Ephesians," *JBL* 82 (1963): 101; and note 4 above.

6. H. Chadwick quoted in Kirby 54.

7. See Barth, *Ephesians 1–3;* Kirby; and Swain.

8. See Arnold.

9. E. Best, *HBD*, ed. Paul J. Achtemeier (San Francisco: Harper & Row, 1985) 269.

10. A. Borland, "God's Eternal Purpose," *EQ* 34 (1962): 29–35.

11. Markus Barth, "Traditions in Ephesians," *NTS* 30 (1984): 3–25.

12. F. W. Beare, "The Epistle to the Ephesians," *IB*, ed. G. A. Buttrick et al. (New York: Abingdon-Cokesbury Press, 1953) 10:694.

13. Swain 4.

14. J. L. Houlden, *Paul's Letters from Prison* (Philadelphia: Westminster Press, 1977) 259.

15. C. Leslie Mitton, *Ephesians* (Grand Rapids: Wm. B. Eerdmans, 1981) 129.

16. Paul J. Kobelski, "The Letter to the Ephesians," *The New Jerome Biblical Commentary,* ed. Raymond E. Brown, Joseph A. Fitzmyer, Roland E. Murphy (Englewood Cliffs, N.J.: Prentice-Hall, 1990) 888. Arnold (p. 86) believes that at 3:1 "the author interrupts himself to establish his apostolic credentials (vv. 2–13)."

17. Barth, *Ephesians 1–3* 377; and J. L. Blevins, "The Church's Great Ministry: Ephesians 3," *Review and Expositor* 76 (1979): 512.

18. Arnold 86.

19. Houlden 302.

20. Cf. Kirby (pp. 126ff.), who sees extensive baptismal *berakah* as the basis for chapters 1–3.

21. Arnold 86–87.

22. Swain 69.

23. Kobelski 888.

24. A. T. Lincoln, "The Use of the Old Testament in Ephesians," *JSOT* 14 (1982): 16–57.

25. R. G. Bratcher and E. A. Nida, *A Translator's Handbook on Paul's Letter to the Ephesians* (New York: United Bible Societies, 1982) 84.

26. Houlden 302.

27. Nils A. Dahl, "Ephesians," *HBC*, ed. James L. Mays et al. (San Francisco: Harper & Row, 1988) 1217

28. Barth, *Ephesians 1–3* 374.

29. Houlden 304.

30. Barth, *Ephesians 1–3* 18–21; and "Traditions."

31. Jerome Murphy-O'Connor, "Who Wrote Ephesians?" *Bible Today* 18 (1965).

32. Arnold 90.

33. Barth, *Ephesians 1–3* 13.

34. Eduard Lohse, *A Commentary on the Epistles to the Colossians and Philemon* (Philadelphia: Fortress Press, 1971) 57–58.

35. Houlden 278.

36. See Lohse's excursus on the meanings of the term, in Lohse, *Commentary*.

37. The classic *abba* discussion is found in Joachim Jeremias, *The Prayers of Jesus* (Philadelphia: Fortress Press, 1978), but more recent work has been done by James Charlesworth of Princeton Theological Seminary.

38. Barth, *Ephesians 1–3* 368.

39. See, e.g., Bratcher and Nida 86.

40. See, e.g., the discussion by Barth, *Ephesians 1–3* 395–397; Houlden 304; Mitton, *Ephesians* 134; and Rom. 3:37–39.

41. Caird 18–19, 56–59.

42. Beare 674.

43. Arnold 99.

44. Mitton, *Ephesians* 129.

45. Mitton, *Ephesians* 134.

46. Blevins 514.

47. Foulkes 104.

48. J. O. F. Murray, *The Epistle of Paul to the Ephesians* (Cambridge: Cambridge University Press, 1933) 60; and M. R. Vincent, *Word Studies in the New Testament,* 4 vols. (New York: Charles Scribner's Sons, 1903) 3:385.

49. Barth, *Ephesians 1–3* 394.

50. Foulkes 104.

51. Arnold 99.

52. Arnold 99.

53. Swain 69.

54. Swain xii.

Index of Biblical References